BIG BAD

A SMALL TOWN MURDER MYSTERY

KIRSTEN WEISS

MISTERIO PRESS

Contents

COPYRIGHT

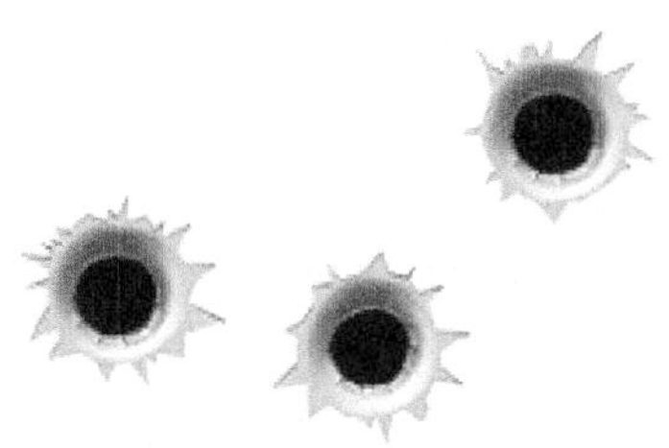

This book is a work of fiction. Names, characters and incidents are either the product of the author's imagination or are used fictitiously. Any resemblance to actual persons, living or dead, is entirely coincidental.

Visit the author website to sign up for updates on upcoming books and fun, free stuff: KirstenWeiss.com

Line drawings for the mystery game by Articult.
misterio press / print edition June, 2022
ISBN-13: 978-1-944767-80-8

About Big Bad

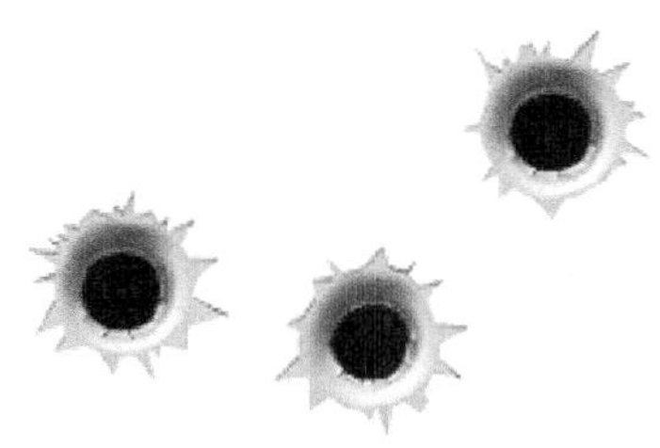

Hi. I'm Alice, a thirty-something ex-bodyguard. I live to sleep in, but I rarely get the chance now that I'm living above my small-town's dinner theater. Between self-absorbed actors slamming doors at all hours and the theater cat that won't leave me alone... I swear he knows I'm allergic. Also, he led me straight to the corpse of the theater's leading lady.

Thanks, cat.

Now my brother, the murdered woman's co-star, is determined to solve the crime. He thinks his improv and questionable sword fighting skills somehow qualify him as a detective. Whether I like it or not, I'm going to have to solve this murder—and fast—before he gets in over his head. Or gets it taken off.

Big Bad is the second book in the Big Murder Mystery series. If you like laugh-out-loud mysteries, relationships with heart, and stories about figuring out where you belong, you'll love *Big Bad*. Buy the book and start this quirky mystery today.

Murder mystery game in the back of the book!

Chapter One

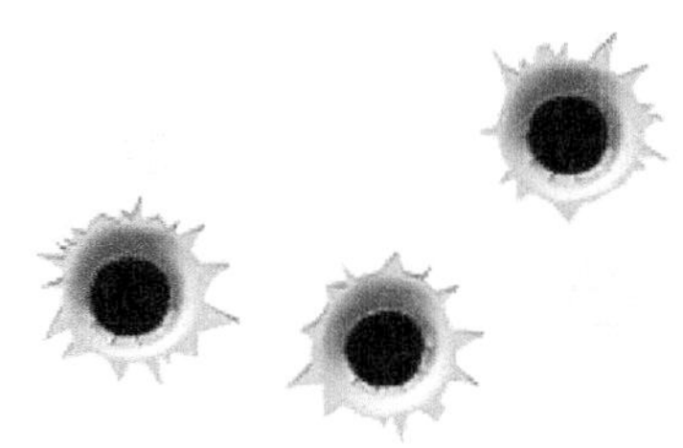

Prurient jokes aside, I really did like to watch.

There was a certain Zen to surveillance. You had to concentrate, or the object of your surveillance might get away. Worse, you might get clobbered by an unwary driver or by a very wary accomplice.

I liked the focus. But on this October morning, I was questioning the life choices that had led me to this Reno suburb.

I drummed my fingers on the Jeep's steering wheel. I was back in the surveillance game. Good. Unfortunately, I was working for a PI rather than as part of a personal protection team.

But beggars couldn't be choosers. I'd tried—oh, how I'd tried—to get another surveillance gig with a personal protection firm. They didn't *all* laugh at me. Some had hung up on me. Others simply hadn't bothered to return my calls.

Desperate or not, I still wasn't sure if contracting for this particular PI, Fitch Rhodes, was such a hot idea. Fitch and I had done some heavy flirting before I'd taken this assignment. The last time I'd dated a co-worker, I'd married and divorced him. My judgment when it came to men wasn't the best.

I trailed the client's ex-husband down a residential street lined with ranch homes. Pumpkins and plywood witches and blow-up ghosts decorated the wide lawns.

Bulging eyes rolling, Fredo growled in the seat beside me. A string of drool dripped from one of his snaggle teeth. The little gray dog hated all things Halloween—plastic skeletons, jack-o-lanterns, paper ghosts.

It was going to be a long month.

Taking a dog on a surveillance gig could work for or against you. If your quarry noted the dog, odds were they'd notice the dog a second time—and notice you.

As a blond beanpole, I was memorable enough. Wigs could fix the blond, but there was nothing I could do about the tall. Most women weren't scraping six feet.

Fredo was ugly enough to be memorable. But he was also short enough not to stick above the car window. And dogs made a good excuse for strolling down residential streets where you didn't belong. The dog, plus my jeans and respectably stylish brown sweater gave me some cover.

Two blocks ahead, my subject's Tesla pulled to the side of the road. I pulled over as well and reached for Fredo, extracting him from his doggy car restraints.

The sub, a tall, good-looking dentist in his forties, crossed the street toward his ex-wife's ranch house. I frowned. According to my intel, the kids were in school. He had no reason to be here.

The ex-couple was involved in a fresh custody battle. Fitch's client was convinced her ex was drinking and driving with their kids in the car. I'd seen a lot of drinking over the last week, but nothing to endanger his two kids. In short, I'd been a major disappointment. But hey, you got what you got.

I walked Fredo toward the house. My subject rang the bell, and after a moment, the door opened. There was a brief discussion, and the sub walked inside. The hairs on the back of my neck stood at attention. Fredo ripped fake spider webs from a nearby bush.

I had no reason to do anything here but wait outside. I was supposed to be catching my sub in the act of drinking with the kids, and the kids were away. But something had pinged my internal radar when the door had closed behind those two. Plus, I was nosy.

I released Fredo's leash. As expected, he ran straight to the pumpkin on the concrete step. Spider webs trailing, he lifted his leg. I hurried after him, making a show of recapturing his leash.

I took the opportunity to glance in a front window as I tugged the dog away from the Halloween decor. Neither my subject nor our client could be seen inside the elegantly decorated interior.

Something thumped behind the white-painted door, rattling the doorknocker—a lion with a ring in its teeth. I stilled, staring at the door, and an oily chill slithered up the back of my neck.

It would have been easy for me to talk myself out of the apprehension that clutched me. But doors don't just thump on their own. And ignoring your instincts was a good way for bad things to happen.

I returned to the front door and rang the bell. It buzzed angrily.

If nothing was wrong, this assignment was about to come to a crashing halt, and I could have used the money. If my subject saw me, odds were high he'd recognize me later. Disguise or no, I'd be made. Fitch would have to bring in someone else, and that wouldn't make him happy. But I'd learned not to ignore my bad feelings.

No one came to the door. I pressed the bell again, this time longer. Stomach tight, I peered through the narrow window beside the door. The newly redecorated hallway had been done up in tasteful grays.

I rang the bell a third time, waited, tried the door. *Locked.*

"Come on, Fredo." I walked him past the garage and around the corner of the garage. A high, white fence blocked the view of the narrow side yard from the next-door neighbor.

I checked the high gate blocking passage to the back yard. It was padlocked shut. I *could* crawl over the six-foot fence, but it wasn't my first choice. Frustrated, I looked for somewhere to tie Fredo's leash. I settled on a hose hook beneath a garage window.

Looping the dog's leash around it, I straightened in front of the narrow window. Through its film of dirt I had a decent view of the interior. A blue Audi. Behind it, a set of metal shelves full of garage stuff and a door to the interior of the house.

The door bumped open. The sub backed through it, dragging Fitch's client in front of him, his hands hooked beneath her arm pits. He lurched, jostling the shelves, and ricocheted against the Audi.

I darted from the window and bit back a curse. Striding toward the front of the garage, I called Fitch.

"Let me guess," he said. "You're bored and thought, I'll find out what fascinating things Fitch is up to right now—"

"Get the cops to your client's house. She's hurt. Ambulance too." It would be quicker if Fitch explained to the cops. I had a feeling I'd be too busy.

A car started inside the garage.

"What's happening?" he asked, all business.

I was going to have to bang on the window and let the sub know he'd been caught. I really hated that idea, but it might dissuade him from doing anything worse. "Attempted murder."

I swallowed, hoping it hadn't been an *actual* murder. The running car told me my sub was going for the old fake suicide-by-carbon-monoxide plot. TV has given too many wannabe bad guys terrible ideas. But the nice thing about clichés is they're easy to predict.

Without any real expectation it would open, I tugged on the garage door handle. The door flew upward, banging loudly. I sucked in a startled breath.

The dentist and I gaped at each other. He was feeding a hose through the Audi's cracked driver's window. His ex, in the car, slumped lifeless against the door.

Fredo dropped to his stomach and panted. The dog cocked his head, looking interested.

Moving in slow motion, I took the phone from my ear and snapped a photo of the scene. Cell phone cameras really have revolutionized the surveillance biz. "So," I began, "I'm a—"

The dentist dropped the hose and charged, racing down the narrow aisle between the metal shelves and the Audi. I grabbed the top of the metal shelf and pulled. He ducked. The shelves crashed against the Audi and missed him completely.

"Whoops." *Sorry car*. Also, dammit, I'd barely even slowed him down. This is what came from stepping out of my career comfort zone.

Bent double, eyes burning with fury, stumbling over paint cans and plastic toolboxes, he was still moving forward. The dentist emerged from beneath the shelf in a wrestler's crouch. Fredo cocked his head, his ears twitching.

Fear punched my chest. I stepped backward. "Now, let's think about this—"

His arms swung wide, reaching for me. I dropped the phone and skipped backward.

He moved fast, his head up, his shoulder angled inward toward my gut. This wasn't just a random wrestler's crouch. This guy had trained in actual wrestling. My insides turned to seawater.

I didn't feel like a trained and toughened bodyguard. I didn't feel like someone who'd once worked in war zones. I didn't feel like a martial arts expert. I felt like a wannabe PI who was in over her head.

I stepped forward to meet him, and I tripped over the dog. Fredo yipped. I stumbled, my arms windmilling.

Time did that weird slo-mo thing. The air smelled like exhaust, the car engine rumbling. I could see every bristle on the dentist's unshaven face. I had a lover's view of the gold flecks in his eyes. And I was in big, big trouble.

Once and only once, I dropped my martial arts instructor to the ground. He'd thrown me in a demo. I fell in a spot he hadn't expected, and he'd tripped over me. All he'd suffered was mild embarrassment, which he'd laughed off. I was about to drop in front of someone who wanted me dead.

There was a rule in the dojo: don't go to the ground. Unless you're a jujitsu master, and I wasn't, rolling around on the pavement was the last place you wanted to be.

I did an awkward kick-ball-change on my tippy toes, and the dentist was on me.

"Hell." Grabbing him by the hair, I slammed my knee into his face. Sharp pain pierced my thigh. He grunted a curse and fell flat on the concrete. Then he began to rise.

Being a firm believer 'tis better to give than to receive, I kicked him a couple more times to make sure he stayed down.

He did.

I yanked one of the dentist's teeth from my thigh. "You okay?" I asked Fredo. A spider web hung from his nocked ear. The dog grinned, panting.

And then I started shaking.

Chapter Two

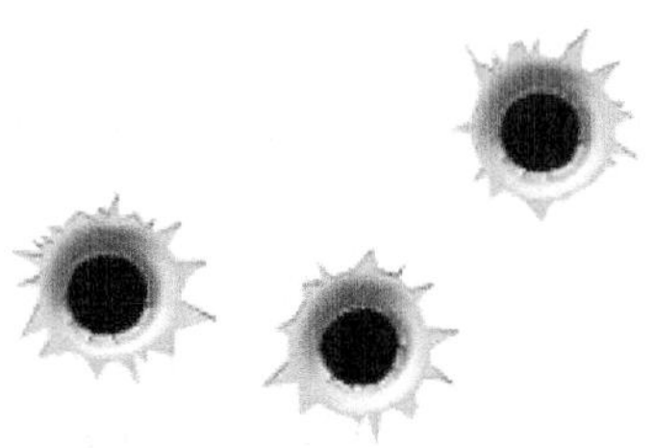

There were a lot of things I could ignore when I was tired enough. Actors shouting. A bathroom ghost. The fact that yesterday I'd nearly gotten killed by a dentist, which was just mortifying.

Eighteen pounds of howling, flying fur and scratching claws was not one of those things. I sat bolt upright on my bed. The paperback on my stomach slid to the floor.

The theater's black cat, Sammie, dug his claws through the thin fabric of my t-shirt, piercing my skin, and I hissed. He spring boarded off my chest just in time for Fredo to make his own landing.

"Oof." Glancing warily at the apartment door, I retrieved the book from the uneven wood floor. "Knock it off, you two."

Sammie leapt onto my dresser and out of reach, knocking a stick of deodorant to the rag rug. Fredo scrambled off the bed and barked up at the cat.

I snarled. "I said, cut it out."

Fredo and Sammie froze for a moment. Their heads swiveled to face me. The dog barked, and they resumed tearing around my micro apartment.

I flopped back on my bed. The cat was a good part of the reason for the cheap rent on this apartment. The near-nightly crowds in the mystery dinner theater below were the other.

Laughter and voices floated up through the floorboards, and I yawned. I'd spent too much time at the police station last night explaining what I'd seen and why I'd broken into the garage.

You'd think having the ex-wife there to testify would have sped things up. But it hadn't seemed to.

Fitch then demanded I fill out the report forms that night, before I forgot any details. I filled out the forms. In a fit of pique, I might have added more detail than was strictly necessary. When my employer asks for a report, he gets it. We have a totally professional relationship, after all. Though the way he'd been glaring at me last night…

I scrubbed my hands over my face and yawned again. Outside the window, twilight had turned the sky a deep, blue gray. I'd slept the day away, and it had left me feeling disconnected and disoriented. I needed to get out.

Stumbling to standing, I tripped over the red sweater I was knitting my brother for Christmas. I tossed it on my bed, took two steps to my front door and stuck my head outside the apartment.

On the opposite side of the hall, the door to Gloria's dressing room was closed. I relaxed. If the theater's diva hadn't come pounding on my door to complain about the racket yet, odds were she wouldn't bother me now.

Quietly returning inside, I glanced at the laptop on the card table that made up my dining nook and hesitated. I opened it, turned it on, and checked my email. There was one from a personal protection firm, and my heart jumped. I opened it.

Dear Ms. Sommerland:

Thank you for your interest in Williams and Shield. While your resumé is impressive, we do not feel you are a good fit at this time…

I slammed the laptop shut and stood there, my fingers pressed to its top for a long moment. Then I grabbed an athletic jacket and tucked my wallet and phone into the back pockets of my jeans. When I'd come to Nowhere, Nevada, I'd brought a lot of stretchy, professional, travel clothes. They worked well for stakeouts. But I'd gotten in the habit of wearing jeans and tees around town.

I stepped into the old-west theater's hallway and closed the door behind me, shutting the animals inside. The cat had a nasty habit of wandering into the dinner theater during performances. He was looking for scraps—a sign of high intelligence. Jane, the stage *and* food service manager, could have been on one of those cooking shows. And though Sammie technically wasn't my cat, I'd agreed to try to wrangle him when possible.

Behind the door, Fredo loosed a single, woeful bark.

I tiptoed past Gloria's dressing room and down the stairs. Sometimes discretion really was the better part of valor.

In the prop room, the improv cast crammed around an XXL pepperoni pizza on an extra-extra-small table. Costumes for knights and ladies, bootleggers and flappers, miners and showgirls, hung along two walls. Swords and knives and fake tommy guns lined a third. Other props—telephones and typewriters, pennants and pitchforks—were stacked randomly throughout the room.

"Hey, Alice." My brother Charlie swallowed. "Vittoria dropped this off. Want a slice?"

My stomach rumbled. Since this was a town of big things, the local pizza parlor had decided on super-large pizzas as a gimmick. But they hadn't sacrificed quality for size. They'd even had XXL insulated carriers made for delivery. "Thanks."

"You see Gloria?" Charlie wore a court jester's costume, which was appropriate. My brother is pure of heart, but he's not the most together guy. On the other hand, I hadn't exactly been winning points in the productive-adult department either.

I ambled past a suit of armor and snagged a slice of pepperoni. "No. I thought Gloria was in her dressing room." A crumb of pizza crust had snagged in my brother's neatly trimmed beard, and I flecked it away.

Charlie shrugged, and the bells on his hat tinkled. His longish blond hair curled from beneath it. "Nope. It's empty. I knocked."

A middle-aged woman built along the lines of a Teutonic opera singer—and with the decibel level to match—shook her head. She reached up to steady her conical, medieval hat, the gauzy fabric of her pink dress rippling at the motion. "I'm still not sure how she managed to claim that dressing room as her own," Kristie said. "Speaking for the other ladies of the cast, we wouldn't mind sharing."

A Hollywood-handsome man in a tunic strode into the room and looked around. "My better half's still not here?" Jed frowned. "Where's Gloria?" Jed was almost as tall as me. That made him endearing, even if his wife had told me off Tuesday for walking past her dressing room too loudly.

"Have you tried calling her?" Kristie asked.

"Yes," he said, "but it keeps going to voicemail." He shrugged, his silky tunic rustling. "She's probably in her car."

A slender, mousy woman in an apron sidled into the room. The pencils pinning her brown hair in a bun dangled loosely, about to make a break for the floorboards. "Er, the natives are getting restless." She pushed her thick glasses higher up the bridge of her nose.

Jed adjusted the sword in his knotted belt and nodded. "I'm sure she'll be here any minute. We can start the show without her."

"Or make her the first murder victim." Kristie boomed a laugh, and her conical hat trembled. "Then she can play dead for the rest of the show."

Jed smiled. "It would serve her right for being late. Are we agreed then? Gloria's the victim tonight? That way if she doesn't make it in time, we're in the clear."

"Or, hey. Maybe Alice wants to step in?" Charlie tilted his head, bells jingling. Heads turned to stare at me.

A creeping sensation inched up the back of my neck. I swallowed the last of my pizza. "What?"

"You've seen every show," Charlie said. "You can improv with us."

"It might not be fair to throw your sister into the fire," Jed said, smiling.

Thank you. My brother was the actor, not me.

"Come on," Charlie said. "It'll be fun. You could be a part of something."

"Why?" I asked. "I know who I am, and I know my limits, and I don't need to be a part of anything."

My brother gave an exasperated huff. "Why do you have to be so—"

"Fair enough." Jed clapped Charlie's shoulder. "So we're agreed? Gloria dies?" The rest of the cast glanced at each other and nodded. "Then *en garde*." Jed drew his sword and aimed it toward the open door. "Let the show begin."

The cast trailed out, leaving me with the last slice of pizza. It seemed a shame to let it get cold. I reached for it and hesitated. A golden sphinx smiled enigmatically at me from a set of speakeasy props.

I abandoned the pizza, backed from the room, and checked my phone. No new messages from Fitch. I made a face, unsure whether to feel disappointed or relieved. Even though yesterday's surveillance had nearly ended in disaster, I'd hoped for a new gig. I needed *something* until I could restart my old life.

Leaving through the theater's rear door, I stepped into the crisp October night. A gibbous moon hung over the Sierras to the west and dimmed the stars. To the east, a three-story lawn flamingo wearing an eyepatch squinted over the two-story building.

I wound through the rapidly filling parking lot and walked around the theater to Main Street. I'd say living in a town trying to make its name with the world's largest collection of the world's biggest things was unique. But honestly? It was just odd. It was even odder at Halloween, when there was a fake corpse pinned beneath the world's biggest corkscrew.

Chapter Three

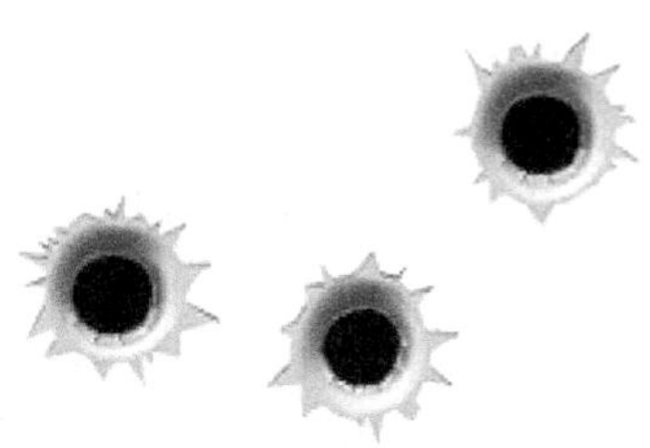

Just because someone looked dead, it didn't mean they were dead. Yes, I *have* made that mistake before (don't ask). And Gloria's face looked so pink and healthy...

Hurrying past the mini fridge, I knelt beside her. I took her pulse. I couldn't find one, and my insides flipped over and dove to the thin carpet. And then I dialed 9-1-1. I put the call on speaker, explaining to the dispatcher while I gave Gloria chest compressions through her stiff blue corset. Or whatever it was medieval ladies wore.

Oblivious laughter and chatter drifted up the wooden stairs from the theater. I glanced at the clock on her dressing room table. It was eight-fifty. The dinner theater was wrapping up, the guests trickling out, and I felt cold.

I bent to give Gloria mouth-to-mouth. The scent of bitter almonds wafted from her lips, and I recoiled. I sat back and took her pulse again.

My hands fell loose to my sides. She was really dead. And this hadn't been a heart attack or a stroke. I'd read enough Agatha Christies to know the smell of bitter almonds meant cyanide.

Bells tinkled behind me. Charlie, in his jester's costume, swung from the door frame into the cramped room. "Oh, you're here." He frowned. "Is that Gloria? Is she okay?"

I brought a shaky hand to my forehead. "No." I met his gaze. "I'm sorry. She's dead. The police are on their way."

"Oh my God." My brother straightened, paling beneath his blond beard. "Gloria can't be dead. I saw her this morning."

I didn't point out a lot could change between morning and night. Sudden death is never easy to process. I still hadn't and was now moving on habit and instinct. "I've been giving her CPR. But I think it's cyanide poisoning."

He let go of the door frame and blinked. "What? No. Murder?" He pulled off his jester's hat and crushed the hat between his hands. "The black knight," he whispered.

Oh, boy. The black knight was one of those local stage myths, like the ghost in my bathroom. He lurked around the theater and heralded... I don't know what he heralded, but it was no doubt apocalyptic.

"The knight?" Kristie breezed into the room behind him in a waft of pink gown. "*He's* not coming around again soon." She seemed to notice Gloria, and her chest swelled. "Nice." Her voice reverberated through the small room. "Gloria picks *now* to play dead? How typical."

"She's not playing," I said in a low voice. "She's dead, and we need to secure the scene. The police are on their way."

"Secure the scene?" Kristie stepped backward and onto Charlie's foot. "Wait. You mean this really *is* murder?"

He winced, hopping on his good foot. "Maybe we should—"

"So you finally made it." Jed strolled into the crowded dressing room and stopped short. "Gloria?"

Hastily, I rose, hands extended. "The police are on their way. I'm sorry, Jed, but—"

He pushed past me and dropped to his knees beside his wife. Grasping her shoulders, he shook her lightly, his handsome face twisted with worry. "Gloria?"

I laid my hand on his shoulder. "I'm sorry, Jed." A futile ache expanded in my chest. "She's gone."

"Gone?" He looked up at me, his hazel eyes wide and uncomprehending. "You mean dead? But she can't be dead. She can't be..."

"We need to make way for emergency services," I said quietly and pocketed my phone. "We need to step outside."

Kristie pointed at a fallen glass beside the dressing table. The remains of a yellowish liquid spilled from it. "Poison," she hissed.

"That's Gloria's pineapple juice," Charlie said. "She drinks it before every performance. So that means she *was* planning on performing tonight."

"She's in costume." Kristie twisted the gauzy material cascading from the top of her hat. "Of course she was planning on performing."

"Look," I said, raising my voice. "The longer we stay here, the greater the chance we contaminate the scene for the police." Aside from my years in countersurveillance, my past life had given me some experience in crime scenes. The police really did not like civilians wandering around them.

"*You're* here," Kristie said.

Lilyanna Gomez stuck her head into the dressing room. "What's going on?" She was a delicate-looking brunette costumed in humble, peasant-like attire. A thick scarf draped over her head like a nun's habit. Briefly, I closed my eyes.

"Charlie," Lilyana said, flushing delicately, "would you mind helping me with...?" Her eyes widened. "Gloria? What happened?" She hurried to Jed, kneeling beside his wife, and laid a slim hand on his shoulder.

I exhaled slowly. *Who next*? I liked Lilyanna, but come *on*.

"She's not... dead?" Lilyanna whispered.

"I'm sorry," I said, "she is. The sheriff will be here any minute, and—"

"Eh, probably not." Charlie rubbed his foot. "There's that big Halloween thing over in Hot Springs tonight."

Kristie arched a brow. "*The Town* of Hot Springs."

"Right," my brother said. "*The* Hot Springs." He pointed at an open laptop computer on the dressing table. "Look. Gloria's computer's on. Maybe there's a clue on it."

I sucked in a breath to shout. They might play amateur detectives in murder mysteries, but that didn't mean they were the next Miss Marple.

"Alice is right," Kristie said, surprising me. "We need to leave the clues for the sheriff. Everyone out. Chop, chop." She clapped her hands and bustled everyone, me included, from the room. We clustered at the top of the narrow stairs.

"Now what?" she asked me.

Good question. Before becoming a bodyguard, I'd been an MP. I'd been the equivalent of a beat cop, and not for very long. I knew the basics, but not much more. "Usually the police don't want witnesses talking to each other. We might mess with each other's memories."

"Right." Kristie nodded. "Everyone downstairs and to their separate corners." She glanced at Lilyanna, rubbing Jed's back. He hung his head, his face slack. "Except for Lilyanna and Jed," Kristie whispered. "The poor man's obviously in shock."

I nodded. Better to leave Lilyanna to comfort the widower. It wasn't a skill I excelled at.

Kristie trotted down the stairs, followed by Jed and Lilyanna. My brother and I glanced at each other and followed.

The next day, I drooped beside the Sagebrush's counter and stared at my cheeseburger. Arrangements of mini pumpkins and paper leaves lay artistically scattered by my elbow. The scent of pumpkin pancakes mingled with the smell of the grill.

Fredo growled beneath my sky-blue barstool, but no one heard amidst the comforting chatter of the lunch patrons.

The Sagebrush had relaxed it's "dogs outside only" policy for the cold-weather months. The caveat was the dogs had to be well behaved. Fredo wasn't, but the Halloween decorations were all well out of his reach.

Molly Haanson, the Sagebrush's owner, topped up my coffee. "Rough night?"

I smothered a yawn. "The sheriff didn't get to the theater until nearly midnight." A pair of deputies had made it earlier. They'd stood guard and waited for the big man to arrive while we cooled our heels. "He should be voted out."

She snorted. "Good luck with that. The Town of Hot Springs pays his salary." She shook her head. Her blond hair was done up in a bun and laced with silver-gray at the temples. She wore the Sagebrush's Prussian-blue uniform that bared her forearms, scarred with burn marks from kitchen accidents.

"He's a county sheriff. Why does Hot Springs foot the bill?" Something tugged my shoestring. Fredo yanked at it with his snaggle teeth.

"They've got the biggest tax base in the county," she said. "It's all those hotels and restaurants and resorts, and he takes good care of them. They love Sheriff Randall in Hot Springs. Though they've got their own police force, so I'm not sure what they need him for." She shook her head. "It is a lovely town," she concluded doubtfully.

"But there was a m—dead woman *here*," I said, irate.

Old Mr. Washington, on the blue stool beside mine, nudged my elbow. "I heard you found the body."

"The theater cat did," I said. "I just followed Sammie."

He swiveled toward the elderly man beside him. They gave each other knowing looks.

"What?" I asked.

"It's a well-known fact that cats can see ghosts," Mr. Washington said.

"Not that old *ghost in the theater* yarn again," Molly said warningly.

"Looks like there may be another ghost now," Mr. Washington said. "You ever see him?" he asked me.

I shook my head. "Not a peep. Not even a boo."

He snorted. "Boo Peep. Good one."

Beside him, his friend chortled. It hadn't been that funny, but I was pleased I could leave 'em laughing. The bell over the café's glass front door jangled, and we glanced over our shoulders to look.

Gert Magimountain creaked inside and looked around, his wizened face drawing into a scowl. Angry tufts of white hair sprang from above his ears.

Mr. Washington and his buddy swiveled to face front. In a single, unified motion, they picked up their mugs and drank.

"Sommerland," Gert said. "Report."

I blinked. "Excuse me?"

"The murder." He stalked toward me. "You found the body. You didn't call. Whatcha thinking?"

Fredo sat up and panted happily. I wished Gert would take the dog, since Fredo obviously liked him better than me.

"Why would I call you?" I asked slowly. Gert ran the antique store on Main Street. He also rented motorbikes and other random bits of equipment people might need. He'd *also* tried to kill me on several occasions, but I liked to think we'd moved beyond that.

He blinked furiously behind his thick spectacles. "Because I'm the mayor."

Mr. Washington coughed. It sounded a lot like *temporary*. Gert scowled at him.

I cleared my throat. "Sorry. I didn't think to call. It was pretty late."

"I don't sleep much anyway. Molly, coffee." Our temporary mayor thumped onto the empty stool beside me. "Well?"

"I found Gloria—"

"You said the cat found her," Mr. Washington said.

I swiveled to face Gert before Mr. Washington could add more helpful comments. "The cat and I found Gloria in her dressing room. She appeared to be dead, but I applied CPR and called 9-1-1. I couldn't revive her."

"And?" Gert's bushy brows drew downward. "I heard Gloria Jackson was poisoned."

"I'm sure we'll have to wait for the coroner to make that determination," I demurred.

"And I heard you said it was cyanide," Gert snapped.

"I smelled bitter almonds," I said, "and her face was flushed pink. Those are both signs of cyanide poisoning."

I'd looked it up after the sheriff had searched my room and given me permission to retreat to it. And I'd learned that if you ingest enough, it can quickly cause unconsciousness, followed by death.

It must have been a large dose. Gloria couldn't have been at the theater long before the show started. She hadn't finished dressing. A gray, heavy feeling settled in my chest. If any of us had dared open the door to check on her, maybe she could have been saved.

"Actors." Gert shook his head. "Always trouble."

Mr. Washington leered. "Oh, I don't think it was Gloria's *acting* that got her in trouble."

"You think it was something at the school?" Gert asked.

"School?" I parroted.

Gert waved a gnarled hand. "She's—I mean, Gloria *was*—the admin assistant at the grammar school."

Someone had conned a private school into open in Nowhere. I suspected Mr. Washington's son, our town benefactor and financer of the Big Things, had been behind it.

Mr. Washington chortled into his coffee. "Right. The school."

I studied him. What was going on here? "Was she involved in something else?"

Mr. Washington made a show of looking around, then leaned closer. "Spicy pictures," he said in a low voice.

"Wait," I said. "You mean... pictures of Gloria? How? Where?"

Mr. Washington shrugged beneath his loose gray jacket. "I never saw 'em. My nephew told me if she wasn't careful though, she'd be fired."

My mind churned through the web of Nowhere relations. "Your nephew who works at the meadery?"

"That's the one. He's got another job at the mini-mart now too. A real portfolio career."

I nodded wisely.

"He hates those Viking helmets," Mr. Washington continued. "They're too heavy. Says they give him a headache."

"Not the plastic ones?" I said.

"No," he said. "The metal ones the staff has to wear."

"I thought the staff brought those from home," I said.

"Forget the helmets," Gert said. "We got a murderer in Nowhere. We all should be wearing helmets if we don't solve this and fast. What's an unsolved crime going to do for tourism?"

I drew a breath. "The sheriff—"

"There's that whole murder tourism thing," Mr. Washington said. "People like that. And it's Halloween soon. We could do a ghost tour of the theater."

Oh, hell no. I lived there.

Molly set down her coffeepot with a bang. "The poor woman isn't even cold, and you want to profit off her? Shame on you all."

We shriveled on our seats. The bell jangled behind us, and we turned, hoping for a reprieve from Molly's glare. Cane tapping, Mrs. Malone strode into the café.

Gert adjusted his bowtie and slipped from the stool. "Artemesia. Would you like to join us?"

"I need to speak to Alice," she said.

"Everyone out," Gert said, shooing the old men off their bar stools.

Mrs. Malone sighed. "At a table, if you please." She cocked her head toward an empty corner booth.

I grabbed my coffee and Fredo's leash, and we followed. "What's up?" I slid into the booth across from her.

"What's up? *What's up*? Someone was murdered in my theater, you found the body, and you wonder what's up?"

"It was terrible, but the sheriff's got everything under control. He said the show could go on tonight. They've only closed off the dressing room, and—"

"Only the dressing room? The sheriff doesn't care about this murder."

"He seemed pretty interested." When he eventually got to the theater.

"Did he?" Her mouth puckered. "Because it doesn't sound like it to me. He let a Halloween extravaganza in Hot Springs divert him from a Nowhere murder. What does that tell you?"

I leaned back against the blue Naugahyde and jammed my hands into my pockets. That and other experiences with the sheriff told me Nowhere might not be a priority. But that was a big *might*.

She ground her fingertip into the table. "It tells you *we* need to investigate."

Chapter Four

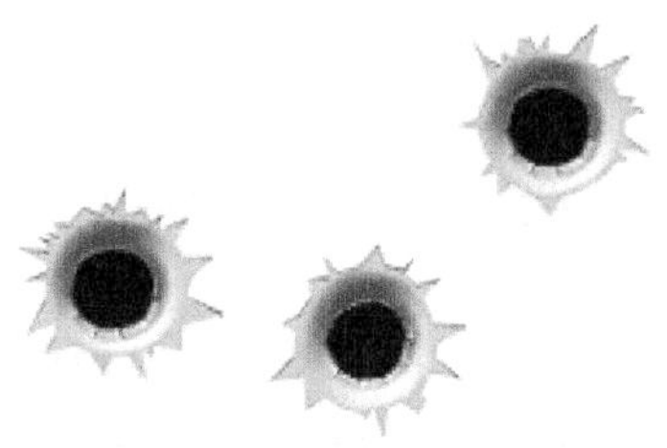

A glass crashed in the café. Fredo started beneath our table, and I guess I jumped a little too.

"We?" I blurted stupidly. The dog tried to clamber into the booth beside me, but I pushed him away. I was pretty sure Molly didn't want the dog on her furniture.

Mrs. Malone sniffed. "Don't worry. You'll purely be the muscle."

Hell no. I'd never been much of a bodyguard. There was a good reason why I'd stuck mostly to surveillance.

My stomach rumbled. I glanced at the counter and my waiting food. The diner smelled like lunch—burgers and fries and other good things—and it was really distracting. "In the first place, my specialty is countersurveillance, not muscle—"

"Excellent. We'll need to surveil all the suspects."

"In the second..." What was second? I brightened, remembering. "Second, the sheriff is investigating. The police don't like it when civilians interfere."

The older woman arched a gray brow. "Do you really think the sheriff will notice?"

That was actually a good point. "And third," I said, "neither of us are private investigators."

"But you work for one." She sneezed. "Did you have to bring that dog?"

"I don't *work* for Fitch. It's short-term contract employment until I get back to personal protection." Annoyance pinched my lips. Just because Mrs. Malone had the world's biggest collection of true-crime novels...

Mrs. Malone's upper lip curled. "Now, you're just hairsplitting."

"And fourth, no."

"No? No?" Her mouth pinched. "We have a contract."

"What contract?"

"Our rental agreement."

Baffled, I wrinkled my forehead. "Is a rental agreement. It doesn't say anything about amateur detecting."

Mrs. Malone thumped her fist on the laminate table, and the salt and pepper shakers jumped. Fredo looked up. "It says you will perform any additional tasks related to the theater as the need arises," she said. "The need has arisen."

"What? I don't remember that." Had that been in the contract? In all honesty, I hadn't read it that closely.

"It's not my fault if you didn't read the contract."

"But—"

"Why do you think you got such a good deal on the rent?"

"Because there's a cat that won't leave me alone, and a noisy theater beneath me five nights a week. And the theater's haunted, I might add."

"Don't tell me you believe *that*."

I folded my arms. "I'm not doing it. I could get in serious trouble with the cops, contract or no. You know how they feel about me."

"I'll give you a month's free rent."

Whoa. Really? I had to play this cool. I arched a brow. "Three months."

"Two."

"Three."

"Two, and I won't evict you for blowing all the theater's fuses last week with that ancient hotplate."

I sucked in a breath. The theater's fuses were a lot older than my hotplate. Though my hotplate was a little old. "Now wait a darn minute—"

"I also expect you to stop using that hotplate." She checked her gold watch and edged from the booth. "Be at my house at three. We can review the murder board there. Leave the dog."

"Murder board?"

She swiveled on her sensible heels and strode from the café.

Murder board? I shook my head. Still, two months' rent wasn't bad. Granted, the rent wasn't that high. I suspected Fitch got paid more for his cases.

But I wouldn't be working on this full time. And I didn't have any better offers at the present. Besides, I'd already gathered some good intel about Gloria and naughty pictures, so the way I figured it, I could take the rest of the day off.

Someone tugged at my sleeve, and I twitched. Clyde, a pudgy blond man about my age (mid-thirties—okay, late thirties) blinked up at me with guileless blue eyes. "I heard you're investigating the murder," he said. "I want to help."

How had he heard that? *I'd* only just learned I was doing it. "I'm not investigating the murder." I paused, curious. "And how could you help?"

"I know everything about the cast. I was Gloria's biggest fan. I saw every show. I even wrote a murder script for them."

Beneath the table, Fredo growled.

"Do they even use scripts?" I asked. "They're improv players."

"Yes, but they need to know whodunit and how. The script's basic, but it's a framework for their improv."

"Were you at the theater last night?"

He crammed into the booth to sit across from me. It was a tight fit. "Ah, no. Events conspired against me."

"Who do you think wanted Gloria dead?"

He looked around the crowded café and lowered his voice. "I suspect her sister."

"Gloria has a sister?"

"Jane."

I blinked. "Jane? The woman who manages the restaurant in the theater? And who's also the theater manager? She's Gloria's sister?"

"I know," he said. "They don't look a thing alike. But that's because they're only half-sisters."

I looked longingly at the counter, where my cheeseburger was cooling. "Why would Jane want her dead?"

He shook his head sadly. "I'm afraid Jane always envied Gloria's talent."

Molly stopped by our table. "You want your burger and fries to go, hon?"

"Sure. Thanks." It looked like I was going to have to reheat them anyway. She bustled away, and I turned to Clyde. "What about the other players?" I asked.

"Kristie is just as she appears, the group's mother hen. And Jed adored his wife. Your brother, ah, well, I don't think he's particularly motivated toward crime."

He could have dropped the "toward crime" part and still described my brother accurately. Maybe Clyde really *did* get the cast of characters. "Anyone else?"

"It has to be someone at the theater, don't you think? Security's not particularly tight there, but I'd think someone who didn't belong would have been noticed. Don't you?"

I did think so. "Thanks. That's helpful." I rose, holding Fredo's leash, and made for the counter. Molly strode from the kitchen and handed me a bag. I paid and headed for the door.

"Wait," Clyde called from the booth. "What do you want me to do next?"

I turned, walking backwards toward the glass door. "Keep a low profile."

"And what else?"

"Keep your eyes and ears open."

He nodded eagerly. "Right. Gotcha."

I escaped out the door and flipped up the collar of my jacket. Did *everyone* in this town think they could play detective? And yes, I know that sounds hypocritical. After all, I was playing detective. But surveillance is a key detecting skill. And I *had* discovered the body. I was also justifying what I was about to do. But everyone does that.

Fredo and I walked to my brother's treehouse, nestled in a neat residential neighborhood. And no, *treehouse* is not a euphemism for some fancy home in the trees. Charlie lives in a child's treehouse. It sleeps one uncomfortably. And it's in the front yard of a home he doesn't own. I glanced at the FOR-SALE sign spiked into the dead lawn.

Shielding my eyes, I squinted up into the big pine. "Charlie?" The air had a snap to it, and that worried me. My brother said his sleeping bag went to minus something or other, but he needed a better home.

My brother's shaggy blond head popped out the window, and he smiled. "Hi, Fredo." He waved. "Cool. You're here. Come on up." His head vanished inside the treehouse.

I tied Fredo's leash to the realty sign, climbed the makeshift ladder hammered into the tree, and crawled through the opening in the floor.

Charlie sat cross legged on his sleeping bag. Beside him, a duffel lay on the uneven wooden planks. He finger-combed his loose hair behind one ear. "I was going to call you. What did you learn about the murder?"

"Only that Nowhere's got an unusually large supply of amateur detectives. What's going on with the house?" I angled my head downward and toward the ranch house below.

His face fell. "I think it's going to sell. I'm going to have to move soon."

"Any idea where?" I asked warily. I wasn't going to let my brother go homeless, but space was limited in my studio apartment.

Airily, he waved the concern away. "That's not important."

"It seems kind of important."

"No, no, there are bigger things in play here."

Nowhere had a population of 8,372. Bigger things in play than murder didn't seem likely. "Like what?"

"Listen." Charlie edged forward on his sleeping bag. "I know how we can catch the black knight."

"Who?"

"The black knight who's been creeping around every time we do our medieval show. He's like a character in a bad movie, except he's real."

I folded my arms. "Have you actually seen this so-called black knight?"

"That's what I've been trying to tell you. The black knight was *there*."

Oh, brother. "The black knight, if he even exists—"

"Oh, he exists." Charlie nodded vehemently.

"Might not be connected to any of this," I finished. "According to you, he's been hanging around for months."

"More like six weeks."

"Whatever. I've never seen him."

"Yeah, that's because he's probably terrified of you."

At least something was going right. "Let's table the black knight as a suspect for now. In fact, let's table the whole idea of investigating anything. That's what the sheriff's department is for."

I shifted uncomfortably on the wooden floorboards. I had just promised Mrs. Malone I'd investigate in exchange for free rent. But that was me, and he was talking about *we*. A small animal scrabbled across the peaked roof, and we looked up.

"The sheriff's department's not going to solve this crime," Charlie said. "I mean, just look at them. You can't look at them because they haven't been around. But I've got an idea. All we need to do..." He spread his hands wide, palms out. "...is reenact the murder," he finished triumphantly.

"Reenact... In all my time working for a private investigator—"

"Huh. Three weeks?"

"More than that. I don't think I've ever heard of him using that technique."

"Augh." He let his head drop backward. "You're always telling me to play to my strengths. I'm an actor. Acting out the murder is playing to my strength."

A chill breeze carrying the scents of woodsmoke and autumn drifted through the window. I pulled my jacket tighter. "And we can't reenact it when we have no idea how she was killed."

He angled his head. "Come on. Cyanide. You said it yourself. Bitter almonds. Flushed face. Someone put cyanide in her pineapple juice. Everyone knew she drank the stuff before a performance."

"Everyone? Or just the other people in the theater?"

"See," Charlie said. "I knew you'd be good at this. That's exactly the sort of question a real detective would ask."

"Except I'm not a real detective. I'm not even a trainee detective. And the sheriff is investigating the murder."

"Oh, come on. It took him hours to get to the theater last night. He doesn't care about Nowhere. He's a pawn of Hot Springs. *The* Hot Springs," he sneered, then shook his head, sobering. "Gloria really loved that juice. Death by pineapple, the unkindest cut of all."

I folded my arms. "I'd say death by cyanide is unkinder."

"Yeah. You're probably right. Still, it was *in* the pineapple juice. So what do you think?"

I flopped back against the wall of the treehouse. "About what?" I asked, exasperated.

"About recreating the crime?"

"I think it's a bad idea."

"What?" His pale brows drew downward. "No way. It's a great idea."

"It's too soon for something like that. We can't recreate something we know so little about." *Dammit.* I'd just agreed with the premise of the two of us fighting crime together.

"What's to know? Poison in the pineapple juice. Boom. Done."

Oh, what the hell? Charlie knew this town better than I did. And I could see where this was going. My brother was going to do what he wanted.

But I threw out a few more halfhearted objections. "When was it put in her juice? Did it go into her glass or into the carton? If it went into the glass, then the poisoner probably put it there when Gloria was in the room with him or her. How did they distract her?"

He snapped his fingers. "Gloria had a mini fridge. It could have gone into the juice in advance."

"Who had access to her dressing room? Did Gloria keep it locked?"

"Uh..." He grimaced. "I sort of steered clear of it. But her husband might know."

If only Charlie would be wise enough to steer clear of the sheriff. He'd tried to arrest my brother before. Twice. I worried it might be becoming a habit. "Did Jed use her dressing room too?"

"I think so." My brother screwed up his face. "But sometimes he just came to the theater already in costume. I think he liked to change at home."

"But it wouldn't have looked odd to anyone if he'd gone inside?"

He slumped. "No."

A stiffer breeze whipped through the window, and the treehouse groaned. "The sheriff will test whatever's left of the pineapple juice," I said. "He'll have a better idea if someone poisoned her in advance or in person."

"But he's not going to tell us what he finds out."

"Which is why we should stay out of it." Despite the chill, beads of sweat broke out on my forehead. Charlie was going to get in real trouble with the sheriff if he didn't watch out.

My brother frowned. "But... we all worked together. Gloria died in *our* theater, on our watch. We can't ignore a murder in our theater."

"It's Mrs. Malone's theater," I said glumly. I really needed to take another look at that contract.

"Mrs. Malone's theater, our theater, it doesn't matter. We're murder mystery players, and one of our own was killed. If the three of us can't figure this out, then who can?"

"Wait. Three?" I pointed to the roof. "You're not including the squirrel, are you? Because that thing's a menace."

"Charlie?" a feminine voice called up. Fredo barked cheerfully from the lawn.

"That's Lilyanna," my brother said. "I asked her to come so we could plan our next steps."

My hands briefly clenched. I like Lilyanna. She's sweet, and she's thoughtful, and I suspected she had a crush on my brother. But she was also convinced she'd been abducted by aliens and was exactly the sort of person the sheriff was itching to toss in jail. "There are no next steps."

"In our investigation." He leaned out the window and waved to her. "Come on up."

Augh. Now Lilyanna was investigating too? And Lord only knew what Mrs. Malone and Gert would get up to. What was wrong with this town?

"No, don't come up," I shouted. I didn't think the treehouse could hold three adults. "I'll come down."

"But we need to work together," Charlie said.

"And we will," I promised hastily. All I had to do was keep Charlie, and Mrs. Malone, and Gert out of the sheriff's way. No biggie. I'd just nose around, throw them a few nonsensical clues, and let them think they were helping.

It would work.

Right?

My pulse quickened unpleasantly. It was a terrible position for a fight. He was three steps above me. All he had to do was push me down the stairs and shoot me. Or just push me down the stairs. Or just wait for Fredo to do the job.

I gripped the railing. The smart play would be to pretend I didn't see anything, to smile, to keep going. "The theater's closed," I said. "And put back that laptop."

"Beat it," he growled, walking down the middle of the narrow wooden stairs. "This is a crime scene."

So that was a weird thing to say if he was a criminal. "I know it's a crime scene. I live here." And I really didn't like what that said about me. "What are you doing with Gloria's laptop?"

"You live in a haunted theater?"

"It's not haunted." How did everyone know about the ghost but me? And how did *he* know? He wasn't from Nowhere. I definitely would have noticed him. Broad shouldered, mid-forties, and a square jaw spoiled by a brutally blunt haircut. He looked at least six-feet tall, but it was hard to tell from this angle. "And I said, put that computer back."

"Police. Get out of my way."

That explained the haircut but not the suit. "Let's see some ID."

He sighed and pulled back his jacket, exposing a badge on his belt. "Aiden Guthrie. Homicide."

"Oh. You're a detective." Because no beat cop wore Armani. Come to think of it, most detectives didn't either. Unless... *Oh, damn.* He was from Hot Springs. He nodded, seeing me catch on. "About time you got here," I snapped. "She was killed yesterday."

His mouth compressed. "I was busy."

"In Hot Springs?"

"It's the Town of Hot Springs."

At least he wasn't lying about being from Hot Springs. Only people from Hot Springs called it *The Town of*. It was unbelievably pretentious.

Yagh!" He skipped backward and pointed at Fredo. "What the hell's that?"

I folded my arms. “It’s a dog.”

“If you say so,” the detective said doubtfully. Fredo growled. “Oh, yeah, you’re the bodyguard who offed that scumbag Koppel,” he continued. “Good work.”

“I didn’t—It was a car accident,” I said hotly. “Koppel stole my car. It’s not my fault he crashed it. I loved that car. You’re a detective. You should know this sort of background about the person who found the body.”

Briefly, I closed my eyes. I shouldn’t have said that. Though if he knew who I was, he already knew I’d found the body.

He grunted. “That’s a lot less interesting. I should have guessed after reviewing your statement.”

“What’s that supposed to mean?” I was extremely interesting.

“It means we’ll talk later.” He pushed past me.

I’d guessed right. He really was six-feet tall.

“I can wait,” I said. “Seriously, I can wait for days. Weeks.”

“Huh.” He kept going, unimpressed.

My ax throwing partner for the night strolled from the room, her ax dead center in the target. I squinted at it. I’d been practicing for months, and I still felt glee when I even *hit* the target.

Nowhere doesn’t have much, but it does have a state-of-the-art Viking bar. The axe throwing section was decked out in blond wood, fake Viking shields hanging from the back wall between high, round tables.

With a sigh, I stepped across the blue and red throwing lines painted on the floor and moved to retrieve the ax for her. It was an unwritten Viking bar rule: loser put the axes back.

“I thought I’d find you here,” a man said behind me.

I jumped a little and turned. “Am I that predictable?”

Fitch Rhodes, private investigator, grinned at me. Broad shoulders. Mid-forties. Taller than me. And occasionally my contract-employer. I suppressed a girlish shiver, the *employer* part being the most relevant.

"That's not bad." He nodded at my partner's ax, still in its target. He wore jeans and a green Henley that brought his eyes.

"Were you watching me throw?" I asked, glancing at the door through which my partner had vanished.

"No," he said, "I just got here."

I yanked the ax free. "Yeah, well, I've been practicing."

"If only your report writing was that on target."

"It's all in the wrist," I said. "Well, not really. You see, you have to judge the distance—"

"Speaking of the theater—"

"Were we?"

He pushed up the sleeves of his green shirt. "It beats talking about what happened in Reno."

I set the ax on the table. "I—"

"You got lucky."

"What did you want me to do? Wait for the police to arrive while your client asphyxiated?"

"I want you to not get killed."

The thing was, I *had* been lucky. I hadn't wanted to take on the dentist. He could have handed me my head on a plate.

I'd like to say I'd planned to keep him crouched over by dumping the shelves on him. But I hadn't. The fact that he'd come at me in a wrestler's crouch, that I'd managed not to fall on my butt, that I'd surprised him by bringing my knee up that fast...

I'd been lucky, and that scared me. Things could have gone very wrong very fast. There was a reason I specialized in countersurveillance. It was the same reason my close protection gigs had all been situational, providing protection in spaces men weren't allowed.

What I didn't understand was why this particular incident was still gnawing at me. I'd been in a physical situation a couple of months back—one equally dangerous, if not more so. But I'd had a weapon then, and that had evened the odds.

"You okay?" he asked.

"Yeah," I said slowly. "I just... I don't usually get into fights like that." Maybe I'd strayed too far outside my comfort zone. Maybe I needed to get back to it. I was surveillance, not a fighter.

"Are you shook?" he asked.

I frowned. He didn't need to belabor the point. I'd been belaboring it enough on my own. "No. Just second guessing myself."

"You ever been punched in the face before?"

I laid my forearm on the high table and raised a brow. "Excuse me?"

He folded his arms, his biceps bulging. "You've never been punched in the face, have you?"

"No," I said dryly. "Hard as it may be to believe, I haven't."

"That's why you're shook. Once you get punched in the face, you know it's not so bad, and the next fight's easier."

"It may not be so bad for you. But if a guy your size hits a woman my size, I may not get up again." And I wasn't exactly small. But there were physics involved, namely Newton's Second Law of Motion: *force = mass x acceleration*. Men had advantages in all of those factors.

"You're right." Fitch cocked his head thoughtfully. "On second thought, don't get punched in the face. I heard you had a murder at the theater. What's the story?"

Relieved by the change of subject, I said, "Let's grab a beer."

We ambled into the beer hall. I unloaded the axes. We ordered at the bar and found a corner table. A gaggle of gamers dressed like medieval marauders rolled dice at a nearby table. The dice clattered, and three gamers cheered. The fourth, huddled behind an open hardback, scowled.

"How's your client?" I asked.

He scraped his hand across the top of his wavy hair. "Mad as hell about the damage to her car. She was threatening to sue. The car was only a few months old."

My face heated, guilt mingling with anger. *I'd* dropped that shelf on her car, not Fitch. "Are you kidding me? I saved her—Hold on. Did you say she *was* threatening?"

"When she learned you were *the* Alice Sommerland," he said, "she backed off and decided to pay me a bonus instead. You'll see a cut."

That just made me feel worse. "Using me to scare a client—"

"It wasn't me." He raised his hands defensively. "One of the local cops filled her in on your history."

"Oh." If my cruddy reputation had gotten Fitch out of a potential lawsuit, well, at least it was good for something. Still, I didn't like being painted as one of the bad guys. "Thanks." I shifted on the wooden chair. "Got any more surveillance work coming up?"

"Not right now." He eyed me. "Nothing from your old company?"

"No," I said shortly. My old company was run by my ex-husband. I'd like to say I'd forgiven him for cheating on me and leaving me to hang out to dry when a case had blown up in our faces. But I guess I'm not that big of a person.

"Tell me about this murder," he said. "Who was Gloria Jackson?"

I sighed. Two jobs in a row probably had been too much to hope for. "She's the theater's diva."

"How much of a diva?"

"She was the only one with her own dressing room, so she stepped on a lot of toes. Her husband's a player at the theater too, and he had access. Her sister, Jane, is the theater manager. She also manages the actors and the dinners, so she had easy access."

"Those are your two top suspects?" he asked.

"I wouldn't say they're my suspects. It's not like I'm investigating."

A waiter in a horned helmet dropped off our beer steins, slopping foam over the sides and onto the wooden table.

"You hiring me?" Fitch asked.

I choked in my beer. Like I had the money for a PI. Besides, I'd gotten an inside look at his investigations. They didn't seem that complicated. If he could do it, so could I. But unease quivered in my gut.

"Skoll." Fitch lifted his stein in a toast and swigged down a gulp. "Who found the body?"

"I did."

He set down his beer and stared. "You did?"

"I was just following the cat."

Fitch shook his head. "Alice, this is the second time in Nowhere you've found a murder victim."

"It does seem like bad luck, but I have a theory."

He rolled his eyes. "I can't wait to hear it."

"It's a small town."

"And?"

"And what?" I spread my hands. "It's a small town. The odds of a bad thing happening to the same person twice aren't that low."

"That's not a theory. It's a statement."

"It's true though."

"Imagine you're a cop," he said.

"I'm trying not to." I'd been an MP in the Army, the military equivalent of a beat cop. It didn't qualify me to investigate murders, but it didn't disqualify me either.

"You're called to a murder in a small town," he said, his green eyes serious. "A stranger, an out-of-towner, has found the body. Naturally, you suspect her, because we all hate strangers and would rather it not be an inside job. But it turns out an insider *did* do it, and the stranger's off the hook."

I braced my elbow on the table, my head on my fist. "This is all sounding strangely familiar." As it had happened to me a few months back.

"Now imagine that stranger decides to stick around. And whadaya know? She finds another murder victim. How does that stranger look to you?"

"What a rotten run of luck. I'm starting to feel bad for her."

He cocked an eyebrow.

"All right." I sipped my beer. "I take your point. It doesn't look good." Maybe a day would come when my reputation as a killer of a villainous blackmailer wouldn't dog me, but that day was in the distant future.

"And you *live* in that theater. You had access."

My heart skipped a beat. "But no motive. I barely knew the woman."

"You said she was a diva. Did she ever give your brother guff?"

I laughed. "I'm sure she did, but do you think Charlie would have noticed?"

"Not the point. You're protective of your little brother. Everyone knows that."

"I'd have to be nuts to kill someone just because they were bossy to a relative." I sipped my beer again, more slowly. It *would* be nuts. But if I were the sheriff...

I slumped, numbness spreading through my center. *Oh, damn.*

"What are you doing about it?" he asked.

"I'm trying to keep half a dozen townspeople from interfering in the sheriff's investigation. Everyone thinks they're an amateur detective. My brother. Mrs. Malone. Gert..."

"The lunatic with the antique store?"

"That lunatic is interim mayor."

He whistled. "This gets better and better."

I sank lower in my chair. Talking things over with Fitch hadn't exactly filled me with positivity. I'd been so busy worrying about my friends getting arrested, I hadn't considered how I might look.

But what was I supposed to do? The fact was, I *had* found Gloria. I couldn't pretend otherwise. I propped my head on my hand. "Look," I said. "I can't hire you. I just can't afford it right now."

He nodded. His agreement was mildly annoying.

"But if you were investigating..." I trailed off. "How would you go about it?"

Chapter Six

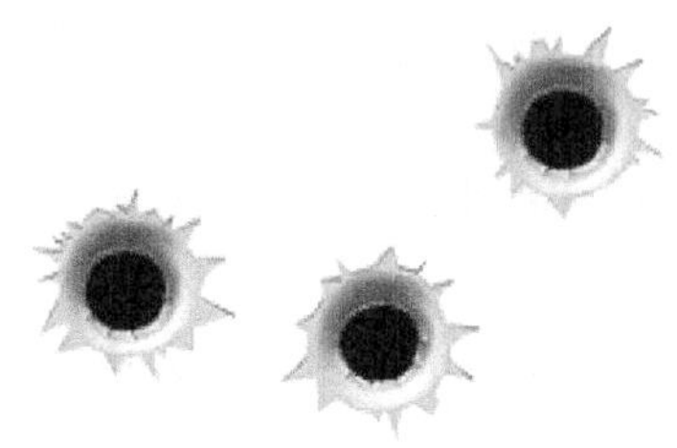

Nowhere'd had a Halloween parade for as long as I could remember. And for as long as I could remember, it had been weak. Nowhere's a small town. There's just not that much to parade.

But the Big Things had changed that. We cruised past the giant mushrooms, covered in webs and menaced by oversized spiders, and a shiver ran up my spine. Not because it was scary. It wasn't. Not even close. But because for the first time since I'd been home, the changes to the town seemed *real*.

A belly dance troupe billed as the Danse Macabre swayed ahead of us in black gowns and skeletal faces. Two floats ahead, a steampunk team of vampire hunters menaced a giant octopus. Behind our car a jet of fire shot into the air—the fire juggler. And behind him, the theater troupe, in 1920s costumes, brandished prop tommy guns at the crowd.

I sat beside Gert on top of the seat in the metallic green Caddy convertible. The air was clear with an October chill, and I pulled my black parka tighter.

He nudged me. "Wave."

I waved, feeling ridiculous. As a kid, I'd wanted to be part of the parade, even if it had been small and silly. So a part of me was secretly thrilled I'd finally made it.

"I don't want people thinking I need a bodyguard." Gert scowled. "Because I don't. I'm only letting you tag along because of Mrs. Malone. Got it?"

"Got it. It's the only reason I'm doing it too."

"Yeah, well. Good."

A thick crowd of tourists and locals lined Main Street. Outside their shops, owners handed out candy.

"Who *are* all these people?" I motioned toward the belly dancers.

"They're here for the Halloween Faire," Gert said. "That's faire with an *e*. Mrs. Malone and I will need you to check the security on that."

I fidgeted my foot. Mrs. Malone and I would be chatting about that. Maybe I could get another couple weeks' rent out of the job. "And how is that connected to the theater?"

"Your brother and the others from the theater will be performing, of course. Charlie's even created a mystery game based on the faire. Now, he's got real Nowhere spirit, unlike *some* people I could mention," he said pointedly.

That stupid contract. I glanced over my shoulder. Lilyanna, in a beaded flapper's dress, died dramatically in my brother's arms. Charlie scooped her up, walked a few paces, and set her down again. They ran to the spectators and handed out flyers.

BANG.

I started to reach for Gert, but he'd already dropped down in his seat. This was a good thing, because the bang hadn't been a gunshot. A car had backfired. I didn't know if anyone in the crowd had seen my paranoid reaction, but at least Gert hadn't. He blinked rapidly, his blue eyes magnified through his glasses. Head whipping around, Gert reached beneath his jacket.

"You're clear," I said quickly. "It was only a backfire."

He withdrew his hand from his jacket, and I relaxed. Gert had an arsenal of antique weapons. They were as likely to blow up in his own face as shoot someone.

I glanced over my shoulder. Charlie lay sprawled in the street, and my chest seized. It *had* been a backfire, but why was he—?

My brother sat up and waved, and my shoulders dropped. Charlie must have taken advantage of the noise to improv another murder.

I shook my head. He really *was* a good actor. What would he have become if he'd ever left Nowhere?

Gert crawled back onto his perch beside me. "You can never be too careful," he muttered.

The parade edged forward. Horns from a high school band blared somewhere ahead. *The school.* Gloria had worked at the local grade school. Her colleagues might be a good place to start. I glanced over my shoulder again. Jed wasn't among the theater paraders.

But starting with the victim's husband maybe made more sense than with her school. "Gert, do you know where Jed lives?"

"Don't you?" he asked.

"No," I said patiently, "that's why I'm asking."

"He's across the street and down one from Charlie's treehouse."

"What?" That was... Okay, it wasn't *that* weird. It was a small town. There weren't that many streets and houses to choose from. But still... It didn't mean anything that my brother was the murder victim's neighbor.

Did it?

Jed lived in a green Craftsman style two-story house with a porch and shingled, sloping roof. I walked through its rock garden, an artistic tumble of rocks and scrub plants. There was a lot of talent in little Nowhere, and my thoughts drifted back to the parade I'd just left.

Climbing the porch steps, I glanced across the street and down a house. The FOR-SALE sign was still in the yard beneath Charlie's treehouse, and I lightly bit my bottom lip. Even in Nowhere, the housing market was heating up. My brother was going to have to move soon.

I knocked on the green front door. A few moments later, I rang the bell.

Jed opened the door and frowned. "Alice?" One corner of his button-up shirt was untucked from his khaki slacks, and his thick, brown hair was mussed, as if I'd just woken him from an afternoon snooze on the couch.

"Hi, Jed." I hesitated. "Can I come in?"

In answer, he stepped forward and hugged me. Awkwardly, I patted his back. I'm not really a hugger.

"You tried to save her," he said, his voice muffled against my black jacket. He stepped backward, opening the door wider, and I walked inside.

The house smelled like vanilla. It was decorated in the Scandinavian style—angular wood furniture and stark colors. He led me into a pale living room, and we sat opposite on hard wooden benches with thin, ivory cushions. I guessed he didn't want me to stay long.

"How are you holding up?" I asked in a quiet voice.

He braced his elbows on his thighs, his hands dangling between his knees, and looked down. "I'm not sure how I'm supposed to be holding up." A triangle of wan, early afternoon sunlight slanted through the curtains and across Jed's scuffed boat shoes. One of the gray laces was untied.

"I don't think there are rules in a situation like this," I said. Though I was pretty sure hassling a new widower for clues was outside the bounds of good manners. "Is there any way I can help?"

His jaw worked. He looked out the living room window to the street beyond. "I guess I don't know that either."

I nodded, abashed. On the mantlepiece, a clock ticked beside wood-framed photos of Gloria and Jed, and I resisted the urge to get up and study them, to give him time to gather himself. The fireplace was made of river stone, lovely and romantic, a place for couples to gaze together at its flickering flames, and my heart tightened.

I rubbed the finger where I'd once worn a ring and cleared my throat. "Have the police given you any information? Any leads they might have?" They shouldn't have since Jed had to be the prime suspect. But you never knew, and I didn't quite trust Sheriff Randall to do the right thing. I didn't think the sheriff was a bad guy, but I did think he was a careless one.

"No." Jed laughed hollowly. "All they've done is ask me questions."

I wrinkled my brow. "Like what?"

"Like how was our relationship? Did we have any problems? Who knew about her pineapple juice habit, and who had access to her dressing room?"

"*Did* your wife have any enemies?"

"No," he said. "How could she? Gloria worked at a grammar school. Her hobby was acting in the local dinner theater. She was innocent."

Not according to Mr. William's nephew. "What else was she interested in?"

He straightened slowly. "What else?"

"All I knew about her was that she was terrific at improv. There must have been more to Gloria than that."

He ran his thumb along the edge of the couch's wooden arm. "She..." He swallowed, looked toward the entry to the kitchen. "She liked cooking."

People lie to me all the time. Most of the time, they're half-lies, evasions. I was fairly certain Jed had just delivered one to me.

He knew about the dirty pictures. Or about *something*. "There are a lot of great recipes online these days," I said, bland. "They're going to put traditional cookbooks out of business."

Jed paled. "Yes. Yes, I suppose so." He rose. "Well, thank you for your condolences."

I hadn't offered any yet, though I should have. I stood. "Please let me know what you need, and I'll help however I can."

"Yes," he said. "Thank you. Everyone's been so generous." He hustled me out the door.

I returned to my Jeep and drove back to the theater. Fredo and Sammie had expressed their displeasure at my absence by playing tug-of-war with one of my bargain throw pillows.

Resigned to my fate as a new dog owner, I cleaned up the stuffing. Then I took Fredo for a walk and returned to do some serious internet research at my card table.

Gloria had a social media page that she'd barely used. There were no death threats on it. More interesting, Clyde McGarrity had created a fan website dedicated to her work.

Welcome to ***Adoring Gloria Jackson****, your online resource for everything Gloria.*

Born Gloria Glover, December 16, 1978, Gloria is best known for her roles as Queen Esmerelda in A Medieval Murder, The Woman in Green, *in* A Roaring (20s) Homicide, *and as Sal in* A Miner Murder.

NOTICE: ***Gloria Jackson was brutally murdered before what would be her final performance on Friday, October 19th. The killer remains at large. Anyone with information should contact me through the form on this website.***

What would be her final performance? Had Gloria planned to quit the dinner theater? Or was that just an awkwardly worded addendum?

I scrolled down.

Photos. Lots of photos. Gloria and Jed dancing at the Dog & Wine. Gloria mingling with guests at the theater. Gloria shopping at the minimart.

I whistled, the hairs rising on the back of my neck. This wasn't a fan site. It was a stalker site. At least there weren't any shots of her in her backyard. Or front yard for that matter. Clyde seemed to have limited his stalking to public appearances. But still. *Yeesh.*

I scanned the photos, looking for a clue. Aside from a picture of my brother mock strangling Gloria at the theater, there was nothing incriminating.

There was a hacking sound, and Sammie coughed a hairball onto my rag rug. He looked up at me, his green eyes unrepentant.

I glared at the cat. "You've got the whole theater to roam, and you do that here?" The black cat looked down at the mess on the wood floor and back up at me. Since berating a cat is pointless, I cleaned the floor and shooed Sammie into the hallway. "Go haunt a ghost."

He looked uncertainly at Gloria's dressing room, barricaded with police tape. The cat's ears flicked. He swaggered down the stairs as if he'd meant to do that all along.

I shut the apartment door, heated up a mug of tea on my hotplate, and returned to my computer. Jed had been more active on social media than his wife, but it was all vacation, hiking, and theater pics. If he had a girl on the side (did he?) they weren't chatting about it in online.

I drummed my fingers on the desk and stared out the window at the head of the giant flamingo rising behind the bowling alley. I'd like to say the flamingo stared back, but it was hard to tell with the eyepatch.

I considered calling Buck. My ex-husband had resources that I didn't. But I shoved that consideration right down where it belonged. Things with Buck hadn't been complicated until recently. We'd married. We'd divorced. I'd agreed to keep working for his company. I think I'd thought I was being mature or something.

And then the assignment I'd been on had gone sideways, and I'd taken the public blame. I was trying to be adult about the fact that he'd let me take the blame.

I slouched back against the chair. At some point, people would have to forget. They'd forget I was the face of the bodyguard team that had failed to protect an infamous blackmailer from himself. They'd forget the conspiracy theories. They'd forget, and life would return to normal.

Eventually.

Chapter Seven

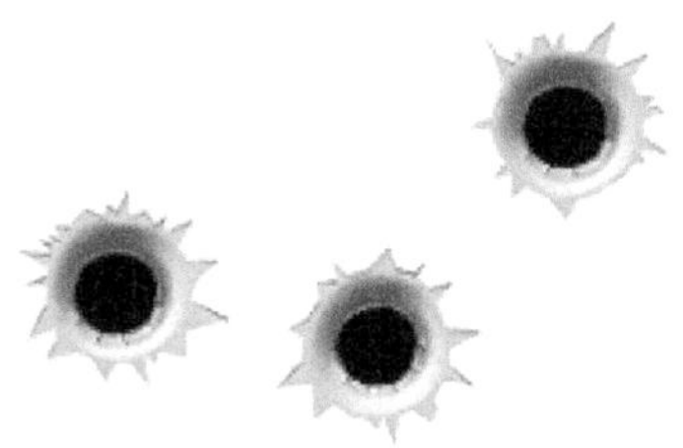

One of the exciting things about the recent changes in Nowhere was that the town now had good food. Granted, it's hard to mess up pizza, but the Pizza Wheel went above and beyond with a crisp sourdough crust and tangy tomato sauce. The players had been having their pizza delivered before every Friday performance. The pizza was good enough that we were eating lunch at the pizza parlor again that Monday.

The dimly lit parlor was full of tourists bundled up in sweaters, their bulky jackets hanging from hooks on the sides of the booths. Kristie and Jane sat opposite us. I squeezed beside Charlie and Lilyanna. Lilyanna wore her beekeeper's uniform. Her net hat lay on the table.

Jane tightened her ponytail and sat back against the wooden booth. Her nose twitched. "It's so nice to eat someone else's cooking for once," she said wearily. The theater manager looked down at a fresh grease stain on her plain blue sweater. Grabbing a paper napkin, she blotted at the stain.

Kristie's broad face creased. "I suppose you'll be leaving us for greener pastures soon too," she said to her in a petulant tone. She curved a hank of gray hair behind her ear.

"Greener pastures?" Jane asked.

A teenager in the red and white Pizza Wheel uniform bustled past carrying a red, oversized insulated carrier. He climbed into a red van, parked at the sidewalk. Another XXL making its way out into the world. Capitalism was a beautiful thing. Most of the time.

"Leave us, I mean. It's not the same without Jed—I mean Gloria," Kristie boomed. She brushed a crumb from the front of her silky, crimson blouse, snug against her ample curves. "I suppose I'm worried he'll quit the theater and that will start an exodus. Do you think he will?"

I winced. They say the things that irritate you about others are things that you don't want to examine in yourself. I'd been wondering about Jed's future plans, too, though for different reasons. And the question seemed tactless.

"I think..." Lilyanna picked up her beekeeper's hat and rearranged the netting. She set it down. "Don't you think a big part of the fun of it for Jed was working with his wife?" The young woman gasped, her eyes widening with regret. "Oh, I didn't mean—" She reached forward and grasped Jane's hand. "I'm so sorry, Jane. We've been so focused on Jed, but Gloria was your sister. The theater must be a terrible place for you now too."

Jane blinked rapidly. "No." She looked at her crumb-strewn plate. "I don't know. I don't know what I'll do now. I did like the theater, you know. I wasn't only working there because of Gloria. I have a—" She bit her bottom lip.

Kristie quirked a brow then smoothed her face so quickly, I almost missed it. "I'll talk to Jed," she rumbled. "We need to find out what we can do for him and—not to be crass—what he's thinking about with the shows going forward. I'm sure that hotel in Hot Springs he works at keeps him busy. It's amazing he's been able to put in as much time as he has."

The front door opened, allowing a beam of piercing autumn light into the pizza parlor. The other patrons winced and looked away. Gert strolled inside, the door closing behind him.

"If you're going to try to convince him to stay, I'm not sure it's the right thing," Jane warned.

"But we need to know, one way or another," Kristie said. "If he's done, that means we've lost *two* players. We'll have to modify the murders in the short-term and find substitutes in the long."

"Uh, I don't know," Charlie said. "Isn't it a little too soon?"

Jane frowned. "No, she's right. I should have thought of it myself."

"Of course you didn't think about it," Lilyanna said. "How could you, when you're grieving? You lost a sister."

"Half-sister," Kristie murmured.

Half-sister or no, Jane been awfully stoic about the loss. But people mourned differently. I glanced at Charlie, in a faded t-shirt and board shorts despite the cooling weather. The thought of losing my goofy little brother… My throat tightened.

Kristie patted Jane's hand. "Don't worry. We're here to help you too."

Gert ambled to the counter. The manager hurried to take his order.

"What about you?" Lilyanna asked the theater manager gently. "Will you stay?"

Jane blinked. "Of course. It's my job."

"It's a hazard," Gert said loudly. He motioned toward the giant pizza cutter on the wall beside us. The manager, Vittoria, emerged from behind the counter to speak to him.

I shifted. "Did Gloria have any enemies?"

The women at the table stared. Charlie coughed and gave me a sidelong look. But someone—most likely someone associated with the theater—had killed Gloria. And I hadn't seen the sheriff since the murder. He wasn't interviewing suspects or collecting evidence. So, okay. It wasn't just about Mrs. Malone and rent reductions. I'd taken an interest.

But it was more than an interest. A sense of unease, of unsettledness, had haunted me since last night. The feeling that the killer wasn't finished, that something else, something awful was going to happen.

"Look," Charlie said in a low voice, "I told you, the killer had to be the black knight."

Not that again. But I bit back my objections, curious how the others would react to the idea. So far, none of them had. "Fine," I said, "but who's the black knight?"

Gert strode toward us, the pizza parlor's manager at his heels. "Look at those hooks." He pointed at the giant pizza wheel. "One good earthquake, and that wheel will fall, maybe on some kid."

"It would have to be a big earthquake," the manager, Vittoria, said in an exasperated tone. "The wheel's pretty heavy."

"Quakes happen in the Sierras all the time," he snapped. "And look how close that booth is." He knocked on our table. "If the wheel's as heavy as you say, it could kill someone. And look at that blade!"

Charlie stretched in his chair and yawned. "It's no biggie, Gert," my brother scratched his stomach through the thin tee. "There must have been a city inspector or two who's already seen and approved it."

The manager glanced at us. She flushed and took a step back, then motioned toward me. "You brought your heavy too? Is she some sort of enforcer?"

I stared stupidly at her for a moment, then realized she was talking about me. "I'm just here for the pizza."

A lot of people thought those of us in the personal protection biz were dumb thugs. But you had to think and be aware to do the job well. There were strategies and psychologies involved. And why was I getting defensive? No one had called me stupid. Though the word "heavy" sort of implied it.

"Alice is assisting as my bodyguard," Gert said.

My shoulders tensed. "No, I'm not."

"I see how things are being run around here now," Vittoria said, acid in her voice.

"Yes," Gert said. "They're better."

She cast me a dark look and stormed into the kitchen. I squeezed from the booth, my hip brushing an empty pizza tray. I grabbed it before it could fall to the thin, crimson carpet. "Hold on, Gert. You can't tell people..." I began, but our temporary mayor had already made it to the door. "I'm not his bodyguard," I told the table.

Gert strode outside. Light and a chill breeze flooded through the slowly closing door.

"I'd better talk to Vittoria." Lilyanna rose. "She's practically part of the theater." She hurried into the kitchen.

"I'm not Gert's bodyguard," I insisted.

"You *were* riding in the Cadillac with him at yesterday's Halloween parade," Kristie said, arch.

"That was just a one-time thing," I said.

"Okay, everyone." Charlie clapped his hands together. "Focus. Let's figure this out. Who's the black knight?"

Jane and Kristie stopped frowning at me and swiveled in their chairs to face my brother.

"It's got to be Clyde," Kristie's voice crescendoed. "You said the knight didn't start showing up until after we'd thrown Clyde out of the theater. It's his way of sneaking into the medieval shows."

I slid into the booth. "Hold on. *Charlie* said? Has anyone else here seen the knight?"

The others exchanged uneasy glances. "I've seen him," Kristie said.

Jane grimaced. "The thing is, it's a medieval murder. A lot of people come in costume. There was always a knight or two around."

"So you don't know that there was *one* black knight. It could have been guests showing up in the same type of costume." I glared at Charlie. Just when I'd started to believe the knight might be a real suspect, I find this out.

"It's not a random costume that different people keep wearing," he insisted. "He was acting weird. I've seen him lurking around the theater."

"It's true," Kristie said. "But I can't see Clyde committing murder. Can you? And he *adored* Gloria. He was practically obsessed with her. Not in a bad way, of course."

"Of course," I agreed, not because I believed it, but because the two women were still looking at me like I really was Gert's henchwoman. "But Gloria must have had an enemy. *Someone* killed her."

"Not everyone got along with my sister." Jane shot a meaningful glance at Kristie, one Kristie didn't see.

"Because Gloria finagled a dressing room and everyone else had to share?" I asked.

"Gloria was a favorite of Mrs. Malone," Kristie said. "That's how she got the dressing room. Though why she was a favorite is something I never understood."

"You're saying there was something between those two?" I asked.

Kristie shrugged.

A shadow fell across our table. Clyde, my wannabe informant from the diner, grabbed the back of a chair from a nearby table and pulled it out. "May I?" he asked tonelessly, brushing his blond hair out of his eyes.

The players groaned.

"I suppose you're going to have to change your play now," Clyde said heavily. He set the chair at the open end of our booth and sat, his broad stomach pressing into the table. "The good news is, I've written something for a smaller cast of characters."

His eyes were pink and his broad face splotchy. But the authorial impulse must have been stronger than the throes of fanish obsession if he was pitching a script.

"We're improv," Charlie said.

"We don't need a new play," Kristie said shortly. "And especially not from you. You've been banned from the theater."

"That was a misunderstanding," Clyde said. "I'd do anything for the theater, and for Gloria. And I know she'd want the show to go on."

"Was it a misunderstanding when I caught you trying to climb through Alice's window?" Charlie asked. "You're lucky I didn't call the cops."

"Wait," I said. "What?" When had that happened?

"The sheriff wouldn't have come in time anyway," Clyde said.

"When was he climbing through my window?" I asked.

"It's okay," Kristie said. "It was before you moved in."

Charlie slapped the flat of his hand on the table. "Out." He glowered at Clyde and pointed toward the front door.

Clyde's eyes widened. "You can't throw me out. My wife manages this pizza parlor."

Clyde and Vittoria were married? I really needed to catch up on Nowhere relationships. "Actually," I said, rising. "I'd love to follow up with you on that thing we talked about the other day, Clyde," I said vaguely.

His broad forehead creased. "Oh," he said. "Oh, right. I know—"

"Outside." I motioned toward the wooden door.

"Right." Knocking his chair back, he followed me onto the sidewalk.

We paused near the parlor's glass door. Pumpkins had been stacked in a pyramid beside it. The sky was mercilessly blue, but the afternoon was cold, and I zipped up my jacket. "Tell me more about this play. Have you written many for the theater?"

"Yeah," he said, "but they keep insisting on doing improv. It's just dumb. A real mystery needs solid clues and red herrings."

"And a strong leading lady."

A tour bus chugged past, spewing exhaust. We held our breaths, waiting for the cloud to dissipate.

He exhaled gustily. "Gloria." His shoulders slumped. "I can't believe she's gone."

"Were you two close?" I asked.

"Gloria understood me like no one else did."

Uh, huh. "Friends like that are special." I paused. How did Vittoria feel about this relationship? At the police station, the dentist had complained his ex-wife never understood him – like *that* was a reasonable excuse for attempted murder. "I didn't realize you and Vittoria were married."

"For ten years now. She's a peach. She gets me too, but differently."

"You're lucky." I *think* Buck had understood me – maybe too well. Given how things had turned out, it was a depressing thought. "Tell me more about Gloria. You were close to her. Was she worried about anything?"

"Her behavior did change at the end. She became more abrupt with me, like something was bothering her."

That was interesting, if true. Or maybe Gloria had just gotten fed up with Clyde. "Any idea what was going on?"

He shook his head. "She was a woman with many burdens. People don't understand what stars like her go through."

Stars in dinner theater? I refrained from comment. "Did she have a conflict with anyone in particular?" I asked.

"Her sister." He lowered his voice. "Jane's a lovely woman, but she could never hold a candle to Gloria, you understand? And their mother always favored Gloria. Jane wasn't her real daughter, you understand. She came from her husband's prior marriage."

Gloria, with her flash, would be a tough act to follow. I got the sense Jane hadn't bothered to try. "And Gloria's husband? Did Jed understand your, um, relationship?"

"No." Clyde laughed shortly. "He actually threatened to kill me if I came around the theater again. Actors." He rolled his eyes. "I knew it was all bluster."

So Jed had known about Clyde's interest in his wife. Why hadn't he mentioned it when we'd talked? "Did you see anything unusual the night of the murder?"

He glanced around. Tourists wandered the sidewalks and darted in and out of shops. A woman dressed like a witch with a pointy black hat walked a terrier past us. "Maybe. I saw Jane go into Gloria's dressing room the night before she died."

I stiffened. "What time was this?"

"After the Thursday night show. She was very... furtive."

She was also the theater manager and had every right to go into that dressing room. And Gloria had died on a Friday. But the nice thing about poison is you can leave it around any old time for your victim to consume. But what had *Clyde* been doing up there? "Was Gloria in the room at the time?"

"No." He rubbed his fleshy chin. "That's what makes it so strange."

"Where exactly were you when you saw this?"

"I was in the room across the hall. The cat was quite friendly."

He'd been in my *apartment*? I needed a new lock. "Clyde," I ground out.

"Yes?"

"Don't ever go in that room again."

"But—"

"*Ever.*"

Chapter Eight

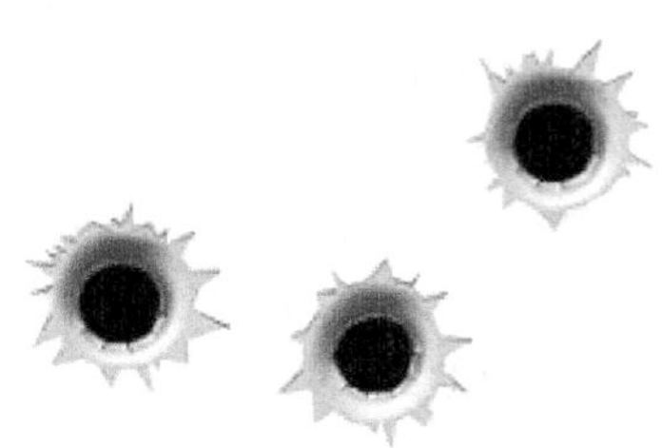

“Honestly, I only ducked into your apartment while I waited for Jane to leave.” Clyde stepped back. His heel bumped the pumpkins near the pizza parlor’s glass door. The pyramid trembled but didn’t fall.

I narrowed my eyes. “How long was she in there?”

“Not long. Just a minute or two. And then I left my newest script on Gloria’s dresser.”

“And then?”

“And then I left the theater. And that was all. I swear.”

My lips flattened. I wasn’t sure if he’d crossed the line from fan to stalker, but I wasn’t taking any chances. And I hadn’t noticed any script in Gloria’s dressing room. ““What about Friday night?”

“Friday?” he squeaked.

“You must have come back on Friday to see how she reacted to your script.”

He shifted his weight. “I might have, ah, stopped by before showtime. But I didn’t see her.”

“When before showtime?”

“About thirty minutes before the show started.”

If Gloria had reached the theater before showtime, she’d been cutting it close. I grilled Clyde some more.

Unfortunately, he hadn't seen anyone loitering at the theater on the night of Gloria's death. He also hadn't seen anyone aside from himself sneaking into her dressing room.

The little man's eyes brightened. "Would you show your brother my script?" A crowd of teenagers brushed past us and into the brick pizza parlor.

I liked my brother too much to dump what was bound to be a literary stinker in his lap. "N—" On the other hand, I was a little curious myself. "Yes." I held out my hand.

Expression gleeful, he gave me the script. "Thank you. You won't regret it." Clyde squeezed past the exiting players and retreated inside the pizza parlor.

Charlie stopped beside me. "Why is Clyde so happy?"

Lilyanna smiled at my brother, adjusted the netting on her beekeeper outfit, and ambled in the direction of the theater with Kristie. Jane walked in the opposite direction, toward the Sagebrush.

"I told him I'd give you his latest script," I said, glancing after the theater manager.

My brother's head dropped forward, his shoulders hunching beneath his thick, multi-colored jacket. "Are you kidding me?"

"Don't worry. I really just want to read it myself."

He unbent. "Oh. This is part of our investigation. Good idea." Charlie made a grab for the script.

I pivoted, keeping Clyde's script out of reach. "I said I wanted to see it."

"I want to see it too. Besides, Kristie was right. Clyde's got to be the black knight. There may be proof in there."

"Fine." I handed the bundle of paper to him. Maybe Charlie *could* find something. More importantly, I wanted to talk to Jane. "But I read his script next." I hurried down the sidewalk after the theater manager.

My quarry stopped and bent to scratch her ankle. Straightening, she turned down the alley with the big paperclip on its wall.

"Jane?" I called, jogging after her. In the shade of the brick alley, the temperature dropped a good ten degrees, and I shivered.

She waited, adjusting her thick-rimmed glasses. "Did Clyde try to give you one of his scripts?" She smiled faintly.

"Tried and succeeded."

"Poor Clyde." She shook her head. "I feel for him. We've all had unattainable dreams at one time or another."

A breeze rustled the paper ghosts on the giant metal clip. I jammed my freezing hands into my jacket pockets. "Which dream do you mean? To see his play acted or to get close to your sister?"

"I thought they were the same dream—to see his play acted *by* my sister." Jane hugged herself and shuddered, flipping up the collar of her navy parka. "Now, I'm not so sure."

"What do you mean? The guy's a borderline stalker, and he may have crossed the border."

"He wasn't a stalker. He was a super fan. Gloria never felt threatened by him."

Maybe she should have. "He admits to being in her dressing room the night before she died, after the show."

She cocked her head. "Dropping off a script?"

"That's what he says. He said you were in there before him."

"Was I?" She frowned, then her expression cleared. "Oh, yes. She called to tell me she'd forgotten her wallet. I picked it up and dropped it at her house."

"How'd you know about the script?"

She grimaced. "The next evening, Gloria came down to the kitchen to toss it in the industrial garbage bin afterward. She didn't want to hurt his feelings if he saw it in her own waste bin."

"That was... thoughtful." Or thorough. And why would she assume Clyde would see it in her waste basket? Was she in the habit of letting him in? Or was he in the habit of letting himself in?

Jane's smile flickered. "Gloria cared about her fans."

"What time was this?"

"About fifteen minutes before curtain. Well, we don't really use the curtain much, but you know what I mean."

Then Gloria had died right before the show had started Friday night. "Weren't you worried when she didn't appear on stage?"

Jane flushed. "I was so busy with the dinner, I didn't realize she never went on stage. And then when the meals were out and I didn't see her, I just assumed the players had gone ahead with their plan and made her the first to die."

I nodded. It was all perfectly logical. But it seemed odd that Jane hadn't mentioned any of this before. Maybe she'd been trying to spare Clyde some humiliation. But Clyde hadn't been around when we'd discovered Gloria's body.

She stared down the alley at the yarn store across the street. "I know what people said about my sister. That she was a diva. But she was also a great actress. Too good for Nowhere, but... Neither of us could bring ourselves to leave. You know how that is."

Uncomfortable, I rubbed the back of my neck. I could leave Nowhere any time I wanted. My stay here was only temporary, and everyone knew it. But guilt niggled at me. And why should I feel guilty? It didn't make any sense.

"Have you seen the ghost yet?" she asked.

I coughed, startled at the change of subject. But I couldn't blame her for moving the conversation away from her sister. She and Gloria might not have been close, or even full sisters, but they were still sisters. "You mean the theater ghost? No."

"That's good." She laughed. "He hangs out in your bathroom."

I jumped a little. "*My* bathroom? I thought he haunted the ladies room downstairs."

"No, according to the story, he's been spotted in yours. I wouldn't worry about it though. He hasn't been seen in months."

"Yeah, because I moved in and no one else has been in there for ghost hunting or other reasons." Also, there was no such thing as ghosts.

But my scalp prickled, because I believed in other things, like instincts and intuitions. They'd saved me on more than one occasion. If those existed, why not ghosts?

That was the problem. Once you started believing in one weird thing, it was a lot easier to believe in others. "Who was spending time in my bathroom before I moved in?" I asked.

"Everyone. The players used it as a dressing room. Aside from Gloria, I mean, since she had her own."

I hunched my shoulders inside my thick jacket. The players couldn't have been happy about being kicked out when I'd taken the room over.

"We were thrilled the theater was getting the extra rental income from your apartment," she said quickly.

"The theater gets it? But I'm renting it from Mrs. Malone."

"But she uses that to support the theater. All your rent money has been going to advertising and costumes. That means more profit to share amongst the cast."

Huh. Mrs. Malone was more than a landlord, she was also a patron of the arts, at least until it came to the Big Things. She thought those were ridiculous.

I shook myself. "Look, I'm sorry to press. She was your sister, and I can't imagine what you're going through. But whoever did this is still out there. If Clyde wasn't involved, then who?"

She blanched and looked again toward the end of the alley, lit with sunshine. "I already told the sheriff this, but..."

"But what?"

Another tour bus rumbled past on Main Street. Its exhaust funneled down the alley. We held our breath, waiting for it to pass.

She met my gaze. "I heard Kristie and Gloria arguing last week."

That wasn't much of a surprise. Gloria had gotten into it with lots of people. It went with the diva territory. "About what?"

"I couldn't hear. My sister was shouting and Kristie..." She bit her bottom lip.

"Kristie was what?"

"Laughing," Jane blurted. "In fairness, there was no sense taking my sister's tirades seriously. They always blew over. But... it only made Gloria angrier."

"Have Gloria and Kristie argued before?"

"No. You know Kristie. Or maybe you don't. She's the group's mother hen. Kristie takes care of everyone. Sometimes she does divulge awkward truths though—not intentionally, of course. I expect one of those truths set Gloria off." She swallowed, blinking rapidly. "My sister was..." Her lips trembled.

My chest squeezed. I lowered my head to stare at the pavement. A black beetle attempted to traverse a crack between the pavement and the brick building. It stumbled, tried again, made it to the brick, and fell off onto its back.

"Again," I said, "I'm so sorry for your loss. If there's anything I can do..." I winced internally. I was piling platitudes on top of platitudes and wasn't sure how to stop. "How can I help?"

"There's nothing, but thank you." She whipped off her glasses and wiped her sleeve across her eyes. "Both our parents are gone, and... I knew one of us would go first. I just didn't think it would be so soon."

She returned her glasses to her face. "At least she had Jed. I've never seen a man adore a woman like he did her, even if she was difficult. Maybe it's because he's so easygoing, nothing ever bothered him. Everyone loves him."

Everyone? It seemed an odd thing to say, and an arrow of suspicion struck me. Did Jane love him?

"He has a knack for seeing the best in people," she continued hurriedly. "And then people are better around him because of it. I wish I had more of that." She colored. "I was actually heading to his house now to see how he was doing. Do you want to come with me?"

"No," I said, "thanks. I stopped by the other day. Give him my best though."

"I will." She nodded and walked down the alley.

I stared after her for a moment then returned to my apartment above the theater. So far, all I had was gossip. I needed evidence—like those dirty pictures old Mr. Washington had mentioned.

In my cramped and possibly haunted bathroom, I splashed water on my face. I blotted my cheeks with a rough towel then studied myself in the mirror.

Behind me, something pale shifted in the glass. I yelped, my heart jumping, and whirled. The black cat eeled out from behind the shower curtains.

I exhaled slowly. The cat had brushed against the filmy curtain. It had only taken a dash of fevered imagination to think I'd been joined by something inhuman. *Ghosts. Ha.* Shaking my head, I opened the bathroom door, and Fredo edged backward, his tail thumping.

I shooed the cat from my apartment and took the doggo for a walk. When I returned, Sammie was lying on my bed.

I braced my fists on my hips. "How are you getting *in* here?"

"Maybe the ghost let him inside," Charlie said in my ear.

I jumped. "Gagh. What are you doing here?"

He handed me the script. "I read Clyde's script. It's terrible."

I tossed it on the bed beside the cat. Sammie didn't even flick an ear.

"What's next in our investigation?" Charlie asked.

"I'm going to the minimart."

"Cool. I could use some coffee."

The minimart *did* have surprisingly good java. And since I knew I'd have to basically arm wrestle my brother to get him to back off, I didn't argue. We climbed into my Jeep Commander and drove to the outskirts of Nowhere.

The minimart stood on one side of the mountain highway in the shadow of towering black rock. Lilyanna, dressed in a white rabbit suit, waved at us from the parking lot. A red Tesla was the only other car there.

"I didn't know Lilyanna was working today," I said.

"Odd hours are just one of the many perils of a portfolio career." Charlie sighed.

"How's your portfolio career coming?"

"I've just been hired to paint the interior of the cannery."

"That's a big job."

He shrugged. "I'll do it apartment by apartment. What about you? Any new gigs from *Fitch*?"

I shot him a look, because I had not imagined his emphasis on Fitch's name. He grinned.

"No." I pulled open the handle of the minimart's glass door, plastered with flyers. Charlie beelined past me for the coffeepot near the register.

I walked inside and straightened. Two well-dressed and muscular young men were at the slushie machine. I'd encountered them before. They were trouble, and I'd talked them out of making more. I nodded to them.

One nudged the other. He glanced at me, and his eyes widened. The two hurried from the store. I studied a lottery display and discarded the idea of buying a ticket. I wasn't feeling that lucky.

The shop owner, Mr. Graham, braced his elbow on the cash register and scowled. "Thanks a lot." His checked button-up shirt strained across his gut. Wisps of graying hair made a valiant attempt to cover his head.

"What did I do?" I asked. The minimart smelled of nacho cheese, and my stomach tried to convince me I was hungry.

"Hot chocolate?" Charlie asked me and pointed at the gleaming machine beside the coffeepot.

"Why not?" I asked. It might divert me from my irrational nacho craving.

"You scared off my best customers." Mr. Graham gestured toward the front door.

"Sorry," I said. We all had to make a living, and I didn't like that I'd just made that harder for Mr. Graham. "Is Mr. Washington's nephew working here today?"

"Terrence? He's out back. Why?" He straightened. "If Magimountain's got a problem with my staff, he can talk to me."

"Gert? No, I just wanted to ask—"

His face reddened. "And if he's got a problem with me or my shop, he can talk to me directly to instead of sending his enforcer."

"Okay, but... Wait, you think I'm his enforcer too?" I laughed. "No—"

"Aren't you?"

"No—"

"You were his bodyguard during the parade," the shopkeeper said. "And I heard what happened in the pizza parlor today."

Whoa. I shouldn't have been surprised though. Word *really* gets around fast in a small town. "You've got the wrong idea. I don't work for Gert."

He folded his arms, resting them on the swell of his stomach. "You've gotten pretty chummy with him lately."

"That's because..." Not a whole lot of people knew Gert had tried to kill me last summer on behalf of the Estonian mafia. I decided to keep it that way. "He's just Gert."

"He's gone power mad. He told me I had too many flyers in my windows." He motioned toward the glass front door. "This is a minimart, not a... Mazda. I don't need visibility. What I need is sales."

"Nice alliteration," I said.

"Hmph."

My brother ambled to the counter and laid a dollar and some change on it. "Thanks for the coffee."

"You're welcome," Mr. Graham said. "Now tell your sister to tell Gert to back off."

Charlie handed me a warm paper cup filled with cocoa. "Tell Gert to back off."

"I will." I pulled my wallet from the back pocket of my jeans. "I mean, I won't. I don't work for Gert."

Charlie tilted his head and squinted at me. "You sort of do."

"No, I don't," I gritted out and laid a couple dollars on the counter.

A lanky, twenty-something man walked from the back of the shop. His dark hair was cropped close to his scalp.

"Finished." He brushed off his hands on his canvas apron. "What do you want me to do next?"

"Terrence?" I asked.

"You can't talk to Terrence," Mr. Graham said. "He's got nothing to do with Gert. Leave Terrence alone."

I sputtered. "I'm just..." Why was everyone convinced I was the kind of person to do awful things? It was enough to make a girl feel misunderstood.

Charlie laid his hand on the counter. "This is murder, Mr. Graham. We need to talk to Terrence."

Terrence's angular face paled. "Murder? Me?"

"Maybe we should speak privately," Charlie said and led him outside.

"I'm really not working for Gert," I told the store owner and strode after my brother. The bell above the glass door jangled behind me.

"Go ahead." Charlie stopped in a spot of sunshine and motioned to Terrence. "Ask your questions."

I blew out an exasperated breath. "Your uncle, Mr. Washington, mentioned you knew about some risqué pictures of Gloria Jackson."

His face cleared. "Oh, you mean her JustGroupies account."

"Just what?"

"It's a website," Charlie said. "Stars and models post photos there for fans, and fans pay to see them."

"Porn?" I asked.

"No," Terrence said, flushing. "Burlesque. It's an art form."

"Okay." I rolled my eyes. "Art."

"No, really," the young man insisted. "Burlesque got its start in the 1840s. By the early 1900s, it was a combo of striptease and vaudeville. It was provocative, but not porn."

That was a relief. I've seen plenty that I hadn't wanted to see in my work. I didn't want to add dirty pictures to the list. "Can you show me her pictures?"

Terrence laughed. "I'm not a member. A friend of mine is. He's a big afficionado of the form, which is how I know so much. He's always talking about it. And just as a warning,

I'm pretty sure there's other stuff on JustGroupies besides burlesque."

"But you saw Gloria's photos on there?" I asked.

"She has—had an account. It's under a different name, but it's her."

"What name is it under?" I asked.

"Glinda Love."

I raised a brow.

"Honestly," Terrence said. "It's just burlesque."

Chapter Nine

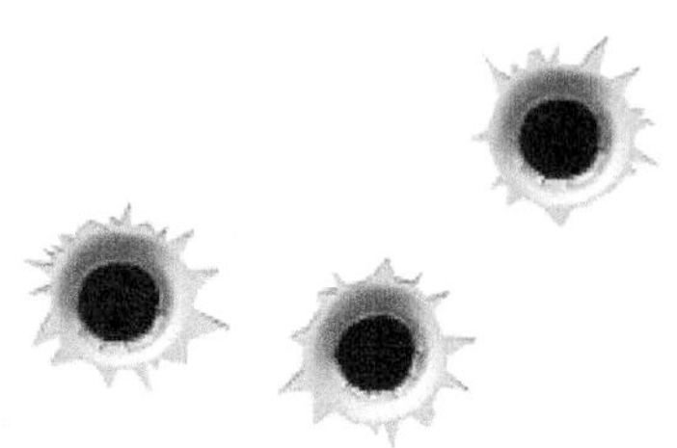

Charlie and I returned to my Jeep in the minimart parking lot. While my brother slurped his coffee, I signed up for a JustGroupies account on my phone. And it *was* just burlesque.

True, there was a lot more than burlesque on that site. Bikini shots by burgeoning starlets. Pouty photos of women eating cake. But Gloria's, aka Glinda's account, was different. She'd done pictures in high-waisted bikinis and fifties lingerie. There were artful shots posing in bathtubs and slipping on stockings. The photos implied everything and gave away nothing.

"Lemme see," Charlie said.

"You're too young."

He snatched the phone from me and whistled. "Wow. I had no idea Gloria had this whole other secret life."

"We all have secrets." It was my bad luck that my worst moment had been spilled across the internet last summer.

I bit the bullet, and though my finances were tightening, I bought several of her photos for download.

"Why are you paying for those?" Charlie asked. "You can look at them for free. The watermark doesn't exactly block anything."

"Evidence," I said. "These photos may or may not have anything to do with her murder, but like you said, she had a secret life." And I wanted proof in case the photos were taken down.

Charlie sniffed. "Have you thought of an air freshener? Your car smells like dog."

"Noted." Just to see what happened, I typed *JustGroupies Murder* into the search engine. A slew of articles appeared, but none about Gloria. Over the last two years, four women with JustGroupies pages had been murdered. Two by obsessed fans. Two more by furious husbands.

In each JustGroupies crime I found, the killer had been caught. Also in each, the killer had claimed he'd somehow been used or taken advantage of by their victim. The victim had "led them on" or "cheated." Each murder had been violent—stabbings, strangulations. Crimes of misplaced passion.

But Gloria had likely been poisoned. Her murder had been bloodless. Planned. It didn't fit the pattern. Still, Clyde deserved a deeper look.

"So what next?" Charlie asked.

"I'm thinking Gloria's school. I'd like to talk to the people she worked with."

He grimaced. "I can't go undercover there. They all know me."

"Really? How?" I hadn't been thinking about undercover—there didn't seem much point in a place as small as Nowhere. But if Charlie thought he couldn't go to the grammar school, all the better.

"We did a murder mystery for the principal's fiftieth birthday. It was great. We tailored the story to his life and—" He gave his head a quick shake. "You don't care about that stuff. Never mind."

Of course I cared. But in fairness, I'd been away for years. My actions had said otherwise. Feeling even more misunderstood, I fastened my seat belt. "I care. It's interesting. What was the theme?"

"Medieval," he said. "The school had looked up his family's coat of arms and everything." He scratched his blond beard. "Think we've got a coat of arms?"

"No way. The Sommerlands were likely lowly peasants in the old country."

"Maybe not. It would be worth checking out. Maybe doing one of those DNA searches or family trees or something."

I shrugged and started the Jeep. It kind of did smell like dog. "I guess everyone's connected to someone. So where to?"

"I'll come with you to the school and wait in the car."

I smiled. Charlie was worried I'd later head off on some new adventure without him. But all I had planned was some reading and a hot bath.

School was out when we arrived. At Charlie's insistence, I parked around the corner then walked to the school's office. It was set in a smaller concrete building slightly set aside from the classrooms. I was a little worried the admin staff had gone for the day, but I was in luck. The office was open. It was like every school office I've ever been in. Bland colors. Cheap, laminate furniture. And the sterile stench of bitterness.

A woman wearing a pink cardigan with a sprig of embroidered flowers over the heart looked up from an ancient computer. "Can I help you?" She didn't quite smile, and she touched her graying hair, swept into a bun.

I didn't recognize her, so I guessed she commuted from out of town. And Charlie's talk of going undercover had given me an idea. "I'm a friend of Gloria's. Is she here?" I asked, to see her reaction.

The woman sucked in a breath, her chin lowering. She removed her reading glasses. "Oh. I'm so sorry. She's... Well, there's no way to say this gently. She's dead."

I took a step backward and pressed a hand to my chest. "What? What happened?"

She blinked rapidly. "Gloria was... She was... Well, it seems like someone killed her."

Abruptly, I sat in one of the gray plastic chairs lined up against the wall. "Here? At the school?" Charlie wasn't the only one who could act. But, okay, he was loads better.

She stood so she could see me better over the high counter. "No. At the theater."

"She loved that theater," I whispered.

"Yes, she was... quite a performer."

"Did you know her well?" I asked.

"No, I've only worked here a year," she said. "I'm from Inspiration."

I nodded. I'd been right about her not living in Nowhere. Inspiration was a town even tinier than ours and higher up in the hills.

She frowned. "Do I know you? You look kind of familiar."

Dammit. My notoriety last summer possibly made me the worst candidate on the planet for undercover work. I adjusted my jacket. "Maybe you saw me with Gloria? We were tearing up Reno a couple weeks back."

She shook her head. "I rarely get to Reno."

I chuckled. "Good thing. We may have broken a few of the school's morality clauses."

She sucked in her cheeks. "Oh."

"Sorry," I said, contrite. "I was joking. I shouldn't have been. Er, *does* the school have a morality clause?"

"Yes. And they take it quite seriously."

Then they might not have appreciated Gloria's cheeky photos... *if* they'd found out. "Well," I said, "I really was joking. Gloria was a stand-up person."

"Yes," she said doubtfully. "She was."

She had some bits of juicy gossip, I could tell. Now if I could only get her to spill them. "But she could be a bit of a diva," I said ruefully.

The secretary gusted a breath, her shoulders dropping. "That's the truth. She didn't always make life easy. But she was a good person," she added.

"I know. That's why I can't imagine who would have wanted to kill her."

She shook her head. "I can't believe it either. It must have been someone from the theater, don't you think?"

I slumped in the plastic chair. The evidence did seem to point in that direction. I wasn't really worried about Charlie landing on the sheriff's radar. But I'd gotten to know the theater folks a bit. I didn't want the killer to be any of them.

"I wonder..." I began.

She cocked her head.

"Jed," I said. "He works at the theater."

"Oh, but he would never..." She fiddled with a mesh pencil cup. "You know how crazy he was about her. He worshipped the ground she walked on. I wish I had that sort of love in my life."

I nodded, but my recent divorce had pretty much killed my faith in happy endings. And Jed was a good actor. Could his adoration have been an act? "Still," I said. "There was that one time..." I trailed off hopefully.

"But that was silly," she said. "Just some misplaced jealousy. He was so embarrassed the next day. Gloria laughed about it."

"Yeah." I stood. "I'm sure it meant nothing. And that was... how long ago?"

"It's been at least three months."

"Right. Ages." But three months wasn't that long ago, not really. I hesitated, trying to figure out a way to get more details and failing. "Well, thanks for letting me know. Will the school have a memorial of any kind?"

"I don't know. We'll probably wait and see what Jed's planning."

"That makes sense." I glanced around, but no one had entered the office while we'd been chatting. "Has Jed cleared out Gloria's desk yet?"

"This morning," she said.

Drat. "Oh, good. Then I guess there's nothing I can help him with here. Thanks." With no other clues at the school to follow—or at least none that were obvious to me—I returned to my Jeep.

Charlie blinked and yawned, lifting his head off the window. "Learn anything?"

"The school secretary said there was a jealous-Jed incident about three months back. Know anything about it?"

"Jealous Jed? That doesn't sound like him. She's got to be mistaken."

"Right." Sometimes I worried my brother's tendency to only see the good in everyone would get him into trouble. "I'm headed back to my apartment. Where do you want me to drop you?"

He stretched and yawned again. "Home, James."

I drove him to the treehouse and watched him climb the ladder nailed into the pine. When his sneaker had vanished through the hole in the floor, I drove home.

The dinner theater was closed on Mondays. I liked the quiet, but there was something eerie about the old building's emptiness. The theater was just big enough for the silence to be creepy.

I climbed the stairs to my apartment and glanced at the police tape over Gloria's dressing room door. How long would that stay up?

I opened the door to my apartment and stared. Books and broken crockery lay on the floor. My patchwork quilt had been pulled halfway off the bed. The bureau drawers were closed, and I opened them. Nothing was disturbed inside. So… not a burglar.

A *Fredo*. My jaw clenched. "Fredo?"

The dog crawled from under the bed, his bulgy eyes rolling.

I bent and picked up an open, upside-down book, its spine cracked and pages wrinkled. "Did you do—?"

YEOOOWWWWL. Something landed on my back. I yelled and straightened.

The cat launched off of me and onto the bureau. He sat, lifted a paw, and licked it casually.

"For Pete's… Is this mess some sort of twisted revenge? Were you two mad I left you alone?" I pointed at the cat.

"Or was it just you?" Because cats understood revenge better than dogs.

The ebony cat didn't pause in his ablutions. Yeah, Sammie had to be the ringleader. *Cats.*

Something creaked in the bathroom, and I froze. Its door was cracked open. A shadow shifted behind it.

Heart thumping, I pulled my kubotan keyring from my jacket pocket. I crept toward the bathroom. Stealth at this stage was pointless, but… habit.

I adjusted the kubotan in my hand. It was metal and roughly the length and shape of a pen, but wider. Its end could be used for hooking and striking, and the keys could be flicked as a weapon as well. The shadow moved beneath the door.

One… Two… I kicked it open. The door banged against the wall and ricocheted back, but I was already through.

The bathroom was empty. I paused, kubotan hand raised. The shower curtains rippled like a living—or unliving—thing. I ripped them back. No one stood inside the clawfoot tub.

I frowned, turning in the cramped space. I'd *seen* a shadow move in here. *Twice.* Where…? A chill breeze wafted across my neck, and the shower curtains undulated.

The curtains. Had they caused the moving shadow? I raised my hand to the vent fan in the wall. Air brushed against my palm, and I relaxed. So, not a human, not even a ghost. Just me and my overactive paranoia. A heavy door slammed downstairs.

I shooed Sammie from my apartment, shot Fredo a warning look, and climbed down the steps. "Hello?" I called.

No one answered. Watchful, I prowled through the gleaming and empty kitchen. I walked into the dining area beneath the stage. Kristie, in a red velvet tunic and black leggings, stood on stage and frowned.

"Oh, hi." I climbed the steps to the stage. "I thought I heard someone down here."

She brushed her graying hair away off one temple, and her round face creased. "I'm sorry if I startled you." Her voice echoed across the stage, and I winced. Man, she could project. "I just came here to think," she continued. "We rarely use the stage in our performances, but I think there are ways we could."

"Oh?" I strolled toward her.

Something rattled metallically above us, and we looked up. Rippling darkness plummeted downward.

Unthinking, I hurled myself at Kristie, shoving her toward the back of the stage. She yelped. The curtain hit the floor behind me, its metal rod splintering the wood with a dull crash.

Kristie stumbled, regained her balance, and pressed a hand to her chest. Her face went from white to pink. "That's—That could have—Oh! I'm going to give Jane a piece of my mind."

I straightened, my heart thudding. "Is that... Is that normal?" I strode to the curtain pulleys. They were out of reach now, unhooked from the wall and swinging high above me. If they hadn't been hooked properly, they could have slipped off naturally. But what were the odds?

"In this place?" She snorted. "Lights going out, scenery falling to bits? Jane really needs to do a better job with safety issues."

I jogged into the kitchen. It was empty. The metal door to the parking lot stood open. I returned to the stage. "Jane's not here. Did you leave the back door open?"

"Yes, I left the door open. This place gets so stuffy." She picked up her oversized purse, lying near the front of the stage. "I'm calling Jane. She's responsible for all the equipment, including the stage. That could have killed us."

Yes, it could have. I looked up. Above us, the walkway swayed.

Chapter Ten

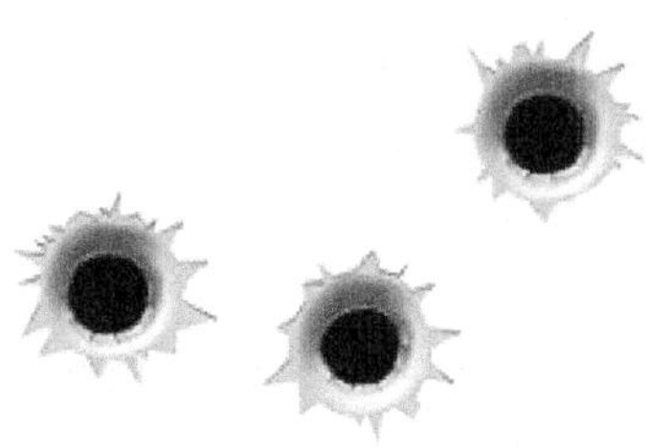

Sometimes, you needed to play to your strengths. I wasn't certain this was one of those times, but I also wasn't sure what else to do. So that night I was back on surveillance. At least I didn't have to feel guilty about knitting on duty since I wasn't getting paid.

A small animal skittered across the treehouse roof, but I didn't look up as I peered through my video camera, mounted on a tripod. I'd set it up beside the open window, which had an ideal view of Jed's house.

Since it was Monday and the theater closed, he was home. The widower was making things easy for me, working at a computer that overlooked the dark street. His back was to me, so the screen was visible.

A blue Ford Explorer pulled to the curb below me, and Fitch stepped out. The PI reached back into the car and retrieved a grocery bag. The SUV's lights went off. He strode across the dying lawn to my tree. "Alice?" he whisper-shouted. "Are you there?"

Frowning, I crawled to the opening in the floor. "Get up here before you burn me."

Moving like a cat, he climbed the ladder nailed into the tree.

"How'd you find me?" I asked when his head emerged through the floor.

Fitch hauled himself inside. "Your brother told me you'd be here." He set the bag down and crawled to my window. "See anything good?"

"It looks like he's trying to get into his wife's JustGroupie's account but doesn't know the password. Gloria's side hustle was burlesque photos."

He quirked a brow. "Burlesque? Is that a euphemism for—?"

"It's an art form."

"Yeah," he said dryly. "I've heard that too." He looked around. "Your brother's got a nice place here."

"He's going for the rustic look."

"Achievement unlocked." He nodded toward my camera. "I like a contractor who uses her own equipment."

It beat checking equipment in and out of his Reno office. I didn't get paid for my travel time. Or had the equipment remark been a double entendre? *Nah.* I was reading too much into this. "So why are you here?"

"Just thought I'd check out the scene in Nowhere. I brought snacks."

My stomach growled. It was a little unfair. How was I *not* supposed to be attracted to a man who brought snacks? Especially one who looked like one of those muscular ancient Greek statues. "What have you got?"

He pulled from the paper bag a collection of dark objects. I switched on Charlie's electric lantern to low. Fitch had brought a wheel of brie, a jar of fig jam, crackers, a charcuterie board, and skewered grape tomatoes, mozzarella, and basil.

My jaw slackened. This was a whole other level of stakeout food. And I'd pegged Fitch as a junk food guy. "Another stereotype, dashed."

Fitch brandished a skewer. "It's got pesto."

"It had damn well better."

"I'd usually just go for a power bar while on a stakeout, but the guy at the counter told me women like this stuff." He pulled out a bottle of fizzy lemonade.

Right. Sure. *Women* liked it. I eyed the lemonade. "Since you're here, can you give me a break and watch the house? I've got to use the ladies' room." I'd been on liquid restriction for the last four hours, but that only works for so long.

He looked around. "Where's that?"

"The house." I nodded at the empty house below us.

"How'd you get the key?"

Keys. Ha. "I left the back door unlocked when the realtor gave me the home tour this afternoon."

He grinned. "It's a good thing you're on my team."

"I'm my own team." That hadn't come out right. I shrugged and climbed down the ladder and did what I needed to do in the empty ranch house. When I returned to the treehouse, Fitch had laid out the spread on a picnic blanket. And he hadn't forgotten the paper plates and plastic utensils.

He poured me a glass of lemonade. "Skoll."

Ignoring the fact that this looked more like a romantic picnic than a stakeout, I took the plastic glass, abandoned my knitting, and resumed my post at the window. I wasn't sure what Fitch's game was, but I was curious to see how it would play out. "Anything happen while I was away?"

"Still trying to figure out his dead wife's password."

"Poor guy." If I was being honest, there were two reasons I'd chosen Jed to surveil. First, the spouse was always the most likely suspect. Second, the treehouse really did make surveillance convenient. I looked through the camera.

Jed paced the living room, his movements quick, jerky, his fists clenched.

"The life of an amateur hacker." I shook my head. "I imagine learning how to pick locks is just as frustrating," I hinted. I really wanted Fitch to teach me how to do that.

"Here." He handed me a plate. Our fingers brushed, and I felt a shiver of awareness. But Fitch didn't remark on it. It was annoying, but okay, we were going to be professionals. Having a romantic treehouse picnic.

Fine by me. I was *not* going to date another guy I worked with, even if he did look like a Spartan warrior and smelled like cedar and nutmeg. I'd learned my lesson on that score.

I set the lemonade in the crude windowsill and tried some brie and crackers. "Have I thanked you yet? Because this is a serious upgrade from my usual surveillance food."

"Mine too. But we've got added cover with the treehouse," he said. "May as well take advantage with real food. Where's your car?"

"Around the block."

"I'm surprised you didn't buy a ride that was more inconspicuous," he said.

My old ride had been wrecked last summer by a self-destructive blackmailer, the creep. The next car I'd rented had been taken out by a crossbow. (Long story). It must have put me on some secret rental company blacklist, because I'd been stuck with rideshares until I'd bought my Jeep Commander.

I loved my new, super-sized Jeep and was trying not to. I was a little worried loving a car would doom it.

"I wanted something I could live in if I had to," I said. Plus, it was a nice, neutral black. In theory, that made it less conspicuous. But in reality, beige would have been better. I'd just liked the black.

"Is that a possibility?" His forehead wrinkled. "Living in it?"

I turned to face him and wiped a dribble of olive oil from the corner of my mouth with my thumb. "I meant for camping, not permanently. My financial situation isn't that desperate." But it would be desperate were it not for Mrs. Malone's deal on the rent. My stomach rumbled again, this time louder.

"Hey," he said, "you eat. I'll take over."

"Thanks." Bringing Charlie's half-finished red sweater with me, I shifted from the window.

Fitch took up the camera and watched the house. I sat cross-legged and watched him. Even from the back, he was easy on the eyes.

Maybe I was being too high-minded. After all, I *was* only a subcontractor. This wasn't like the situation with my ex. I grabbed a skewer and slid a grape tomato from it, popping it into my mouth. It was delicious.

Something skittered across the roof. Involuntarily, I glanced up.

Fitch cleared his throat. "That guy who got killed on your watch, Koppel..."

"Yeah?" I asked, gaze on the ceiling.

"Any idea where he was running to when he crashed your car?"

"It's a mystery," I lied. It was the sort of information you didn't share with people you liked. I'd been warned to keep my mouth shut and fully intended to. It hadn't been anything criminal, and it was nobody's business but the crazed mafia family the blackmailer had belonged to. And if Fitch had thought gourmet bread and cheese would get him the scoop, he had another think coming.

On one knee, Fitch swiveled to look at me, the camera held at chest level. His eyes gleamed. "Damn. You know something."

I stuffed more cheese into my mouth before I said something stupid. "I know a lot of things," I mumbled.

"Does the FBI know? Scratch that. If they knew, the press would know. The FBI leaks like a sieve. And if the press knew, you'd be off the hook. And that means—"

"You've got a big imagination."

His dark brows drew downward. "Whatever you found out, it must be big."

"It's irrelevant. Toomas Koppel isn't my problem and isn't my business anymore."

The detective's gaze turned flinty. "His family put the squeeze on you." His jaw hardened.

Dammit. He was putting together way too much, way too fast. "Unless they're committing a crime, my clients get confidentiality, just like yours. Thanks for the pesto, but—"

"Gagh!" Fitch jerked away from the window. His knee landed on the charcuterie plate. It skidded from under him, and he toppled against me.

I collapsed beneath his weight. Something squished beneath my back. Fitch landed between my legs, his back to me.

"This really wasn't how I'd pictured this evening going down," I gasped.

A blur of brown fur flew over our heads. A squirrel raced up one wall and chittered angrily.

Fitch rolled off me. "Where is it?" he snarled. A fluffy tail vanished through a window.

"I forgot to mention the treehouse has a squirrel problem." I braced myself on my elbows.

"That was no normal squirrel."

I sat up and crossed my legs. "What other kind is there?"

"It could be rabid."

"There *was* a lot of nuclear testing in the fifties out in the desert," I said. "Who knows what it did to the wildlife?"

He lifted his knee. With a disgusted look, he peeled a slice of salami from his jeans. "You okay?" His eyes widened. "Incoming!"

Fitch pulled me roughly to him. We rolled, his muscles hard against mine. Something scraped my hair, and I caught a flash of brown fur. The squirrel sprang out the window he'd come in through.

Fitch lay on top of me, pressing me to the floor, and looked around. "It's definitely rabid."

This is what he was thinking about? *Now*? "He's been living with Charlie for months. He's developed a thing against men." I was starting to sympathize. "And I'm having a little trouble breathing here."

Fitch looked down at me and his face reddened. "Sorry." He rolled off me and looked at his palms. "Why are my palms sticky?"

"I landed in something. How bad is it?" I turned.

"Er, is this a jacket you care about?" He grabbed a paper napkin and swiped ineffectually at the back of my jacket.

I sighed. I'd really liked that jacket.

He squished up the napkin and tossed it into the paper bag. "It was the squirrel's fault."

I grabbed another napkin and reached behind me. "What's happening at Jed's?"

Fitch glanced out the window through the camera. "Hold on. Something's changed."

"Let me see." I wadded up the napkin and dropped it on the floor.

He handed me the camera, and I peered through.

In his living room, Jed punched his fist in the air and did a victory dance. I shifted my view to the computer screen. Ice hardened my veins. He was in Gloria's JustGroupies account.

I swore. "He's going to delete Gloria's account." I set down the camera and scrambled for the hole in the floor.

"What are you doing?"

"Stopping him."

Chapter Eleven

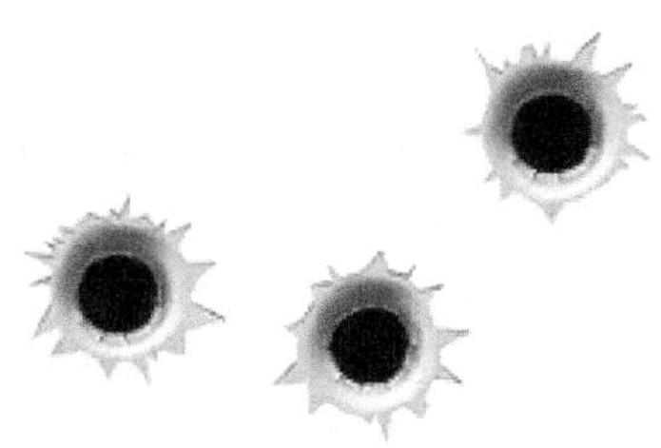

"Hold on," Fitch said, peering through the opening in the treehouse. "Something's happening."

I paused, one foot on the makeshift ladder nailed into the pine. "What?"

"It's your brother."

My heart jumped sickeningly. "*What?*" I scrambled across the treehouse and got a splinter in the process. Putting my eye to the lens, I peered through the camera on its tripod.

Charlie stood on Jed's doorstep. The door opened. The two men talked, and Charlie walked inside. I cursed, my hands growing clammy on the uneven floor.

"What's he doing there?" Fitch asked.

"Investigating." Charlie *knew* I was surveilling Jed from his treehouse because he'd given me permission to be here. I should have been more suspicious when Charlie hadn't insisted on being part of the fun.

I gazed through the camera. My brother walked into Jed's living room followed by Jed himself. Charlie turned to him and motioned with his arms.

Fitch squeezed next to me and looked through a miniature camera of his own.

"You brought your own?" I asked.

"I always bring my own."

"Then why were you borrowing my camera?"

"Yours looked better quality."

I shrugged. Mine *was* better. I returned my attention to the camera lens. Jed's hands fisted, and his face reddened.

"Uh, oh," Fitch said.

"Time to break this up." I fumbled down the ladder and dropped to the ground. Fitch and I ran across the street. A man shouted inside Jed's house, and I ran faster. The PI beat me to the door and rang the bell.

I banged on the door. "We know you're in there," I shouted. Why had Charlie pulled a stunt like this? *Why*? He *knew* we suspected Jed...

And that was why. He believed in Jed and wanted to prove him innocent. And maybe he believed in me too, in my ability to protect him.

The door opened beneath my raised fist. Jed's hair was mussed, his eyes slightly pink. His elegant gray shirt and trousers were wrinkled. "Yes?"

My nails bit into my palms. "We're here to collect my brother. And to talk to you about that JustGroupies account you were about to delete."

The blood drained from his face. "You... How...?"

"Can we come in?" Fitch asked.

Jed took a step backward, opening the door wider. Fitch and I glanced at each other then walked inside the short hallway cluttered with shoes and jackets.

"This isn't a good time," Jed said.

"It never is," Fitch said.

"And who are you?" Jed asked.

"This is Fitch Rhodes," I said. "We work together."

"Oh, hey." Charlie emerged from the living room. "I thought I recognized your voices. What's going on?"

"What are you doing here?" I asked.

"Running lines. Well, practicing our improv."

My fury leaked from my pores, leaving my muscles limp. They'd been *acting*? Fitch smacked his forehead.

"What's going on?" Charlie asked.

Face hot, I turned to Jed. Now that he knew we'd been watching him. I might as well blunder onward. "Tell us about your wife's side hustle."

His shoulders sagged. "We'd better sit down." He led us into the living room. The scent of vanilla had faded since the last time I'd been here. Fitch, Charlie and I squeezed onto a hard, ivory sofa.

I sat forward, mainly to get some breathing space. Also, even though Jed might be a killer, there was no use getting jam on his couch. It might be uncomfortable, but I suspected it hadn't been cheap.

Jed dropped onto a matching, armless, leather chair with a Scandinavian vibe, its back to the gray stone fireplace. "Gloria..." Jed blew out his breath. "She was an amazing woman."

Charlie rested his elbows on his knees. "Oh, totally. She was the best."

Jed nodded. "She took some burlesque classes as part of her acting training."

"It's a classic American art form." Charlie straightened, motioning airily.

"Art," Fitch said. "Yeah."

"And in one of the classes, they were photographed in costume." Jed crossed his legs. "Gloria's pictures were fantastic, so she posted them online."

"And that's when she discovered she could make money off them?" I asked.

"Let's just say there was a demand," Jed said. "And JustGroupies is great. People pay if they want to see the entire portfolio. They pay more if they want to download pictures without a watermark. It was extra income. We were planning a Paris vacation."

"Paris, the City of Lights," Charlie said. "Plus, the Moulin Rouge. That's sort of burlesque."

"Exactly," Jed said. "We've always wanted to go there. It's been a lifelong dream."

"So you were okay with the pictures?" Because I found that hard to believe.

"Are you kidding? It was terrific. It made Gloria happy. It made money. And it was only burlesque."

"It's Americana," Fitch said.

"Theater history," Charlie agreed. "In fact, in the 1920s mystery game we sell at the theater—"

"So why delete her account?" I interrupted. I'd bought that game, *Flappers and Fall Guys*. I hadn't played it yet, because I didn't have anyone to play it with. Since this was a little embarrassing, I didn't want that topic to proceed any further.

Jed shifted in his chair and looked toward a media console, against one wall. "Gloria was being blackmailed."

"Whoa," Charlie said. "That's terrible."

"Over the photos?" I asked.

"Yeah." Jed uncrossed and recrossed his long legs. "Burlesque may be fairly tame, but she could have lost her job at the school. And they had an amazing healthcare plan for us both."

"Who was blackmailing her?" Fitch asked.

In a jerky motion, he ran his hands over his head. "I don't know. That's the problem. I got another email today demanding more money. I figured the only way to stop this was to close Gloria's account. Then there's nothing to blackmail anyone over."

"Unless the blackmailer already downloaded photos," I said.

Jed opened his mouth. Closed it.

"Would you have paid the blackmail?" I asked.

"Of course. Gloria's name means something. She was part of this community. Not everyone would understand."

"I'd like to see that email," Fitch said.

"You can't," he said miserably. "It's deleted."

"You mean *you* deleted it," I said. "If it's in the trash—"

"No," Jed said. "I mean it deleted automatically after I read it. And it's not in the trash. I checked."

I glanced at Fitch. "Is that possible?"

He nodded. "It's easy to set up. Most email programs have that function."

Jed rose and paced in front of the scarred table. "Gloria said she felt like she was being watched. Now I'm starting to feel the same way."

"Watched?" I asked. "Did she ever talk to you about Clyde McGarrity?"

"That's not fair," Charlie said. "Clyde only took pictures of her in public and with permission." I shot my brother an exasperated look.

"He's right," Jed said. "Clyde might be... overly enthusiastic about his scripts. But he always asked permission to take photos."

"Really?" I asked, disbelieving. "I've seen some of his photos, and they looked candid."

"We stopped posing after a while," Jed said. "It got boring. Clyde would ask if it was okay to take pictures, and then we'd ignore him. He gave us copies of everything."

"Was he interested in the both of you?" I asked. "Or only in Gloria?"

"Gloria," Jed said promptly. "Clyde was her biggest fan, and she appreciated his devotion to the craft."

Charlie snorted and turned it into a cough.

"She appreciated the fandom, not his scripts," Jed amended.

"How did this blackmailer approach Gloria?" Fitch leaned forward, his shoulder brushing mine, and my stomach quivered. I edged away on the couch, closer to my brother.

"Typed letters under her dressing room door," Jed said. "Emails that vanished after they'd been read."

"Do you have any of the letters?" Fitch asked.

"I think so."

"Find them," Fitch said. "We'd like to examine them. When did these demands start?"

"About a year ago." Jed returned to his chair, and the leather squeaked beneath his slacks.

"How frequent were they?" Fitch asked.

"Every couple months."

"And the blackmailer wanted money?" I asked.

Jed nodded. "It was eating into the profits from her account, let me tell you."

My brother squinted. "But why would the blackmailer kill Gloria?" He straightened on the couch. "I mean, whoever it was, they were getting money from Gloria. Wouldn't that be killing the golden goose?"

"Yes, but it's possible..." Jed said slowly.

"What?" I asked.

"Gloria was furious about the blackmail. She thought if she could discover who was behind it, she could take them down."

"Was she close to figuring it out?" Fitch asked.

Jed nodded. "She thought so. But she wasn't sure, so she wouldn't tell me."

"Everyone hates blackmailers," Charlie said.

"I know. Look what happened to that guy you were guarding last summer," Jed said, "Toomas Koppel."

"He was driving too fast and crashed into a tomato truck," I said flatly.

Jed gave me a pitying look. "No one believes that. Look, it's okay. It probably would have been better if he'd gone to trial, but no one blames you for... you know."

My face tightened. "There was no *you know*. He stole my car and crashed it. End of story."

Charlie patted my arm. "She's kind of sensitive about it," he said to Jed.

"Because it wasn't my fault!" *This*. This was why no one wanted to hire me. Never mind the police and FBI reports—

Jed shook his head. "I don't need to know what he had on you—"

"Nothing." My fists clenched. "He had nothing on me. And he died in a car accident."

"But if Gloria's blackmailer was exposed," Charlie said, "he or she'd be done. This is a small community. Everyone would know."

“Not to mention blackmail is a crime,” Fitch said.

“So Gloria was willing to pay the blackmail to keep her secret,” I said. “But she must have known if she exposed the blackmailer, her secret would be out too.”

“But the blackmailer would be destroyed as well,” Charlie said. “Gloria was all for going down with the ship. She just didn’t want to be the only person going down.”

“Right.” Jed came to sit on the coffee table in front of my brother. “*You* understand.”

“Gloria was part of our crew,” Charlie said sadly.

We got Jed to promise he’d tell the sheriff about the JustGroupies account and the blackmail, and the three of us left.

We walked to the treehouse. Fitch and I retrieved my surveillance equipment and cleaned up the mess. Charlie waited below. The treehouse couldn’t handle the weight of more than two adults.

Fitch and I climbed down, and my brother drew me aside. “What was going on up there?” he whispered. “I didn’t want to say anything, but you’ve got a massive jam stain on the back of your jacket.”

“Squirrel,” I said shortly, and Charlie shuddered.

“It may be rabid,” Fitch said. “Better watch for it.”

“No,” Charlie said. “It’s just got a really bad attitude.” He pointed to a slice of salami stuck to Fitch’s sleeve. “Hey, is that salami?”

I shook my head.

“It’s all yours,” Fitch said.

Chapter Twelve

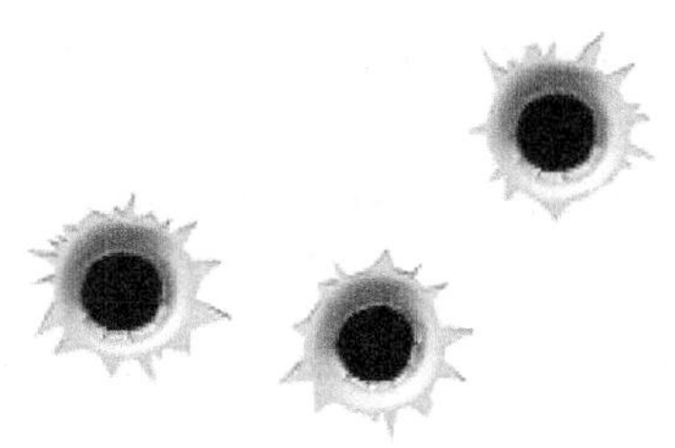

The nice thing about living in a theater? A person could sleep in. Nothing was going on before noon. Unless that theater had a cat.

An unholy howl awoke me, my arms prickling with goose flesh. My apartment was dark and empty. I rolled over and closed my eyes. *Owwwwwooooo!*

I sat up. Fredo snored at the end of my bed. I flopped back down again.

Owwoowoo!

"Blagh." I threw off the covers, stumbled over a dog toy, and made my way to the door of my studio apartment.

A masculine figure loomed in the corner. I patted the training dummy's rubbery head and yawned. "Hi, Bob."

I opened the door. The cat sat in the hallway and licked his paw. He glanced up at me and waltzed inside.

"I'm not your doorman. You can't just stroll in here any time you want. I was sleeping."

Sammie hopped onto the bed, batted Fredo's nocked ear, and curled up beside him. The dog snorted and rolled over.

"I need a real apartment," I muttered, got up, and pulled on a pair of sweats. A workout and hot shower later, I felt marginally human. I took Fredo for a walk, and we returned to the theater.

I eyed Gloria's dressing room door, still barricaded with yellow police tape. It wasn't much of a barrier. I mean, a barrier that weak was just begging to be ignored. Plus, the cops hadn't exactly been around to *do* anything with the dressing room. It obviously wasn't serious.

I put Fredo inside my apartment. Closing its door behind me, I reached for the dressing room's doorknob. Heavy footsteps sounded on the stairs, and I drew back.

Detective Guthrie strode around the corner. Over his boxer's nose, his eyes narrowed. "I figured I'd find you here."

Oh, damn. "I *do* live here." Today he was wearing a Brioni suit—it looked like a Vanquish II, and yes, those were Roman numerals, because Brioni was Italian. And incredibly expensive. I think you had to pay for them in gold or Bitcoin or something.

And why did a good suit make so many women drool? I mean, other women, not me. I was definitely not drooling.

"What are you doing standing outside the victim's door?" he demanded.

"See above regarding living here." I folded my arms.

He stared down at me. This doesn't happen a lot since I'm nearly six feet myself, so it was kind of exciting. "Move it," he said.

"Moving it." I stepped aside, but he managed to brush against me anyway as he stepped into the dressing room.

He snapped on gloves. "Weird that you were on the scene so quickly."

"Like I said, I live here—"

"I meant Koppel. He stole your car, and you were right there after the accident." He put the last word in air quotes, his gloved fingers making plasticy, rustling sounds.

Annoyed, I flipped my hair off my shoulder. "His mistake was drugging me. If he'd just let me sleep, I never would have known he'd taken my car. Once I knew I'd been drugged, I knew something was up."

He nodded his head. "Uh, huh." His thin lips pursed.

"What brings you back to the crime scene?"

He walked inside the dressing room without answering, and I figured I was out of luck. Then, he said, "Mr. Jackson contacted us with new information about his wife being blackmailed. I'm here to do another search of the room, make sure nothing was overlooked." Somehow his tone managed to imply that if something *had* been overlooked, it wasn't his fault. He pulled out the dressing table's drawer and felt the table's underside.

Rats. I'd wanted to search the room. But at least Jed had called the sheriff's station, like he'd said he would.

"Any idea who the blackmailer is?" I leaned against the doorframe.

He dug through the contents of the drawer. It looked to all be makeup. "Nope. Anyone tried to blackmail you?"

"No." Why would they? Only an idiot would try to blackmail someone who's reputation was already mud. "I heard there was poison in her box of pineapple juice."

He returned the drawer and walked to the wardrobe. "Just the glass." He ran his hand along the top of the wardrobe.

That was new. It implied someone had slipped the poison in not long before she'd died. "So you're looking at all the people in the theater."

"How'd he get your car?" He opened the wardrobe doors and moved the costumes aside.

This again. "Koppel drugged me. We were staying in adjoining rooms under the same name. All he had to do was ask the valet for the keys."

He grunted and pulled the shoes down from the wardrobe shelf, then ran his hand along the shelf. "Doesn't seem very smart."

"He thought the drugs would keep me down—"

"I meant you." He returned the shoes to their place. At least he was neat.

"Gee. Thanks."

He reached into the pockets of the costumes in a methodical fashion. "But most killers aren't smart."

"I didn't kill Toomas Koppel," I said, exasperated. "I've never killed anyone."

"You did break that guy's arm in Paris." He shut the wardrobe doors.

My mouth went dry. He'd been looking into me. The Paris incident wasn't common knowledge and hadn't made it into the press. "He took a swing at me. The Paris police let me off. There were witnesses. Cell phone video."

He lifted the mirror above the dressing table from the wall and looked behind it. "Still, breaking his arm might seem a little extreme to civilized people."

Had I imagined the emphasis on *civilized*? I didn't think I had, and I wasn't sure what it meant. But I got the feeling that beneath that classy suit, he might not be all that civilized himself.

"It stopped him from coming after me and my client," I said neutrally. I hadn't planned to break the guy's arm. I'd just hit him as hard as I could, knowing it was a possibility something would break and not liking it. I hadn't had much choice.

But I wanted to be one of those people who could think out moves split-seconds in advance and didn't care if arms got broken. A person who didn't need to be lucky... like I had been with the Reno dentist. I felt a little nauseated at the memory.

"Huh." He replaced the mirror. "Put the police tape back the way it was, will you?" he asked, striding from the room.

"Sure." I smiled. "No problem."

He jogged down the stairs, his expensive shoes soft on the hollow wood. My timing was the pits. If I'd raided Gloria's dressing room earlier, I might have gotten a look at her laptop. But at least he'd left the door open. I took a step toward the room.

"Hey, you're up." Charlie bounded into the hallway. "I thought we could get breakfast at the Sagebrush."

I scrubbed a hand over my face. "Why are you up so early?"

"We're having a meeting of the Medieval Battle Society, remember?"

"Oh, right."

"They took the police tape down." He motioned toward the tape coiled on the floor.

"I'm supposed to put it back again."

We stared at each other. Then we walked into the dressing room.

"Where's her laptop?" Charlie asked.

"Homicide detective took it."

"Bummer." My brother picked an e-reader off the dressing table and swiped it. "*Bound by the Earl*, by Alyson Chase. Looks spicy." Charlie swiped the screen. "Gloria doesn't have her email set up on this." He set the reader against the big mirror over the dressing table.

"Too bad." Now I couldn't sneer at the fancy-pants detective for missing it. The e-reader wasn't evidence. I checked the inside of the copper wall sconce beside the door for bugs.

Charlie dropped into the chair in front of the dressing table and swiveled. He heaved out a breath, his cheeks puffing. "Hard to believe a murder happened here," he said heavily.

Pulling my mini flashlight from my pocket, I peered under the chaise lounge. I ran my fingers along the underside of its wooden base.

"What are you looking for?" Charlie asked.

"Surveillance devices. Someone was blackmailing Gloria. Maybe they just happened to find out about Gloria's side business, but maybe they were surveilling her."

Charlie whistled. "Good thinking."

I checked the other likely places for bugs and found nothing. Hands on my hips, I stared at the high wardrobe. A spot heated between my shoulder blades, as if I were being watched. I glanced over my shoulder. Charlie sat sprawled in the chair, his head back, staring at the ceiling.

I shook myself. *Paranoia.* But I crossed the hall to my apartment, unearthed my bug sweeper, and returned to the dressing room.

Most surveillance devices emitted a signal. Some only emitted that signal when they downloaded their video or audio to their owner. This made them harder to detect with devices like mine. I turned my device on. Its bank of lights lit up, then went blank.

I turned slowly. A light on the screen flickered red. I looked up. Charlie scratched his stomach. I moved toward him. The light glowed steadily red. A second red light lit.

"Charlie," I said excitedly, "turn your phone off."

He pulled his phone from the pocket of his jeans and turned it off. "Done. Why did I just do that?"

I stepped closer. A third red light came on.

"The e-reader. Turn that off too."

"Yeah. Sure." He grabbed it and pushed a button. The screen came to life and died.

The lights on my bug finder went blank. Well, that was disappointing. I'd been picking up the e-reader and not a bug. "That must have been it."

"Is that a bug finder?"

"Yeah." I continued scanning the room and found nothing.

"Why didn't you start with that?"

"Redundancies. I like to double check my work."

He snapped his fingers and pointed at me. "And that's why you're the best."

I shot him a look.

"Except for that whole Koppel incident," he admitted. "But that wasn't your fault. You were counter surveillance, not close protection." He checked his watch and leapt to his feet. "We've got to get to the Sagebrush."

"Are you that hungry?"

"Yes, but that's not why. Jane's meeting us there for an interview."

My neck tightened. "She... Gloria's sister?" When had *that* been decided?

"And we're buying her breakfast. Well. You. You're buying her breakfast."

Fortunately for my wallet, Jane was not the sort of person to buy the most expensive thing on the menu. We sat in our jackets on the café's back patio, in the center of a cluster of heat lamps and tables that gave us a view of the Sierras above the high redwood fence. We weren't the only ones there. The diner was packed.

Fredo lay by my feet and gnawed on my shoestrings. I hadn't had the heart to leave the snaggle-toothed dog in my apartment. And with Sammie around, it would just be asking for trouble.

Jane's gaze bounced from my brother to me. "You said you had news about my sister?"

What *had* Charlie told her? I might not be a private detective, but I knew we should be keeping our evidence close.

"That's right." Charlie swallowed and laid his hands on the wire-mesh table. "Alice? Show her."

I pulled my cellphone from the pocket of my jacket and called up a pic I'd downloaded of Gloria. "Here." I handed her the phone.

Jane looked at it and sucked in her breath. "That's—"

"Gloria," Charlie said. "I know."

"Was this for a... show?" she asked.

"No," I said. "She's got a JustGroupies account where she sells the photos."

"You mean there are more?" She swiped my phone screen. Her mouth pinched. "This is—"

"In fairness," Charlie said, "burlesque is an art."

"People aren't buying these for their artistic quality," she snapped. "How could she do this to— her family? She works at the school! What would happen if these got into the hands of the kids? She'd be a laughingstock. She'd lose her job."

Charlie stretched his legs beside the table and crossed them at the ankles. "Which brings us to your sister's blackmailer."

"What?" Her eyes widened behind her glasses. "She was being blackmailed?" Charlie nodded. "Poor Jed," she whispered.

"Poor Jed?" I asked, incredulous.

"He wouldn't be in this situation if it weren't for these pictures," she said. "I suppose he's trying to protect her reputation now?"

"Um." I glanced at my brother. "Yes."

"Gloria never thought of the effect her actions had on others." Jane fumed. "Never."

"Do you have any idea who might have been blackmailing your sister?" I asked.

A waitress sped past our table carrying a tray filled with steaming plates. The scent of pancakes and bacon wafted on the October air, and my mouth watered.

"Of course not. If I had, I would have tossed them off the theater roof. Gloria was my *sister*. We might not have always gotten along, but she was family."

"She never said anything to you about the blackmail?" I asked.

"No. She probably knew how I'd react about what she was being blackmailed over. She *was* being blackmailed over these photos? There wasn't something else?"

That was a good question. "Did Gloria have something else to hide?"

Jane slumped in her metal chair. "I don't know. Gloria stopped confiding in me long ago."

"Did she ever complain to you that she felt she was being watched?" I asked.

An odd expression crossed her face. "Yes, she did. At first she thought it was Clyde. But when I asked her if she'd done anything about him, she told me it wasn't him."

"So she knew who it was?" Charlie sliced into his breakfast burrito. Meat and beans spilled onto his plate.

Jane blinked rapidly. "No, I... I don't know."

"When was this?" I leaned closer.

"About two weeks ago," she said. "Should I tell the sheriff about this?"

For the love of Mike. She hadn't already? "Yes," I said evenly. "It might be nothing, but I think you should. What time did you arrive at the theater the night of Gloria's death?"

"Five o'clock," she said, "like I always do."

"Did you see Gloria?" I asked.

"Not after she dropped Clyde's script in the kitchen garbage."

We finished breakfast, and I got no more useful information out of Jane. Charlie left for his Medieval Battle Society meeting, and Fredo and I returned to my apartment.

I checked my email. There was nothing from any of the overseas protection companies I'd applied to, and that was disappointing. I sat back in my creaky chair. How long was I going to be stuck in Nowhere? It wasn't terrible, but it wasn't great either. It was like an airport—an in-between place you'd rather leave. Purgatory.

The sticky note I'd stuck over my webcam lit from behind. I frowned and peeled it off. My webcam's blue light was on. I typed "webcam" into the computer's search box, and a list of commands for the camera popped up.

Annoyed, I clicked one. A new screen popped up. I scrolled down and turned off my camera. The light glowed electric blue. I toggled the off button. The light kept glowing. A chill rippled up my back. I re-read the screen instructions, toggled the button again.

But the webcam didn't turn off. Unease slithered inside my chest. It was probably nothing. Probably just a defective light. But there was a reason I kept a sticky note over my webcam. I didn't want some creeper watching me through it.

And I was pretty sure someone was doing just that right now.

Chapter Thirteen

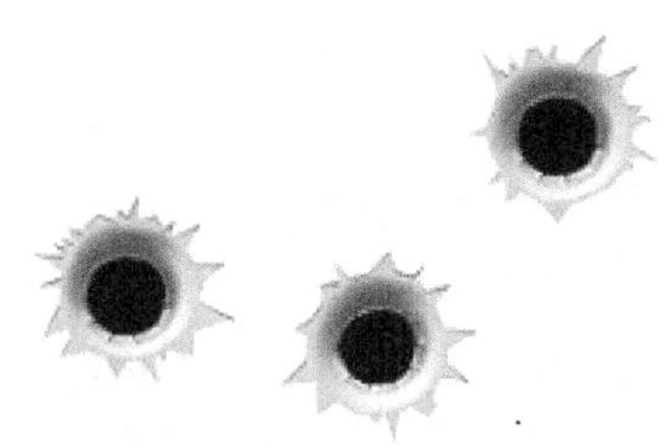

I slammed the laptop shut. On his dog bed, Fredo raised his head. The gray dog's ears swiveled like antennas.

I massaged the back of my neck. The malfunctioning webcam still might be a computer glitch. But if someone *had* gotten into my computer, what else had they accessed?

I rebooted the laptop. This time, the webcam light stayed dark, and my muscles relaxed. I clicked over to my VPN, which protected me from most attempted hacks. It was off. I didn't remember turning it off.

Keeping an eye on the webcam, I turned on the VPN and relaxed a little more. But *could* I afford to relax?

Gloria had thought she was being watched, and now Jed felt the same. Had someone been surveilling them through their laptops? And if so, who? Because this sort of thing went well beyond Clyde's low-tech lurking.

Light from my apartment's small, square window slanted across my table. I drummed my fingers on the table.

I needed Gloria's history. Unfortunately, that meant consulting Clyde or Jed. I called Charlie instead.

"Talk fast," he said, "my battery's about to run out and I've got no power in the woods. Medieval Battle Society practice," he added by way of explanation.

"I need Clyde's contact info."

"I'm coming with you."

"No, I just need his phone number—"

"He's home now," my brother said.

"How do you know...?" Why did everyone know everyone else's business in this town? "Never mind. I just need his phone number."

"Cool. I'll meet you there." He rattled off an address. The line went dead.

I redialed. The call went straight to voice mail. I cursed, unsure if Charlie was avoiding me or if his phone really had died. Either were possible. Not that it mattered. I knew where Charlie was headed. And *why* hadn't I decided to pester Jed instead?

"Stay," I told the dog, and I left the theater, drove to Clyde's house.

Clyde and Vittoria lived in a neat, two-story cabin with a granny cottage next door. The latter was covered in fake spider webs, wafting in the cool breeze. Their phantom-like strands gestured at rows of crooked Styrofoam gravestones. In front of those, bones stuck from the ground, faux-skeletons emerging from the graves.

Other than the graveyard, they'd gone with the natural look in their yard—pine trees and earth, stones and manzanita. Between the landscaping and the decorations, it looked like a miniature ghost town.

Red eyes glowed off and on in one of the granny cottage's windows. Since Charlie hadn't arrived yet, I walked to the window and peered inside. A long table down its center was covered in a miniature hobbit village.

"Hey," Charlie said in my ear, and I jumped.

"You didn't need to cut out of your Medieval Battle Society," I said.

"We weren't getting anything done. All anyone could talk about was the murder."

"Did you learn anything?"

He rubbed the back of his blond head. "Only that Gloria wasn't really well liked. I don't get it. I mean, I know she could be a diva. And pushy. And demanding."

"So, a diva."

He stared fixedly at me. "Well, yeah. But it's not like she was a bad person. Not usually, at least. I mean, it was no reason to kill her."

"That is true. How do you know Clyde's home?"

"He works from home. He's a financial analyst." Charlie scratched his beard. "I think."

I pointed my thumb at the window. "Have you seen this?"

Charlie glanced inside. "The hobbit miniatures? Yeah. Vittoria's really into Tolkien. Her big dream is to go to New Zealand and see the spot where they filmed. You know, with all the life-size hobbit houses?" He frowned. "Or maybe they're hobbit sized."

Someone once told me that all one needs to be happy is good work, someone to love, and a dream. Gloria's dream had been Paris. Vittoria's was New Zealand. I just wanted to get back to my career, but I wasn't sure my dream was making me happy. "Let's say hello."

We walked to the front door. A gargoyle knocker scowled from beneath the peep hole. I lifted its heavy metal ring and knocked.

"Oh, hey," Charlie said casually. "I was wondering if I could maybe crash at your place for a little while."

"Did the realtor tell you to move it?"

"Yeah," he said, expression glum. "She told me they paid cash. They move in next month. And I don't think they'll want to rent me the treehouse."

No kidding. "Yeah," I said, "you're probably right."

"So, if I can't find anything in time, can I stay?"

What was I going to say? No? He was my little brother. And truth to tell, I'd rather he crash with me than stay in a treehouse. It was starting to get cold at night, and it was just embarrassing. "Sure. But it's only temporary." I love Charlie, but he's the kind of guy who needs incentives.

"Right, I'm working on a new place. Don't worry."

"I'm just saying, I'm not sure how long I'll be there." I rang the bell again. "If a protection gig comes through, I'm out."

"Yeah, yeah. Sure. I get it."

Clyde opened the door. "Perfect." His round face beamed. "You're both here. Come in, come in."

Had he been expecting us? Baffled, Charlie and I glanced at each other then followed him inside the cabin. The interior was as decorated as the outside. A miniature Halloween village glowed on an occasional table in the hallway.

In the living room, pumpkins, electric candles, and autumn leaves lay along the fireplace mantel and windowsills. A pyramid of pumpkins was stacked beside the fireplace. The room smelled like pumpkin and caramel.

"Nice," Charlie said. "Who's the Halloween fan?"

"Both of us, but Vittoria gets credit for the decorations. She loves the holidays." Clyde waddled to the open dining room. He grabbed two sheafs of paper off the table, covered in an orange and black cloth. "I want to see how these scripts flow." He handed each of us a stapled stack of paper. I glanced at the title, *This is Murder.*

Charlie let his head drop back so he could see the beamed ceiling. "Seriously? Another script? You *know* we do improv."

"We're actually here to ask if you'd noticed anyone watching Gloria," I said. "You spent quite a bit of time with her. Did you notice anyone else who was around her a lot? Someone who showed up in your photos?"

"Other than Jed?" Clyde rubbed his fleshy chin. "Hm... That's an interesting question."

"And?" I asked.

"I'll tell you after you run these lines," he said.

"Oh, come *on.*" Charlie groaned. "This is murder."

"Yes," Clyde said brightly. "That's the name of my script. Turn to page one hundred and fifty-two. Charlie, you're Slate. Alice, you're Blueberry."

"I'm a blueberry?" I flipped the pages.

"No," Clyde said. "Blueberry is your name. From the top, please." He turned a dining chair so he could face us and sat.

I found the page. It looked like I went first. "You fiend," I read. "This is blackmail."

"What's the scene's foundation?" Charlie asked. "Who am I?"

That line wasn't in the script. Had I missed a page? I flipped forward through the pages. Or had I been distracted by the pumpkin caramel scent? Where was it coming from?

"You're a fiendish blackmailer," Clyde told him.

"Got it." Charlie dropped into a hunch and twirled an imaginary mustache. "Do you want the world to know your secret identity as Captain Blueberry? Buahahahaha!"

I spotted a pumpkin shaped air freshener plugged into the wall and nodded. *One mystery solved.*

"That's not the line." Clyde's forehead wrinkled and he flipped through the pages.

"It's improv," Charlie said.

"I don't want you to improv. And Alice, can you read your lines a little less woodenly?"

"Yeah," Charlie said. "Maybe if you stood and moved around a little, you'd give the lines more energy."

"He's right," Clyde said.

"This is the first time I've seen the script," I said, affronted. What did they expect?

Clyde motioned toward us with his hands. "Just keep reading."

I stood and read the next line. "I will never pay."

"Pay? Who said anything about money?" Charlie waggled his brows and leered.

"Then what do you want?" I stepped forward and cracked my shin against a coffee table. I sucked in a pained breath with a hiss. "Ow. Dammit."

Charlie slunk toward me. "I want you to discover someone *else's* secret and tell me, and then *you* blackmail *them*. And if you don't, I'll destroy you both. It's the Devil's Pyramid Scheme. Buahahaha!"

Clyde threw his script to the beige carpet. "Will you be serious and stick to the lines? *Devil's Pyramid Scheme*? You're not Mephistopheles, and that's not part of the script."

"I can't help it," Charlie said. "I'm improv."

"I thought the *Devil's Pyramid Scheme* line was pretty good," I said.

"It's not original," Charlie admitted.

"Read *my* lines." Clyde retrieved the script from the carpet.

"Fine," Charlie said. "It's your line, Alice."

"I won't. I won't do it," I read.

"Then I'll tell everyone *you're* the secret shopper." Charlie bounded onto the coffee table, knocking a stack of National Geographics to the floor.

"She's not a secret shopper," Clyde shouted. "*I'll tell everyone your secret*. The line is, *I'll tell everyone your secret*."

"You wouldn't," I read hastily. "It will ruin me."

"I will, and that's the point," Charlie read dully from the coffee table.

"Don't push me, Slate." Focused on the script, I stepped backward. This time my calf hit the couch, and I sat with a thump. "Oops."

"Forget it." Clyde crumpled in his chair. "Just forget it. Clearly, Charlie has all the acting talent in your family. I'm sorry Alice, but it's just the truth."

"It's my first time reading the lines!" I hadn't been *that* bad.

"This is hopeless." Clyde twisted and slapped his script onto the dining table behind him.

"I told you," Charlie said, "you don't give an improv troupe scripts. You give them scenarios."

"Does this mean we're done?" I asked.

Clyde's face sagged. "We're done."

"Good." I set the script on the coffee table beside Charlie's feet and bent to pick up the fallen magazines. "Did you see anyone hanging around Gloria?"

"No."

"No one?" I asked, disappointed. I returned the magazines to their spot.

"I told you, she spent most of her time with Jed, and he's her husband."

"Did you know about her JustGroupies account?" I asked.

"Of course I did," he said. "I've downloaded every one of her photos. I wanted to support her talent."

"Then why didn't you mention it?" I clambered to my feet.

"Gloria was conscious that it might not go over too well with the school. I respected that."

Or he might have been blackmailing her over the account. Or Clyde's fandom could have turned unhealthy. And how did Clyde's wife feel about the photos? "Does your wife know?" I asked.

"Does his wife know what?" Vittoria asked from the open doorway.

CHAPTER FOURTEEN

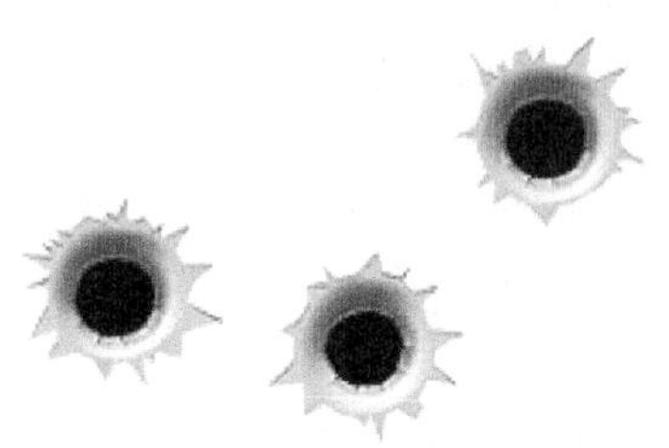

"WHOOPS," CHARLIE SAID FROM atop the coffee table. "I guess she knows now."

"Knows what?" Vittoria strode into the living room. She dropped an XXL pizza delivery bag on top of the piano.

Her husband smiled. "Alice was asking about my fandom."

"I don't care what she was asking about, what's she doing here?" Vittoria clawed both hands through her brown hair. "And get off my table." Charlie hopped to the carpet.

Clyde straightened. "She wanted my help figuring out who might have killed Gloria."

Vittoria's green eyes narrowed. "She works for Gert. You know those two are making my life a living hell at the pizza parlor. What are you thinking, letting her inside our house?"

No one ever listens. "Why do people still think that? I told you, I don't work for Gert."

She rolled her eyes. "You're his *enforcer*."

"No," I said. "I'm really not."

"Oh, please." She glared. "You're investigating the murder on Gert's behalf. Get out of my house."

"Okay, okay." I backed up, then realized I was moving away from the entryway and not toward it. "I'm going. But I'm telling you, I'm not working for Gert."

"Gert says you are," she said. "And it's obviously true. Do you know how much it's going to cost to put extra braces on that big pizza cutter? It's also not going to look as good. And we don't need them in the first place. What do *you* know about hanging outsized pizza cutters?"

"Nothing," I said, "but—"

"You tell Gert he's only temporary mayor. He's got no right to push us around."

We stood in awkward silence. I folded my arms. If people were going to take me for an enforcer, I might as well look the part.

"Your Halloween decorations are really cool," Charlie said feebly.

"Thanks." Her mouth flattened.

"So you knew about Gloria's JustGroupies account?" I asked.

"Of course I knew," she huffed. "I could hardly miss the credit card bill."

"What did you think of it?" I asked.

"I think we're all doing what we can to get by, and your boss is trying to ruin my livelihood."

"Okay," I said meekly. "We'll just go."

"You do that." She followed us to the front door and slammed it behind us.

Charlie and I walked past the spiderwebbed shack. That had gone badly. But at least I knew that Vittoria knew about the JustGroupies account. She could have been the blackmailer. But so could Mr. Washington's nephew.

With a sharp tug, I zipped my jacket higher. I also now knew that Gert was still telling people I was his muscle. My jaw hardened. That was going to stop.

I dropped Charlie off at the treehouse and drove to Gert's antique store. A CLOSED sign hung in its dusty window, but I rattled the door in frustrated impotence anyway.

"Hey! Hey, Alice!" a man shouted. Jim, the owner of the Viking Bar down the street, waved at me.

I waved back and smiled. Small business owners are the best. They work hard, they take risks, and for whatever reason, they tend to be good with people. Jim was no exception. About Charlie's age, he was a blond two inches taller than me, and with much broader shoulders.

"What's up?" I asked.

His face darkened. "Are you kidding me? What the hell, Alice? Gert's talking about closing down the ax throwing."

"I didn't— Can he do that?"

He shrugged. "How should I know. *I'm* not his lackey."

"Neither am I. I don't work for Gert."

"That's not what he's saying. And if you don't work for Gert, what are you doing here?"

I glanced toward the shop window. In its display, a jackalope snarled silently back at me. "I'm here to tell him to stop telling people I work for him."

He raised one hand, palm out. "Alice, just stop. You were riding with him in the parade."

"Mrs. Malone blackmailed me into that."

He raised a brow. "That's a new one."

"Okay, technically, it's not blackmail since I have to help her out with theater business. She put it in my rental contract. She's also giving me a discount on the rent. Fair's fair."

Jim barked a laugh. "Mrs. Malone doesn't miss a step. Why didn't you read your contract?"

"So you believe me?" Was it possible?

He frowned and cocked his head. "I guess working as Gert's hired gun doesn't really fit your style," he said slowly.

Thank you. "Have you seen Gert around?" I asked, suddenly giddy. For all their quirks, the people of Nowhere had mostly believed I hadn't been involved in Toomas Koppel's car accident. Until now, I hadn't realized how much that had meant to me, and how much the lost of that faith had stung.

"No," he said. "Did you try Town Hall?"

Town Hall. Obvious. I guess I still wasn't used to Gert actually being the mayor, even if it was only temporary. "No. I will now. See you around."

I walked to Town Hall. Gert wasn't there either. His assistant, an iron-haired woman with a permanently disapproving look, told me he was consulting with Mrs. Malone.

Ten minutes later, I banged on the door of her quaint, two-story, red-painted cabin. The flowers in the window boxes had been replaced with mini pumpkins and gourds.

A shadow darkened the door's diamond-pane window. The door opened. Mrs. Malone frowned out. "About time you got here." She turned and marched inside on her sensible shoes. Her black skirt, decorated with jack-o-lanterns at the hem, swished in time to her movements.

Bemused, I followed. "Is Gert here?"

I answered my own question when I walked into the dining room. Gert sat at the wooden table drinking from a coffee mug. I jammed my fists on my hips. "Gert, you've got to stop telling people I work for you."

Mrs. Malone lowered herself into a dining chair. "But you do work for him."

"Not when it comes to bullying local business owners."

She waved away my objection. "It hardly matters when a woman has been murdered and the sheriff has no interest in solving the case."

"I'm sure that's not true," I said.

The old lady quirked a brow. "Are you? How often have you seen his deputies in Nowhere lately?"

"I saw his homicide detective this morning, searching Gloria's dressing room."

"He should have done that the night you found her body," she said. "Did you wonder why he wasn't there?"

"He was in Hot Springs." Gert set his coffee on the table. "For their pumpkin festival."

"They don't grow pumpkins in Hot Springs," I said, indignant. Where did they get off having a pumpkin festival? Besides, Hot Springs had its own police department. I shook myself. And that wasn't the point. "And what was the sheriff's detective doing in Hot Springs if they've got their own department?"

"He's only the sheriff's detective temporarily." Mrs. Malone sniffed.

"A temporary detective?" Were there agencies for that? I rubbed the back of my neck. "But if he works for the sheriff—"

"He doesn't." Gert polished his thick glasses. "The sheriff's borrowing the Hot Springs homicide detective. Our sheriff's department doesn't have one." He replaced the glasses on his nose. "What's so confusing about that?"

"The sheriff recently decided it would be more efficient if a detective devoted to the craft managed county homicides," Mrs. Malone elaborated. "Something about his nerves."

Gert cackled. "Heh."

She shot him a sharp look and he subsided. "Hot Springs was happy to oblige."

"One homicide detective for the county still seems kind of... under resourced," I said.

Mrs. Malone braced one elbow on the dining table. "And this surprises you? You think every police department in every state and every county runs the same way?"

"Well, no, but—"

"But what? We're a small, sparsely populated county. We have to share resources. It's happening all over the country. You should know this."

"But was there a homicide in Hot Springs Friday night?" I asked.

"Hardly." Mrs. Malone sniffed. "They were auctioning off a crystal pumpkin, and he was on guard duty."

"A homicide detective was guarding a glass pumpkin?" I asked, disbelieving. On the wall, the wooden bird popped out of its clock and cuckooed.

"Crystal, and it's quite valuable. I was given to understand that there was some miscommunication, and they couldn't locate the detective right away to come here." Mrs. Malone slipped on a pair of reading glasses, unfolded a piece of paper, studied it, and handed it to me. "Here's the map."

"Map of what?" I asked.

"The Halloween Faire, of course," she said. "I'd like you to review it for safety concerns. Set-up begins on Friday at the rodeo grounds. You'll need to walk the grounds for—"

"Security," I finished for her. "We've gone over this before. I'm busy. I've got other work to do, work which I need to pay the rent."

She lowered her head and peered at me over her reading glasses. "Do this and you won't have to pay for two more weeks rent. Are we agreed?"

"No," I said, folding the map.

"No?"

I turned to Gert. "I've got half the businesses in town yelling at me because they think I work for you. If I do this, they'll keep thinking it."

"What nonsense," Mrs. Malone said. "You work for me."

"And you'll tell them that?" I asked Gert.

He shrugged. "Her. Me. As long as the job gets done." He took a sip of coffee from his chipped mug.

"Well," I said. "Okay. It's a deal." After all, the gig at the Halloween faire couldn't take more than a few hours.

She nodded. "And of course, I'll expect you to work there over the weekend."

"The whole weekend?" I bleated.

"How else are you supposed to provide security?" she asked.

"I'm not a security guard. I'm—"

"Now," she said, "what have you discovered?"

"What?" I asked.

"Our murder investigation," she prompted. "What have you turned up?"

"Oh. According to her husband, Gloria was being blackmailed over her JustGroupies account."

"Her what?" Gert asked blankly.

"It's a website where people can pay to look at photos," Mrs. Malone said, surprising me. JustGroupies seemed modern and sketchy. Neither were Mrs. Malone's style. "There's a monthly membership fee," she said, "and extra if you want to download unwatermarked copies."

I grasped the back of a dining room chair. "Um, yeah."

"I suppose she was selling dirty pictures?" Mrs. Malone asked.

"Burlesque," I corrected.

"That's real American art." With his mug, Gert gestured toward a faded wall calendar—a Yosemite scene, not a pin-up.

"And yet it was saucy enough for her to pay a blackmailer?" Mrs. Malone asked. "Of course it would be. She worked at the school." She blew out her breath. "Disappointing, but that's human nature. What else?"

"Clyde and Vittoria both knew about the account," I said. "Clyde was a customer." I didn't mention Mr. Washington's nephew. The poor kid had a portfolio career. I felt like we were connected.

"So one or both of them could have been the blackmailers." She paced beside the bookcase, stuffed with true crime novels. "But why kill Gloria if she was paying?"

"Jed said Gloria had an idea who was blackmailing her and wanted to expose the person," I said.

"Do you believe it?" Mrs. Malone asked.

I shook my head. "I don't believe anything anyone tells me. I just file it away to ponder later."

"Good girl," she said. "How were the demands made?"

"Letters shoved under her door and emails that disappeared after opening. Jed's trying to find some of the letters for us."

Us? Why had I said that? I was a lone wolf. Even when I'd been in personal protection, I'd been a contract employee... Until Buck had started his own company and I'd gone to work for him. And look how *that* had worked out.

"Excellent." She nodded. "What's this about disappearing emails?"

"Apparently it's easy to do. But I think..." I wrinkled my brow. "I think someone was trying to spy on me through my webcam. Either the blackmailer or the killer—if they're not the same person—has serious tech chops. Are any of the players at the theater in tech?"

"I don't think so," she said. "Jed is a manager at one of those fancy hotels in Hot Springs. Clyde's a financial analyst. His wife manages the pizza parlor. Kristie is a systems engineer, whatever that means. And Charlie... Well, you know your brother."

"And the blackmail may have nothing to do with her murder," I said. "Jed says he was supportive of his wife's JustGroupies account, but he could be lying. Jane may have had a motive—"

"Jealousy." Mrs. Malone paused beside a tall, brass lamp. "She always stood in her sister's shadow."

"Half-sister," I corrected absently.

"It's the same thing," she said.

"Is it?" Because I'm not sure it was for Jane. "Anyway, Clyde may have strayed from fandom into stalking," I continued. "So there's motive."

She snorted. "Clyde? A killer? I think not."

"I'm just saying, we don't know enough about our suspects."

"You mean *you* don't." Gert sipped his coffee.

"Fine," I said. "I don't."

Mrs. Malone arched a smoky brow. "Then hadn't you better do something about that?"

Chapter Fifteen

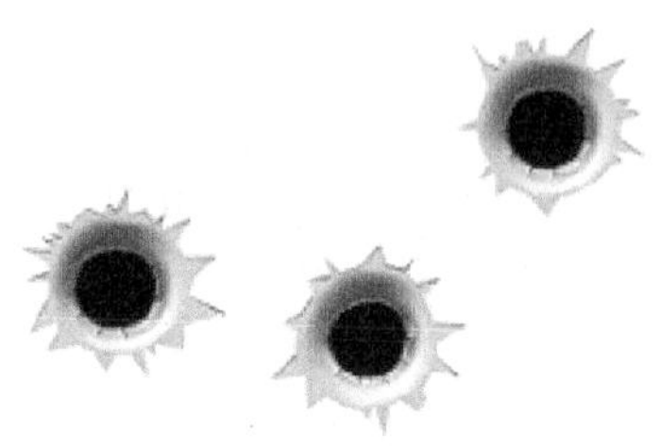

I climbed the narrow steps to my apartment. Behind its wooden door, an unearthly wail lifted the hairs on the back of my neck. Wary, I unlocked my door. Even more warily, I stepped inside. The cat hissed beside my ear.

"Gagh!" I jumped away, annoyed that despite my precautions, I'd still been startled.

Sammie perched on the top of the bookcase. The black cat was in full Halloween mode, back arched, fur standing on end.

I scanned the apartment. Everything looked okay. Bed, made. Windows, closed. Laptop, on table. What had put the cat on edge?

For a wild moment, I entertained the idea he'd seen a ghost. Then I noticed my bare-chested boxing dummy, its white martial-arts gi pooled on the floor behind it.

I scooped up the gi and hung it over the dummy's shoulders. "At this point, you have to know it's not real," I said to the cat. I found the white belt and tied it around the dummy's waist.

There was a gentle sneeze. Fredo crawled from beneath the bed, his bulging eyes rolling.

"You too?" I unfolded the fair map from my jacket pocket. Edging aside my laptop, I spread the map on the small table.

The Nowhere rodeo grounds had been divided into four kingdoms—five if you counted the food court. I studied the map. *Old West Vampires*, *Silk Road Spooks*, *Haunted Olde England*, and the *Goblin Grotto*. Vendor areas were disbursed between the kingdoms.

It all seemed simple enough, and I didn't see the need to waste more time on it. "How would you like to assist in an investigation?" I asked Fredo.

The gray dog eyed me suspiciously.

I leashed Fredo. We strolled toward the location of my next suspect interviewee: Kristie Naysmith. Kristie didn't have any pets. But she'd once cornered me at the theater and told me at length how much she loved animals. I figured Fredo would make a good icebreaker.

Kristie lived in a stone cottage with a steep, shingled roof and half-circle windows. Pumpkins climbed the wooden steps to the front porch. It was the perfect home for an earth goddess. Or a forest witch.

A cold breeze sighed in the nearby pines, and I stared into their shadows, lengthened by the slanting afternoon sun. No fairytale monsters emerged, which I confess was a little disappointing.

Growing up in Nowhere, I'd spent a lot of time fantasizing about going on adventures in magical lands. The town's black rock spires and pine forest had seemed on the edge of potential, as if something *might* happen.

But nothing ever did. Now the town felt weirder than wyrd. But I appreciated Kristie's attempt at some forest magic—at least décor-wise.

Fredo trotted to a pumpkin and lifted his leg. Picking him up, I climbed the stairs. One of Fredo's many failings was he tended to run *into* steps instead of up them. It might have had something to do with his weird eyes.

I rang the bell. It cackled. Fredo started in my arms and howled.

Kristi opened the door, and her brown eyes widened. "Why Alice," she bellowed, and Fredo twitched again. "What brings you to my door? And your wacky little dog, too."

Wacky was a diplomatic way of describing Fredo. "I need your help."

She smiled. "Come inside. I was just going to have tea in my garden. Why don't you join me?"

It seemed a little cold for that, but I was on her turf, so I'd put up with it. "Thank you."

Black broomstick skirt swaying, she led us into a homey, red-tiled kitchen. She handed me a teapot, grabbed two mugs, spoons, and a jar of honey, and walked out the back d oor.

The backyard was a clearing encircled by pines. A creek burbled behind it, backed by a manzanita-covered hillside. She nodded to the two Adirondack chairs and the crackling covered firepit between them.

I set the teapot on the firepit's circular ledge. Nudging the footstool out of the way, I sat on the edge of one chair. The yard was free of Halloween décor, so I put Fredo down and lengthened his leash, giving him room to wander. Instead of taking advantage, he dropped to the ground by my feet.

She settled herself, adjusting her long skirt. "Now, how can I help you?"

"It's about Gloria. It turns out she... Well, she had something of a secret life."

"Oh?" She laced her hands over her broad stomach.

"She had a JustGroupies page where she sold burlesque photos."

She laughed and crossed her legs at the ankles on the sloping wooden ottoman. "Is that all? Gloria is—was a performer."

"Did you know about the account?"

Kristie poured tea into my mug. "What?"

"Did you know about the photos?"

"I had no idea. But Gloria was never one to confide in me."

"It seems someone was blackmailing her over them."

"Honey?" She held out the jar.

"Thanks." Forcing a smile, I scooped a teaspoon into my tea and managed not to get too much on my finger. I swirled it into the tea, spoon clinking against the mug. "Did you notice anyone watching Gloria?"

She shook her head. "No. There was that knight, of course, but well, you know."

I knew the knight was an iffy suspect at best. "What about any conflicts between Gloria and the other actors?" I asked.

She pressed her knuckles to a plump cheek and cocked her head, thoughtful. "Not at all."

"What were you two arguing about?" I sucked the honey off my finger.

"Hey! There you are." Charlie rounded the corner of the stone house. "I've been looking all over for you."

"And you found me," I said, irritated. It was like my brother had a homing device. I stilled. *Had* he found my collection of tracking devices?

"Would you like some tea?" Kristie asked.

"No, thanks," he said. "Mrs. Malone said you'd be here," he told me.

"Mrs. Malone?" Kristie asked. A crow alighted in a nearby pine, and a pinecone thudded from its branch to the ground. Fredo's ears twitched.

"We're helping her investigate Gloria's murder," Charlie said.

I shook my head. Not that I'd been particularly subtle with my questioning earlier. But I hadn't wanted to just come out and *say* it.

"It's okay," he told her, "we've done this sort of thing before. What did I miss?"

"I was just asking Kristie about her argument with Gloria," I gritted out.

Kristie tapped her chin. "I can't remember us arguing."

"You were overheard," I said. "The week before Gloria died."

She sat up in her chair, her mouth pinching. "Overheard by whom?"

"Jane." Charlie shot me an apologetic look and sat on my wooden footrest. "Jane told me you'd been arguing." In the pine, the crow flapped his wings. Dried needles showered to the dirt. Fredo got to his feet and growled.

"Poor Jane." Kristie shook her head. "To lose a sister like that, and to have so much unfinished business."

"Unfinished?" I asked.

"Jane and Gloria were always at odds. It's the age-old story. One sibling flying high, and the other ignored. Gloria got all the attention as a child. And then there was Jed—" She shook her head and took a sip of her tea.

"And then there was Jed what?" Charlie leaned closer to her, his elbows on his knees.

She smiled wanly. "I shouldn't say."

But I could tell she wanted to, and I was losing patience. "No," I said. "You should. Someone poisoned one of your fellow players."

Kristie stared into her mug. "No. No, it isn't right, even if Jane hasn't done a very good job of hiding it." A branch in the firepit popped. Sparks shot upward and were captured by the wire mesh lid. Fredo started and hid behind my legs.

"Hiding what?" Charlie asked.

"A private desire," she said. "I'm sure Jane's feeling horribly bad about it now. *Jed* has nothing to regret, however."

"Are you suggesting... Jane's in love with Jed?" I asked.

"What?" Charlie said. "No way."

Kristie smoothed her black skirt. "I'm not suggesting anything, and neither should you. But the way she acts around him..."

Charlie squinted. "Jane? And Jed? Really?"

"Oh, I'm *not* saying they ever acted on it." She squeezed her shoulders closer. "Just a touch of unrequited love. Besides, Jane *couldn't* have been the black knight."

Ugh. I massaged the bridge of my nose between pinched fingers. How'd we get back to the knight again?

"Why not?" Charlie asked.

"Who said anything about the knight?" I asked.

"Because Jane was in the theater kitchen when the knight appeared outside the theater two weeks ago," Kristie continued.

My brother snapped his fingers. "See? I'm not the only one who thinks there's something weird about the guy. He's real."

Whatever. "I'm just saying, it's a little too much for someone dressed as a black knight to have been the killer. It's undignified. Nowhere isn't a cartoon." And I was starting to sound like Mrs. Malone.

"In fairness," Kristie said, "Jane was right. We don't know if there's a black knight or lots of people enjoying the same costume. I believe a costume shop in Reno sells them."

"And we have no reason to believe the knight's got anything to do with the murder," I said.

Kristie paled. "I'm not so sure of that."

"Why?" Charlie asked.

Finger shaking, she pointed at the hillside, thick with dry brush. "Because he's right there." A figure in black tunic, pants, and helmet ran up the hill.

Charlie leapt to his feet. "That's him." He raced through the clearing and hurdled the narrow stream.

"Charlie, wait." I thrust Fredo's leash into Kristie's hand and jogged after my brother. It was bad enough that he was chasing an idiotic Halloween costume through the woods. Now he was forcing me to do it too.

My brother hopped and wove through the manzanita, his arms high. Its bare branches clawed at his clothes. "Ow, ow, ow!"

"Charlie!" I puffed after him, the bush's sharp spurs catching my jeans and jacket.

Charlie broke through the manzanita and ran up the rock and boulder-strewn hill.

"It's probably some kid," I shouted. *Chasing a black knight.* This was worse than the time I'd had to guard a slushie mascot.

The black knight scrabbled over a field of smaller rocks.

"Get back here," my brother yelled.

The knight's foot skidded behind him, dislodging a good-sized rock. It bounced down the hill and knocked others loose. Rocks and earth clattered down the hillside. Charlie dodged sideways.

I passed him and kept running. Rocks bounced past. One thudded against a pine, and the tree shuddered, needles raining down.

I kept going. I can be a little competitive, and now that the chase was on, I wanted to win. The knight—or whoever—was close. Dust plumed on the hillside. Pulse hammering in my ears, I stretched for the knight's black tunic. I could just...

A gray coldness settled in my chest, turned my skin clammy. I'd learned the wrong lesson from my battle with the killer dentist—that I could fight and win. But that had never been me. Not without a weapon. The dentist had been a fluke.

I dropped my hand. My knees slackened. Gasping, I bent and braced my hands on a black rock to stop them from shaking. Dust stuck to my damp skin. The knight crested the hillside and vanished.

I exhaled slowly. *Okay*. The shaking, the adrenaline dump, this wasn't normal. I was freaked out more than I should have been—a delayed reaction from the deadly dentist. But I'd work through it. I rose and turned.

The hillside was a wreck, bushes uprooted. A lone rock skittered down the hillside. Stones had come to rest in the creek, and the muddy water rippled around them. I stared, shocked by the destruction.

"Are you all right?" Kristie shouted from the bottom of the hill.

Heart banging, I stepped from behind the pine and scanned the hillside. "Charlie?" I coughed, crooking my arm to cover my nose and mouth from the billowing dust. The wind soughed in the pines, blowing the cloud westward.

My throat closed. I couldn't see my brother. "Charlie?"

Chapter Sixteen

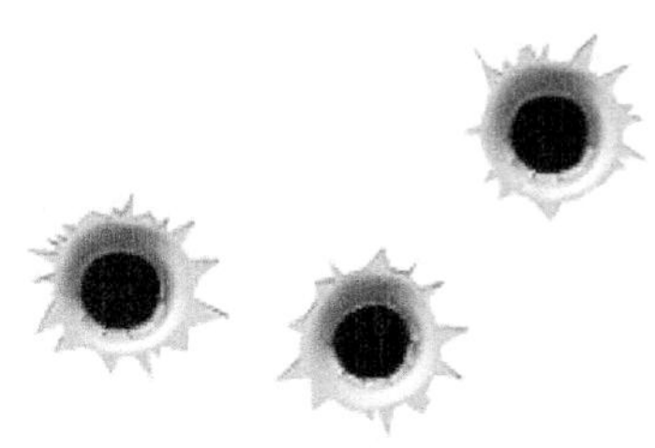

Frantic, I raced down the rock-strewn hillside. Loose gravel slid beneath my shoes. "Charlie!" Dust hung in the air. Why hadn't I been focused on my brother instead of the knight?

Charlie has done a lot of reckless things in his life. If there was a lake, he'd find the highest cliff around to jump into it. And then he'd stay down, the greenish water rippling as if it had swallowed him. But he'd always popped up again, laughing and spitting water. Usually at me. But this time, I'd been the reckless one. My head dizzied.

I scrambled over and around fallen rock, slipping more than once in my haste. "Charlie!" I'd seen him throw himself toward the western side of the hill. If I hadn't chased after the knight, if I hadn't left him… There'd been a tree…

"Here." Charlie coughed. A pale hand shot from the earth.

I gasped a hysterical laugh. He was alive. But how badly was he hurt? I hurdled a small boulder and stumbled to reach him.

Charlie lay on his back. Boulders formed a ring around him, leaving him unscathed, though his face was a mask of dirt. "Wow," he said. "Wow!"

I sagged onto a smooth, flat rock. He was okay. It was enough to make me believe in guardian angels. I wanted to kill him. "Wow?" I snarled. "You could have been killed."

He lifted his head. "I *told* you he was real."

"Are you hurt?"

He sat up. "The black knight. You saw him too."

I'd abandoned him to chase after that damn knight, and he could have been killed. Charlie wasn't the one I was furious with. I braced my elbow on my knee, my head in my hand, and laughed shakily. Standing, I extended a hand to my brother.

He grasped it and hopped to his feet. "Did you see where the black knight went?"

"No," I said, scanning the hill above us. I was pretty sure the knight had been above the avalanche, but what if he'd been caught up in the slide?

We spent the next hour searching, Kristie calling out unhelpful ideas from the base of the hill. We finally gave up when I spotted a knightly footprint leading away from the mini disaster scene.

Gritty with dust and dirt, I followed Charlie down the hillside. "Careful," Kristie shouted.

It was a little late for that. Using freshly strewn boulders as steppingstones, my brother and I crossed the stream, clouded and widened by the avalanche.

"Lemonade?" Kristie held up a pitcher. "You must be thirsty after climbing up and down that hillside."

"Thanks," Charlie said.

We returned to the grouping of Adirondack chairs. Kristie had added glasses and a tray of sugar cookies decorated in Halloween shapes.

Fredo lay coiled beside the firepit and pretended to sleep. Hardened orange frosting flecked the fur around his mouth.

Charlie dropped into my chair and poured himself a glass. I perched on the arched, wooden footstool.

"Did you find anything?" she asked anxiously.

"We found tracks above the slide," I said. "They were leading away. The knight's long gone." A stellar jay fluttered into a nearby pine, then to the ground. It pecked at some birdseed, strewn on the earth.

Kristie smiled benignly at the bird and sat in the chair on the other side of the firepit. The smoldering branches crackled. "I'm glad to hear it. I wouldn't want Clyde to be hurt—assuming he's the knight."

"That knight moved fast," I said. "No offense, but Clyde's not exactly built for speed."

"You'd be surprised what people can do when properly motivated," she said. "And that tunic could be hiding a multitude of sins."

"At least we know you're not the black knight," Charlie joked.

She laughed easily. "Me? The knight? What an idea. That would be far too much work."

I studied the cookies. "Speaking of work," I said. "What do you do when you're not at the theater?"

"I'm a systems engineer for a medical company."

"Right," Charlie said. "A systems engineer." He frowned and leaned over the arm of the Adirondack chair, closer to the firepit. "What's a systems engineer?"

"The company I work for has all sorts of internal systems," she said. "I make sure they run smoothly and update them as needs be."

"You're talking about software systems?" I asked. She nodded. "Did you build them yourself?" I snagged a bat-shaped cookie from the tray and bit off a black wing. It had a sugar cookie/gingerbread flavor, and it wasn't half bad.

She laughed. "Heavens, no. The programs are all off-the-shelf. Anyone can buy the software. I'm just the poor soul who has to read all the manuals and understand how to use them. The best part is, I get to work from home."

"Do you know anything about hacking?" Charlie asked.

She flipped back her hair. "The company has a security team to make sure that doesn't happen. That's the one system I *don't* manage. Why? Are you looking for a hacker?"

"He's asking for a friend," I said, dropping cookie crumbs on my jacket. I brushed them off, but it was already filthy from the rockslide, so it didn't make much difference. "Do you know of anyone in town who might have those skills?"

She shook a plump finger at me. "Tell your friend they could get in big trouble if they try it. Hacking is a serious crime. You might ask Jane though."

"Why?" I asked.

"She has a degree in computer science."

"I thought she had a degree in cooking," Charlie said.

Kristie frowned. "No, poor thing. She wanted to go to the Cordon Bleu, or even the Culinary Institute of America. But their parents thought Gloria had frittered away her college funding studying to be an actress. They didn't want Jane to go down the same path. They insisted on a practical degree. And since they were paying..." She shrugged.

"Bummer," Charlie said.

"She shouldn't feel so insecure about it," Kristie said. "Jane's a wonderful cook, even if she isn't formally trained." She shook her head. "So many thwarted desires."

"What do you mean?" I asked.

"Jed's been a hotel manager in Hot Springs forever, it seems. All he wants is to open his own hotel. But I'm afraid Gloria's career always came first, and that's where the money flowed."

"Do you think he resented that?" I asked.

Her brown eyes widened. "Oh, no. I wouldn't say that at all. He was very supportive of Gloria. *Very* supportive."

My mouth flattened. Like the player in *Hamlet*, Kristie was protesting too much.

I tucked Fredo under my arm. Half a ghost cookie dropped from his jaws, and I frowned. I hadn't seen him take it. Where had he learned to be such a sneak?

We thanked Kristie and left with a supply of Halloween cookies on an orange paper plate. Charlie slid the plate onto the dashboard and buckled himself into my Jeep. "Hey, can you drop me at the post office?"

"Sure." I strapped Fredo into his dog harness. "Are you expecting a package?"

"I sent off to a genealogy company. You know, to find out if there are any coats of arms in my past."

I snorted and got in the car. "Good luck with that."

"This is a serious company. I gave them a DNA sample and everything."

I started the Jeep. "You know the government can access those samples. They've used them to track down criminals."

"But I'm no criminal."

"What if I decide to commit a crime, and they find me through you?" I pulled into the residential street.

He snorted. "You'd never commit a crime."

"Thanks, but I still don't trust those companies."

"That's because it's your job not to trust them. You're paid to be suspicious. Your life depends on being suspicious."

"Yeah." When he put it that way, it didn't sound like a good thing. I like to think of myself as an optimist, not a cynic. But life seemed to be pushing me in the latter direction.

I dropped him at the post office and returned to my apartment above the theater. Cautiously, I unlocked the door and peered inside. Sammie didn't seem to be around, but I wouldn't have put it past him to lie in wait.

I unhooked Fredo from his leash. He trotted around the small room, sniffing. When no ball of black fur came hurtling out to attack, I relaxed and opened my laptop on the table. I booted it up, made sure my laptop's VPN was on, and adjusted the sticky note on the webcam. But instead of typing, I frowned at my e-reader, lying on the couch.

There'd been an e-reader in Gloria's dressing room. I rose and retrieved mine. A tiny camera eye stared from the top of the device.

I strode from my apartment to the dressing room. The door was unlocked, though police tape still crisscrossed the doorframe. I ducked beneath it and walked inside. Her e-reader lay on the dressing table.

I squatted, studying the device but not touching it. It had a webcam on it too, and my insides jumped. Had someone been watching my brother and I as we'd searched her dressing room?

Returning to my apartment, I started a new internet search. Jane had one of those all-photo social media pages, filled with pictures of food. My stomach growled, which seemed impossible after all the cookies I'd eaten.

I searched the internet some more. But aside from her food pics, Jane was an online ghost.

I typed in Kristie's name. She was on the same professional networking website where I had an account. As a paying customer, I got to see all her professional details. I scanned down her resume, and my mouth puckered.

She'd graduated from MIT summa cum laude. And she had a PhD from UC San Diego in software engineering. I scrolled down and clicked on her dissertation.

I whistled. "Are you kidding me?"

She'd written a dissertation on thwarting hackers.

I sat back in my chair. Kristie had acted like she didn't know anything about hacking.

Kristie had lied.

Chapter Seventeen

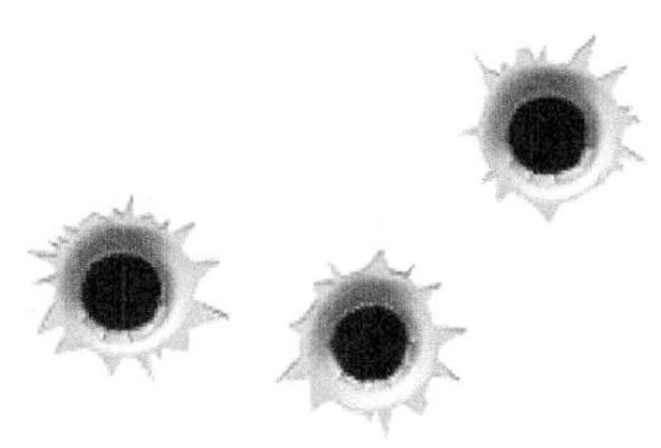

Blinking in the bright Wednesday morning light, I edged outside the old-west theater. The universe—or maybe the town—seemed determined not to let me investigate on my lonesome. If Charlie wasn't dogging my footsteps, Gert or Mrs. Malone were sure to turn up.

I peered around the corner of the wooden building. A tour bus chugged down the street. It screeched to a halt in the bowling alley's parking lot and disgorged a load of elderly tourists outside town hall. They milled on the sidewalk and shivered in the October chill. Cameras emerged from pockets and purses.

But I had bigger fish to fry and another appointment with Kristie. I'd called last night and told her I thought I'd lost my favorite knife in the rockslide behind her house. She'd invited me to return and look. I didn't think Kristie would admit to her lie, but I wanted to see how far she'd take her pretense of ignorance.

I scanned the street again. No sign of Mrs. Malone or my brother. Satisfied I was alone, I started for my Jeep Commander.

"There you are," Gert said.

I hunched my shoulders and grimaced, turning to face our temporary mayor. “Is it theater business?”

The elderly man nodded, his chin dipping into the thick, gray scarf knotted around his neck. “I’ll need your help at the rodeo grounds.” He wore a long gray parka that covered his knees, and he looked ridiculous in it.

“I thought they weren’t going to start setting up for the festival until Friday?”

“It’s a faire with an *e*, not a festival,” he said.

“It’s only a faire with an *e* because you and Mrs. Malone are trying to outclass Hot Springs.” And that was a losing battle.

“It’s a faire with an *e* because of its historical elements,” he said.

“Vampires are historical?” I leaned against my black Jeep.

“And no,” he continued, ignoring me. “Friday’s when we want you to start *working* there. But they’ve already begun the setup, and I want to do a walk-through with you.”

“Why?”

“For security.”

“I’m a counter-surveillance specialist.”

“But you do look for potential risks to your clients,” he said. “At least you *did*.”

“I can’t right now. I’ve got an appointment.”

“With whom?”

“One of our murder suspects, Kristie Naysmith. I think you said murder takes precedence,” I said craftily.

He rubbed his knobby chin. “I suppose I did. Of course it takes precedence.”

“Great. I’ll meet you at the rodeo after I’m done.”

“I have a better idea. I’ll come with you.”

Oh, come on. “You can’t—”

“Hey, Gert. What’s up?” Charlie, in a faded yellow t-shirt and board shorts, strode through the parking lot toward us. He was actually wearing flip-flops in this weather. I don’t know how he stood it.

I straightened off the car and exhaled slowly. It didn’t take a psychic to figure out what was going to happen next.

"Alice and I are going to interview a suspect," Gert said.

"Cool," my brother said. "I'll come too."

I groaned. I was being punished. Nowhere was conspiring against me. Like all strange and unsettling places, Nowhere had its own minor deities or spirits of the place. And they seemed to get a kick out of watching me flail.

"What was that?" Gert asked.

"Nothing," I mumbled.

"And afterward we're going to the rodeo grounds," Gert said.

"Even better," Charlie said. "I want to see where they're setting up our stage."

A flurry of high-pitched barking emerged from the theater, and something crashed.

Stupid Nowhere gods. I hung my head. "Let me get my dog."

"How many sheriff's deputies are going to be at the fair?" I started my Jeep. Fredo wriggled in his harness between the temporary mayor and me.

"One." Gert clipped in his seatbelt. "And don't forget the *e*."

"The *e* is silent. You can't possibly hear it. How did you—?" I paused, hands on the wheel. "Only one deputy? How many people do you expect?"

"Ten thousand a day," he said. "That's what we did last year."

"And there's only *one* deputy?" That was just… reckless if the faire-with-an-e was as big as they'd projected.

"I'll bet Hot Springs has got dozens of deputies," Charlie said from the back seat. Fredo yipped.

"Nowhere has never been a priority," Gert said bitterly.

"But it's a hazard," I said. "We get more deputies for our summer rodeo. Why not the faire?"

"That's because the deputies want to *watch* the rodeo," Gert said. "And your car smells like dog."

"I know," my brother said. "I told her she needs an air freshener."

"No," Gert said, "this car needs a deep cleaning. I know a guy..."

Tuning them out, I shook my head and pulled from the theater's parking lot. I turned onto Main Street.

We might not be as cool as Hot Springs, but Town Hall *did* look picturesque. Pumpkins lined the hay bales near its low, brick steps. Sheaves of corn stood sentry outside its double doors. And then there was the giant lawn flamingo with its monstrous eyepatch.

"Tell me more about this black knight," Gert said. "When did he start showing up?"

"Forget the black knight," I said. "He can't possibly be connected to the murder." But why had he been lurking around Kristie's? I understood why he'd run. No one in their right mind would want to be caught in that getup. But why be there at all?

My brother rolled down his window, and an arctic gale blew through the car, flapping his t-shirt. He rolled it back up. "Like Kristie said, the knight started appearing around the time we banned Clyde from the theater."

"You can't ban citizens from the theater," Gert said.

"He was ruining it for the other guests," Charlie said. "He kept interrupting our jokes and saying our lines before we could get them out."

"I thought you were improv." I turned left and drove past an abandoned brick building.

"We are," my brother said, "but lines get recycled. We *are* doing the show five nights a week."

"This was when, exactly?" I asked, curious despite myself. I glanced in the rearview mirror.

"About a month ago." Charlie twisted in the back seat and rested his crossed, bare legs on the opposite window ledge.

"And then the knight showed up." I aimed the Jeep toward Kristie's neighborhood.

"Yeah." Charlie yawned. "He didn't say anything, so at first it didn't bother us. Guests are encouraged to come in costume. But then it started to get creepy, especially because he never talked. But it's a generic costume, so we weren't sure if it was the same person or a different one."

"And so you banned the knight," Gert guessed.

"He *can't* be connected to the murders," I muttered. Black knights only killed people in fantasy novels.

"Gloria banned him," Charlie said. "She was getting really wigged out about the guy."

"Gloria in particular?" I asked sharply.

"Well, yeah." My brother laced his hands behind his head and rested it against the window. "But in fairness, he was creeping out everyone. Well. Okay. We were all creeping each other out talking about knight sightings."

"Did you ever see Gloria and the knight together?" I asked.

"Oh, yeah." Charlie waggled his tennis shoes, leaving a streak on the inside of the window. "She lost it one night during the cocktail party and threw her champagne at him. The glass broke on his helmet." He laughed. "You should have seen the mess. Of course, I had to clean it up. Anyway, that's when she banned him."

I turned into a residential section of homes. Moderately wealthier, the houses were spaced widely between pines and desiccated scrub oaks.

"But he kept coming around?" Gert asked.

"Not *in* the theater," he said. "But we spotted him a few times lurking outside."

"It's just childish." I grumped. But I'd seen the knight with my own eyes. He wasn't a phantom. And he'd been surveilling us. I didn't think he'd set off the landslide intentionally, but it was weird. *Black knight. Bah.*

"And then he showed up at Kristie's house yesterday and started the landslide," Charlie concluded.

"Landslide?" Gert yelped. "There's been a landslide?"

"Just a small one," he said. "No one was hurt."

"You need to tell me these things." Gert twisted in his seat to glare. "I'm the mayor. This may involve county works. Why didn't Kristie call town hall?"

"I don't know," I said.

"Well, she should have," the old man complained.

I pulled into Kristie's gravel driveway. "She can tell you all about it now."

A wisp of smoke coiled from the chimney of the stone cottage. The half-circle windows in the eaves and above the door were dark.

Gert clambered from the Jeep. "Black knights, bah."

I tensed. Hearing my own thoughts echoed by an elderly failed hitman was just... Well, it wasn't good.

"Sounds like a coward to me," he continued, "hiding beneath his helmet. In my day, we looked you in the eye before we punched you in the face."

"Those were the days," I agreed and turned to retrieve Fredo.

"Uh..." Charlie hopped from the car. "No one got punched."

"And he might have nothing to do with the murder." I looped Fredo's leash around my wrist. "We can't jump to conclusions. He's a suspect, but that's it."

"He was surveilling us in Kristie's yard," Charlie said. "The black knight's a—you know—a thing."

We climbed the wooden steps to the front porch. Fredo studied the pumpkins through narrowed eyes.

Gert nudged a pumpkin with his toe. "That's a quality gourd."

I rang the bell. It cackled inside the small house.

"So what's the play?" Gert asked. "You want me to be the bad cop?"

"Since none of us are cops," I whispered, glancing at the closed, arched door, "no."

"I meant metaphorically," he said.

"I know, but I don't think it will work. Just let me ask the questions."

"Why are you whispering?" Gert bellowed. "How am I supposed to hear anything if you whisper?"

I massaged my temple. What was the point? Why was I even trying? I should have staked out Kristie last night. I was good at stakeouts. But no, I had to play detective. Doing a few jobs for Fitch didn't make me a PI. It made me a contractor, with all the extra taxes and insurance costs.

Charlie cupped his hands and pressed his face to a paned window. "I don't see her. Does she know we're coming?"

"I called her last night," I said.

"You gave her a warning?" Gert scowled. "She's probably on the lam. Nice going."

"She's not on the lam," I said. "Why would she be on the lam?"

Gert sniffed. "You tell me, genius."

"She's not on the lam," I said. "There's smoke coming from her chimney. If she'd left last night, and she'd been reckless enough to leave a fire burning, the fire would be out by now."

"Well, who lights a fire in the morning?" Gert asked.

Charlie scratched the back of his head. "Someone who wanted to stay warm?"

"She's got heaters for that, doesn't she?" Gert asked.

"She's very earth mothery," I said and pushed the cackling bell again. "Maybe she just liked the look of a fire."

We waited some more. Fredo lunged for a pumpkin, and I hauled him back.

"This is a waste of time." Gert huffed and creakily descended the steps. "She's probably in her yard and can't hear us."

The whole street could hear us. He shuffled around the corner of the stone house. Charlie and I shared a look and followed.

"Are you sure Kristie was expecting you?" my brother asked in a low voice.

"I told her I lost my favorite knife in the landslide and wanted to look for it."

"You lost the knife I gave you?"

"No," I said. "I didn't lose any knife. It was just an excuse."

"Maybe she thought you'd just look for it on your own. I mean, you don't really need her around to help you."

We rounded the corner of the house and emerged in Kristie's back yard. The Adirondack chairs sat in their same grouping beside the unlit firepit.

Gert stood beside the creek, which had widened since we'd last seen it and made a pond of a flowerbed. Gloomily, he shook his head at the rocks. "We'll have to call county works."

"Uh, Al?" Charlie tugged on the sleeve of my jacket.

"What?"

"Kristie's door is open."

I turned to look. The paned glass door that opened onto her deck stood wide open. An acrid scent wafted from inside.

"Watch Gert." I handed Charlie Fredo's leash.

I climbed the deck's steps and stuck my head through the open door. "Hello? Kristie?"

She didn't respond.

"Kristie?" I called more loudly and stepped inside the kitchen. A floorboard creaked beneath my shoe.

The acrid smell grew stronger, and my eyes watered. I followed the smell into a living room. Drying herbs dangled from the varnished ceiling beams. A fire crackled in the fireplace. Kristie lay prone before it on a sheep-skin rug, blood staining its white wool, a short sword in her chest.

Chapter Eighteen

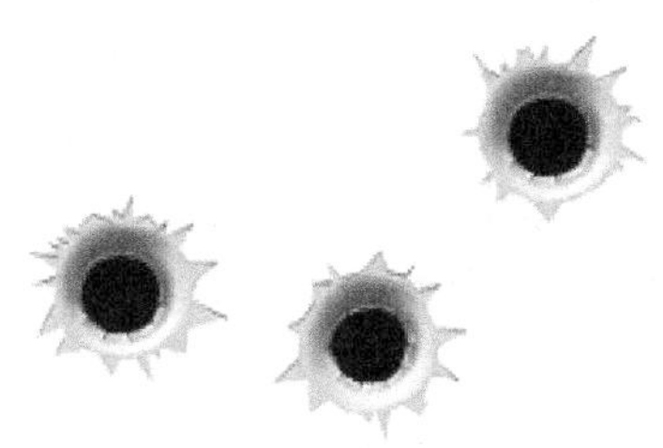

I stood, unmoving, the scene and the strangeness settling around me until it clutched at my throat, smothering. Kristie was dead. I stood, and it felt like months passed.

And then I moved.

There was no way Kristie *couldn't* be dead with that sword in her chest. But I pressed my fingers to her throat anyway, searching for a pulse. There was none.

Sickened, I backed away, careful not to step in the blood soaking the rug. I pulled out my phone and managed to call nine-one-one on the second try. My hands had been shaking too badly on the first.

That duty done, I took pictures with my phone. I tried not to think of yesterday, when the three of us had been companionably sipping tea.

Photography was a mindless habit when you've spent time in countersurveillance. Everything got photographed. Taking pictures also created a sense of distance. For a short time, I could fool myself into thinking what was behind the lens was separate, unreal.

I finished at the fireplace. A computer hard drive smoldered inside it—the source of the sickening, acrid smell.

"Hey, that landslide was worse than we thought." Charlie ambled into the room with Fredo. "Gert's called—" He stopped short, swaying slightly. "Is that...? Is that Kristie?"

I couldn't blame my brother for denying the obvious. I'd been intentionally doing it myself. "I've called the police," I said. "We should get out of here so we don't accidentally tamper with any evidence."

"That's—that's Kristie." He took a wobbly step toward her.

I rested my hand on his shoulder. "I'm sorry. She's dead. And we should step outside and wait."

Fredo trotted toward the body, his whiskers twitching. I scooped him up before he did anything I'd regret.

"Yeah. Yeah. Right." Charlie turned and stumbled into Gert.

"What's that stink?" the old man asked.

"I think it's murder," Charlie said, face green.

"What? What's happened?" Gert stepped sideways and past Charlie. His eyes widened behind his thick glasses. "Oh, crud. Another? Whose sword is that?"

"Uh, I think it's mine." Charlie winced.

His sword? This could *not* be happening again. "Are you sure?"

Last summer, a man had been stabbed with an antique-looking knife. Suspicion had fallen on my brother for a lot of reasons. One reason was the knife had looked like something he'd use in his medieval re-enactment society. If this was his...

The whole town knew the story about Charlie and the knife. And the whole town knew he'd been a prime suspect. Anyone could have used it with the aim of implicating my brother.

"Pretty sure it's my short sword," Charlie said, his voice taut. "I keep it with the props at the theater."

"Aren't the prop weapons supposed to be dull?" I asked.

"The sides are dull," he said, "but the tips are pretty sharp."

I turned to study Kristie's body. Rivulets of blood stained her right temple. She'd likely been struck with something in the head before the stabbing. That might have made it easier to use the blade. Nausea choked my throat at the thought.

"We need to get out of this house," I said. "We're probably leaving DNA evidence all over the place."

Grumbling, the men followed me into the back yard. Gert sat in an Adirondack chair and pulled out a cell phone.

"Who are you calling?" I asked.

"Mrs. Malone. This is theater business."

"Maybe we should keep this quiet until the sheriff arrives," I said. Fredo barked once. I'd like to have taken it for agreement, but Fredo wasn't an agreeable kind of dog.

Gert glared. "You want to leave Mrs. Malone out of the loop?"

Charlie nudged me. "That's, uh, probably not such a good idea."

I sighed. Why bother? The news would be all over town soon enough. Besides, Gert was already calling. He jiggled his foot with impatience.

"Who's back here?" Detective Aiden Guthrie strode around the corner of the house. His arms went limp at the sides of his sleek suit. He'd downgraded this morning to a Saint Laurent. It looked good on him. "You again. Did you call this in?" he asked accusingly.

"Yes." I pointed toward the paned back door. He'd gotten here fast. Too fast if he'd come from Hot Springs, which meant he must have been in the area. It worried me a little that he'd been spending quality time in Nowhere. "She's in there."

"Mr. Mayor." He nodded to Gert and jogged up the steps and strode inside.

Gert smoothed the front of his long parka and shrugged. "He looks a little wet behind the ears."

"Not to me," I said, grim.

The detective returned outside and pulled out a black Moleskin journal and a Mont Blanc pen. "Okay. Who found the body?"

"I found the body," I said.

"Sure you did. Why'd you go inside the house?"

I glanced at Gert and Charlie. Weren't we supposed to be separated so he could ask these questions privately? "I had an appointment with Kristie. The back door was open, and she didn't respond to my calls. There was a strange smell inside. I was concerned and went in."

"Just you?" He scribbled in the notebook.

"I came to check out the landslide." Gert nodded toward the flooded flowerbed.

The detective's dark brows slashed downward. "There was a landslide? When did that happen?"

"Yesterday," Charlie said. "See, there was this black knight, and we chased him up the hill. Then somehow—I think it was an accident—he triggered a landslide."

"A black knight." Detective Guthrie slid his notebook into the inside pocket of his suit jacket. It didn't make a single crease in the fabric.

"Oh," Charlie said, "it's not as weird as it sounds. He's been stalking the theater for weeks now. He's probably the one who killed Kristie."

"No," Guthrie said. "That's not weird at all."

"Kristie said the knight's costume came from a shop in Reno," I said before things could go too far off the rails.

"Right," Charlie said. "I just can't figure out how he got my short sword."

"*Your* sword?" The detective lifted his brows.

Shut up, Charlie. I glared at my brother.

"I think the murder weapon's mine," Charlie said. "At least, it looks like mine. I mean, not *mine*, mine, but it's from the theater. It's one of the props." A siren wailed in the distance.

"Anyone could have taken it," I said. "The prop closet isn't locked. And the actors bring backpacks and duffel bags in and out of the theater all the time. That sword is only about, what? Fourteen inches long?"

"Fourteen and a half," Charlie said.

"It wouldn't have been hard to smuggle it out," I said. "Heck, Kristie might have taken it herself for some reason."

"But why would she?" Detective Guthrie asked.

Since I didn't know the answer to that, I said, "It looked to me like someone hit Kristie in the head and then stabbed her. It would be interesting to know what she was hit with."

The detective gave me a long look. "I want each of you to go to a different corner of the yard and wait. Someone will be by soon to take your statements." He strode up the stone steps and inside the house.

"He seems okay," Charlie said.

"He seems like trouble," Gert said.

We edged a little away from each other. I hugged myself to keep my teeth from chattering. In the shade of the hill and the pines, it had to be at least ten degrees colder. Two paramedics entered the house. After a few minutes, they returned outside.

"You can't trust cops," Gert said out of the side of his mouth. "A dumb cop is the only kind I want to have around. Then we can control the situation. And this guy doesn't look that dumb. Trouble."

A well-built, sandy-haired paramedic glanced toward us. He shook his head.

"There's nothing left to control," I said bleakly. "Kristie's dead. This is already out of control."

Sheriff's deputies arrived. The coroner. The two fire engines seemed like overkill, but when you call nine-one-one, you get everyone and his brother.

The sheriff, however, did not appear. Deputies took more detailed statements from Gert and Charlie. I got Detective Guthrie and recited to him the chain of events.

He returned the cap to his pen and slid it into his breast pocket. "We're done here. You can go now."

"Is the sheriff on his way?" I asked.

The detective's mouth firmed. He shook his head. "He's busy in The Town of Hot Springs. They've got a planning meeting going on."

A spark of heat flared in my gut. "This is a murder. And it's probably connected to the murder of Gloria Jackson."

"I'm sure he'll give it his full attention when he's finished in The Town of Hot Springs."

My face tightened. "You can just say Hot Springs, you know."

His shoulders jerked, as if he'd smothered a laugh. "You're one of those."

"One of whats?"

"A Nowhere snob."

"What?" I wasn't a snob. Nowhere had absolutely nothing to be snobbish about.

"What about the Black Knight?" Charlie trotted up to us, Gert trailing behind. I rubbed my forehead. *Shut* up *about the stupid knight*. It made us look insane.

"Did you ever see the Black Knight with a sword?" the detective asked.

Charlie's brow furrowed. He cocked his head and squinted. "Uh..."

"Young man," Gert said to the detective, "is this your first murder investigation?"

"No." He slid his notebook into the same pocket his pen had vanished into. "And you three can go now."

We left, Gert muttering under his breath as we rounded the corner of the house. "There's nothing worse than a half-way competent cop."

"What makes you think he's only half-way?" I asked.

"You can't trust cops," he barked.

I shook my head. Gert still had scars from his time in the USSR, where cops had been the enemy. Actually, they were still the enemy in most parts of the world.

Gert checked his watch. "We're late. Drive to the rodeo grounds."

"Now? After all this?" I asked.

"The faire isn't going to be canceled because of this murder," Gert said.

"Can I still come?" Charlie toed the ground. "It's just... Kristie and I weren't close or anything, but... We knew her," he burst out. "We worked with her. I feel literally sick." He pressed his hands to his stomach. "And if anything happened to you—"

"You can come," I said, my chest tightening. This sword business... If someone had framed my brother, I wanted to stick close.

"Fine," Gert grumped. "But I'm not paying your brother."

"You're not paying me," I pointed out.

Gert folded his arms. "Well, I'm not paying him either."

We drove to the rodeo grounds. Gert led us to the entry, a wooden arch at the edge of a dirt parking lot.

He pulled out his map and handed it to me. "They've chalked the walking paths," he said, pointing. "I want you two to walk them and let me know if you see any pinch points that could cause people to back up. We don't want a stampede."

"What are you going to do?" I asked.

He lifted his chin. "I have faire business to attend to," Gert said, and I swear I could hear the *e* on the end of *faire*. Gert strode across the parking lot.

Charlie took the map from my hands. He turned it one way, then the other, frowning. "This is confusing."

"Let's just walk the chalked paths."

Whoever had designed the paths had done a decent job. They wove back on each other in ways that would make the fairgrounds seem larger than they were. And they'd been widened at points where people might potentially be slowed down. Simple vendor shacks lined the trails between the occasional pine.

"What do you think?" Charlie asked after an hour of tramping around the labyrinth of dusty trails.

"As long as they don't let too many people in and have the exits well marked, it should work."

I called Gert and gave him my report. He told me he'd find his own ride home, and Charlie and I drove back into Nowhere. We ate a late lunch at the pizza parlor. I had a Caesar salad with chicken, but I didn't taste it.

Some of my shock at Kristie's death had dissipated as we'd walked through the fair grounds. But enough lingered to kill my appetite.

The manager, Vittoria, stopped by our table when we'd nearly finished. "How was your meal?" she asked with a perfunctory air.

Charlie looked down at his untouched metal plate. "Great. Great. Maybe I'll take mine to go. I mean, it's hard to enjoy. Not because anything's wrong with the pizza or anything. Because of the other murder."

Vittoria's eyes widened. "The *other* murder? Who? What happened?"

"Kristie," Charlie said quietly.

She took a step backward and covered her mouth with her hand. "Someone else from the theater? I need to tell Clyde." She hurried away. Annoyed, I shot my brother a look.

"We're going to have to tell everyone anyway," Charlie said glumly. "We're down *two* actors now. Not that that's the most important thing here. But everyone's going to have to know."

"It's true, no one told us to keep our mouths shut." But someone should have. I drummed my fingers on the table. "And I guess they'll hear soon enough."

"Jane should be at the theater by now," Charlie said. "She starts food prep early. I think she has to, since she's also theater manager."

We paid and walked back to the theater. As Charlie had predicted, Jane was there. But she wasn't in the kitchen. She sat at a table in the dining area. A slender redhead in clingy, earth-toned clothing strode up and down the stage.

"No," said the woman from the stage. "I'm not *feeling* it here."

"We only start the play up there to get everyone's attention," Jane said wearily. She propped her head on her fist, knocking her glasses cockeyed. "Then we move into the crowd. It's interactive theater."

"I'll need a different costume," the woman said. "The one you gave me is a wreck."

Jane stiffened. Swallowed. Rose. "You can choose which one you want." She turned toward us and blinked. "Oh. Charlie. Alice. This is Autumn Winter, from Hot Springs."

"The Town of Hot Springs," Autumn corrected from the stage.

Jane's smile thinned. "Yes, The *Town* of Hot Springs. She's got improv experience and has agreed to step in for Gloria."

Charlie's eyes widened, and he approached the stage. "Autumn Winter? I saw you in Reno at that... that... casino. You were terrific."

"Thank you." Autumn bowed her head modestly, her silky hair swinging forward. "Jane, where's my dressing room?"

"Ah." Jane shuffled her feet. "I'm afraid we haven't been cleared by the police to use Gloria's—the dressing room yet."

Autumn rolled her eyes. "I'm sure there's some place I can use." She swept off the stage.

"Wow," Charlie said. "How'd you get her?"

"I got lucky," Jane said.

"Uh, maybe not so much," Charlie said. "We have some really bad news."

She gripped her hands together. "You're not quitting, are you?" she asked in a pleading tone.

"No, no, no," my brother said. "Nothing like that." He winced. "Well, something like that."

She wrung her hands. "You *are* quitting, aren't you? Gloria was the core of the players. Of course you're—"

"Kristie Naysmith is dead," I interrupted.

Jane swayed. She pressed her hand to the wooden tabletop. "What? How?"

"It's unclear," I said.

Charlie shook his head. "It wasn't that un—"

I stepped on his foot, and he winced. "But it looks like murder," I said. Charlie rubbed the top of his foot with the sole of his other shoe.

"But this's..." Jane clawed a hand through her mousy hair. "We have a show tonight!" She shook herself. "Sorry. This is terrible. Poor Kristie."

"Does she have any family?" I asked.

"Two grown kids," Jane said. "She's an empty nester."

"And where are they?" I asked.

"New York, I think." She shook her head. "What an awful thing for them." She paced the rough wooden floor. "This is a disaster. We have a sold-out show tonight. We can't cancel."

"Do we need five players?" Charlie asked.

"We won't have the proper number of suspects without them," she said. "Where are we going to get a fifth player on such short notice?"

Charlie and Jane looked at each other. They looked at me.

I crossed my arms and uncrossed them. Shifted my weight. "Why are you looking at me like that?"

"It's easy," Charlie said. "All you have to do is memorize a few set responses. And if you don't get them word for word, that's even better. It feels more natural."

"Responses for what?" I asked.

Jane eyed me. "I think I've got something that will fit."

Oh, no. No, *no, no.* "I can't act. Charlie, you *know* I can't act." I backed away and bumped into a round table.

"Are you talking about Clyde's script?" he asked. "Because that was terrible. No one could read that well. Besides, you can be the first to die."

"No," I said.

"No, what?" Mrs. Malone asked from behind me, and I started.

"Have you heard about Kristie?" Jane asked the older woman.

"Yes." Mrs. Malone, bundled in a thick, blood-orange colored coat, leaned on her cane. She shot me a seraphic smile. "And I see you've already found a substitute."

Chapter Nineteen

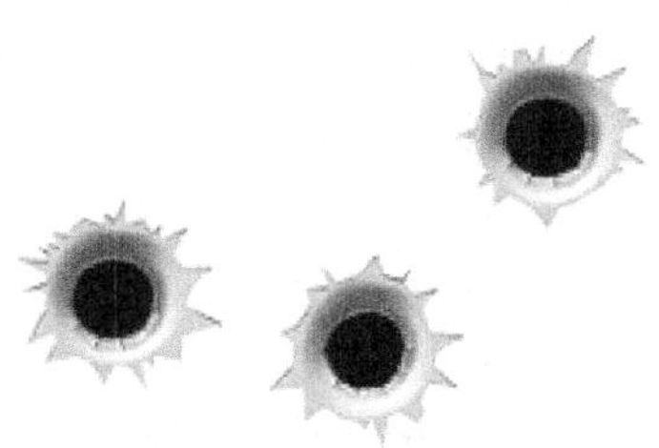

"Darling Dan may be rolling in cabbage," I muttered, climbing the stairs to my apartment. "But I ain't goin' to the big house. I saw him with Fran with my own two eyes."

All this nineteen-twenties slang was going to be my downfall. It was hard enough remembering the clues I needed to reveal at tonight's show without throwing a bunch of tomatoes and cake eaters on top.

It didn't help that that homicide detective had searched the prop room this afternoon, either. I don't know if I was more unsettled that only he had come, or that I'd clearly developed a thing for expensive men's suits.

My hip bumped the banister. "Darling Dan... rolling in cabbage. Darling Dan... rolling in cabbage." Achieving the landing, I made my way to my apartment, and reached the doorknob. I halted, my hand outstretched.

The black cat sat beside the door. He looked up at me and meowed, a pained expression on his whiskered face.

"Couldn't get in on your own? Ha." I opened the door.

A woman shrieked. "Get out!"

I pushed the door wider. Sammie slunk inside.

Autumn threw a sparkling red shoe at the cat. He leapt aside, evading it easily, and hopped onto the bed to join Fredo, curled into a furry gray ball.

"Why'd you let that cat in here? I'm allergic." The actress tugged up the straps of her flapper dress, the color of black ice.

"What are you doing in here?" I asked.

"This is my changing room," she said without looking my way. "And I wouldn't mind some privacy."

"Is not. This is my apartment. I live here."

She snorted. "Nice try. What are you? The phantom of the opera? Who lives in a theater?"

"I do. That's my dog." I pointed at the fur ball on the bed.

She blinked. "That's a dog? I thought it was a throw pillow."

"It's—he's got ears!"

The actress tossed her hair. Closer, I could see the red was flecked with gold. It made her even more revoltingly beautiful. "You'll have to wait until after the show," she said. "I'm busy in here. Now go on, go away, and take the cat. I'm ah—ah—allergic." She sneezed.

"I'm not—This is my apartment," I sputtered. "How did you even get inside?"

"The door was unlocked. Zip me up, will you?" She turned her back on me.

My fists curled into a quick, evil-crone clench. But the sooner Autumn was done, the sooner she'd be out of here. I zipped up the beaded dress and frowned. "Isn't this Lilyanna's dress?"

"Who?"

"Lilyanna Gomez. She plays the ingenue." And I was feeling oddly defensive of her, though I hadn't seen her around much lately. Though it was hard to actually *see* Lilyanna under her rabbit and beekeeper costumes.

"This dress suits me better than the rag that theater manager gave me." The actress strode into the bathroom. "Where's the makeup table?"

"In the dressing room across the hall," I said.

"Can't you bring it in here?" she called. "Oh! It's so cold in here. Do something about that draft, will you?"

My hands twitched. "It's not a draft. It's the ghost."

She popped her head from the bathroom and gasped. "Ghost?"

"You know, like in *Macbeth*? Or was it *Hamlet*?"

Her mouth made an O. "Don't say that name," she shrieked.

"Hamlet?"

"No, the Scottish play."

"*Macbeth*?"

Autumn scowled. "Stop saying that! Every actor knows its bad luck. Where's the salt?" She strode from the bathroom to the hotplate in my tiny, open kitchen.

"Hey!" I moved toward her.

A colorful saltshaker whizzed over her shoulder and past my head, thunked to the wall and dropped onto the bed. Sammie yowled. Fredo's eyes bugged open. He gave a startled bark.

I picked up the ceramic saltshaker, which miraculously, hadn't shattered. Autumn turned and dusted off her hands.

"What the hell," I snarled. "I got that in Casablanca." It had cost me less than a dollar, but still. I treasured the memories of guarding a client there at Rick's Café. It was nothing like the club in the movie, but still, Rick's. Casablanca.

"You throw salt over the left shoulder to ward off bad luck," she said.

"You're not supposed to throw the whole shaker."

She looked significantly at the animals on the bed. "You haven't gotten rid of them yet?"

Heat raced from my chest to the top of my head. I drew in a calming breath. It didn't help. I sucked in another breath to tell her off.

Garment bag over one arm, Jane stepped into my apartment. "Oh, there you are, Autumn. Good news. The sheriff's department said we can start using the real dressing room again."

"Finally." Autumn huffed and strode past us into the hallway.

"Finally," I said. The cat dropped from the bed and sauntered after the actress.

Jane smiled weakly. "I see you two are getting to know each other."

I folded my arms. "Did you let her in here?"

She adjusted her glasses. "No, I thought you did."

"Aiiieee!" Autumn shouted. "Get out!" A door slammed, and the windows in my apartment rattled.

Sammie came to sit in the middle of my apartment's open doorway. Casually, he licked a paw.

"Strange how cats like people who don't like them," Jane said. "How are you coming with those lines?"

"Dan may be rolling in darlings, but I saw him in the big house with Fran."

Her smile thinned. "I'll send Charlie up in a few minutes to practice with you." She handed me the garment bag. "I think this will fit." Jane bustled to the door. "We'll kill you in the first act," she muttered and shut the door behind her.

I unzipped the garment bag. Inside was a drop-waisted blue dress with a white collar. It was the flapper version of Alice's of *Wonderland* fame, and I groaned. "You can't be serious," I said to no one.

I strode to the door and checked the lock. It hadn't been broken, and I was sure I'd left it locked. I always did. How *had* Autumn gotten inside?

Striding to the closet, I opened my gear bag and took out my bug detector. I swept the apartment. But I couldn't find any surveillance devices or anything out of place. It was almost... spooky.

I grabbed a glass of champagne from a passing waitress's tray and gulped it down. Above, the lights in the theater's wagon-wheel chandeliers glowed softly. Guests laughed and chattered around the tables excitedly in nineteen-twenties costumes.

"What exactly did you see?" A short man in a fedora squinted at me. He held his pen over his notepad.

"They were in the cabbage," I said desperately.

"Cabbage? They were in the garden?"

"Uh, yeah. Yeah, the garden."

"Doing what?"

Sweat trickled down my forehead and stung one eye. "He had his arm around her. I got embarrassed and left."

"And what time was this?" he asked.

"It was last week, around three, when the missus was at her bridge club."

He tapped his pen on the pad and nodded. "Excellent. Thank you." He strode into the crowd of costumed diners.

I sagged and scanned the crowd for another drink. Waitresses in sequins whizzed through the circular tables carrying glasses on silver trays. One headed my way, and I smiled in anticipation.

Visualizing, moving, pretending none of it mattered—none of these tips were getting me through this show. And I know alcohol is a weak, evil crutch. But I was desperate.

"Here she is," Charlie, aka Dashing Dan boomed behind me.

In a white suit and eyepatch, my brother escorted two costumed guests toward me. He slung his arms over the couple's shoulders. "Morganna! Tell these two where I was this afternoon."

"Yeep." I turned and hustled into the crowd. Jiminy cricket, how was I supposed to know? And why was I thinking in old-timey swear words when I couldn't even remember my lines?

The theater plunged into darkness. I smacked into an empty chair and froze.

"What's happened?" a woman asked at my elbow.

The mutterings grew. Most were excited, expectant. Because the obvious thing to happen next would be for the lights to come on, revealing a fresh corpse. It was exactly what I dreaded, because that wasn't in the script. Or it wouldn't have been if we had scripts.

I really hated improv.

"It's all right," Jane shouted. "It's just a blown fuse."

"Is this part of the show?" a male voice asked.

"Charlie?" I said in a low voice, my stomach butterflying.

"Here," he said from a few feet away, and I relaxed. "Just give it a minute or two."

The lights came on to a mixture of cheers and sighs of disappointment. I looked around. No body lay unartfully on the stage. No shrieks of horror met my ears.

I hurried from the dining area and checked the kitchen. It wasn't as gleaming as it had been before the show. Every surface was covered in dessert plates. A plate crashed, and I scampered away.

Jogging upstairs, I checked inside the dressing room. No dead bodies there either. I rattled the knob on my door. Still locked. I checked my hotplate. It was on.

Autumn Winter. She'd used my hotplate. Stealing my apartment to change in was one thing, but leaving a girl's hotplate on was a whole other level of wrong. I unplugged it and returned downstairs.

Just in case, I prowled around backstage and even checked the parking lot. But I didn't find anything suspicious. Sometimes a blown fuse is just a blown fuse.

"Costumes Caramel, how can I help you?" a woman trilled.

I sat cross-legged on my lumpy bed and doodled in a notepad. "I'm calling about a black knight costume." Fredo snored in a patch of morning sunshine on the quilt.

"The black knight is of our most popular," she said.

My stomach gave a little jump. "You've got them? Do you keep records of who you sell your costumes to?" A bus horn honked outside, and Fredo's gray ear flicked. From his spot beneath the card table, Sammie looked up.

"Why do you ask?" she asked cautiously.

"Someone's been using a black knight costume to harass members of a local theater—"

"Oh my God, this isn't about the theater murders, is it? In Nowhere?"

I winced. "Yes." The murders had been outré enough to attract the attention of the local media. My name hadn't cropped up so far, but I'd developed an allergy to being a news story, local or otherwise.

"I don't know if we can," she breathed. "That information may be private."

"It's really important."

"So is our customer's privacy."

For a costume shop? I pressed the end of the phone into my forehead. This was the last costume shop on my list, and they sold the black knight costumes. I *needed* this info. "I'm working for a private investigator—"

"Ooh! You're *working* the theater murders case?"

"Ye-es?" My voice cracked. How much trouble would impersonating a PI get me into? More importantly, would it blow back on Fitch? Fredo yawned and rolled onto his back, exposing his pink belly.

"Then if it was a credit card purchase," she said, "we have a record. But there's not much info. Just the name and zip code."

"That would be enough. I'm looking for someone from Nowhere, Nevada who may have purchased one of your black knight costumes."

"During what time period?"

"Ah, I'm not sure," I admitted.

"I don't know. I mean, that could be a big search. I'd have to ask my manager."

"Is your manager available?" I asked.

"No," she said, drawing out the word. "But I'll give her the message."

"Do you know when she'll be back?"

"She's out sick."

In other words, no, she didn't know, or just didn't want to say. "Okay. Thanks. I'd appreciate any help you could give me."

We exchanged contact info. I hung up and drummed my pen on the pillow. It didn't have the same snap as on the table.

Maybe the costume company would come through. Maybe they wouldn't. I grimaced. But I'd sort of pretended to be a PI, and if that got out...

It was time to give Fitch that bad news.

Chapter Twenty

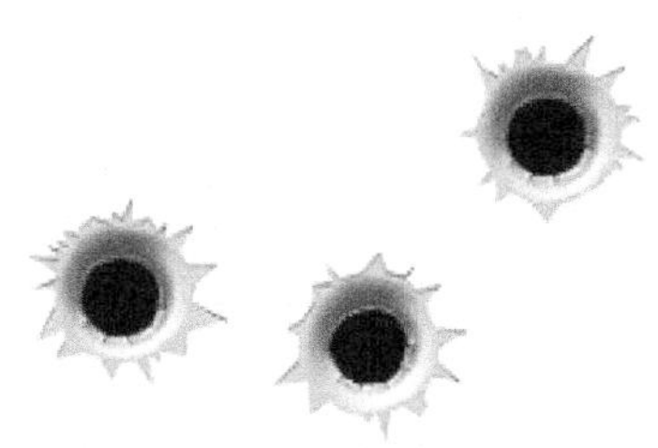

I could have called Fitch from my apartment. But then I wouldn't have been able to delay the inevitable. So I walked down to the park and found a sunny bench. Children ran shrieking through the cobwebbed mushrooms, overseen by giant spiders.

"What *exactly* did you tell her?" Fitch asked.

I hunched on the bench, cell phone to my ear. "I told her I was working for a private investigator." My gaze flicked to the Japanese tea garden fence. That part of the park was still closed—something about a koi problem.

The PI sighed. Even though we were talking on the phone, my skin reacted as if his breath had tickled my ear. I grimaced. Sure he was built like a Greek statue—one of those muscular ones from the Hellenistic period. But I was a professional.

"You didn't use my name?"

"No."

"But you still brought me into this," he said. "Because we do work together."

"I know," I snapped.

"But at least you didn't lie, and you didn't represent yourself as a PI."

"Well, I wouldn't." The knot between my shoulder blades loosened. Maybe this wasn't so bad.

"All right," he said. "What's in it for me?"

"In it? For you?" The day was bright but cold, and I hoisted the zipper on my jacket.

"You dragged me into your little illicit investigation. If the cops find out, they're going to be asking me about it. So. What's in it for me?"

"Free tickets to the Halloween Fair?" I asked brightly.

"Try harder."

I winced. "A behind-the-scenes tour of the theater? I can get you a backstage pass," I wheedled.

"I'll take it, plus the tickets to the fair, *and* an update on our case."

"*Our* case?" Now Fitch was chiseling in on the investigation too? Not that I was protective about it or anything, but there were a lot of "investigators" involved now. Though he'd be the only one with any real experience. Plus that actual detective from Hot Springs. I shivered.

"You said you worked for me on your theater murder case. If the cops ask me about it, I need to make it real."

I exhaled heavily. "Fine." Since I didn't actually know what I was doing, a debrief wouldn't hurt. It might actually get my own thoughts in order. "So far, it's featured more murders than I would have liked."

"Beginner's luck," he grumbled.

"You call this luck?" I asked, incredulous. A shadow fell across me. I looked up.

Gert glared, his thick glasses flashing in the sunlight. "What are you doing just sitting around?"

"Ah, Fitch," I said, rising, "I've got to go. Can you stop by the theater tonight? Say five?"

"Sure. We can grab dinner." He hung up.

I stared at the phone. *Dinner*? He'd said it casually, and we'd be talking over a case. But I wasn't so sure about these mixed messages. Or was I just looking for mixed messages?

"We're supposed to do the walk-through." Gert jammed his fists into the pockets of his woolen coat. His scarf was wound highly enough to obscure his chin.

"We did the fair walk-through yesterday," I said.

"Faire with an *e*. And that was before most of the stands and decorations were put up."

"Then why didn't we just go today?"

"To be thorough. Mrs. Malone and I already told you this. Did you forget?"

I guess I had. There was only so much multitasking my brain could handle. I needed to stop with this portfolio career business and get back to personal protection.

"Of course I didn't forget," I said. "I was just waiting for you to finish up at your shop." I motioned to his antique store across the street.

"Good help really is hard to find," he muttered and strode away.

I looked around. But since no one was lurking behind the mushrooms or trying to kill me (yet), I followed. We drove in Gert's blue Prius to the rodeo grounds.

The fair was starting to take shape. Pumpkins, sheaves of corn, and wooden cutouts of haunted trees decorated the paths. A section of the rodeo area had been turned into a petting zoo. Cheesecloth ghosts and black fabric ghouls floated on wires above the dirt roads. There was even a pumpkin patch.

We made our way to the stage. A haunted castle set had been added to it, with more spooky tree cutouts. The flat pieces of scenery looked three-dimensional. Whoever had painted the set had real talent.

Gert nimbly climbed the steps to the stage, and I followed behind. Hands on his narrow hips, he stared out at the empty audience area. "Where are the folding chairs? Why hasn't the seating been set up yet?"

"They're probably waiting for tomorrow morning," I said.

"Sounds shifty to me. They need to be prepared. Where is that dratted woman?" He looked around.

"What dratted woman?"

"Jane, from your theater."

"She put all this together?" I asked, surprised. What *couldn't* that woman do? If she'd turned her talents to murder, I didn't like my odds of catching her.

"Of course she did. I told you, this is theater business."

I sensed movement and glanced over my shoulder. A castle wall creaked, angling forward. It took me a beat too long to realize what I was seeing. The painted wood rushed toward us. Roughly, I shoved Gert sideways.

"Whatcha—?"

I leapt after him. Pain nipped my heel. BANG. A cool breeze fluttered my hair.

We gaped at the castle wall now lying flat on the stage where we'd been standing.

"I could have been killed." Gert gripped his scarf.

My neck stiffened. *He* could have been killed? What was I? Chopped liver? I bent to rub my scraped ankle. "It wasn't that heavy." But one or both of us could have been hurt.

"That was intentional," he snapped. "Who did that?" He strode between the castle pieces that remained upright.

"Gert. Wait." I straightened.

"I'm being hunted." He vanished backstage. His voice floated from behind a crenelated tower. "No one's here."

I studied the fallen piece of scenery then squatted beside it. The sections of painted wood had been buttressed with two-by-fours. They'd work fine inside a theater, but outdoors, a strong blast of wind could knock them over.

But there hadn't been a blast of wind. I tugged down my jacket. There hadn't been *any* wind. I shook myself and focused on the problem at hand. The scenery would need to be braced somehow at the top as well, maybe with cables.

"Well?" Gert asked behind me.

Still kneeling, I pivoted to face him on the stage. "You were right—"

"I knew it. Someone's trying to kill me." Brushing back his coat, he pulled a Glock from his waistband and scowled. "It was bound to happen sooner or later."

Since he kept the gun aimed downward and his finger was off the trigger, I didn't voice an objection to the weapon. But I admit, it had startled me. I just hoped he hadn't noticed.

"Sure," I said. "About the walk-through, these scenery pieces aren't stable. They need to be wired at the top so they don't blow over, like this one did." I motioned to the painted castle.

"Blown? I didn't feel any wind before it fell. Did you?"

"No," I said, uneasy. "But it might not take much." Though what did I know about physics? "Who can we talk to about bracing this scenery?"

"Jane, of course. I need a real bodyguard."

"I am a real bodyguard. Just because my specialty is countersurveillance—"

"But you're not *my* real bodyguard."

I arched a brow and stood. "Why do you think you need one? You're an ex assassin with the Estonian mafia."

"I can't be watching for trouble all the time," he said. "And who says I'm *ex*?"

Whatever. "No one's going to mess with you when you're packing heat like that."

Gert holstered the weapon. "Yeah. Well. I'm not the man I used to be." He stared at his scuffed brown shoes.

"No one is." I tilted my head. "Why do you think someone wants to hurt you?"

He clawed at the wisps of hair on his balding head. "To kill me."

"To kill you," I said flatly.

"I'm being sent a message."

"And what's the message?"

"Resign."

I paused. "You think the Chamber of Commerce wants you dead?" Because the way he'd been hassling the local business owners, the idea wasn't that off-the-wall.

He scowled, sunlight glinting off his spectacles. "There are forces at work. People who don't like an independent-minded man in the mayor's office."

"Maybe the job's not worth it?" I said casually.

He looked up, expression fierce. "You're saying I should quit? Gert Magimountain doesn't quit. Do you know what it means to..." His mouth pinched.

Means to whom? Means to quit? Whatever he'd been about to say, I didn't press. Gert had been a force back in the day. Maybe becoming temporary mayor meant more to him than I'd realized. Maybe he was trying to get something back, to prove something.

It was an impulse I understood. I stared out at the empty space where the audience would sit. "You could be a great mayor," I said.

He blinked at me. "You think? I mean, sure I could. I *am*."

"Sure. Maybe just... ease up on some of the businesses."

"You're right," he said slowly.

At *last*. I smiled. "Thanks. I'm glad you—"

"It probably *is* one of the business owners who's out to get me."

I clenched my teeth. "That wasn't what I—"

"Makes sense. I *have* been ruffling feathers." He rubbed his narrow chin. "Good thinking. I knew there was a reason Mrs. Malone kept you around."

Frustrated, I motioned toward the stage. "This was an accident, Gert."

He snorted. "That's what *you* think."

"I feel awful." In the theater kitchen, Jane adjusted the net over her mouse-brown hair. Flour dusted the sleeves of her shapeless gray top. "You two could have been seriously hurt."

"As you planned." Gert's jaw jutted forward.

Her eyes widened. "What do you mean?"

"He doesn't mean anything," I said hastily. "And you weren't the only one with wobbly decor." I'd had to make a run to a hardware shop in Reno for enough cable to attach to all the false fronts and stage scenery.

"Where were you this morning between ten and eleven AM?" Gert demanded.

"I was home," she said.

"Ah, HA." Gert snapped his fingers beneath her nose. "No alibi."

"Not that she needs one," I said.

"Let me see your license," Gert said.

"My what?" she asked.

"Food service license," he snapped.

She pointed to a framed certificate on the kitchen wall. He strode across the black fatigue mats to peer at it.

"Those castle sets were impressive," I said. "Who made them?"

She flushed. "I did—"

"You *see*?" Gert said. "She made the set that nearly killed me."

Jane shot me a hurt look. "You were trying to entrap me?"

"No," I said. "No. That wasn't what I meant—"

"Good job, Alice," Gert said. "We'll see about you." He stormed from the kitchen.

"I wasn't trying to trap you," I said. "The sets really are amazing. Gert's just... Gert."

"Hey," Fitch stepped into the kitchen, and my stupid heart skipped a girlish beat. He was wearing a blue fisherman's sweater that brought out the wicked in his eyes. "Gert said you were in here, and I should interrogate the suspect?"

"There's no suspect." I smiled at Jane. "Gert just had a near miss and is a little wound up."

"If you say so," she said doubtfully.

"And this is my friend, Fitch," I said. "Fitch, this is Jane, the theater manager. Or stage manager."

She sighed. "I do it all."

"She really does," I said. "She even manages the dinners, and they're amazing."

"I've heard." Fitch shook her hand. "This place has a reputation."

"I love the theater," she said. "But it would be nice to branch out."

Fitch angled his head. "And do what?"

She blushed. "I always wanted to own a tearoom. There's one on the coast that does tea and Tarot, and it… I just love the atmosphere."

"Why don't you do it?" he asked.

"Oh." She adjusted her hair net. "Gloria needed me here."

And now Gloria didn't. But Jane would have to be certifiable to decide killing Gloria was easier than saying *no*. "I was just going to give Fitch a backstage tour."

She smiled. "Don't let me hold you up."

I took Fitch's arm and led him upstairs. "That was the victim's sister?" he asked in a rumbly voice that tickled deep inside my chest.

I nodded and stopped at the dressing room's closed door. "The police let us have the room back. Unfortunately, Jane gave it over to our newest star, Autumn Winter. So there's not much left of the crime scene."

Fitch jaw slackened. "Autumn Winter?"

I laughed. "I know. I can't figure out if it's a stage name or—"

"*She's* here?"

"Not right now. She'll be here later."

"I saw her in Reno. She's fantastic. Your dinner theater is coming up in the world."

Save me from starstruck groupies. "Lucky us." I opened the dressing room door. "*Voila*. The murder scene." We walked inside.

He bent to open the mini-fridge. "This is where Gloria kept her pineapple juice?"

I nodded. "One thing I did find out. The poison was in her glass and not in the box of juice."

He grunted. "The box would have been easier. Was the dressing room door kept locked?"

"No."

Fitch leaned against the dressing table, and it creaked beneath his weight. He seemed to fill the small room. "Tell me about the other woman who was killed, Kristie Naysmith."

"She was sort of the theater den mother, though..." But *had* she been? I frowned.

"Though what?"

"She had a tendency to say the wrong thing at the wrong time."

"Intentionally?"

"The others say she was just gaffe-prone." I pushed my hair out of my face. "But it seemed to me she knew exactly what she was saying. Kristie was the one who mentioned that the black knight costume could be found at a shop in Reno."

"Black knight costume?"

I braced my shoulder against the frame of the open door. "Someone in a black knight costume has been haunting the theater. We saw him when we went to Kristie's house, watching us. We gave chase but he got away."

"In a *knight's* costume?" Fitch's dark brow sketched upward.

"Half a costume. Just the helmet, really. He was at the top of a hill, we were at the bottom. And there was a landslide."

He doubled over, laughing. "A black knight?"

"Someone could have been hurt," I sputtered.

He wheezed. "Nowhere. Unbelievable."

"And the next day," I continued, annoyed, "Kristie was stabbed with a sword."

He straightened, chuckling. "Which points toward the mysterious knight... or someone in the theater."

I sighed. "It was Charlie's sword, but it was stored in the prop room, which is kept unlocked."

"Did you see this knight around the night Gloria died?" He opened the tall wardrobe.

"No," I said. "But I think Lilyanna mentioned seeing him. The police already searched the wardrobe."

He shut the wardrobe doors. "She mentioned the knight? Did you follow up?"

I grimaced. "No."

"I dunno. Poison points to someone who had easy access to this room. In fact, all signs point to someone from the theater."

"If only someone who was a real detective could infiltrate it..." I hinted.

He stepped closer, forcing me to look up. My heart beat a little faster. "Nice try," he said. "I'm only here so the cops don't bust my chops. I work for pay."

"But you'd get to meet Autumn Winter. In fact, the theater needs another player." And my Alice-in-Wonderland dress was a little too on-the-nose.

"I'm not an actor."

"Come on," I wheedled. "You're a PI. You must go undercover all the time. That means improv."

"Well, yeah, but—"

"And you've already seen the twenties-show." Tonight was medieval, but who was counting? If twenties slang had been bad, all the *prithees* and *thous* were a nightmare.

"They all know I'm a PI."

"I don't think that got out. Charlie knows, and Mrs. Malone and Gert—"

"Is that all?"

And now Jed. "But Charlie hasn't told anyone, and the others would have no reason to."

"Why not?" he asked.

"I swore my brother to secrecy, since I thought I might be working with you later. The theater's a paying gig," I added.

His absinthe eyes narrowed. "How much?"

"Ah, I'm not sure. There's a profit-sharing agreement. But think of the groupies."

He brightened. "There are groupies?"

"Tons," I lied.

"And you'd owe me a favor." He pointed at me.

"Ah... Yes. I'd owe you a favor." Which I knew I'd pay dearly for. Later. Good thing I was all about living in the now.

"Deal."

"Great. Look around, do your detective thing. I'll talk to Jane and be right back."

I jogged down the stairs and found Jane bending over a drawer in the kitchen. "So, Jane."

She closed the drawer and turned to me. Wisps of hair had escaped her prim bun. "Are you having trouble with your lines? I'm working on finding another substitute, but—"

"I've found one. But I don't think he's going to fit into my costume."

Chapter Twenty-One

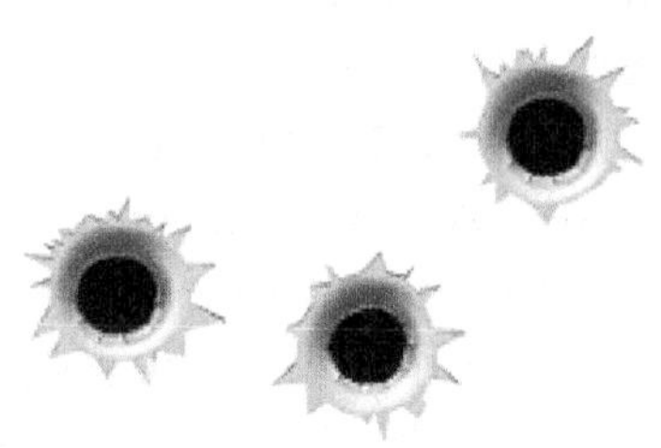

The fair opened at noon. I was there at eight getting better acquainted with the staff and vendors. I stepped inside the medic tent, a red cross painted across its front flaps. A mini heater hummed beneath a plastic table.

A well-built, sandy-haired man in jeans and a navy-blue fleece jacket stood at another long table and set out bottles of water. He looked over his shoulder at me. "Hey. Tell me you're not hurt."

"I'm not hurt." I squinted at him. "Have we met?"

He turned to face me fully and snapped his fingers, recognition lighting his rugged face. I stiffened. I hated it when people recognized me. "You found the woman who'd been poisoned and skewered," he said.

"And you were the paramedic at the scene," I said, relaxing. I figured it was better to be known as the woman at the scene of Kristie's murder than as the bodyguard who'd let dirtbag Toomas Koppel die.

"Not that I could do anything about it," he said disgustedly.

"Wait. You said she'd been poisoned *and* stabbed?" And Gloria had been poisoned too. Had it been the same poison?

He nodded. "I didn't figure out the poison angle myself. My cousin works in the coroner's office."

I stepped closer to the mini heater and warmed my feet. "So… she was poisoned first, obviously." Which would make it easier to stab her. But why stab her at all? Just to make a point? To frame the black knight? "I thought she'd been hit in the head before the stabbing."

"The head wound came from her fall, probably after the poison took effect. Whoever stabbed her, rolled her over to do it."

The killer had wanted to see his victim's face when he'd done the deed. That was creepy. "Shame on me for assuming."

"Don't feel bad," he said. "I thought the same thing when I arrived at the scene. There were no other signs of trauma to her aside from the short sword in her chest."

The mini-heater hummed. I moved a foot closer.

"I, uh, don't suppose your cousin mentioned the time of death?" I said, enjoying the warming sensation in my toes. I have a tendency toward chilblains, a Victorian-sounding condition which is really irritating. Literally.

"He estimates she was stabbed around nine AM. He's still trying to work out the poisoning angle."

"I suppose it was the same poison used on the victim in the theater," I said nonchalantly.

"Yeah, that's what my cousin said."

"Well, it's good to meet you." Talk about a lucky break. But this was a small town. I was bound to get to know everyone sooner or later. "I'm helping with security at the fair."

"Then let's hope we don't see each other again. If all goes well, the worst I'll be dealing with is dehydration or possibly shock." He laughed. "Have you *seen* the prices at the food court?"

"I don't think I want to know. Take care." I nodded and left the tent.

The fair was coming to life. Vendors bustled about, decorating their booths with spider webs and mini pumpkins. Skeletons posed climbing the walls and on the roof of one particularly ambitious stall.

The food court had been decorated with more pumpkins and corn sheaves. The black-painted stands pressed close against each other. Most were closed at this hour. But the window of one was open, and fair workers lined up there for water.

I walked past a cauldron bubbling over a fake fire and got in line. When I reached the open window, Jane smiled out at me. "Hi, Alice. What are you doing here so early?"

"I've got to set up some cameras for crowd control," I said, surprised to see her here. "I didn't know you were volunteering at the food court too."

With the back of her gloved hand, she brushed a blot of orange frosting off her temple. "I'm not a volunteer. This is my stand. I'm doing some last-minute decorating. I didn't want to bring a load of frosted cupcakes here only to have them fall over in the car and get mashed up." She reached down and set a tray of bats and Frankenstein's monsters and ghosts before me.

I sucked in a breath. "Those look amazing." The frosting had been molded to create a 3-D effect.

"It's a little more frosting than I'd normally slap on top of a cupcake, but it's for Halloween."

"You'll sell out fast. Can you set two aside for me and Charlie?" I reached for my wallet.

"Of course I will. And put away your wallet. You don't have to pay."

"Yes, I do. Those are worth it." I checked the price menu and handed her some bills. The paramedic hadn't been kidding about the prices. "I didn't realize you were a baker, too."

"I actually prefer baking to cooking, but the dinner theater is steady income. And Gloria..." She swallowed and hurriedly looked away. "Which would you like?"

"I'll take a vampire and a ghost."

"Sure. Come back any time to pick them up."

"Thanks. I'll see you around." I wandered, checking out the other stalls. The meadery had a booth, and so did the pizza parlor. Both were closed at this early hour.

I returned to my Jeep and excavated my things from the back. Hefting the carrying bag with my equipment over one shoulder, I studied the ladder unenthusiastically. Finally, I set the ladder over my other shoulder.

Ladder biting into my muscles, I trudged like a pack mule to the front gate. I stopped to chat with the man who'd be taking tickets and set up the ladder. I'd already confirmed with the gatekeeper that they'd be counting the number of heads. If we went over max capacity the fire marshal would have *my* head.

The gatekeeper held the ladder for me while I installed a security camera up high. I climbed down, checked my map, and nodded. "Thanks." Reluctantly, I returned the ladder to my shoulder.

"You want me to come with you?" he said. "I can carry that ladder."

I shook my head. "I wouldn't dream of interfering with your duties." Mrs. Malone wouldn't let me hear the end of it.

I crossed beneath a metal pergola twined with fake autumn leaves and walked to the next install spot. It was a pine tree in the steampunk-vampire-old-west Halloween section. Shacks with old-west false fronts lined the curving pedestrian road.

Clambering onto the ladder, I screwed the camera into the pine. Fantastic metal devices trundled past spewing steam.

"Alice?" Jed, in a blue suit with something gold embroidered over one breast, craned up at me.

"Oh, hi, Jed." I climbed down. "What brings you here?"

He brandished a sheaf of black paper. "Marketing. I'm dropping off brochures for the hotel I work at."

"A Hot Springs hotel advertising in Nowhere?" I raised my brows.

Jed half-laughed. "I know. But the hotel paid for space at the fair's information booth, so..." He shrugged. "And since I live here, I was the one appointed to bring them over. Though in *fairness*—ha-ha—I was also the one who suggested we buy space here."

I grinned. “I’m not sure if that makes you a Nowhere patriot or a traitor.”

Jed gave a quick shake of his head. “Gloria would have...” He blinked rapidly. “She loved Halloween. Any excuse, really, to dress up.”

“She was one of a kind,” I agreed. “Are you going to perform in the mystery theater shows here?”

“Gloria and I... I made a commitment. I intend to see it through. And I hear we have two new players.”

Fitch had been a smash hit last night. Though I’d been lying about the groupies, several women had taken him out for drinks at the speakeasy afterward. I forced a smile. “The show must go on.”

“So everyone keeps telling me.” Jed looked down at the bare earth.

“How are you holding up?” I asked in a low tone.

“Everyone keeps asking me that. I’m not sure what to say anymore.”

“You don’t have to say anything. People will understand.”

“Well. I’d better get these to the information booth.” He strode away.

I gathered my gear and made my way to the next install point, at an emergency exit in the medieval Halloween land. Someone had done a bang-up job painting realistic-looking stones on the exit’s wooden false front.

The exit signs were big and bright and obvious above the turreted wooden gate, and I nodded. If there was an emergency, people would easily find their way out. I checked that the gate latch worked smoothly from the inside, then climbed the ladder. This camera would go on the EXIT sign high above the gate.

I set the bag with my equipment in it on the ladder stand and removed the drill. Bracing one hand on the wooden sign, I penciled in the spots where I’d need to drill.

Something moved beneath me, and I glanced down. A werewolf in a black jacket rushed toward the ladder.

“Hey,” I said. “Watch—”

He lowered his shoulder and caromed into the ladder. The step jerked from beneath my feet. I bleated an expletive. The base of the ladder skidded in the dirt, and I was airborne.

CHAPTER TWENTY-TWO

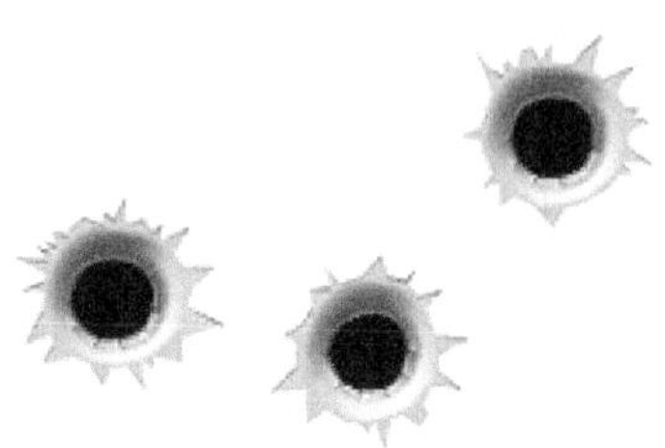

THAT WHOLE TIME SLOWING down thing happened again. It gave me time to think about dentists and werewolves, black knights and blackmailers. My life hadn't been anywhere near this peculiar before I'd landed in Nowhere.

And then time sped up again. I made a wild grab for the exit arch, and for once, things went my way. My hands caught its edge. The ladder clattered to the ground beneath me. The curve of uneven wood tore into my palms, and I gasped at the flash of pain.

I swore again, adrenaline pounding through my veins. Dangling above the ground, I glanced over my shoulder. The werewolf raced around a bend in the dirt trail and disappeared behind a jewelry stand.

My fingers slipped a fraction, scratching the flesh. So that hurt, but it was only a few fingers.

I was higher than I liked, but if I let go, I probably wouldn't do more than twist an ankle. And I might not even do that. Still, I really didn't *want* to let go.

The phone rang in my jacket pocket, because of course it would. People only call me when its inconvenient.

"What on earth are you doing up there?" Mrs. Malone asked from beneath me, and I dared a glance over my shoulder.

Leaning on her cane, she glared up at me. She wore a festive yet professional pumpkin-orange blazer and black pantsuit. I guessed there were sensible shoes at the bottom of that outfit but couldn't really tell from that angle.

I grunted. "Trying not to fall." My phone jangled.

"Well, it seems a silly way of going about it." She righted the ladder. "How many times have I told you not to go to the top step?"

"Never." My foot touched metal, and the tension in my body released. Shakily, I applied more weight, but I couldn't quite convince myself to release my grip on the arch. "We've never discussed ladder safety."

"Didn't you read the warning label?"

I forced myself to let go of the arch and grabbed the nearby wooden post for balance.

"Well?" she asked.

Climbing down, I rubbed my palms on my jeans. "I didn't knock it over. Someone dressed like a werewolf pushed it over."

She rolled her eyes. "First a black knight and now a homicidal werewolf. How ridiculous. I expect you to stop playing silly games and do the work you've committed to."

"He may know something about the murders," I said, exasperated. My phone stopped ringing. I glanced down. Mrs. Malone really was wearing sensible shoes—black trail runners.

She cocked her head and arched a brow. "You *were* on the top step, weren't you?"

"I know a werewolf sounds ridiculous, but... I've got to find him." I hurried away.

"Wait," she shouted after me. "Come back here. I'm not finished talking to you."

I jogged around the bend and stopped at a stall where an artist was setting up her watercolors. "Did you see a person dressed as a werewolf go by?"

She pointed. "He's probably headed to the medieval section."

"We're *in* the medieval section."

Her brow wrinkled. "Oh. Right."

I speed walked down the dirt track. Anger flared at the front of my skull. If I hadn't managed to grab that arch, it could have been a bad fall. I strode past Halloween carnival games, swagged with orange and black bunting. A man in a black-and-white striped shirt adjusted a wheel with a jack-o-lantern painted in its center.

"Have you seen a werewolf go past?" I asked him.

"Just missed him. He was headed toward the steampunk zone. Or whatever it's called."

"Thanks." I raced on, stopping to ask vendors and barkers if he'd been seen. They all pointed me in the same direction.

I slackened my pace at the steampunk section. A metal dragon huffed a cloud of fog, obscuring the pedestrian road. More slowly, I moved through the swirling murk, my scalp prickling.

Something clanked to my right. I reoriented, walking toward the sound. CLANK.

The gray cloud parted. A massive, black metal wheel rolled past. Atop it, rode a man dressed in a gas mask and leathers.

"Have you seen a werewolf?" I called. I was starting to feel like a character in a children's story. *Have* you *seen my cheese*? Or something. It had been a long time since I'd read a children's book.

The contraption stopped. The man looked down at me. He pointed. "That way."

"Thanks." I continued past creepy clockwork and a stand selling metal jack-o-lanterns wearing goggles. The road curved, and another entrance to the food area appeared.

I strode inside and to Jane's cupcake stand. A smile lit her plain face. "Back for your cupcakes?"

"Not quite yet. Did you see a werewolf come by?"

She shook her head and brushed a floury hand across the front of her black apron. "No. Why?"

"He shoved me off a ladder."

The hand on her apron stilled. "Oh, no. Are you okay?"

"Yeah, I'm fine. But I'd really like to find him."

Her hand clenched, bunching the black fabric. "You don't think it's the same person who was dressing as a black knight? Because if he shows up for one of our shows, the players may riot. They're getting really paranoid about that guy."

"Me too," I muttered.

"Ask Vittoria." She angled her head toward a stand decorated with pizza slices nearby. "She just opened. She may have seen something."

"I will. Thanks." I strode to the pizza stall.

Waves of heat blossomed from the stall's front window. Vittoria hefted a block of cheese as long as my arm into a mini fridge on a stand.

"Hi, Vittoria."

She turned. Her medium-length brown hair was in its usual working ponytail. She wore a zip-up hoodie emblazoned with a white pizza wheel. And her face was nearly as red as her hoodie. "Oh, hey, Alice. What's up?"

I bit the inside of my lip. The last time we'd spoken, she'd still been holding a grudge. "I don't suppose a werewolf came through here?"

"A werewolf?" She frowned. "No. Should one have?"

"I guess not," I muttered. I must have lost him in Steampunk Halloween.

"Is everything okay?" she asked.

"Yeah. There's just a lot to do."

"Tell me about it. My helper's out sick. I don't suppose you want to sling slices today?"

"Ah..." I backed away. That explained her sudden friendliness. Vittoria wanted a favor. "I don't think I'll have the time."

"Don't worry." She smiled. "I didn't really expect you would. And Clyde should be here any minute to help."

"Clyde's around?" I asked, my ears pricking.

She laughed. "He'd better be."

"Okay. Thanks." Keeping my eyes peeled for black knights and werewolves, I returned to the emergency exit.

Mrs. Malone paced in front of the wooden arch. "There you are." She pointed at the black security camera on the dirt. "I presume that's supposed to be above the exit and not lying where anyone could trip over it."

My jaw clenched. "Yes. Thank you for keeping guard."

"I wasn't. I was waiting for you to finish your work for the festival and solve these murders. I've given you quite a deal on the rent, young lady, and you've been delinquent with your reports."

Reports. I hung my head. Arguing just wasn't worth it. "I'm working on it."

"Oh? How, exactly?"

"I'm trying to track down the costume shop in Reno where the black knight got his costume." I pulled my phone from my pocket.

"I thought you were chasing a big bad wolf?"

"I was. There's a black knight and a werewolf, okay? And they could be the same person."

She banged the end of her cane on the earth. "That knight's obviously just some theater stalker."

"But the knight was watching Kristie's the day before she was killed. And *someone* drove a sword through her chest."

"What sort of fool would dress up in costume to commit murder?"

"Someone who didn't want to be seen?" And it had worked in both cases. No one would give a werewolf a second look at a Halloween fair. Just like they normally wouldn't pay much attention to a knight at a medieval murder mystery.

But if it was the same person, why switch costume? Had the black knight get-up become too hot to handle?

She sniffed. "Werewolves. Knights. It just seems ridiculous."

At least we agreed on that. I checked my phone. "Ha! The costume shop called back."

"Alice, I insist you—"

I raised a finger and pressed the green dial button.

"Costumes Caramel, how can I help you?"

"Hi, this is Alice Sommerland returning your call?"

"Oh, yes, the private detective."

"Actually, I work with..." *Never mind.* "Yes. Were you able to find out who bought any black knight costumes over the last few months?"

"Yes, we sold two, actually. One to a Persimmon Landers and another to Clyde McGarrity."

"Who is it?" Mrs. Malone whispered. "What did she say?"

"McGarrity," I repeated. "From Nowhere, Nevada?"

"Clyde." Mrs. Malone grimaced.

"I think that's the zip code." The costume shop manager rattled off a string of numbers.

"That's Nowhere's zip code," I said, dour. So Clyde's interest in the theater *had* turned into an unhealthy obsession. It didn't prove he was the killer, but it didn't look good either.

"I'm sorry it took so long," the manager was saying. "The clerk you spoke to forgot to give me your message until this morning."

"It's fine. I appreciate you taking the time to check your records."

"No problem. I did it for the police two weeks ago and had the names on hand."

My brain stumbled. "Two *weeks* ago?" The police could only have known about the costume shop connection since Kristie's death. That had been two days ago. And Gloria had been killed a week ago.

"What happened two weeks ago?" Mrs. Malone asked.

"Yes," the manager said. "Why?"

"What?" Mrs. Malone tapped her cane. "What's going on?"

"Nothing," I said. "Do you remember the name of the officer who called? I'd really love to talk to him. Or her."

"No, I'm afraid I don't. And it was a woman, if that helps. I think she said her first name was something with a... C?"

"What is it?" Mrs. Malone demanded.

I covered the speaker with my hand. "A woman claiming to be a sheriff's deputy called the costume shop two weeks ago. She asked the same question I did," I whispered.

"But Gloria was killed one week ago," Mrs. Malone said.

"I know." My gaze clouded. So who'd made that call?

Chapter Twenty-Three

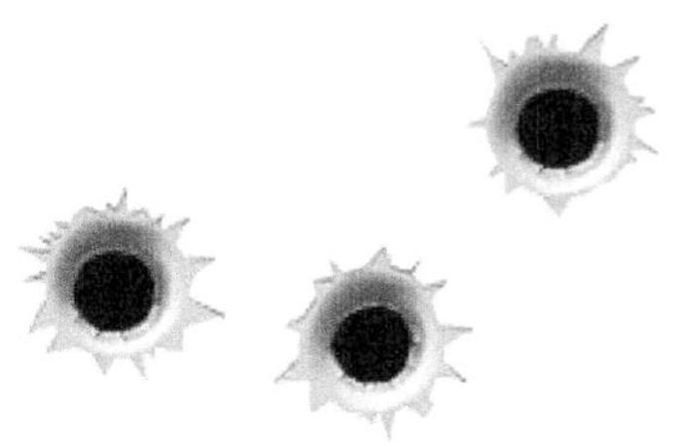

"Has anyone else called about the costume?" I asked the shop manager. An electric saw whirred somewhere on the fairgrounds, and I stuck my finger in my other ear so I could hear the phone better.

"No," she said, "only you."

A woman cursed, and I glanced down the wide dirt path. In front of the jewelry stall, the owner righted a stand dripping with beaded necklaces.

"Thanks," I said, dissatisfied. "You've been very helpful." We exchanged a few more pleasantries and hung up. The saw whirred to a halt and fell silent.

"Well?" Mrs. Malone demanded.

I slid the phone into the rear pocket of my jeans. "I told the detective about that black knight when we found Kristie's body. It doesn't sound like anyone from the sheriff's office has followed up yet."

She arched a brow. "Are you surprised?"

"Well, no, but I'm still disappointed." But if I hadn't seen the black knight myself, I might have dismissed the story too.

Mrs. Malone brandished her cane at the mountains to the south. "Hot Springs has always gotten the most attention from county services. It's because they have the biggest tax base. Gert still hasn't been able to get anyone from county to even look at that landslide."

I shook myself. "At least we know who bought that costume: Clyde."

"Shocking," she said dryly. "Let's go."

"Where?"

"To confront Clyde, of course. If he's been harassing the players, this is theater business. Besides, it's also part of your investigation, which you're being well paid for."

My shoulders slumped. *That free rent.* I *really* needed a new apartment.

We found Clyde waddling away from the rear of the Pizza Wheel stand, a canvas satchel slung crossways over his broad stomach. He'd eschewed the fair's Halloween theme for a fisherman's hat, brown windbreaker, and khakis.

Through the open door, I could see his wife bustling back and forth in the tiny booth's kitchen. The smell of baking cheese, garlic, and tomato sauce drifted across the open space, and my stomach rumbled.

He motioned us toward a green picnic table and sat on one of its benches. "Oh, hey. I just ordered. I thought I'd better get here before the fair opened to the plebes. If you put your order in now, we can eat together. Now, I've been making some changes to the script—"

"No, thank you," Mrs. Malone said in a freezing voice.

Clyde dug into the canvas satchel and pulled out a sheaf of papers. "I think my killer was a little too obvious. So I added more red herrings."

I slid onto the bench across from him. "You're the black knight."

He blinked. "What?"

"You bought the black knight costume from Costumes Caramel in Reno," I said.

He grimaced. "An impulse purchase. Vittoria wasn't happy about it. We've been saving for a trip to New Zealand to see the hobbit houses. It's been a dream of hers—"

Mrs. Malone slammed her wrinkled hand on the picnic table. "Forget the hobbit houses," she said. "Why did you kill those two women?"

He reared backward in his seat, his chin tucking. "What?"

"You were *seen*," Mrs. Malone thundered.

He pulled his satchel to his chest. "Seen where?"

"Seen in your black knight costume," I said.

"But I haven't worn that since I bought it in the costume shop."

"A likely story." Mrs. Malone scowled and sat beside me on the picnic bench.

"No," he said. "Really. I don't even know where that costume is. Vittoria and I had a blow-out when I got home with it, and I put it somewhere in her she-shed."

Maybe he did, maybe he didn't. But I'd play along for now. "Is the shed kept locked?"

"Sometimes. I mean, there's a padlock, but sometimes we just hook it over the latch instead of actually locking it. So... no." His round face fell.

Then anyone could have taken the costume—assuming they'd known it was there. "Who else did you tell about it?"

"Um... I don't know. I mean, it wasn't a big deal. I might have told a few people at the theater about our argument though." He waggled his head. "I guess I should have just returned it. But Costumes Caramel is really hard to return things to. I can't blame 'em. People are always buying costumes and then returning them after use."

"You used it to sneak into the theater after you'd been banned," I said.

His knuckles whitened on the canvas bag. "What? No! Really I didn't."

"Where were you Wednesday morning?" I asked.

"Uh..." He scratched his head beneath his floppy hat. "Where was I? I was home—"

"Alone?" Mrs. Malone asked.

"No, Vittoria was with me. At least, until I went to Gert's antique shop."

"Why'd you go there?" I asked.

"He's been giving Vittoria a lot of guff about that pizza wheel being properly braced. I thought... Gert said he was having some wi-fi connectivity problems at his shop. I thought if I helped him, maybe he'd back off."

"Corruption," Mrs. Malone hissed.

"How is it corrupt?" he asked. "It's just a little computer assist."

"How long were you there?" I asked.

He fiddled with the hat's cord. "He told me to come at eight. I was there until noon."

And we'd found Kristie around eleven. If this was true, he might have an alibi. "Where's the costume, Clyde?" I asked.

He raised his hands helplessly. "I don't know what happened to it. I mean, I'll go find it if you want and prove it to you. It's still in its wrapping."

"And the werewolf costume?" I asked him.

"What werewolf costume?"

Vittoria strode to the table and set a soda in a large paper cup in front of her husband. "Can I get you two anything?"

I wouldn't have minded a slice of peperoni, and I opened my mouth to say so. "Ye—"

"No," Mrs. Malone said. "We're here on business."

"With Clyde?" Vittoria asked.

"Have you seen my black knight costume?" Clyde asked her.

Vittoria's green eyes narrowed. "What do you mean *have I seen it*? Didn't you take it back?"

He rubbed the back of his neck. "Ah, I got really busy with the script, and work, and—"

"You've got to be kidding me." Her hands clenched. "You said you'd take it back and get a refund!"

"I will, I will," he said. "It's still in its box, so I'm sure they'll take it back."

"This is so..." She huffed a breath and strode away, her back rigid.

"I, uh, should probably go talk to her." He began to slide from the picnic table.

"Stay right there," Mrs. Malone said.

He froze, his hands pressed to the green tabletop, his elbows bent, as if about to lift himself from his seat.

"This nonsense with your script is done," Mrs. Malone said. "The players are improv. If you have ideas for scenes they can *improv*, you may submit them to me. You will cease bothering the players. Are we understood?"

"Yes, ma'am," he squeaked. "And congratulations on your two new players. I heard they're both a hit."

"Congratulate Jane. On second thought, do not congratulate Jane. She's a busy woman."

"May I go?" he asked.

She nodded graciously, her dyed-black hair stiff and unmoving. He practically tripped over his own feet in his haste to get away.

Mrs. Malone sniffed. "You can have the rest of the day off, Alice. But I expect you here tomorrow before opening."

"Yes ma'am."

She extricated herself from the table and strode away. Something crashed inside the Pizza Wheel booth.

Maybe pizza wasn't the best idea today after all.

"Clyde denied using the costume, but he didn't deny having it." I paced Fitch's spartan office. Aside from his PI license, he didn't have a thing on the walls. The only decoration was a dead spider plant on top of a metal filing cabinet. And I hadn't believed spider plants were killable. Lesson learned.

Fitch peered into a wall mirror the size of a postcard and adjusted a fake mustache. It made him look like Magnum PI—the original one, not that weak 2020s remake.

"He seemed truthful." I sat against the window frame, and the back of my navy jacket brushed the miniblinds. They rustled a reproach, and I glanced over my shoulder. The window had an uninspiring view of the concrete building opposite. "But the only way I would know is if I broke into their she-shed and checked to see if the costume had been used."

"Don't do that." He smoothed his mustache.

"Is it enough to know he's got the costume, and we can just assume he's lying? He's snuck into the theater in the past. He could have stolen Charlie's short sword."

"No, but you can assume everyone's lying. Everyone does," he mumbled.

"And what do I do with this costume shop info? Tell the sheriff?"

"Leave it be for now. You don't want to be accused of usurping an investigation."

"Usurping?" I raised a brow. "Is that a plot line from the theater's medieval mystery?"

"It's what they call interfering in an investigation in Nevada. Does this mustache make me look like Tom Selleck?"

It wasn't a bad look. "Like a Tom Selleck wannabe."

"Meh." He peeled it off, wincing.

"Are you going under cover?" I asked.

"It's for our next show." He studied the mirror and ran his hand over a lock of dark hair.

Our? "Did you learn anything at the last show?"

"Yeah, to go with the flow."

I rolled my eyes. "I'm not talking about improv techniques. I mean about the murders."

He turned to me. "Everyone claims to be shocked and baffled by Kristie's death. I don't believe any of them, because they're actors."

"Not all of them. What did you think of Jane?"

"Who?"

"The theater manager."

"Oh, right." He returned to the tiny mirror. "I got the feeling she resented her sister more than she lets on."

I got that feeling too. But it didn't add up to much. Shaking my head, I fiddled with the pull for the miniblinds. "This is getting embarrassing."

"Don't feel too bad. It takes time to gain people's confidence when you're undercover. Especially when everyone suspects you're undercover. The whole cast knows I'm a PI. Charlie's incapable of keeping a secret, which you should know." He shot me an accusing look.

"I was referring to your sudden-onset narcissism."

Flushing, he turned to face me. "It turns out I'm good at improv. Must be from all the undercover work. And since this isn't a paying case, I get to enjoy myself. It's a rule."

"Well, don't go so deep undercover you forget why you're there," I grumped.

"Because you were too chicken for improv?"

I crossed my arms. "Yes. Because I was too chicken for improv."

He grinned. "And now you owe me."

"Right." And I was more curious than worried about what that was going to cost me.

Chapter Twenty-Four

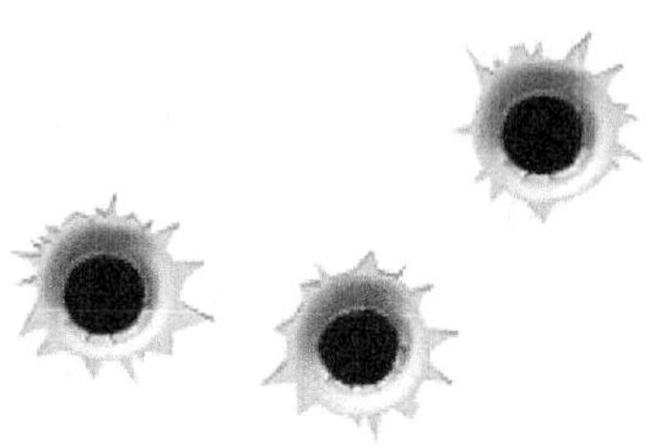

Fairgoers milled on the black-and-white screens. A cool breeze flowed through the cramped security tent. It ruffled my hair in a seductive invitation to be anywhere but here. The air in the tent was starting to get manky.

I rose from the bank of monitors and stretched. "I'm going to do a walkthrough," I said to Mrs. Malone.

"Good idea," she said. "Are you sure these cameras cover all the pinch points?"

I bit back a smile. Mrs. Malone had been doing her research. Generally speaking, a pinch point was also a bottleneck, any place people can get caught.

But in my world, a pinch point was a place where people had to go—like your driveway. If you wanted to get your car out, you couldn't avoid your own driveway. Bad guys loved pinch points—or at least their potential victim's pinch points.

"Every exit is covered," I said, "and so are the three tightest bends in the trails." I pointed to the screens, my borrowed SECURITY windbreaker rustling. "Do you want me to get you anything from the food court?"

Mrs. Malone folded her arms across her ample chest. "No, thank you, and I suggest you avoid it as well. It's all junk food. And don't forget your radio."

I patted it on my belt and left the tent. The air smelled like autumn and candy apples. Smiling, I merged with the costumed crowd. Our security tent was close to the center of the fair, in the Silk Road Spooks section. Middle eastern music warbled over the loudspeakers of a nearby stage. Belly dancers swayed and drummers drummed. Little kids bounced along to the tunes.

I stopped to duck my head into the first aid tent. The EMT from the other day wasn't there. Another EMT treated a woman who'd spilled coffee on her arm. I waved and left the tent, wandering down random paths.

At the juncture of two dirt trails, Jed, in a navy blazer embroidered with the Stag Hotel's gold logo, manned the circular information booth. Brochures in curving racks lined its sides.

I stopped in front of him. "Aren't you supposed to be managing a hotel in Hot Springs?" I asked.

"In exchange for letting us promote our hotel, the fair wanted a volunteer. I'm it," the widower said.

"Wow. You're really a jack of all trades, aren't you?"

He smiled faintly. "I don't mind. If I'm going to have my own hotel one day, I'd better get used to it."

"Your own? Someone told me you were planning one."

"Who told you that?"

"Kristie."

He shook his head. "Poor woman. But yes, I plan to start-up a small, boutique hotel. It'll probably be in The Town of Hot Springs, because that's where everyone stays. Something modern with a top-level bar and restaurant."

I picked up a brochure for a Hot Springs spa. What I would give for a massage right now... "You should ask Jane about the restaurant side."

He blinked. "Jane?"

I returned the brochure to its place in the rack. "She *does* manage the restaurant at the dinner theater too. Though I don't think Mrs. Malone will be happy if you steal her from the theater." I grimaced. "Sorry. I'm sure you've already planned all that out."

"Yes, but... You're right, I should talk to Jane. I don't know why I didn't..." He shook himself. "I see Gert's got you working today too?"

"It's not Gert," I said sharply. "I don't work for Gert."

He raised his hands in a defensive gesture. "Okay, okay."

And now I'd overreacted. "It's fine. I'm helping out Mrs. Malone. Were you able to find any of those demand letters?"

"I did find one. It's in my car, but I can't leave the booth."

"When will you be free?"

He checked his watch. "At two o'clock."

"I'll swing by here then, and we can go get it." I wasn't going to leave anything to chance.

I strolled to the food court. It was packed, long lines extending from the stalls, every picnic table full. I walked to the back of Jane's cupcake stall and opened the door.

She glanced over her shoulder. "Hey. What's up?"

"Just checking in," I said. "How's everything?"

"Busy."

"Quick question." I hesitated. Asking where she was when Kristie was being murdered didn't seem like the subtle sort of interrogation technique Fitch would employ. "Were you at the minimart Wednesday morning?"

"The minimart?" Her brow furrowed. "On Wednesday?" She grabbed a pink box and popped it into shape. "Um... No. I was home all morning. Why?"

"No reason. Thanks." I closed the door and walked to the rear of the pizza shack. The back door hung open, and I pulled it wider.

A lanky teenager I knew glanced over his shoulder at me. "You can't come in." Todd wiped his floury hands on his Pizza Wheel hoodie.

"I'm security," I said.

He sneered. "Oh, *you're* Gert's enforcer."

"I'm not Gert's enforcer."

"That's not what he says."

Even teenage Todd was mad at me now? "Was Gert here today?"

"What do you think? He told me I was breathing too close to the pizza. How am I supposed to slice the pizza if I'm not close to it?"

"I don't work for Gert."

He jammed his hands into the pockets of his hoodie. "And then he threatened us with a health code violation."

"Not my circus, not my monkeys." I looked around. "Where's Vittoria?"

"She had to go to the bathroom."

"Okay, thanks. And I don't work for Gert." I shut the door. Stomach growling, I studied the long lines. The sight made me irrationally annoyed. It was clear I wasn't getting food from here anytime soon.

Leaving the food court, I walked down a path lined with medieval-looking shacks. Vendors flogged colorful leather bags and candles, wooden toys and pottery. A jester ambled through the throng juggling colorful leather balls.

I stopped in front of the stage. Charlie and Fitch rearranged folding metal chairs in the audience section.

My brother waved. "Hey, Alice. How's security?"

"So far so good. Fitch, you got a minute?"

"Sure."

Charlie winked at me, and I ignored him. I didn't know what that wink was about, and I didn't want to know. The PI and I walked beneath the shade of a pine.

"You cheated," Fitch said. "You were supposed to get me a free ticket to the fair, but I get in free as part of the players."

"A free ticket's a free ticket. Don't whine."

He grinned. "Not a whine. Just pointing out a fact."

"Jane doesn't have an alibi for the time of Kristie's murder," I said. "Clyde does. Well, he says he does. I have to doublecheck with Gert he wasn't lying."

"The lack of an alibi doesn't make someone guilty. It makes them a suspect."

I clawed a hand through my hair. "This is out of control. I don't know what I'm supposed to be doing or how to evaluate evidence or anything." Being an MP in the Army had been loads easier. We got a call someone was up to no good, we scooped them up and let the Army lawyers figure it out.

He rested his broad hands on my shoulders. "Calm down. It's not rocket science. Aside from the surveillance tech, investigative techniques haven't changed much in the last century. It's still all about who has the means, motive, and opportunity to commit the crime."

"There's too much." I had too many suspects, too many possibilities. Also, his hands on my shoulders weren't exactly calming. I was close enough to notice the flecks of brown in his green eyes and his cedar and nutmeg scent.

"Now who's whining?"

Fitch wasn't wrong. I needed to get organized, write things down, make a list. Act like a detective, even if I didn't feel like one.

"No luck finding work in personal protection yet?" he asked.

"It's still too soon," I said.

"Why can't your old company throw you some work? They know the score. They know what went down wasn't your fault."

"It's complicated," I said shortly.

"So back to detecting 101. I'm assuming you've done your online research?"

"Yeah. It hasn't been all that helpful."

"It's too early to know what is or isn't helpful," he said with an air of maddening superiority. What made it particularly maddening was he was right. *Again.* "Document everything," he continued, "and corroborate what you learn."

Fitch released me and clapped my arm in a we're-just-buddies fashion. "Buck up. When all else fails, there's always going through your suspects' garbage."

"You're hilarious." There was no way I was going dumpster diving. If this was a common PI practice, I was glad my career was personal protection.

"Nope," he said cheerfully. "I wasn't kidding."

"Is that even legal?"

"The Supreme Court ruled that once the garbage has been left out for pickup, it's fair game."

"I need a better shredder." A pinecone thudded to the ground, and I twitched.

"And FYI," Fitch continued, "you just can't go onto a person's property to get the garbage. That's trespassing."

"So I have to wait for the garbage collection day."

"Exactly."

"That's Tuesday."

"Enjoy your weekend."

"Urgh." I stomped away, detoured at a pretzel stand, and returned to the security tent.

"Well?" Mrs. Malone asked from her position at the flickering monitors.

I licked a piece of salt off my upper lip. "All's well. Only minor injuries reported, and no crowd bottlenecks."

"And?" She scooted around in her metal folding chair to face me.

"Jane doesn't have an alibi for Kristie's murder," I said. "And Jed found one of the blackmail letters. It's in his car."

"Why doesn't he get it out of his car?"

"He's stuck working at the information booth until two."

She checked her watch and folded her arms. "Hmph."

Mrs. Malone glowered at me until ten minutes to two. Then she corralled another victim to stare at the video screens. The two of us marched to the information booth. A woman dressed like a scarecrow stepped inside it, taking Jed's place in the circular booth.

"Thanks Terry," Jed said to the scarecrow. "Mrs. Malone. How can I help you?"

"I'm here for that letter," she said.

He shot me a startled look. "You are? I thought Alice—"

"Alice is assisting me and Mr. Magimountain with our investigation."

I covered my face with one hand. Why had she included Gert in this? Now there was no way I was going to convince people I wasn't Gert's henchwoman.

"Okay," he said, drawing the word out. "Well, my car's in the parking lot."

"The staff lot?" she asked.

"No, I parked in the overflow lot. It's closer."

She sighed heavily. "Very well. Let's go."

We walked through the old-west vampire steampunk section. The vendor shacks looked fantastic, decorated with cobwebs and pumpkins and corn sheaves. People with top hats and goggles strolled about.

A Nautilus-shaped contraption the size of a minivan chugged past belching steam. It had a long nose like a jousting lance and was made of a brassy material, with prominent rivets. The Nautilus squealed to a halt, blocked by a crowd watching a duel between cowboys and vampires.

We sidled around the display and to the exit where I'd been pitched off the ladder. A spot prickled between my shoulder blades. I glanced around without appearing to.

No one seemed to be watching. The sensation could have been memory tension, left over from the attack on the ladder. Or it could have been something more.

Mrs. Malone pressed the handicapped button, opening the double gate. We continued through the exit. I stopped to make sure the one-way lock had latched behind us. Mrs. Malone didn't want people sneaking in without buying a ticket.

Jed pointed across the rutted dirt field and toward a lone Prius. "My car's over there."

I nodded. The overflow lot was only a quarter full. It was confirmation the crowds hadn't grown dangerously large, in case my counter at the gate was failing.

We walked toward the Prius. The gate squeaked open behind us, and I glanced over my shoulder. The steampunk Nautilus trundled slowly through the double gate.

"Where did you find the letter?" I asked Jed.

"It was crumpled in the garbage bin by Gloria's desk." He flushed. "I don't normally go through my wife's trash."

"You don't have to explain." Especially since I'd likely be going through *his* garbage this Tuesday. I really needed to get back to personal protection.

Hairs rose on the back of my neck. Casually, I glanced over my shoulder. The Nautilus bumped past a red van.

"You two go ahead," I said.

"My car's not much farther," Jed said.

"Why—?" Mrs. Malone turned and frowned at the Nautilus. "What's that thing doing out here?"

"Probably being taken to a trailer," I said as it approached.

She huffed an exasperated breath. "But the faire's not over. Vehicles and decor are not supposed to be removed from the grounds until after the faire is closed."

"Mrs. Malone," I said, "I think you should head to the car with Jed."

"I should never have left my post in the first place. I'm going back. Tell me what you find." She turned and stomped toward the high gates.

I folded my arms and squinted at the rolling contraption. It seemed to be headed roughly for me, though there were a few cars between us. Experimentally, I wandered to the left. The Nautilus turned, reorienting on me, and put on a sudden burst of speed.

"I insist you stop this instant!" Mrs. Malone stepped in front of the Nautilus.

I stopped short. How had she…? I jolted into a run. Making no sign of slowing, the Nautilus wheeled closer to her.

"Mrs. Malone, no!" What the hell was she doing?

The Nautilus rolled onward, and she stiffened, seeming to realize maybe standing in front of a moving vehicle wasn't the best idea. She dove aside, tumbling to the ground. I swore and raced toward her still form.

Mrs. Malone lay on the ground, her head beside a large stone, a trickle of blood oozing from her forehead.

Chapter Twenty-Five

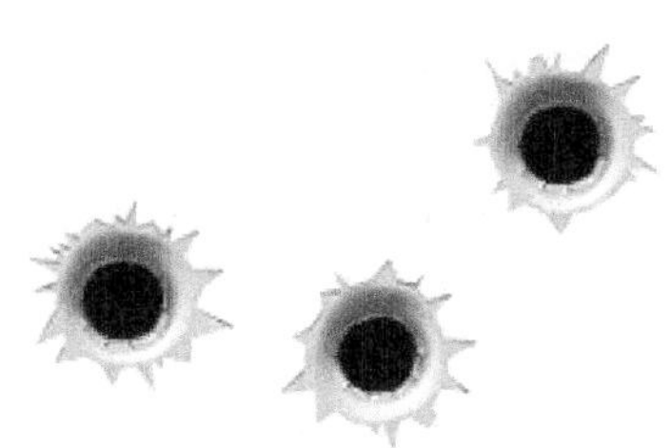

Mrs. Malone's eyes were shut, and she lay unmoving, and my heart thundered as I crouched beside her. The old lady groaned. I buckled, my knee hitting the ground. She was alive. She was alive and conscious.

"Lie still." Mouth dry, I skimmed my hands over her body again, confirming nothing was broken. The only injury seemed to be to her head, but that was bad enough. I swallowed my worry. "The EMTs are on their way."

Two men in blue uniforms jogged through the medieval gate and across the dirt lot. I was glad for the little comms radio I'd carried that had summoned them—the radio Mrs. Malone had insisted on.

"Is she all right?" Jed jogged toward us.

"She hit her head on a stone." And she was damned lucky that was her only injury. It was a miracle she hadn't been run down. I glanced toward the Nautilus on the opposite of the lot. "Did you catch the driver?" It had taken every fiber of self-restraint not to go after it myself. But I couldn't leave Mrs. Malone alone, hurt and vulnerable.

The actor winced. "Sorry. I caught up to it too late." He nodded toward the Nautilus, beside a stand of pines. "Whoever was driving it got away into the woods."

And Jed hadn't bothered going after him, because— My jaw clenched. This wasn't on Jed. "Why don't you get that letter?" I growled.

"Oh. Right." He bobbed his head and hurried toward his Prius.

The EMTs finally reached us, and I backed away. I watched them work over Mrs. Malone and managed to keep myself from interrupting them with questions.

Grouchy or not, Mrs. Malone was a good person. She'd taken care of Charlie and me when our mother had gotten sick. At the time, I'd resented it, had just wanted to be home. It was only as an adult that I'd appreciated what she'd done. And I was going to catch whoever'd done this.

A paramedic glanced over his shoulder at me. "How long was she unconscious?"

"A minute or two," I said tightly. "She came to right after I radioed it in."

He nodded. "We've called in an ambulance. Looks like a possible concussion, and at her age—"

"My age?" Her eyes flew open. "Just how old do you think I am?"

My shoulder sagged. She was arguing. That was a good sign. Being *awake* was a good sign.

"The letter's gone," Jed shouted across the lot. "Someone broke into my car."

"Are you *kidding* me—?" I clamped my mouth shut. Of course it was gone. Of course someone had taken it. Because what made me think anything would go right today?

"There's nothing wrong with my age," Mrs. Malone said. "I'm perfectly fit. I take ballroom dancing class twice a week."

"I'll be right back." I strode toward the Prius.

"They broke a window." Jed motioned toward the glass glittering on the earth and across the seats.

"Who knew you were showing us the letter today?" I photographed the broken window with my phone.

He clawed both hands through his thick, brown hair. "No one. Who would I tell?"

"When's the last time you were at your car?"

"When I got here this morning."

So the break-in could have happened any time. I pulled the radio from my belt. "I'll call the cops. There's a deputy around here... somewhere. Wait here."

I walked toward the abandoned Nautilus and radioed the security desk. They patched me through to the deputy. "We need you in the overflow parking lot," I said. "There's been a car break-in."

"I'm kind of busy right now." His voice crackled. "Someone stole a... Nautilus?"

"The Nautilus is here, in the overflow lot. It was used in a hit and run." I paced the circumference of the steampunk contraption. A door was open in its side. Three low, metal steps extended to the ground.

"Got it," the deputy said. "I'll let the owner know. And I'll be there in five. Out."

I peered inside, keeping my hands close so I wouldn't accidentally touch anything. Colored lights lit an interior panel, but it was obvious they were for show. The Nautilus seemed to be controlled by nothing more glamorous than a steering wheel and pedals.

I took photos of the interior, but I didn't see anything clue-like. I studied the ground around the metal stairs. It was something I probably should have done before walking on it. But the earth here was hard packed, and I didn't see any footprints, not even my own.

Scanning the dirt, I walked into the stand of pines. No helpful gum wrappers or cigarettes had been left behind in the tall, dried grass beneath the trees. I continued onward, until I emerged at a trail that I knew wound around to the front parking lot.

Frustrated, I returned to the overflow lot. An ambulance had arrived, and a protesting Mrs. Malone was being loaded inside. A deputy stood beside the Prius. He scribbled in a notepad and spoke with Jed.

"Alice!" Mrs. Malone waved me over. "Did you catch the driver?"

The paramedics paused, her gurney halfway inside the ambulance.

"No," I said. "But the Nautilus had been stolen."

"Naturally," Mrs. Malone said. "None of the faire participants would have been so reckless." Her face turned gray, and her head thumped to the thin pillow. "Find out who stole that Nautilus, and you'll find our killer. Mark my words."

"We really need to go," one of the blue-uniformed paramedics said. He pushed the gurney deeper into the ambulance. The other paramedic hopped inside with Mrs. Malone.

"I'll meet you at the hospital," I said.

"Forget the hospital," Mrs. Malone said. "You'll finish working at the faire."

I almost smiled. Even possibly concussed, I'd swear she'd slipped in that silent *e*.

"And find that thief," she finished as the paramedic outside closed the doors on her. He retreated to the driver's side of the ambulance.

The ambulance bumped across the lot, dust pluming from beneath its tires. A hollow ache pierced my ribcage. Personal protection only worked if you stayed close to the person you were protecting. I hadn't. But I hadn't thought Mrs. Malone would step in front of a careening Nautilus either.

If she had a concussion—and if she'd been unconscious then she probably did... I kicked a loose clod of dirt and swore.

The Nautilus rolled toward me. I stepped in front of it and waved, and it came to a halt. I walked to the door.

It popped open. A Santa Claus of a man with a thick white beard, brown top hat, tweed suit and spats, leaned out. "Thanks for finding my Nautilus," he said over the droning engine.

I shook my head. "It was used in an attempted hit and run. Do you mind waiting here for a bit? I want the deputy to look it over."

"A hit and run?" His bushy brows lifted. "Good heavens." The vehicle's low hum died.

"Where exactly was your Nautilus stolen from?" I asked.

"Near the bathrooms. I'd left my key in it when I went inside to use the gent's." His cheeks flushed pink. "I should have known better."

"The thief knew it didn't belong to him. You didn't do anything wrong. I'll be right back."

I walked to the Prius and caught the lanky young deputy's eye. He closed his notepad and slid it into the inside pocket of his thick, near-black jacket. "I think I've got everything I need."

"Will I get a police report for my insurance?" Jed asked anxiously.

"Just call the station." He turned to me. "Hey, Ms. Sommerland. I saw the ambulance. What happened?"

"The person who stole the Nautilus tried to run me down. Mrs. Malone got in the way."

"It hit her?" The deputy's brows slashed downward.

"No, she jumped out of the way and hit her head on a rock."

"So there was no actual contact."

"Does it matter?" I snapped. "It was an attempted hit and run."

"No contact, no evidence, no indication for sure that it was intentional. I mean, it's still a stolen Nautilus and leaving the scene of an accident, but it matters."

I glanced at Jed, who stared mournfully at his broken window. "This may be connected to the murders of Gloria Jackson and Kristie Naysmith," I said more quietly.

"Like, a conspiracy?" The deputy's eyes widened with undisguised delight.

Mine narrowed. "Not like a conspiracy." Whenever someone used that word around me, nothing good followed.

The deputy shrugged, the stiff fabric of his jacket rustling. "I'm just saying, the parallels are interesting. Last summer, your client Toomas Koppel, who everybody expected to have bombshell testimony, gets conveniently killed in a car crash. You insist it was only an accident." He put the last two words in air quotes. "And now, a car *accident* nearly takes you out, and you say it's not an accident, it's connected to a murder."

Him too? Sure, I'd resigned myself by now to everyone knowing the story. I just didn't understand why they felt so free to throw it in my face. "I think you should get this in the police record," I said stiffly. "The detective in charge may want to investigate further."

"Oh, right. Don't worry about it."

"The driver's over there." I pointed at the waiting Nautilus and strode away, irate.

The restrooms where the Nautilus had been stolen weren't far from the old-west vendor stalls, but they were out of their line of sight. I interviewed the stall-owners anyway.

A woman wearing a cowboy hat and a leather corset on the outside of her blouse folded her arms and glared. "You're *Gert's* security, aren't you? He told me you might come around."

For pity's sake... "I don't work for Gert."

"There's no law that says I have to have calorie counts printed on my cocoa blends." She motioned angrily toward the rows of shiny brown paper bags.

"I don't care about your cocoa." Though I was a fan of all forms of chocolate. "I'm working for the fair, and I'm trying to figure out who stole that Nautilus. Did you see anything?"

She scowled. "I saw it parked in front of the restrooms, and then it wasn't parked in front of the restrooms."

"And you didn't notice who was driving it?"

"Have you *seen* that Nautilus? You can't see who's inside it."

"Okay. Thank you."

I interviewed the other nearby stall owners. None had seen anything. All had had Gert encounters. He'd told the vendors I'd be making sure they toed his imaginary lines, and he'd actually *described* me. The phrase *blond amazon* had been used.

Fuming, I returned to the security tent. What had gotten into him? Gert had fled the Soviet Union. He'd helped others escape. Now *he* was acting like a dictator. It seemed totally out of character.

But that wasn't what really bothered me as I sat studying the bank of computer monitors. I'd let Mrs. Malone get hurt. The attacker had gotten away. I'd tried to be a detective, and because of it, I'd failed at the one thing I was good at—protection.

Chapter Twenty-Six

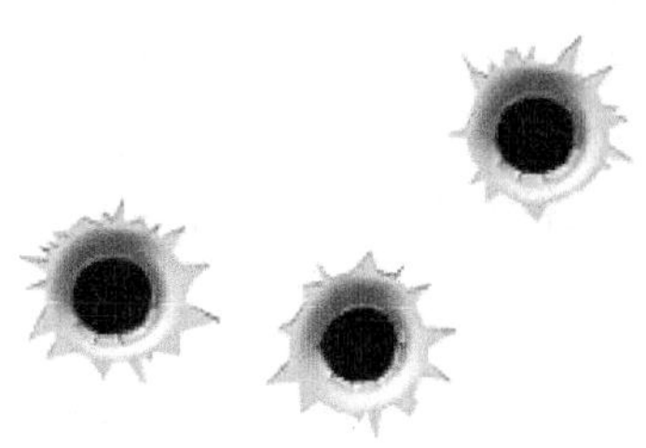

I could hide in the fair's security tent and sulk, but I couldn't avoid the problem. My so-called investigation was a disaster. Plus, the ripe odor in the tent was starting to make my eyes water.

A movement on one of the monitors, a tightening of the crowd, caught my eye. I studied the screen more closely.

Gert stood in the center of the throng and gesticulated. People dressed like cowboys and vampires surged closer. They didn't look happy, and my stomach tightened.

I grabbed my radio off the desk. "Phil," I said to the volunteer sprawled in the folding chair beside me. "Keep an eye on screen D. I'm headed over there."

He yawned and scratched his flat stomach. "Problem?" Phil was a decent guy and an occasional bouncer for the speakeasy on Main Street. He was also massive and knew crowd control. But I wanted to suss out the situation before I brought him in. His size could also seem threatening and set things off.

"I'm not sure, but be ready to call in more security if I make the signal."

"What's the signal?"

I shot him the finger, and he laughed. Striding from the tent, I hurried toward the steampunk western section.

"Hey, Alice." Charlie jogged up to me, his medieval armor clanking. "Where're you going?"

"Steampunk western."

"I heard about Mrs. Malone." He adjusted the helmet beneath his arm. "Is she okay?"

I winced. I needed to get to the hospital. "She hit her head, but she was conscious."

"But she's an old lady. That could be serious."

"I know," I said shortly.

"So what are you doing here?"

"I don't know!" The question was starting to seem existential. What was I still doing in Nowhere? What was I *doing* in Nowhere? What was my point?

"Okay, okay," he said in a conciliatory tone. "Are you going to the hospital later?"

"As soon as the fair closes." And closing time couldn't come soon enough. We walked beneath a wooden entry and into the old-west village of shops.

"Can I come with you?" he asked.

I sighed and dodged a child on a dragon-shaped bicycle. "Yes."

"Cool. Uh, can we stop at your post office box on the way back?"

Shouting rose around the bend in the road. I hurried forward.

"Your sales tax license needs to be in a frame," Gert shouted. "It's not my rule. It's the state's." A mini-pumpkin flew past his ear, and he flinched.

"Hey," I shouted. A few people turned to glance at me. I tapped a black-cloaked vampire on the shoulder. "What's going on?"

"Revolution," the vampire growled.

"Oh, boy," I muttered. "Excuse me." I slithered through the crowd, meeting people's gaze and smiling. For most people, it's hard to attack someone who's looking you in the eyes and smiling. This makes it the second-best thing to do if you're caught in an angry mob. The first best thing to do? Make your way out of the angry mob.

I grasped Gert's shoulder. "Gert? What's going on here?"

He scowled. "It's only a picture frame."

"Okay," I said. "So what's the big deal? Forget about it."

"It's the rule." Gert folded his arms over his thick coat.

"He's a tyrant," a cowboy in a bowler hat and chaps shouted.

"*Sic semper tyrannis.*" The vampire waved his gloved fist in the air.

"Hold on, hold on." My brother made squeaky, pacifying motions. "I'm sure Gert had a good reason for what he did. Right Gert?"

Gert's jaw jutted forward. He looked like a petulant mule.

Charlie nudged him, his armor rattling. "Come on, work with me," he said out of the side of his mouth.

Gert cursed. "I can't just..." His mouth compressed. The old man leaned closer to Charlie and me, his gaze darting. "I'm trying to keep big brother off everyone's backs," he hissed. "There's going to be an inspector here tomorrow."

"That's..." I blinked. Gert's sudden turn to tyranny had never made sense. Unless... "Hold on. That business with the giant pizza cutter. Was an inspector coming to the Pizza Wheel too?"

Gert flapped his arms. "How should I know? But the county's threatening a full investigation of Nowhere's permits. Or lack thereof."

"Do you mean to tell me that all this time you've been hassling people, you've actually been giving them a head's up?" I asked, incredulous.

His blue eyes bulged behind their thick lenses. "Of course I have. You think I want to *help* the ineptocracy?" He spat.

For heaven's sake. "Did you *tell* these people an inspector's coming tomorrow?"

"I'm not supposed to know," he muttered.

I eyed him. How did *he* know? *Not important*. What was important was what to do next. We obviously couldn't tell the vendors, but—

"A state sales tax inspector's coming tomorrow," Charlie hollered. "No one's supposed to know."

A hush fell over the crowd, and then voices buzzed. Abruptly, the crowd disbursed.

Gert shook his head. "If the inspector finds out we told—"

"You think *they're* going to tell him?" I jerked my head toward a vendor shack selling clockwork toys.

"*Her*. The inspector's a woman." He clutched the wisps of hair at the sides of his head. "I hate this job. Government's a filthy business. It's just another form of organized crime. At least back in Estonia, if someone painted graffiti on your business, the mob boss you were paying protection to would take care of it. Here, they fine you if you don't clean it up fast enough. And don't get me started on county services. I don't even know what those bums do."

"Not policing," I muttered, dodging a woman pushing a stroller.

"What?"

"Nothing," I said. "I was just thinking we'd have been better off if the sheriff's department was a little more visible here at the faire."

"Aw, what do they know from faires?" Gert made a dismissive gesture. "They don't know what they're doing."

"They do," I said. "The problem is I don't. I should have stuck to what I'm good at: surveillance."

"You're right." Gert pointed a bony finger at me. "That's what my father always said. Stick to what you know. That's the first..." His jaw sagged, then formed an O. A delighted expression spread across his wizened face.

The hairs rose on the back of my neck. "What? What are you thinking?" As far as I knew, Gert had three specialties: ripping off tourists, smuggling people out of communist countries, and assassination. Actually, he'd never been very good at the latter, but *he* considered it a specialty.

He whipped off his glasses and polished them on the sleeve of his thick coat. "Nothing."

"No." Charlie shifted his helmet to his other arm. "You're definitely thinking something."

"Take the rest of the day off, Alice," Gert said. "I'll make sure the security tent is staffed."

"But—"

"That's an order." He marched away.

"You're not my boss," I shouted after him.

"You!" Gert bellowed at a popcorn vender. "Let me see your permit."

I gripped my hair. "Dammit. He's going into full Nero mode."

"Cool," Charlie said. "Now we can visit Mrs. Malone."

Exasperated, I glared at my brother. Now I wanted to stay at the fair just on principle. But I should visit Mrs. Malone.

We checked in at the security tent to make sure they could survive without me. Naturally, they could. None of us are as indispensable as we like to think.

Getting Charlie in his armor into my Jeep was all sorts of fun. Finally, he got inside, and my brother and I drove to the hospital. After I assured the nurse that no, Charlie didn't need an extraction from the tin-can he was wearing, we learned that Mrs. Malone was in stable condition but would have to spend the night. She was in the process of being moved to another room—a process that apparently took quite some time. So we weren't able to visit her.

I drove Charlie to the post office and waited in my Jeep while he clanked inside. My hands clenched and unclenched on the wheel. I'd been putting this off for too long.

Lifting my hip, I pulled my phone from the pocket of my jeans and called my ex-boss and ex-husband, Buck.

"Alice," he said warily. "What's going on?"

I forced a smile, hoping it would come through in my voice. "I was about to ask you the same thing. Any work for me yet?"

There was a long silence. "Sorry Alice... There's nothing right now. People are still wary after what happened with Koppel."

Hope sank in my gut. I swallowed. But *right now* wasn't forever. "That's got to die down at some point."

"Yeah, I'm sure it will. You're still my best surveillance operative. But..."

"But what?"

"I'm, uh, seeing someone."

"Congratulations." *And?*

"And she thinks... maybe it's not such a good idea if we work together."

Prickly heat washed over my face and neck. "I'm not calling you because I want to get back together," I snapped. "I'm calling you because the last job I had with you tanked my career."

"You're not blaming me for that?"

I pressed the phone against my forehead and mouthed a silent scream. Slowly, I exhaled. "No. I'm just saying, this isn't a social call."

"If we're being professional, then I wish you wouldn't call me anymore."

"Fine," I choked out. "I won't." I hung up and banged my head on the steering wheel. I'd humiliated myself. And I'd done it for nothing. This was worse than the mutton busting incident of my childhood. The rodeo lamb I'd been on top of had run away with me, and Nowhere was *still* talking about it.

The passenger door opened, and I snapped upright. "Got it." Charlie brandished a thick envelope. "Let's see if we're related to someone with a coat of arms." He dropped the file onto the arm rest between our seats. "You okay?"

"I'm fine."

He maneuvered into the Jeep. "You don't look fine."

"Buck told me to stop calling him. He's seeing someone and doesn't think he should give me a job." I started the Jeep.

"What? That's totally unfair. You'd still have a career in personal protection if it wasn't for that guy."

"I don't want to think about it." I pulled from my spot.

"But—"

"I can't fix this," I said. "So I don't want to think about it now. What'd you get?"

"Oh. Yeah." Charlie ripped open the manila envelope and pulled out a sheaf of papers. He flipped to the back of the pages. "Ha! I knew it!"

I drove into the street. "We're related to potato farmers?"

"Only if the potato farmers are Plantagenets," he said loftily and tapped the front of his armor. "Which they're not."

I frowned. "The Plantagenets?" We really were related to royalty? *Weird.* "Weren't they French?"

"Until they crossed the channel to rule England. So?"

"So, I thought we were Scandinavian on Dad's side and Polish on Mom's."

"Yeah, well, we probably are mostly." He flipped more pages. "It says we're Plantagenet on our paternal side. That's Dad."

"I know what paternal... Never mind. I guess Dad's genealogy work didn't go back that far."

"Yeah. I mean, he only had the internet. We've got access to DNA now." He flipped the pages forward. His brow wrinkled. "Huh."

"What?"

He looked up, his blue eyes guileless. "Huh?"

"Yeah, you said that before."

"Uh," he said, "can you take me back to the fairgrounds? I've got to meet Fitch for improv practice."

"Yes, I can." At last, something I was competent at besides surveillance, playing taxi driver. I turned the car, and back we drove to the fair, Charlie poring over his DNA results.

By the time we arrived, the sun had fallen behind the western mountains, and the fair's lights had switched on. Jack-o-lanterns with electric candles grinned from corners, and twinkle lights floated above the crowds.

Charlie clanked toward the stage. Realizing I didn't have anywhere else to be, I followed.

Fitch, in a jester's costume, sat on the edge of the stage, his belled shoes swinging. It was a little revolting that he even looked good dressed as a fool. "Ready?" he asked my brother.

Lilyanna, in a long gown and one of those pointy, medieval hats, emerged from behind the stage castle.

"Yeah." Charlie hopped onto the stage. "I've just got to have a quick word with Lilyanna before we start." He moved toward the back of the stage.

Lilyanna touched his arm. Charlie smiled and leaned closer to her. Alien abductions aside, Lilyanna was a nice woman. I hoped Charlie was waking up to that.

"I heard you had a Nautilus theft earlier." Fitch grinned.

I dragged my attention from my brother's possible love life. "It's not as hilarious as it sounds." I leaned against the stage beside Fitch. "The thief got away and tried to run down Mrs. Malone in the process."

Fitch sobered. "Is she okay?"

I shook my head. "I think so, but she's spending the night in the hospital for observation."

"Your body language says something else is wrong. What's going on?"

I laced my fingers behind my neck and squeezed. "Mrs. Malone's in the hospital. Kristie was killed. The evidence of Gloria being blackmailed was stolen..."

"Okay, back up. What evidence?"

I explained about Jed and the stolen letter.

The PI nodded. "You're onto something."

"Are you kidding? I'm not on to anything. I'm off the case I never should have been on in the first place."

"Yeah. Much better to leave it to professionals like the sheriff."

"Well." Why did that seem like an even worse idea? "Some homicide detective the sheriff's borrowing from Hot Springs, but yeah."

He crossed his arms over his broad chest. "Did the sheriff's department follow up on the stolen Nautilus?"

"They—He—Not really." The deputy hadn't seemed all that interested.

Fitch nodded again. "But of course you don't really know, do you? They could be following up in all sorts of ways. They just haven't informed you about it, because it's none of your business."

But it *was* my business. It was Mrs. Malone, and the theater, and Charlie, and I...

I knew who I was—part of Nowhere, God help me. And I wasn't a total amateur. I was surveillance professional and ex-Army MP. And I needed to be a part of fixing this. I straightened.

He lifted a single eyebrow. "Are you done feeling sorry for yourself?"

I thought about that. I thought about it some more. "Okay. I'm done."

"So what are you going to do about it?"

I hung my head. Because I knew where this was going. And I didn't like it one bit.

Trash collection.

CHAPTER TWENTY-SEVEN

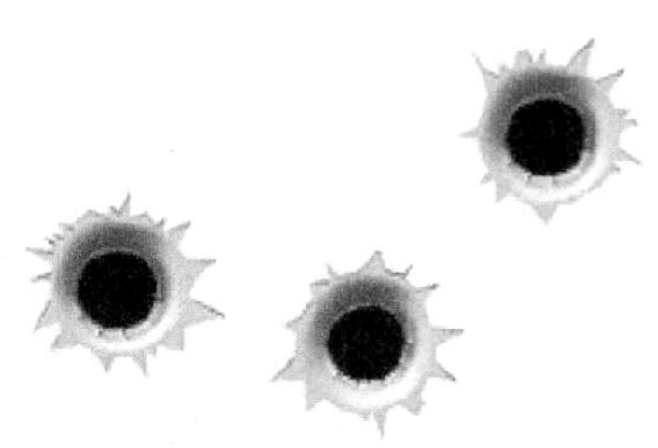

"I GOT THE GARBAGE." Phone to my ear, I leaned against my apartment's street window.

A tour bus rumbled into the bowling alley's parking lot opposite. Fredo and Sammie tumbled around at my feet. I wasn't sure if they were playing or trying to kill each other, but I'd learned from hard experience to stay out of it.

"Congratulations," Fitch said. "You are on your way to being a private investigator."

"Yeah, about that." I rubbed my chin. "Want to teach me how to analyze what I've found?" Mrs. Malone was out of the hospital and back on her feet. She'd called three times demanding more clues for her to unravel.

"Help you dig through trash?" He laughed. "No way."

"This would be an excellent training opportunity," I wheedled. "Since I am doing contract work for you, it would be nice to step up my game."

"Nice try. And tell Charlie thanks."

"For what?"

"He'll know."

"What about teaching me lock picking?" I asked, but Fitch had hung up.

"What's with all the garbage?" Charlie stood, nose wrinkling, inside the open door.

I'd left my door and windows open to improve the airflow. The bags of garbage on the wooden floor were pretty ripe. Even my boxing dummy looked disgusted.

"It belongs to my suspects," I said.

"Blech." He made a face. "You stole people's garbage?"

"Fitch said it's an investigative technique." I was starting to wonder if he'd been having me on.

"Cool," Charlie said. "Want help?"

Did I mention how much I love my brother? How many people do you know who will dig through garbage with you? That's the stuff that *counts*. "That'd be great."

Charlie dropped cross-legged onto the floor and opened a black garbage bag.

"Um, wait," I said.

I ran downstairs, grabbed a blue, plastic tarp out of the back of my Jeep, and returned to my apartment. I spread the tarp on the floor and put the garbage bags on top of it.

I pointed to the names of the people the bags belonged to, which I'd written on the bags. "We need to keep everything we find separate, so we know what belongs to whom." From my open micro-kitchen, I got a pair of rubber gloves and handed them to Charlie. I slipped another pair on my own hands.

"Everything?" Charlie asked.

"We also need to make sure we don't mix up any evidence we might find. If it's not evidence, it can go back in the bag."

He scrunched up his nose. "How do we know if something's not evidence?"

"We use our best judgment, I guess."

Charlie ripped open a bag and dumped its contents on the blue tarp. We recoiled, hands to our noses.

"The things I do for justice," Charlie choked out, and we began sorting garbage.

The first bag, belonging to Jed, was a bust. We opened another of his garbage bags.

"By the way, Fitch says thanks," I said.

"What?" Charlie tossed aside an empty soup can. "Oh. Right."

"Why'd you come over today?"

"What? Uh, I just had to pick something up from the theater, and thought I'd see if you were, uh, home."

I lowered my head, studying him. There'd been too many *uhs* in there. My brother was hiding something. I smoothed a piece of paper on the tarp. A shopping list. Crumpling it, I set the list in the reject pile. "Is that all?"

"I can't believe Jed's throwing this out." Charlie lifted up a rumpled fedora.

"Charlie."

He met my gaze. "Yeah?"

"What's going on?"

"Nothing." He shook his head, frowning. "Everything's great. We're going through garbage, looking for clues. The Sommerland siblings solving crimes."

I raised a brow but said nothing. Whatever it was, he'd tell me when he was ready. We finished that bag and moved on to the McGarrity's trash.

"Something kind of has been bothering me though," he said.

"Oh?"

"You said once that Mom told you to get out of Nowhere. That she hadn't been that happy here."

A gray, guilty feeling settled in my chest. "I shouldn't have said that. I probably misinterpreted what she'd told me."

"So it wasn't true?"

I grimaced. It had been true, but it hadn't been Charlie's childhood, it had been mine. Our mother had died when he was only six, and there were things I was glad he didn't remember. Her outbursts. Her rage. She'd never abused us physically, but I'd grown up in a sea of her anger. "She said it, but... I was young. I could have read more into it than was there."

"But she loved Dad."

"Of course she did."

"But... there were problems."

I pulled out a torn piece of glossy, colored paper and set it beside me. "No marriage is perfect. Why are you bringing this up?"

"Oh. Uh. No reason."

I found another torn piece of paper and fit it against the first. Scrabbing through the bag, I found six more pieces. They made up a tourist brochure for New Zealand.

"Find anything?" Charlie asked.

"No. Just a ripped-up brochure."

"Huh. This is a good picture." He lifted up a photo, its back to me.

"Who is it?"

"Jed. It's a picture of him and Jane. See?" He flipped it around so I could see.

In the photo, the two smiled, Jed's arm looped casually around Jane's shoulders. They were off center, the camera angled upward.

"Where'd you find that?" I asked.

A metal door clanged shut downstairs.

"Jane's bag," he said. "I wonder why she threw it out."

My pulse beat a little faster. "So do I." A *guilty conscience*? It was an innocent enough photo. But throwing it out made it seem like more.

"I'm sure it doesn't mean anything," Charlie said.

A metallic clang sounded from the kitchen below.

"But it might." I stood.

"You're not going to ask Jane about it?" Charlie said.

"Why not?"

"Because she didn't kill anyone."

I peeled off my gloves. "Charlie, it's possible any of these people killed Gloria and Kristie. In fact, it's probable."

"I know, but... It's not Jane. I mean, you know her. Do you really think she could kill her own sister?" he asked.

"There's a reason *fratricide* is a word."

"Huh?"

"Gloria was awful. So yes. She could have killed her own sister."

"Okay, but it's *Jane*."

"And it sounds like she's downstairs. Convenient." I strode past him and out the door.

"Wait—"

I walked down the stairs. Charlie clattered after me. "Wait. Wait. Let me talk to her."

"You? Ha. You don't want to ask her any hard questions."

"Well, no, but—"

I rounded the corner into the kitchen. Jane stood at a metal table, unloading grocery bags.

"Oh," she said, "hi. I was going to try out some recipes, and the kitchen here is bigger than in my apartment. You don't mind, Alice, do you?"

"Not at all."

"Alice was just... looking for a snack," Charlie said.

I shot him a look. There was no way I'd go hunting for food that didn't belong to me in the theater's kitchen, and Jane knew it.

"Then stick around," she said. "You can be my taste tester if you're hungry."

"Thanks," I said. "I actually wanted to ask you about—"

"Those cupcakes from the Halloween Faire were amazing," Charlie said. "Are you thinking of switching to baking?"

She planted her hands on her slim hips. "I might. I mean... Don't get me wrong, I love being theater manager. But it would be nice to do something that was my own."

"Like a cupcake shop," Charlie said.

"Or a tearoom," she said. "Though a cupcake shop would do well here with all the tourists coming through. I'm not sure what big thing you could put inside one though."

"World's biggest cupcake topper." Charlie motioned to the colorful sticks on the counter.

"Start-ups are expensive," I said.

Charlie stepped on my toes, and I glared at him.

"I know," she said. "But Gloria's death... It made me realize maybe I shouldn't put things off, you know? Maybe it's worth the risk." She looked at her sneakers. "Gloria knew how to take risks."

"And then there's Jed," I said.

She flushed. "Jed?"

"Jane, are you in love with Jed?"

Charlie groaned and turned away.

Her flush deepened. "I... He..." Her shoulders sagged. "Is it that obvious?"

"No," I said.

"It's not what you think," she said rapidly. "Jed doesn't even know."

"Did Gloria?" I asked.

She swallowed, her hands briefly clenching. "No, of course not."

But now Gloria was gone, leaving the field clear. And what about Jed? Had he really been so ignorant?

"And what about Kristie," I said. "Did she know?"

"Of course not." She laughed uneasily. "Why would Kristie care?"

And this was the hard part. But it was also necessary. "Because," I said, "I thought she might have been blackmailing you."

Chapter Twenty-Eight

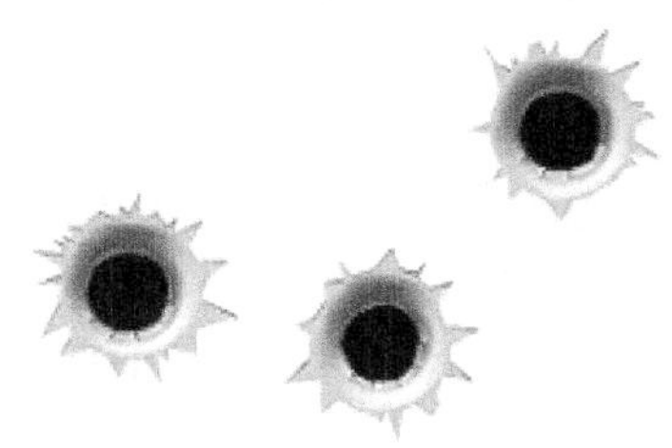

Jane's jaw sagged. Her mouth worked silently. She swayed and grasped the kitchen's shiny metal table.

"Whoa." Charlie hurried around the table and laid a hand on her bowed upper back. Her plain face was pale. Above, the kitchen's florescent lights hummed. "You okay?" he asked.

"You... You knew?" She gasped and steadied herself.

"I was pretty sure Kristie was the one blackmailing Gloria," I said. "She had the tech skills. Before Kristie died, she told me the black knight's costume could be found in a Reno costume shop. When I called the shop, they told me a woman had called pretending to be with the sheriff's department. She'd asked about a black knight costume. The caller had to have been Kristie. They told me who'd bought the costume."

"Who?" Jane said.

I shook my head. "The point is, they told Kristie too, but she didn't say anything. Why keep it secret? And why, weeks later, point me in the same direction?"

"She always liked stirring up trouble," Jane said bitterly.

"Who? Kristie?" Charlie said. "No. She was like the theater mom."

Jane gave a violent shake of her head. "Most people didn't see it. They only saw the mother hen. I only saw the mother hen, until..." She bit her bottom lip.

"Until she tried to blackmail you over Jed," I said.

She nodded.

"How'd she find out about your feelings for him?" I asked.

"She had a photo of us. I don't know how."

"Of *us*?" I asked sharply. "Was Kristie blackmailing Jed too?"

"No. He didn't know anything about it. And it wasn't Jed's fault. I was having a bad day, and he put his arm around me. It didn't mean anything. It was just a friendly hug."

"But it didn't look that way in the picture," I guessed. "Have you still got the photo?"

"I burned it."

"Where was it taken?" I asked.

"In Gloria's dressing room."

I nodded, remembering that e-reader propped against the dressing room mirror. The photo could have been taken by someone using the e-reader. If Kristie had been accessing Gloria's webcams, that made sense.

"I started to suspect Kristie when I saw that burnt drive in her fireplace," I said. "The killer must have put it there to destroy any other evidence Kristie might have saved."

"It wasn't Jed," Jane said.

"How can you be sure?"

She closed her eyes. "Because... Kristie was killed Wednesday morning, right?"

"It looks that way." The hard drive had still been smoking when we'd found her.

"Jed and I were together then."

"Whoa." Charlie stepped backward so fast he bumped into the counter opposite. "You said Jed didn't know you had a thing for him."

"He didn't then. And it's not like that," she said. "He was distraught after Gloria's death. Tuesday night, we went up to that lookout at the top of the mountain, the one where you can see California and Nevada. There was a meteor shower."

"The Orionids," Charlie said.

"Right," she said.

I shot my brother a questioning glance. Since when did he know astronomy?

"It peaks on the twentieth, twenty-first," my brother explained smugly. "We've got an astronomer in our MBS group. Just another reason to join..." he trailed off invitingly.

"We ended up staying there all night," Jane said, "watching the sunrise."

"Okay," I said. "That covers Tuesday night and early Wednesday morning. But Kristie could have been killed right before we arrived."

"And then Jed and I had breakfast at the Sagebrush," she said.

"There'll be witnesses to that," Charlie said.

"What time did you finish breakfast?" I asked.

"Around eight," she said.

"That's no good," I said. "Kristie could have been killed later."

"And then we went back to his place and made love."

"Oh," Charlie said. His arms went limp at his sides.

"I left at noon."

I pulled out my phone and called Jed.

"What are you doing?" Jane asked me.

"Getting confirmation from Jed before you can tell him what you told me."

"No," she hissed. "You can't."

"Hello?" Jed asked.

"This isn't cool, Alice," my brother said.

"Hi, this is Alice. After you had breakfast with Jane at the Sagebrush last Wednesday, what happened?"

Jane buried her head in her hands, her mousy hair falling forward. Awkwardly, Charlie patted her on the back.

Jed sucked in his breath. "Is Jane there?"

"I need to know where Jane was last Wednesday after the Sagebrush," I said. "And yes, she's here."

"We came back to my place. We, er, were together until about lunchtime. Why?"

"Thanks. That's all I need." I hung up. "He confirmed it."

"That's great." Charlie tilted his head. "I mean, not *great*, what with... you know. But—"

"I know." I avoided meeting Jane's gaze. They could have been in on the whole thing together and set up their alibi. Or they could be telling the truth. I thought they were, but I *wanted* to think that. "Did anyone see you at Jed's?"

Jane groaned. "Mrs. Peters saw me leaving. I told her this big story about helping Jed plan for the funeral, but I don't think she believed me."

"I know Mrs. Peters," Charlie said. "I repaired her banister. The flipper she'd bought her house from hadn't bolted it into a stud. She leaned on it too hard and ripped it right out of the wall last weekend. She'll talk to me."

"I have to... Excuse me." Jane fled from the kitchen. The heavy rear door slammed.

"I told you Jane and Jed didn't do it," Charlie said.

"Unless they're covering for each other."

"No way. Did you see how embarrassed she was? The killer has to be someone else. Who've we got left?"

"Clyde McGarrity. He said he lost the black knight costume, but that's not very believable."

Charlie picked up a unicorn-head cupcake topper, pointed it at me, and set it aside. "I don't really see Clyde as a killer. I mean, he's a pest, but he's not a killer."

"He was obsessed with Gloria."

"I really think he was more of a super fan than a stalker."

"Then there's Jane," I said.

He picked up a purple fairy topper and set it beside the unicorn. "But she has an alibi." He moved it away from the paper unicorn.

"Yeah," I said dryly, "from her lover, who happened to be the dead woman's husband. That's no alibi."

"What about Jed's neighbor, Mrs. Peters? She *saw* Jane."

"It depends on what time Mrs. Peters saw Jane leaving his house. Jane could have snuck away to kill Kristie and returned. And let's face it, she had plenty of motive. Gloria treated her like a servant. She was in love with Gloria's husband. And she had access. She was at the theater when Gloria was killed."

"We all were," he argued.

"Including Jed."

"Not a chance. I mean, look at Jed." Charlie picked up a knight cupcake topper and set it between the fairy and the unicorn.

All things considered, I wasn't sure Jed was knight material, but I didn't argue the choice. "Everyone says Jed was devoted to Gloria, but he's an actor. And he picked up with Jane soon enough after his wife's death. Maybe that was heartbreak, maybe he did love his wife. But don't you think he might have been a little too supportive of Gloria's burlesque model career? And with Gloria out of the way, the both of them can live the lives they wanted."

"I'm telling you, Jed didn't do it. I *know* Jed."

"*Someone* killed those women."

"Where was Clyde when Kristie was killed?" Charlie picked up the paper unicorn head and waggled it on its stick.

"He says he was at Gert's antique shop."

"We can verify that." Charlie dropped the unicorn, and it fluttered to the metal counter. "Come on."

We walked to the brick town hall. The shadow of the giant lawn flamingo fell across its entry. The dragon-lady inside told us Gert wasn't in. Charlie and I detoured toward the antique shop.

"I still can't believe Jed and Jane were cheating on Gloria," Charlie mumbled.

"They might not have been. They might have waited until after Gloria was gone."

"Still," Charlie said. "Why can't couples stay together? What's *with* everyone?"

"Everyone? It was just Jed and Jane." And me and Bud. But I wasn't going to think about that now.

"Yeah. Right." He kicked a pebble down the sidewalk.

"Are you okay?"

"Yeah. I was just, you know, thinking about Mom and Dad."

I shook my head. "Forget about it. They weren't cheating on each other."

Charlie stepped over the fake body lying beside the giant corkscrew. "How do you know?"

"What do you mean, how do I know? I just know."

"But you said they weren't happy."

"I said Mom wasn't happy." And I wished I'd never opened my big, fat mouth. "But she was a good person. She stuck around in Nowhere despite that, because she was committed to the family."

"Huh."

"Look," I said, "people go through things. No one's happy all the time. That doesn't mean they're weak or bad, it just means they're people. Where's this coming from?"

"Well. You see..." He cleared his throat. "So, the thing is—"

"Alice!" Jim, the owner of the Viking bar strode toward us glowering. The effect was somewhat diminished by his tunic and helmet. "You've got to do something about Gert. He—"

"After what happened to the last mayor," I said, cutting him off, "the county's auditing Nowhere. A raft of inspectors are coming in to look over every permit. They'll be reinspecting the food service businesses."

He paled. "Damn." A red Pizza Wheel van drove past.

"Gert's not supposed to know," I said, "and he's not supposed to tell. That's why he's been giving everyone a hard time."

He adjusted his horned helmet. "How'd *you* find out?" he asked me.

"I've got my sources. Better you don't ask. Look, Gert hates this even more than you do. The guy fled the Soviet Union. You think he wants to help the Man?"

His mouth puckered, and he blew out a low whistle. "Is this for real?"

"Yeah. Don't tell Gert I said anything. No one's supposed to know."

Charlie scratched his head. "But... isn't everyone supposed to know?"

"Yeah," I said. "So make sure they know they're not supposed to know."

Jim's expression cleared. "Got it. I'll get the word out."

I clapped the bar owner on the shoulder, and my brother and I moved on.

We stopped in front of the antique shop. A CLOSED sign hung in the window. I jiggled the door. *Locked.*

"Weird," Charlie said. "Could he be at the Sagebrush?"

"Maybe. I'm going to check around back."

"I'll try the diner."

We split up. I walked to the rear of the brick building and pulled open the door. "Gert?" I shouted down the cinderblock hallway.

"Bah."

I walked inside and into the shop. Gert hunched behind his dusty glass counter eating a burrito. A jackalope in a fierce pose reared on a shelf behind him.

"The word's going out about the inspections," I said.

"Ask me if I care. What's the point anymore?"

"The point is, you're going to save a lot of people a load of bureaucratic grief. I just can't figure out why you didn't tell them up front about what was going down."

He set his burrito on its paper wrapper. "Because someone would blab. There's always a blabber."

"I dunno." I leaned against the counter. "Small town like this... people will blab to each other, but not to some county inspector."

He shook his head. "You'll see. They'll blab, and I'll be out of the mayor's office in disgrace."

"Is that such a bad thing? I mean, think of your reputation."

Gert cocked his head. "My repu..." He sucked in a breath. "You're right. I've been trying all this time to be the good guy. I'm not the good guy. I'm the bad guy." He shook his fist at the dusty front windows. "Screw my reputation," he roared. "I'm Gert Magimountain, mob hitman."

I stared for a beat. "Right," I said slowly. "You do you. Hey, was Clyde here last Wednesday morning helping you with some internet thing?"

His lip curled. "Yeah. The goombah was here, sucking up to me. What's it to ya?"

"From about eight until noon?"

"Yeah."

"But you left him alone when you came to find me. He doesn't have an alibi."

Gert's eyes narrowed behind his thick glasses. "That's what you think. I checked my computer logs. He was working on my computer until about eleven thirty. I left him here when I went to find you."

I sighed. "Then I'm out of susp…" I trailed off. Because I *wasn't* out of suspects.

That knight costume. It had always seemed so childish. That's why I'd been resisting pegging Clyde or the knight as the killer, even after I'd seen the knight for myself.

I hung my head. How had I not seen it before? There was one other person who could have killed them both. Now I just had to figure out how to bring that person down.

Chapter Twenty-Nine

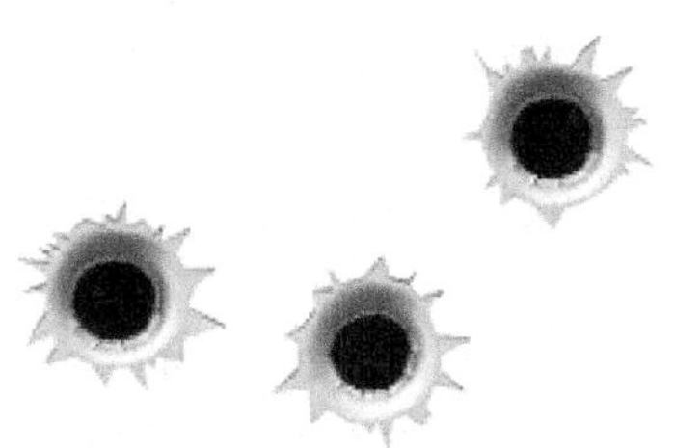

"Suspicion isn't evidence," Fitch said.

"I know that." Phone to my ear, I glared out my apartment window at the bowling alley. Above its roof, the flamingo seemed to wink. The eyepatch was playing tricks on me. "What I don't know is how to get the evidence."

"Here's a crazy thought. You could try surveillance."

"What am I supposed to be watching for?" I turned from the window. It was a perfect October morning. Or it would be, if there wasn't a killer in the theater. "Another murder to be committed? I mean, it's a little late for surveillance, isn't it?"

"See what you can dig up online—"

"Augh." I punched Bob. The rubbery dummy trembled. Sammie and Fredo looked up from the bed. "I've already done that," I said.

"Then do it again. This work takes patience."

But I was all out of patience. "Thanks," I said dryly.

The PI chuckled. "You know you love it. Poking into puzzles, digging into other people's lives. It's interesting."

"It's aggravating."

"Only until you've figured it out. Then it's better than—"

"Than what?" I asked.

"Never mind. Look, I'm kind of busy right now."

I exhaled heavily. "Right. Well. Thanks."

"Anytime." He hung up.

I flopped onto the bed, rumpling the quilt and jostling the animals. *Evidence, evidence...* I drummed my fingers on my stomach. Sammie extended a black paw and tapped my nose.

I sat up. "I'm going to shake some trees." Fredo barked. "Not literally. I'd bring you along if I was really shaking trees." Surveillance was a good idea, but I needed to inspire my killer to do something I could photograph and use as evidence. I called Clyde.

"Have you rethought the script idea?" he asked, breathless.

"I'm not even in the improv group. And it's *improv*. There's no script required."

He sighed. "Right. Then why are you calling?"

"Have you found your black knight costume?"

"No," he said. "I've looked everywhere for it. It's really strange."

Or maybe not so strange. "I do have something you might be interested in."

"Oh?"

"I found some burlesque photos of Gloria that were never posted online, never sold, as far as I can see. Oh hey, is this too early in the morning to call?"

"No, are you kidding? It's nearly ten. These photos—"

"Yeah, I asked Jed if he wanted them, but he wasn't interested. Do you want them?"

"Are you kidding?" He laughed shortly. "Of course I want them. Do you know when they were taken?"

"They look a few years old, professionally done, on photo paper."

"Wait," he said. "They're not digital?"

"No, is that a problem?"

"For burlesque, paper's even better," he said. "When can I pick them up?"

I crossed my ankle over my knee. "Yeah, the thing is, I had to invest a little cash to get these. Long story. I really need to recoup my money."

"Right, right. How much?"

I named a figure.

There was a long pause. "How many photos are we talking about?" he asked.

"Thirty-six."

There was an even longer pause. "I'll get the money, but it'll take me a day."

"Great. You know where to find me. Bye." I hung up. Fredo growled. "I know. I lied, and I'm a terrible person."

Sammie made a gagging sound. I pocketed my phone and stood. "You are *not* coughing up another hairball on my bed." My mother had made that quilt. She might have had issues, but she'd loved us.

I picked up the cat, carried him downstairs, and deposited him, protesting, outside. He shot me a sulky look, flicked his ebony tail, and strolled around the corner of the old-west building.

I stretched and walked to the front of the theater, facing the bowling alley. A golden aspen leaf skittered past, moving toward Main Street.

I walked past the bowling alley. It was a perfect October day. The leaf stopped its perambulations on the sidewalk, and I studied the tall, white aspens across the street at town hall. Their amber leaves clashed with the giant flamingo, but... What are you going to do?

"Hi, Alice!" The owner of the Viking bar strode down the opposite sidewalk and waved at me.

I waved back. "Morning, Jim."

"The word's out," he shouted and pressed a finger to the side of his nose.

I nodded. Maybe Gert would get some relief now.

The owner of the knit shop opened its door and set out a bowl of water for any thirsty dogs. She adjusted the pumpkin beside it, straightened, arched her back, and noticed me.

The older woman smiled and waved. I waved back, and she returned inside.

Up and down the street, doors were opening. People were saying hello to each other. And despite of the morning chill, a warmth blossomed beneath my ribs, and a sensation of...

I frowned. *Contentment*. I hadn't felt it in a long time, so I hadn't recognized it right away. A tour bus drove past me and pulled into the theater's parking lot. The doors squealed open, and tourists emptied out, chattering.

I pocketed my phone and checked my watch. Maybe I'd grab brunch at the Sagebrush. I crossed the street. In front of the pizza parlor, I paused.

The sign in the window said CLOSED, but I tugged on the doorknob anyway. Through the dark glass, I thought I saw movement, and I knocked. After a minute, Todd opened the door.

"Oh, hey. What's up?"

"Hi. Is Vittoria here?"

The teenager shook his head, a shock of brown hair falling into his eyes. "Nah, she doesn't work on Wednesday morning. Want me to leave her a message?"

"No, that's okay. Thanks."

"Hey, I'm, uh, sorry I gave you a hard time at the fair last weekend." His cheeks darkened. "I was out of line."

"It's okay. Everyone was stressed." In a small town, holding a grudge was a loser's game.

His shoulders sagged. "Thanks. See ya."

I continued on. At the stationary shop, I stopped to check out the Halloween decorations in its window. Jane bustled toward me, a bag of groceries in her arms.

"Morning, Jane," I said.

She stopped and blew a tendril of brown hair out of her eyes. "Oh. Hi, Alice. I was just headed to the theater to do some more practice baking, if you don't mind."

"It's not my kitchen. I've got no right to mind."

She shifted the bags in her arms. "Where are you off to?"

"Sagebrush." I folded my arms. "I found some more burlesque photos of Gloria. Jed wasn't interested in them. Do you want them?"

"Oh. No. I don't... I really don't... No."

"Okay. I was thinking of selling them to Clyde."

"Selling?" Her eyes widened behind her glasses.

"He's caused the theater so much trouble, the least he could do is make a forced donation to the pizza fund."

She laughed. "That's not a bad idea. Actually, I've ordered for the actors pizza before the performance tonight." She frowned. "Autumn wants hers with no cheese. She says dairy's trouble for her vocal chords."

"But I'll bet Fitch has no problem with it."

"He's wonderful. It's too bad he's going to have to drop out."

"Is he?" Had he lost interest in the groupies already?

"He says it interferes with his work." She shook herself. "But I've found someone new to take his place, so all's well that ends well."

"Okay, well I'll see you later then." I started to move off.

"Alice... Those pictures..."

I turned. "Yeah?"

She shook her head. "Never mind."

Chapter Thirty

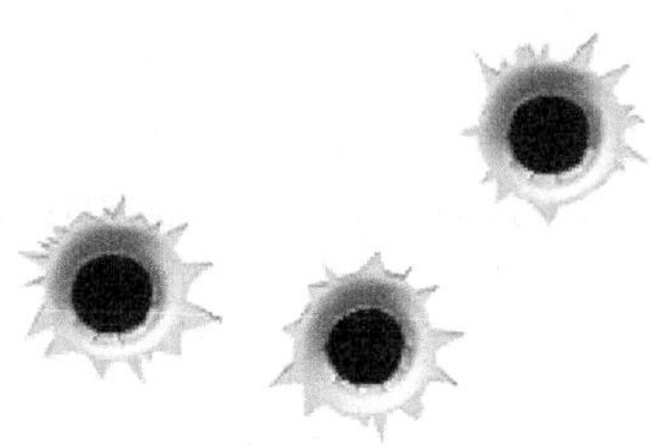

Small towns had this stereotype about everyone knowing everyone else's business. It was for good reason. Some secrets did get kept. But in the case of my non-existent photos, I was counting on word getting around.

I sat at the Sagebrush's counter beside the elder Mr. Washington, aka gossip central. Telling him about the photos was the quickest way I knew for my killer to find out. And then I could give the news a few hours to spread before I spent the rest of the day on surveillance.

"Thanks for telling me about those burlesque photos," I took a bite of my breakfast burrito. Normally I'd just go for the oatmeal, but it was brunch. I was doubling up.

He sipped his coffee. "My nephew helped you out?" The front door opened, and the paper bats above his head danced in the breeze.

"He did. Once I knew what to look for, I found a bunch more."

"They got anything to do with her murder?" he asked.

"I'm pretty sure of it." I shoved aside a dollop of sour cream with my knife. "Well, the ones you told me about did. The new ones I found are going to the theater."

His brow wrinkled. "How so?"

"I'm selling them to Clyde, and the theater will get the proceeds."

"Jed's okay with that?"

I shrugged. "He said he didn't want 'em." And I wasn't sure what I'd do if Jed turned up to tell me he *did* want them. But I figured he was working at the hotel in *The* Hot Springs and wouldn't hear about them right away.

"Hey, Alice?" Charlie came to sit on the empty stool next to me. "Um, can we talk?"

"Sure. What's up?"

My brother raked a hand through his thick blond hair and blinked rapidly. "Ah." He rubbed his beard. "I don't know how to say this, so... I'm just going to come out and say it." He swallowed.

"What'd you do? If you did something to my new Jeep—"

"No, it's not your car."

"Then what?" I swiveled my barstool to face him.

"Sometimes you believe what people tell you to believe, because there's no reason not to believe it. And then, you learn none of its true."

I massaged my forehead. "Charlie, what are you talking about?"

He raised his hand, dropped it. "Dad wasn't my dad," he said quietly.

"Excuse me?"

"That DNA test." He braced one elbow on the counter and leaned close, voice low. "Dad's not my dad."

What? Where'd he get that idea? I shook my head. "That's crazy. There's a mistake."

"That's what I thought. I called the company and had them doublecheck. There's no mistake."

"No," I said, "there is a mistake, they just don't want to admit it. Of course Dad's your dad."

"No, he's not. Some guy in *The* Hot Springs is. Gross, right?"

"Wait. You *know* who the guy is?"

"Yeah. I guess one of his kids took the test or something too..." He drew a long breath. "So. I guess I'm really your half-brother."

I stood and slapped my money on the counter, appetite gone. "No, you're not. Dad's your dad, and you're my brother. The DNA company screwed up."

Old Mr. Williams sat frozen on his counter stool, his coffee mug raised to his mouth. His gaze ping-ponged between us.

"I don't know," Charlie said. "I think these companies are pretty good."

I shoved aside my plate. "This is bull," I told Charlie. "Your father is my father." This was ridiculous. I didn't care what the DNA place said. It was a mistake.

I glanced at Mr. Williams. His coffee mug hadn't budge. This DNA business was going to be all over town by noon, and it was just a dumb mistake.

Unless it wasn't.

"It *is* ridiculous, isn't it?" I said, less certain, to the elderly man.

Mr. Williams blinked rapidly. "I don't... Uh... Are you really asking, or do you just want me to tell you what you want to hear?"

"What do you know?" I demanded.

"Well, there was that time when your mother took a part-time job in Hot Springs, while you were in school. How old were you?"

"Fourth grade," I said. "She quit when..." When she'd become pregnant with Charlie. My mouth went dry. "It doesn't mean anything." This was crazy. The test couldn't be right.

"I think we should find out," Charlie said.

"What do you mean, find out?" I asked.

"Go talk to this guy, my father. Maybe my father, I mean. Ask him if he knew her."

I braced my hands on the counter and stared at the remains of my burrito. No. No. It had to be a mistake.

I rubbed the back of my neck, the muscles twitching beneath my skin. Slowly, my brain started to get a handle on the information. It might be true, or it might not. But if this had knocked me sideways, what had it done to Charlie? He was my brother. That would never change. But if I'd found out I had a different father...

I'd want to know more. A chasm opened in my stomach. I swallowed. "If that's what you want, yeah. Let's talk to him. Just, maybe not today. We need to think about the best way to do this."

"Yeah. Sure." Charlie's head jerked up and down. "I don't want to be all weird around him."

"It's going to be weird no matter how we play this," I said, my voice brisk, professional. "Have you checked this guy out yet?"

"No. I know he's from *The* Hot Springs, but that's it."

"Okay. Why don't you give me his info, and I'll see what I can find?"

"Cool. Thanks." He stared at his shoes, then looked up. "Hug it out?"

I smiled. "Yeah."

We stood and hugged. He handed me a scrap of paper. "Here's what I've got on him."

"This'll help. Thanks."

He hesitated, then pulled me into another rough hug. "Love you, Sis."

A fist tightened around my heart. "Yeah. You too." I watched him leave the diner.

"What are the odds you'll keep quiet about this until I can confirm it?" I said without looking at Mr. Williams.

"You wanted this kept quiet? But I already texted Rich and Bill."

I sighed and shook my head.

Sweating, I staggered to a halt beside a picnic bench beneath a pine. I braced my hands on my thighs and breathed heavily.

Fredo dropped to the ground beside me. The discount cemetery extended below us, its tombstones like chipped teeth.

I pulled my water bottle and a folding bowl from my hip pack and poured water into the latter for Fredo. He lapped it eagerly. I swigged the remaining water and sat on the bench. I'd needed the run to clear my head. It still wasn't clear, but I felt better.

I tried to swallow and found I couldn't. If my mother had cheated... Well, my childhood made a lot more sense. But I still didn't want to believe she had. In spite of what I'd told Charlie about no marriage being perfect, this was...

I shook my head. This wasn't the mother I'd remembered. I pulled out my phone and called Fitch.

"Hey," he said. "I was just going to call you."

"What's up?"

"Uh, you go first."

"There's someone living in Hot Springs I need to check out," I said.

"And you want to know how? Just look him up online."

"I need a real background check. Details. I'll pay for it."

"Is he a suspect?"

"No." Heat raced up my neck and into my cheeks. "He... It's a personal matter."

"Okay. Text me his info. I'll see what I can find. Is that it?"

Relieved, I bowed my head. He hadn't pried. *Yet.* But I knew his curiosity would get the better of him eventually. "After due consideration, I'm going on surveillance in about an hour."

"And you needed my permission?"

"No, a lot of my witnesses are going to be at the show tonight, but I can't keep an eye on them all. I don't think the killer will try anything there, but it would be nice to have some backup."

"Why would anyone try something at the theater?" His voice sharpened. "What did you do?"

"I put it out that I've got more photos of Gloria, and I'm selling them to Clyde."

He groaned. "Goading the killer is not how PIs work."

"Yeah, here's the thing. I'm not a PI. All I've got are a lot of ideas and no hard evidence."

"There's no such thing as hard—I'm in Henderson on a case."

My hand clenched on the phone. What was he doing way over there? "That's seven hours away!"

"Yeah. I'm not sure if I'm going to be back tonight. I was actually wondering if you could take over for me at the theater."

Eyes squinched shut, I smacked my free hand on the top of my head and crunched my hair. *Okay. New plan.* Surveillance tonight was off. I'd just focus on protective detail for everyone at the theater. And I needed Clyde there too.

I exhaled slowly. "Sure. No problem." Whether I liked it or not, I was on my own.

"And there's only evidence," he said. "There's no such thing as *hard* evidence. Consider that PI lesson as thanks for taking over tonight."

"These nuggets of yours are pure gold."

"I should write a book."

But maybe there was a way he could help. We talked some more, and then we hung up.

"I saw that biscuit with Tommy in the garden. I saw that biscuit in the Tommy... biscuit with Tommy in the garden," I muttered. I paced behind the red velvet curtain. A table with leftover pizza stood just off stage, but I could still smell the pepperoni.

The players rarely used the actual stage. They preferred to mingle with the guests around their tables. So it was a good place to be alone and practice. The beads on my dress shimmied with my movements. The chatter of the crowd on the other side of the curtain grew.

Charlie stormed across the stage in his white suit and eyepatch. "There you are. Clyde's in the audience. He said you got him a ticket." A blot of tomato sauce darkened one corner of his mouth.

"Yeah. We need to keep an eye on him tonight."

"That won't be hard. He's not going to leave any of us alone. Thanks a lot."

"Forget Clyde. I've got enough problems with this twenties slang. I'm going to screw it up again. And you've got tomato there." I pointed.

He wiped it away with one finger. "Thanks. And it might have helped if you'd been here earlier. I told you I'd practice with you."

"I was busy," I said evasively. My lead suspect hadn't done anything suspicious. It was demoralizing.

His expression softened. "Look, you know who did it. You know the clues that you have to tell the guests. Just say them. Forget the slang. Pretend you're talking to a friend."

"I'm not an actress," I wailed.

"You've got three clues to give out in the first set. What are they?"

"Lilyanna's character was in the garden with Tommy. You killed a man in Reno, according to rumor. And I'm convinced the maid stole my pearl necklace, though I have no proof."

"Okay. Good. Now all you have to do is remember the names of our characters."

I sighed. "I know."

He clapped my shoulder. "You got this."

"I got this."

He hurried off stage.

"Now." Vittoria emerged from behind the curtains in her red, Pizza Wheel apron. "Give me those photos." She aimed a Walther PPK semi-automatic at my chest.

My chest spasmed inward, like I'd actually *been* punched with a bullet. On the bright side, I hadn't been. Also on the bright side, I no longer had to worry about protecting anyone else. Just me. Plus, I'd been surveilling the right person this afternoon.

"Ah… Photos?" My voice cracked.

I'd thought it would be nice to be right. Vittoria had had access to the black knight costume. Vittoria had reason to hate the woman who'd ruined her dreams of a hobbit-filled vacation. But I wasn't feeling a whole lot of satisfaction right now.

"Don't play dumb," she said. "Where are they?"

"They're upstairs, in my apartment." Where I had weapons hidden in all sorts of locations. Though I hadn't really thought she'd try anything here, this wasn't going to be a replay of the dentist situation.

I exhaled slowly, my pulse slowing. This would be fine. I hadn't planned it this way, but I was good with weapons.

She nodded. "All right. Let's go."

Yes! I had her. I *had* her.

The velvet curtains swooshed open. My stomach torpedoed downward.

Dozens of costumed audience members stared up at us from their tables. And there was no way I could protect them all.

Chapter Thirty-One

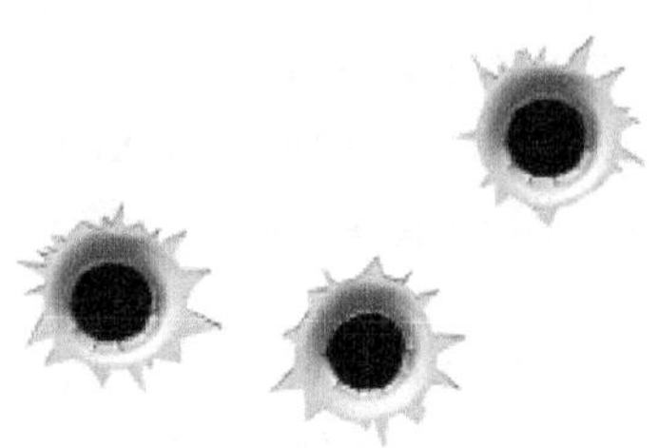

The audience burst into applause.

My mouth went dry. God help me, I wasn't sure if my thumping heart was down to stage fright or to having a gun trained on me. This was worse than the Reno dentist. This was just me, Vittoria and her PPK, and a room full of innocent civilians.

Black spots danced before my eyes. I was panicking. *Stop panicking. Breathe.*

Looking uncertain, Vittoria shifted her weight. But the nine-millimeter she trained on my chest didn't waver. The applause died.

I breathed. "You killed two women, Vittoria," I said using my outdoor voice. "Are you really going to shoot me in front of all these people?"

A chair clattered in the audience. I didn't look its way. Neither did Vittoria. "Kristie didn't give me any choice," she hissed.

"Because she was blackmailing you? She'd hacked into Gloria's e-book webcam, the one she kept in her dressing room. She had you on video putting the poison into Gloria's pineapple juice, didn't she?"

"Web cams aren't 1920s," a woman in the audience said.

"Who's Gloria?" a male guest in a fedora shouted.

"She worked here, at the theater," I told him. "Vittoria's husband, Clyde, was Gloria's biggest fan. All Vittoria wanted was to get out of Nowhere and visit the Hobbit houses in New Zealand. But Clyde spent their vacation money on burlesque photos of Gloria. Instead of killing her husband, she killed Gloria."

"That doesn't seem fair," the man said.

"Move," Vittoria hissed. She motioned with her handgun toward the other side of the stage.

"He wouldn't be spending any more of their money," said a buxom blonde in a beaded headband.

"I was confused," I said, "because I thought another one of the people in the theater had done it. But Vittoria was here that night, delivering pizza for the cast, just like she did tonight."

Charlie stepped onto the stage. My stomach dropped to the molten center of the earth. What was he doing?

"The Pizza Wheel is having a two for one special if you go *right now*," Charlie said. "We'll wait."

A few audience members laughed. I didn't. I wanted to kill my little brother. But at least Charlie was thinking of the guests' safety. He'd come up with a plan to get them out. It had failed, like most of Charlie's plans, but he was still a step ahead of me.

"How'd she kill Kristie?" the blonde shouted.

"And who the hell's Kristie?" Her companion laughed.

I glared at Charlie. *Go away*. Jane, standing in the wings in a shapeless gray dress, shook her head, her eyes wild.

"Kristie was another actress," Charlie said. "She pretended to be a mother-hen type character, but she was a skilled techie and a blackmailer. Vittoria somehow slipped her poison. Then she ran her through with my brother's short sword to try to throw suspicion his way… and at her husband. I imagine she smuggled it from the theater in one of her extra-extra-large pizza delivery containers."

"Wait, you said her husband is Clyde?" A redheaded woman in the audience flipped through her program. "I don't remember a Clyde in this show."

"Right," I said. "He'd bought a black knight's costume with more of their vacation money. Vittoria was furious. He put it away, meaning to return it. But she took the costume, seeing a way to come and go from the theater in disguise."

"Why would she want to do that?" the redhead asked.

I flicked my fingers, motioning my brother off stage. So, of course he ignored that and walked toward me instead. My jaw clenched so hard it ached. *Charlie.*

But my brother wasn't as relaxed as he must have appeared to the audience. Where I was standing, I could see the tautness of his muscles, the stiffness in his step. Behind the velvet curtain, Jane pointed toward the ceiling and grimaced.

"She was looking for a way to kill Gloria," I said and took a step toward Vittoria. "Eventually, she found it. By that time, the entire cast was freaked out by the black knight, and the costume was no good anymore. But all she had to do was wait for the next pizza order to get inside unobtrusively."

I met her gaze. "You switched to a werewolf when you attacked me at the fair." That was why her face had been so red in the Pizza Wheel booth. She'd been moving fast—running and getting out of the costume. She'd probably had it stashed behind the door.

"Hold on," the blonde said. "Aren't *we* supposed to be solving the murder? If you tell us who did it—"

"It's post-modern." A narrow-faced man at the next table leaned toward her. "Time has no meaning. Just go with it and see where it takes us."

"It's very confusing," she complained.

"Why'd you break into Jed's car?" I asked. "How'd you even know he had copies of Kristie's blackmail letters?"

"I didn't," she said. "I saw him park in the lot that morning. He kept fiddling with the lock and checking something on the seat. The way he was acting, like it was important, I was curious. After he left, I looked in the window and saw that file.

I thought he might have something, some evidence about... Something. So I broke in and took it. I didn't know what it was until I'd gotten to my stall."

The red van I'd seen in the overflow lot. It must have belonged to the Pizza Wheel. "And later you left Todd in charge and stole a Nautilus?" I asked, disbelieving.

"I was on lunch break. You were there, the Nautilus was there..." She shrugged. "I wanted you to back off. And I was sick of Gert and Mrs. Malone hassling me about bracing that pizza wheel."

Mrs. Malone hadn't hassled her. But I got why she'd seen the two as a team. "And you used the black knight's costume to stake out Kristie before she killed her as well." I edged closer to Vittoria. Gun takeaways were not my favorite thing to do. But they only worked if I was close enough to grab the gun.

"Right," Charlie said, and I started. He had somehow closed the distance and now stood beside me. "Alice and I saw her, spying, when we visited Kristie the day before she died."

I was close enough. Vittoria held the gun with her right hand. I forced my breathing to even out. Four counts in, four counts out. All I had to do was forward-angle step left, and—

"Enough," Vittoria shouted and raised the gun, aiming at Charlie. "Charlie, put your hands on Alice's shoulders. You two, outside." She motioned with her gun toward the stage steps.

Charlie clapped his hands on my shoulders, immobilizing me. Fury heated the top of my skull. My brother was going to get himself killed. Roughly, I tried to shake him off, but Charlie hung on.

Rage pounded in my ears. How was I supposed to take away the gun if he was hanging onto me? He didn't have a clue, and I couldn't lose him, and this was Reno all over again: out of control and unlucky.

"I think we should do what she says," my brother said to me in a low voice.

But I didn't *want* to do what she said. I wanted to take her gun away and punch her in the face. "Charlie," I ground out. "You need to let go."

"But why did Kristie put a webcam in Gloria's dressing room?" the thin man asked.

"Oh." Charlie maneuvered me sideways, putting himself closer to the line of fire. "I got this. She was blackmailing Gloria over the burlesque photos. They weren't terrible, but Gloria's day job was at a school, so they would have caused problems."

"Let go," I whispered, eyes bulging.

"No," he said.

"I said, walk down the stairs," Vittoria said.

"Which stairs?" Charlie asked, "the stairs behind us or the stairs behind you?"

Vittoria glanced over her shoulder. Everything cleared. The shuffles and murmurs of the crowd fell away. The thudding in my heart and head silenced. Calm certainty washed through my veins, and I knew what to do.

I stomped on Charlie's foot and blasted forward, grabbing her wrist with one hand and the gun with the other. Vittoria's eyes widened. Something whispered past my ear, and there was a loud thud. Vittoria cried out. She sagged sideways and knelt on the floor.

Wrenching the gun away, I kneed her in the face. She went all the way down then.

I tossed the gun backstage, grasped her hand, and twisted it at the wrist, straightening her arm and pinning her. "I'm a trained protection specialist," I hissed. "And I'm not afraid of fighting someone like you."

Blood streamed from her nose. A sandbag lay on the ground beside us. I glanced over my shoulder. Jane stood beside the curtain controls, her face white. Slowly, the theater manager sank to her knees.

The adrenaline rush hit then. I breathed through it and rode that wave, and if my hands shook, the only one who would have noticed was Vittoria.

The thin man pushed back his chair, got to his feet, and slow clapped. Charlie bowed. Uncertainly, more audience members applauded.

"I don't get it," the blonde said.

Chapter Thirty-Two

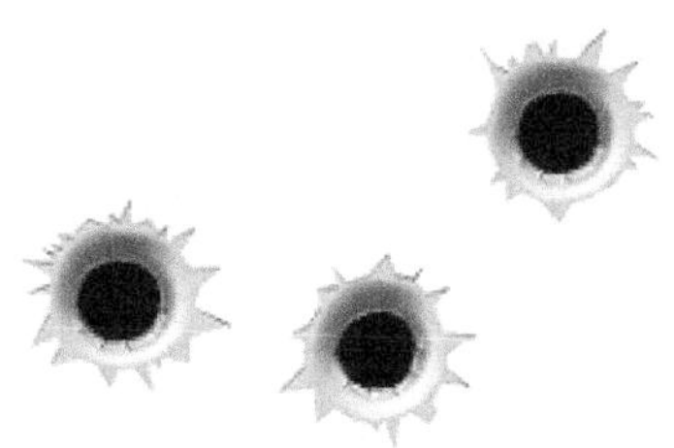

"I didn't know what else to do." Jane sobbed.

We watched Detective Guthrie maneuver Vittoria into the back of a black-and-white SUV. Clyde hurried across the theater parking lot toward them.

"You were there, and she was there," she continued. "And I thought if I opened the curtains and everyone saw, she'd stop. I didn't think she'd try and kidnap you."

"Nice move with the sandbag though," Charlie said.

"I could have killed her," Jane whispered. "And I... I didn't care."

"You may have saved our lives," I said. True, I'd taken Vittoria before the sandbag had hit her, but it wasn't the sort of detail Jane needed to hear right now.

"Gloria was my sister," she went on, as if she hadn't heard anyway.

Clyde grabbed the open door of the sheriff's SUV and pulled it wider. Swiveling in her seat, Vittoria kicked him in the stomach. Clyde went down like a sack of potatoes, and I winced.

"So Clyde had nothing to do with it?" Charlie said. "I was sure he was the black knight."

"Nope. But you were right about the black knight being the killer." And it was stinking embarrassing. Nowhere had become a cartoon. But at least it was *our* cartoon.

"How did you know it was her?" Charlie said.

"Little things," I said. "The torn-up brochure for the hobbit house tours in New Zealand that I found in their garbage. Clyde didn't tear it up. He's not that kind of guy. So Vittoria had done it, which spoke to rage and disappointment." I paused. I'd had plenty of second-hand experience with that. "Clyde admitted she'd been angry about his spending, for example when he brought home the black knight costume."

"Different spending philosophies are one of the biggest drivers of divorces," Charlie agreed.

I shook my head. Charlie rarely came off as the sharpest blade in the drawer, but he was no dummy. My heart spasmed. He'd found out the truth about our parents, after all.

"I figured if word got out there were other photos, she'd act," I said. "I thought she'd try to get the photos from me. But I invited Clyde to the theater, just in case, to keep him under my eye."

"Maybe..." Jane exhaled raggedly. "Maybe I should see those photos."

"They don't exist," I said. "I made them up." I rubbed my bare arms. The night was cold, but the stars above were Sierra-bright.

"Pretty sneaky, Sis," Charlie said, mimicking an old cereal commercial. We laughed harder than the hoary joke warranted. It was silly and dumb, but it was part of our history.

And that history was what counted. Physical DNA had nothing on the DNA of love and memory. "You know," I told him, "you don't need to protect me."

"I know I'm only your half-brother now—"

"You're my brother," I said sharply. "I meant... I do have some personal protection skills." I still had no intention of taking unnecessary risks. But if they were necessary, I'd face them head on.

"Oh yeah, that. But you're my sister. I'm not going to let someone pull a gun on you."

"Wait," Jane said. "Half-brother?"

"Brother," I said firmly.

"By a different father," Charlie said.

I flinched. "We don't know—"

"Yeah," he said, "we kind of do. Or... I mean, I will know. The guy on the DNA test is alive and in Hot Springs. All we have to do is ask him. He may not tell us the truth, but it doesn't mean we can't ask." His Mediterranean eyes turned serious.

"I haven't had a chance to tell you," I said. "Fitch turned up some info on him and sent it over to me. It's on my laptop upstairs." I nodded toward the theater.

"He did? What's it say?"

The detective helped Clyde to his feet and shut the door on Vittoria. He paused, one hand on the roof of the SUV and stared at me. I shivered again, and this time not because of the cold.

"It can't tell us if he's your father or not, but he seems clean, like an okay guy," I said. "It turns out he's really into genealogy. That's probably how the company has his DNA on file. He's even found the family coat of arms."

"No way," Charlie said. "We've got something in common."

And the next time Charlie's maybe-father checked the DNA website, he'd see Charlie on it. He'd know he had a son. Even if I wanted to stop this, I couldn't. And did I *want* to stop this?

The muscles hardened in the front of my throat. I didn't like where this might lead. Charlie's father had money and power. And though there were no signs he'd used that for ill, I wanted to protect my little brother.

He was my brother.

"Uh, Alice," Charlie said. "What if Vittoria tried to kill Clyde to stop him from buying those photos?"

"I had one of Fitch's men watching Clyde. He was safe." He'd called the cops when the curtains had come up and moved to the back of the theater, hoping to step in. But Jane and I had taken action first.

"So why'd you invite him to the theater?" he asked.

"Redundancies. I like to be thorough." And I couldn't have lived with myself if something had happened to Clyde, or Mrs. Malone, or Gert, or any of the people of Nowhere because of me.

"Vittoria wouldn't have hurt Clyde," Jane said. "She didn't kill him when she found out the first time. She killed Gloria instead, and then Kristie. She loved him. And love is strange."

"Yeah." I slung my arm over Charlie's shoulder. "It is that."

I'm Alice, a thirty-something ex-bodyguard, and DNA tests are the Devil. My brother Charlie took one, and it turns out he's only my half-brother. Our parents aren't around to explain things, but Charlie tracked down his real father, in the fancy pants spa town the hill over. Charlie's father is loaded. Or he was until someone killed him.

Now Charlie, high off helping me solve a murder last month, has decided he's going to find his father's killer. I'm not sure if it's pride, or delusion, or… No, that's not fair. Charlie cares. This hurt him. Bad. I'm going to have to solve this murder—and fast—before his rich new relatives eat him alive.

Big Bucks is the third book in Big Murder Mystery series. If you like laugh-out-loud mysteries, relationships with heart, and stories about figuring out where you belong, you'll love Big Bucks. and start the hilarious cozy mystery.

Click here to buy Big Bucks and start reading today!
Turn the page to find a sample chapter of Big Bucks!

Sneak Peek of Big Bucks

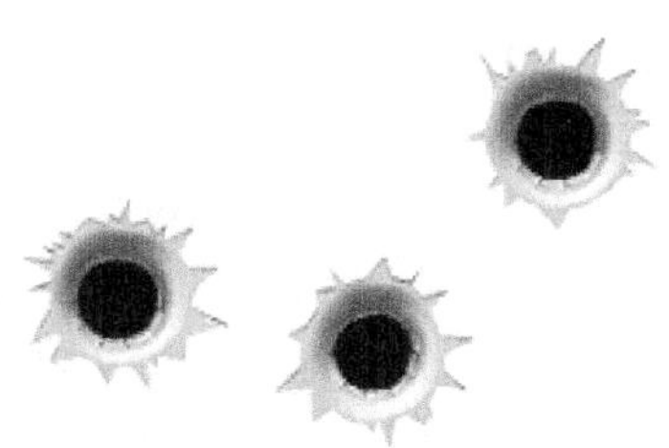

Some people enjoy a challenge. Me? I'm thrilled with easy when I can get it—which isn't often. So invading a wooded estate with no guards or cameras seemed like a day at the spa. Just without the massages, cucumber water, and saunas. I really missed those.

And because the big house was so secluded, the odds of a neighbor reporting me were low. It was unlikely anyone would spot me on the thick hillside. But I'd taken care to wear white to blend in with the patches of December snow between the pines. I was happy with easy, but I also liked to be thorough.

The effortlessness of the surveillance gig should have been a clue that things were fated to go sideways. But if the universe has been sending me warning messages, they've been going to spam.

A breeze rustled the pines, dropping clods of snow to the earth. Kneeling, I peered through my camera on its tripod. Cold seeped through the knees of my white jeans.

The mansion had massive arched windows at the back. They gave me a clear view of a wide, marble stairway leading to the ground floor living area as well as of most of the second floor. It was a nice place if you liked oversized mausoleums.

A woman slumped in a wheelchair at the top of the steps. Her white hair hung lank and unbrushed down her back.

"Dammit." Mrs. Stanton been sitting there over thirty minutes, and I worked to tamp down my anger. This was a job. I needed to stay cool because hot emotions rarely led to good decisions. And this neglect would be going in my report. But it was hard to watch.

I'd been watching her for days now, and she was starting to feel like a friend. Not that I'm in the habit of stalking my actual friends. And I *still* didn't have any video to prove elder abuse, aside from this stretch of neglect.

I double-checked the camera was recording then shifted to look through my second camera, also on a tripod. I scanned the rooms in the upper stories.

A thirty-something brunette, Mrs. Stanton's niece, Irene, sat at Mrs. Stanton's dressing table. Irene tried on a pair of jewel-studded earrings. She turned her head this way and that, admiring, and fluffed her long hair.

I snapped photos, my heart solidifying to something cold and hard. But the niece didn't put the jewelry in her pockets. She carefully returned them to their box, rose, and strolled from her aunt's bedroom.

"Take your sweet time, why don't you?" I muttered.

I shivered and glanced up. The sun was already low on the horizon over the Sierras. Soon it would be gone, and the temperature would drop. I tightened my ivory jacket and flipped up the faux-fur collar. My breath steamed the air.

The niece reappeared at the top of the stairs, and I grunted. "Finally." *Give the old lady a break and some conversation.*

She grasped the wheelchair's handles, bent, and said something to Mrs. Stanton. I stilled, unease spiraling in my gut. Mrs. Stanton turned to her. The older woman's eyes widened, her face contorting. Irene shoved her wheelchair down the stairs.

The wheelchair jounced, tilted. Mrs. Stanton tumbled from the chair.

Swearing, I jolted to my feet, knocking over the nearest camera, and bulleted across the lawn, clear of patches of snow. I was reacting, not thinking. This was never a good move for a personal protection specialist. And it's not like this was the first time I'd witnessed violence. But it still startled the hell out of me.

I raced up the flagstone steps and across a broad patio toward the French windows. They'd be locked. They always were. But I didn't slow.

The wheelchair had plummeted to the bottom of the stairs and lay on its side. Incredibly, the old lady clung to one of the bannisters near the top.

The niece walked slowly down the two steps to her and knelt, then stood. She raised a foot over the old woman's hand.

I cursed, raised my elbows in front of my face as both cover and battering ram, and jumped through the glass doors. Elbows were some of the hardest parts on a body. They were great for fighting at close quarters and for crashing through windows.

At least in theory. I'd never actually done it before.

The glass shattered into harmless pebbles, and the broken panes clawed at my skin. I landed, and my boots slipped on the safety glass. I skidded across the floor windmilling my arms like a cartoon coyote. Regaining my balance if not my dignity, I charged up the stairs.

The niece's eyes grew large as silver dollars. She gaped. "Get out! Get out!"

I jammed my palm heel into her chest. The force of it knocked her onto her butt. Dismissing the niece, I knelt beside Mrs. Stanton.

The niece scrambled to her feet. She tore up the steps and down the hallway. Her shoes clack-clacked on the marble floor. "I'm calling the police. Help! Police!"

That was Irene's idea of calling the cops? I shook my head. "I'm Alice Sommerland," I told Mrs. Stanton. "I work for a private investigator." And I wasn't happy that my last three assignments had been catastrophically exciting.

Don't get me wrong. You didn't get into surveillance if you weren't looking for a certain level of intrigue. But my past surveillance work hadn't been quite so action oriented. I was closing in on forty, and this seemed the wrong time of life to be getting *more* physical.

"Can you put your arm around my neck?" I asked.

"I think so." Her voice quavered. Though in fairness, mine hadn't been perfectly steady either. Her eyes were wide and frightened, and her fear made me angrier.

"Don't worry. I've got you." I was pleased to note the tremor had gone from my voice. *Cool and professional.*

I helped her down the marble stairs. She was light as a bird. And though I'm a beanpole, I'm nearly six feet tall and lean muscled, it was still slow going. I didn't want to injure her more than she'd already been hurt. At the bottom, I righted her wheelchair. I helped her inside it, giving the downstairs a better look.

The end tables were bare, and there were no chairs or carpets in the wide room. I was willing to bet the niece had sold them off. A breeze from outside flowed through the smashed window. I pulled the throw blanket from the back of the wheelchair and put it around her shoulders.

I dialed my current employer, Fitch Rhodes, PI. Just to be clear, I was *not* a PI—just a down-on-her-luck contractor who was very good at surveillance.

"Anything?" he asked, brisk.

I took Mrs. Stanton's hand. It trembled in mine. "Attempted murder," I said. "The cops are on their way. Ah, and they might arrest me. The niece got the call in first." You always want to be the first party to call the cops. The first person to talk is always more believable.

Fitch seemed to know this rule too because he swore long and colorfully. "I'll call and report." He hung up.

"You have glass in your hair," she said.

I reached up and pulled my blond ponytail forward. It glittered. I shook it experimentally. Tiny chunks of glass pinged to the marble floor.

"She moved my Motherwell," she said.

I glanced at her, startled, and she pointed. "I've been staring at that blank spot on the wall for thirty minutes. She moved it."

"You had a Francis Motherwell?"

"I would hardly have said she moved it if I didn't have one," she said dryly. "She's always moving my things. You know Motherwell?"

"I took some art history courses in college." And a Motherwell would go for a pretty penny. Mrs. Stanton would be lucky if it was still in the house.

"I've called the police," her niece yelled from somewhere upstairs.

"Piss off," Mrs. Stanton hollered back.

I blinked. So, that was unexpected.

"See? See what I have to deal with?" Irene shouted. "She's crazy."

"On occasion my husband employed salty language for emphasis," Mrs. Stanton confided. "I do hope you're not offended."

"Ah. No." I sat on the stairs beside her. "I occasionally enjoy some emphasis myself."

She laughed quietly and buried her head in her hands. "Oh, goodness. This isn't funny at all. I do believe I'm a bit hysterical."

"You've got reason for it." I paused. "Your friend, Mr. Harrington, was worried about you."

"Is that who sent you?" Mrs. Stanton raised her head. "Franklin. Such a dear. But I haven't seen him for..." She rubbed her wrinkled brow. "He used to come for tea every Wednesday. I don't know why he stopped."

"Your niece told him you were too ill for visitors."

She sat up straighter. "But I'm not." Twin spots of pink rose to her wrinkled cheeks. "Aside from this." She motioned toward her legs. "But that's not—" She crumpled forward, her head in her hands. "That girl really tried to kill me, didn't she?" she whispered.

"She won't try it again." I reached out to comfort her, then withdrew my hand, uncertain. Comforting shaken survivors hadn't been part of my old career. I wasn't sure what the procedure was. I cleared my throat. "She's..." The words died on my lips.

A metal dog on spindly legs minced through the broken door and across the glass. I froze, ice rippling down my spine. I'd never seen anything like it. But having grown up on a diet of *Terminator* movies, I was prepared for us not to be friends.

The robot dog's head panned right and left. Its glowing blue eyes stopped to fix on me. My temperature dropped several more degrees.

"Mrs. Stanton," I said, without moving my lips. "I'm guessing that's not normal."

"No," she said shakily.

And then I registered the letters in white on its dark-blue back: *TTHSPD*. The Town of Hot Springs Police Department had a robodog. I rolled my eyes. Of course they did.

Two police officers in crisp navy stepped carefully through the shattered French window. Their guns were drawn and aimed at the floor.

I forced my breathing to slow. Cops were human and made mistakes like anyone else. And I wouldn't like it much if they made a mistake with me. I kept my free hand on my knee where they could see it.

"We got a call of a disturbance," the taller cop said. He looked to be in his early forties, just a few years older than me. And though most men looked good in uniforms, his was particularly effective. I had it on good authority that the Hot Springs PD had—I kid not—its own tailor.

"My niece tried to kill me," Mrs. Stanton said in a shaky voice.

"I'm not her niece," I said quickly. "She's upstairs." Probably making off with the jewelry.

"Who are you?" the other cop, a redhead, asked.

"Alice Sommerland. I'm a contract worker for a private investigator from Reno, name of Fitch Rhodes. I've been surveilling the niece due to suspected abuse."

"You're from Reno?" he asked.

I wish. "No, I'm from Nowhere."

The two men glanced at each other, their expressions growing warier. "Nowhere," one said flatly.

"Relax, will you?" I said. "Just because our town hall has a fifty-foot lawn flamingo is no reason to get difficult." Nowhere's collection of record-breaking big things was the envy of... nowhere. "Hot Springs is special all on its own."

"It's The *Town* of Hot Springs," the redheaded cop said.

I snorted. "Whatever."

"We're opening a miniature museum next year," the taller one said.

I swore. I'm a reasonable person, but that was a direct slap at Nowhere's big things. I wondered if our temporary mayor knew. "And what's with the robot?"

"It's a police dog," the tall one said.

I crossed my arms. "Don't get me wrong, but if that's a police dog, you're doing something seriously wrong. It barely comes up to my knee."

Things got weird after that. The cops managed to be super polite while treating me like I was radioactive. The niece tried to claim I was a criminal, which I'd pretty much expected. But between Mrs. Stanton's testimony and my video, which had kept recording, we cleared up that lie quick enough.

An hour later, the first faint stars had appeared in the sky. I stood outside Mrs. Stanton's front gate. The ambulance's taillights faded in the distance. Mrs. Stanton would be okay. Fitch had called Mr. Harrington, and he'd meet her at the hospital.

Outside the mansion's imposing front steps, the police guided a cuffed Irene into a black and white. Bending over,

I pulled the band out my hair and shook it out. More glass pattered to the ground.

I sighed. My new life of low-paid odd jobs in a town called Nowhere stretched before me, and it didn't look half bad. It looked *mostly* bad.

Someday, I was going to get my old career back in the personal protection industry. I had to. But I hadn't been arrested, and no one had died, so I'd call this day a win.

The phone rang in my jacket pocket. I answered without looking. "Whatever you said did the trick," I said. "The cops have the niece in custody."

"What niece?" my brother Charlie asked. "Where are you? I'm at the theater and you're not here."

I tugged on my ear. *Whoops.* Was I supposed to be at Nowhere's dinner theater? I didn't remember agreeing to that. "I'm on a job."

"Cool. You're a detective again? Where?"

"I'm not a detective. It's surveillance." I winced guiltily. "And I'm in Hot Springs."

"It's The *Town* of Hot Springs. They get really tense when you just call it Hot Springs. And why didn't you tell me you're there?"

I grimaced. I'd been trying to give my brother space as he got to know his new family. He'd recently discovered our father wasn't his biological father. His real father was the head of a tech company and lived in a mansion here, in Hot Springs.

I'd gone with Charlie for their first meeting. After the initial shock and suspicion (and a private investigator), Adan Levann had stepped up. The tech gazillionaire had embraced my brother—literally and metaphorically. They'd gotten on so well, Charlie had moved out of his treehouse and into Adan's home.

I admit, I wasn't too happy about him moving to Hot Springs. But I was trying to be a supportive adult. It wasn't as easy as I'd have liked. "I'm on my way home now," I said. "Want to grab dinner?"

"No, no. You stay there. Adan said he wants to meet you. I mean, he met you once, but that was a weird time. He wants to get to know you. And he thinks he can help you with your PR problem."

My heart jumped. Could he? Then I got ahold of myself. I didn't want any favors from strangers. Okay, I wanted them, I just didn't want to pay the inevitable price. "It's fine. I don't need help."

"Yeah, yeah. Can you meet me at the house? I'll be there in thirty minutes."

I started to say no then stopped myself. This was important to Charlie. And if Adan and his kids were part of Charlie's family now, I needed to get with the program. "Sure. Thirty minutes."

We said our goodbyes and hung up. I returned through the gates and found a cop. She gave me permission to leave with my equipment. They kept the memory cards from my cameras as evidence though. I'd expected that too, but it annoyed me anyway.

I collected my cameras, packed them in my black Jeep Commander. Clipboard braced against the steering wheel, I wrote a brief report on the form I kept for such a purpose. Then I drove to Charlie's new home.

When I said Charlie had been living in a treehouse, I hadn't been speaking metaphorically. He'd been crashing in a treehouse. I can only imagine what the private investigator his bio-dad had hired had thought of that.

Since the weather had turned, I was glad Charlie had found less drafty and squirrel-free digs. But the mansion had a San Quentin atmosphere.

At the gate, I pressed a button and announced my arrival to the butler. Yes, Charlie's new father had an honest-to-goodness butler. His dulcet voice informed me I was expected, and the gates buzzed and swung open. Glancing at the modern security camera above the gate, I took my foot off the brake.

I drove down the winding, gravel road and parked beside a blue Tesla in the circular driveway. The sun had sunk behind the western hills. The first pinpricks of stars dotted the sky above the gothic manor's gabled roofline.

I shook my head and climbed the brick steps to the front door. It sprang open before I could ring the bell.

"Hey!" Charlie emerged and gave me a hug. My brother was as tall as me (five-ten), and just as blond. His hair was not as long as mine, but it was past his ears to his chin. He finger combed it behind his ear and grinned. "You rocked the timing," he said. "I just got here." The butler, Shelley, stood behind him looking haughty in his gray business suit and perfect blond hair.

I glanced down at Charlie's navy blazer. He was wearing it over navy board shorts, but that wasn't what raised my eyebrows. The jacket had a yachting emblem over the breast. "Seriously?" I asked. "A yachting jacket?"

He smoothed the gold embroidered logo with his palm. "Cool, huh? It's from Adan's club."

"A yacht club in Nevada? Sure. Why not. Aside from the fact that the state is landlocked."

"It's in California. The place is awesome. There are all sorts of, you know, yachts and stuff. He took me there last week. We flew in his private plane and everything. You're really going to like him." Charlie ushered me, my feet dragging, inside the high-ceilinged foyer.

Adult. I'm a mature adult and this is all good. Black and white marble tiles. An elegant and useless round table in the center, its vase overflowing with freshly cut flowers. Twin curving staircases, carpeted in crimson, ascended to the second floor.

"May I take your jacket, ma'am?" Shelley asked.

"Um, sure. Thanks." I began to shrug free. He whisked behind me and helped me out of my thick jacket.

"Thanks," I said again, feeling awkward. In my job, I'd been around a lot of wealthy people, but I'd rarely been treated like one. It felt weird. Unnatural. Or maybe it was just Shelley.

The butler was six-one and with lean muscles that were built for speed and power. I didn't like letting people get that physically close unless I trusted them. And I didn't trust Shelley.

"Would you like a comb, madam?" he asked.

My eyes narrowed. My hair wasn't that messy.

"There seems to be some glass in your hair," he said.

"It's fine." What was it that was so familiar about the man? I really hoped I hadn't clocked him in a mug book.

"Hey, Shelley, where's Adan?" Charlie asked in a half-whisper.

"I believe you'll find him upstairs in his room."

"Thanks. Come on." My brother climbed the stairs, and I trailed behind. "You need to see my room. It's got its own fireplace and everything."

"That's great," I said gloomily. *Adult. Supportive.* I forced a smile.

"Uh, why is there glass in your hair?"

"I jumped through a window."

"Okay..." He scratched his beard. "Uh, why? I mean, no offense, but I'm usually the one who goes through windows."

That's what *he* thought. "It seemed like a good idea at the time. How's the rest of Adan's family adjusting?" I asked, changing the subject.

His nose crinkled. "They just need to get used to me. Holli's been super cool though."

"Adan's new wife?"

"She's not that new. I mean, they've been married three years. And don't worry about all this." Charlie motioned toward the top of the wide stairs. "I know it's not really my vibe. But this is only temporary, until I find a full-time job."

"Full-time? Are you going to give up your work at the theater?"

"No way. The theater's my family." He colored. "I mean, you're my family too. And so is Adan and—"

"It's okay. I get it." Life had been a lot simpler before genetic testing had become a fun way to pass the time.

"But Adan had this amazing idea," he said. "He thinks I can sell my murder mystery games outside the theater. We're developing a game set in The Town of Hot Springs. Adan's got a contact at the Chamber of Commerce that can help promote it. The murder sites are going to be connected to actual locations in one of The Town of Hot Springs tourist brochures. Cool, right?"

It would have sounded a lot cooler if he'd stop saying *The Town of Hot Springs*. But selling the game outside the theater was a good idea.

"It's a good opportunity," I admitted. And I was impressed Adan was helping my brother with something Charlie loved. It might have been easier to give him a nothing job at Adan's company.

"What was this job you had in The Town of Hot Springs?" Charlie asked.

"An elder abuse case."

"Whoa." He stopped at the top of the stairs, the skin between his blue eyes puckering. "What kind of person would do that? I mean, I know it goes on, but that's terrible."

"Not anymore. I got the woman on video trying to harm the victim. The police have her in custody now."

"*Did* she hurt her?" he asked.

A cold lump formed in my chest. "Not badly." But the knowledge that to her niece, Mrs. Stanton was only money, only a means to an end, only a thing to be rid of… That hurt would take longer to heal than the bruises.

We walked down a long hallway, its thick carpet absorbing the sound of our footsteps. The lump in my chest turned to something else. Adan was the man who could have blown up my parents' marriage. I wasn't sure I wanted to sit down for a friendly chat.

And yet I had so many questions. I just wasn't sure I wanted the answers. The hallway seemed to grow narrower, the thick carpet higher, the air thicker. But I was an adult, and this meeting meant something to my brother.

Charlie stopped in front of a wood-paneled double door. "Are you ready for this?"

"I'm on the edge of my nonexistent seat."

He lowered his chin, tilting his head.

I laughed a little. "I'm ready." I grasped his hands. "I'm happy for you. Really. It's just a lot to adjust to."

"I know. But it's not going to change me."

Wouldn't it? How could it *not* affect him? "No, of course not," I said quickly.

"Okay." He drew a deep breath. "Ready? Ta-dah!" He swung open the door on a darkened room.

I frowned into the shadowy space.

He looked inside. "Oh. Energy saving lights." My brother stepped inside and flicked on the switch. He made a sweeping gesture with one arm. "Ta-dah!"

I gaped. An older version of my blond brother lay face down on the carpet, blood trickling from behind his ear. Adan Levann.

Can't wait to read on? Buy Big Bucks today!

Murder at the Faire RPG

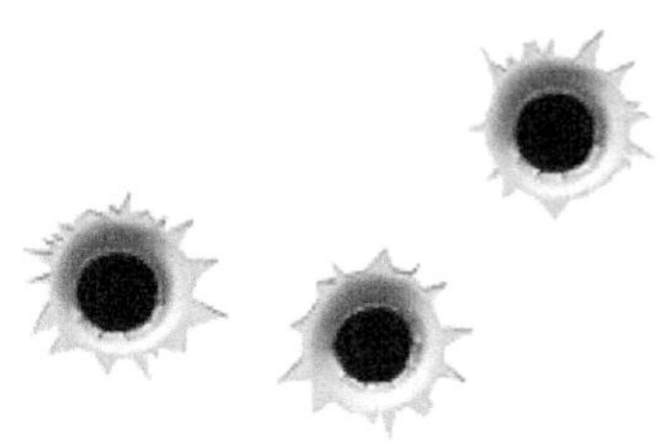

Introduction

Murder at the Faire RPG *Game* is a mystery role playing game (RPG) based on the book and characters created by Kirsten Weiss in *Big Bad*. This short mystery is set at an imaginary steampunk faire in the Sierra Nevadas and is suitable for two to six players but may be adapted for more. You can download a printable, PDF version of the game HERE: https://bit.ly/BigBadGame. The downloadable version includes a brochure to help players navigate the fair and a worksheet so they can keep track of their points.

The player most familiar with the game acts as the Mystery Maven, leading the player characters (PCs) through the game by reading through the game story and playing the roles of non-player characters (NPCs). The Mystery Maven should review the game before playing and should also track the life points of the PCs.

Player Characters choose roles to play (see the next page). Each PC role has certain advantages and disadvantages when it comes to rolling the die. Players will interview suspects and confront danger. PCs are encouraged to ham it up—the game's more fun if there's actual role-playing involved! (PCs may read this rule sheet).

You will need one 6-sided die to play this game. Any roll *over* a three (i.e. 4-6) is a successful roll. Each character can throw the die once per round, unless there is only one PC playing, in which case they get two dice rolls per round.

Interrogations:

When it comes to interviewing suspects and witnesses, PCs with + charisma may add that number to their die roll during questioning. If there is no more information to be gleaned from an interview, the player(s) who did not have a chance to interview the suspect start play in the next round. PCs may keep rolling, taking turns, until all the clues have been exhausted. Any roll *over* a 3 (i.e. a 4-6) gleans an answer from the witness or suspect. If a PC rolls a six, they get to ask two questions.

Searching for Clues:

When searching for clues in a room or space, a roll over a three (i.e. 4-6) gets players one clue. PCs with + awareness may add that number to their die roll when searching for clues. If there are no more clues to be gleaned from the location, the player(s) who did not have a chance to search for more clues start play in the next round. Players can keep rolling, taking turns, until all the clues have been exhausted.

Fighting for survival:

Players with + strength may add that number to their die roll when fighting. Any roll over three (i.e. 4-6) is a successful defense. A roll of a three loses a PC one life point. A roll of a two loses the PC two life points. And a roll of a one loses a character three life points. When life points reach zero, the PC is dead.

Rounds:

A "round" is one cycle of die rolls. For example, there are three PCs in the game plus the Mystery Maven. The PCs take turns questioning a suspect. After three die rolls (as there are 3 players), one round is completed.

Healing:

Once per round, the doctor can heal one PC by rolling the die and adding the number that appears to the PC's life points until the PC reaches his original life points. I.e. the player's original LPs are six and the PC is down to four points; the doctor rolls a five, and the PC will be restored to the PC's original six LPs. If the doctor rolled a one in the same circumstances, the player would get one LP, bring the PC's total to five. During the same round, the doctor may also roll to search for clues or ask an interview question.

The game's afoot!

List of Non-playing Characters:

Larry Lasso – Owner of Lasso Emporium

Hubert Beal – Stagecoach driver.

Gemma Golden – Owner of Gothic Jewels.

Jack Hammer – Improv group leader.

Terrence Madoff – Artist

Lina Love – Owner of Hoopskirts and Honeys western ware.

Maria Martinez – Waitress at the Commodore Tearoom

Haskel Radley – Founder of the Araminta Children's Charity.

Tasha Teasdale – Owner of Deadwood Teas.

Wyatt Westcoat – Author of western steampunk suspense novels.

Commodore Jones – Owner of the Commodore Tearoom and Helga's husband.

Helga Jones – Owner of Aether Couture and Commodore's wife.

Joachim York – Telegraph boy.

Player Characters

[You may wish to give a copy of this sheet to the players in advance, but if you do, ask the characters to introduce themselves, telling the other players their name and one or two things about themselves. Players will have more fun if they're able to interact with each other acting out their roles]

Players will be searching for clues and interviewing suspects. Players will be more successful if they ask open question, which do **not** lead to yes/no answers. Possible open questions include:

- Where were you when...? [time of death]?
- What can you tell me about...?
- Who might have wanted to kill [the victim]?
- Who else should we talk to?
- What else can you tell me?

You may find clues in surprising places (including the brochure), so be sure to explore the areas listed on the brochure after you get it from the Mystery Maven.

To better roleplay your characters, pay attention to the notes in italics at the bottom of the character description. You'll find fun opportunities during the game to let your character quirks shine.

Kennedy – Struggling Science Fiction Author

+3 Awareness

+1 Strength

Life Points: 6

Observant Kennedy writes massive space operas but is thinking of switching to writing steampunk—science fiction set in the Victorian era. It seems to sell quite well these days. But if Kennedy does write steampunk, it will be set in London. In Kennedy's opinion, cowboys ruined the west, and western steampunk is a waste of time and paper. Kennedy is disappointed by the faire, but as a gloomy pessimist, Kennedy is disappointed by pretty much everything. Kennedy's favorite saying is: "This is not going to work out."

Lane – Holistic Doctor

Elliot can heal one life point for any player once per round **in addition to** his die roll (i.e., the healing doesn't take the place of Sawyer's die roll).

Life Points: 9

Lane has a particular interest in herbal medicine and teas. Herbal medicine was the foundation of modern medicine, and Lane is convinced we still have a lot to learn from it. He will lecture anyone who will listen about the evils of the pharmaceutical companies. As far as Lane's concerned, you can't trust putting all those chemicals into your body. Big Pharma only cares about profit.

Lane is determined to keep everyone safe, and that means minimizing any risks the other PCs might take. Lane's favorite saying is: "Sounds dangerous."

MacKenzie - Engineer

+1 Awareness

+2 Charisma

Life Points: 7

As an engineer, MacKenzie is fascinated by the metal contraptions rolling around the faire. But it irritates MacKenzie that so many of the bells and whistles are for decoration only. MacKenzie is only impressed by real and functional tech. MacKenzie is always quick to point out when a flashing light or whistle is just for show. MacKenzie (just call me Mac) is a practical sort and believes in Science. Any character who believes in woo-woo is fair game for MacKenzie's mockery. In MacKenzie's opinion, homeopathy and herbal remedies are bunk.

Morgan - Coffeeologist

+3 Awareness

Life Points: 7

America had a tea party to get rid of its tea, and as far as Morgan is concerned, tea should stay on the opposite side of the Atlantic. Tea is just flavored water. Americans drink coffee! And espresso. And cappuccino and mochacinno... Morgan's favorite sayings are: "Coffee smells like magic and fairytales;" "My birthstone is a coffee bean;" and "Stay grounded," the latter phrase which Morgan will often use instead of "goodbye."

Teagan – Pastry Chef

+4 Charisma

Life Points: 6

Optimistic and upbeat Teagan sees the bright side of everything, even murder. In fact, Teagan's favorite way to begin a sentence is: "On the bright side..." Teagan is determined to keep up morale among the investigation group.

Recently, Teagan has been experimenting with adding tea to pastries and is always on the lookout for interesting flavor combinations. Teagan is deathly afraid of vampires and very interested in sampling all the foods at the faire.

Plot

The Nowhere Halloween Faire is an annual event in small-town Nowhere, Nevada. You've explored its *Silk Road Spooks*, *Haunted Olde England*, and *Goblin Grotto* sections. Now, stuffed with funnel cake and nachos, you're exploring the Old West Vampires section. It's steampunk themed. Steampunk is based in 1800s science-fiction, which typically utilizes steam power and sometimes magic (aether) to power devices. Vampires wearing goggles and bowler hats walk past with old-west cowboys carrying toy laser weapons in this Victorian sci-fi extravaganza.

Players begin the game resting their weary feet at the Commodore's Tea Parlor. They've just ordered tea and scones and are reviewing the section brochure to decide where to go next and to get a break from the whistles of steam, electronic hoots, and ringing bells that are all over the faire.

Commodore's Tea Parlor

The Commodore's Tea Parlor is inside a large, canvas tent. The floor is covered by thick rugs. Copper lanterns strung with twinkle lights hang from the ceiling.

You're enjoying a cup of tea in the parlor when there's a commotion at the back of the tent. A man in a top hat and frock coat bursts through the paisley curtains clutching his throat with one hand and a teacup in the other. He chokes out one word: "Fraud!" Grinning maniacally, he falls to the carpet. The man spasms, knocking over a nearby table. He arches his back and freezes in that contorted position. You call nine-one-one and attempt to render aid, but the man is dead.

PLAYERS EACH ROLL TO SEARCH THE AREA FOR CLUES. Players with + awareness may add that number to their die roll. Any roll over a 3 gets a clue.

Clues:

- "It's the tearoom owner, Commodore Jones," someone shouts. "He's dead."

- "I thought these were *wellness* teas," a woman sobs.
- "Strychnine!" a woman in a blue Victorian dress says. "I'd recognize the symptoms anywhere. That author just talked about it in the Poisons of the Victorians lecture."
- You consult your program brochure and learn that the steampunk writer Wyatt Westcoat lectured on Deadly Poisons of the Victorians at 9:00 this morning in author's alley.
- You check your watch. It is now 11:07 AM.
- You notice a sign advertising that 5% of sales on every tea go to Araminta Children's Charity.
- You see nothing unusual about the cup that lies beside the dead man's outstretched hand.

A young waitress in a corset, pink button up boots, and a western-style saloon-girl skirt sways. "Mr. Jones was poisoned?" She faints. What do you do?

MARIA MARTINEZ

If a player asks you a question and you know the answer (i.e. it's below), you must answer the question honestly. Make the players work for it and have fun with the character. Ham it up!

Mood: Maria is shocked and worried. She drank some tea earlier too. What if it's poisoned as well? She's only worked for Commodore Jones for six weeks and hardly knows the man. What did she get herself into?

Objective: Don't die from poisoning.

If Maria doesn't know the answer, she should simply act shocked and mutter, "I could die. What if I die?"

If PCs ask about flavor combinations with tea and baked goods, she should suggest Earl Grey tea with blackberries.

If PCs ask about the medicinal qualities of the teas, she should say it would be unethical for her to make any claims that the herbs treat specific medical conditions.

PLAYERS EACH MAKE ROLLS TO ASK MARIA QUESTIONS. Players with + charisma can add that number to their die roll. Maria will respond to every die roll over 3.

Clues:

- "I didn't see anything strange. I arrived at work at eight o'clock this morning to help Mr. Jones set up the tearoom for the day."
- "I don't usually serve tea. Mr. Jones doesn't have a tearoom. He sells most of his wellness teas online. Mr. Jones thought having a tea tent at the fair would be a good promotion."
- "He left the tent around eight thirty this morning. When he came back at nine, he was really angry, but he didn't tell me why."
- "He made his own tea. He even had his own special octopus teapot in back, but he refilled it from the hot water urn. I drank tea from that urn!"
- "I haven't been working for Mr. Jones long. I think he's had a hard time filling the position since his last manager, Tasha Teasdale, quit. They really didn't like each other. I don't know why. She's got something against his wellness teas."
- "Who's going to tell his wife? Does she know yet? Helga owns Aether Couture."

The police interrupt your investigation to question you. When they're finished, they let you go.

Author's Alley

Stunned, you wander the fair and find yourself in Author's Alley. Booths line both sides of the narrow dirt road, and authors in Victorian and western clothing stand hopefully behind their tables. A telegraph boy runs through the alley. He blows a shrill whistle. "Wyatt Westcoat! Telegram for Wyatt Westcoat!"

You follow the boy, who is wearing a slouch hat, suspenders and baggy white shirt, and short trousers. He leads you to a wooden table with a western false front and stacks of colorful paperbacks. A freestanding poster of Wyatt in western wear and stroking his long, gray moustache stands beside the table. The author himself grins at you and waves his cowboy hat, exposing longish gray hair. "Howdy, partner! I'm Wyatt Westcoat. Are you looking for a good read?"

The telegraph boy hands him his telegram, blows his whistle again, and races off. How do you respond?

WYATT WESTCOAT

If a player asks you a question and you know the answer (i.e. it's below), you must answer the question honestly. Make the players work for it and have fun with the character. Ham it up!

Mood: Wyatt is horrified when he learns about the poisoning. He didn't know Commodore Jones, but is he going to be liable for the death?

Objective: Don't get sued.

If Wyatt doesn't know the answer, he should simply act shocked and say he has no idea. Wyatt doesn't know anything about the murder, so the PCs will have to explain a bit to him before he'll answer any questions.

If any of the PCs ask for writing advice, he should tell them to get a good editor.

PLAYERS EACH MAKE ROLLS TO ASK WYATT QUESTIONS. Players with + charisma can add that number to their die roll. Wyatt will respond to every die roll over 3.

Clues:

- "Strychnine is a fast-acting poison. It's an odorless powder that's colorless when dissolved in liquid, though it does have a bitter taste. Symptoms usually occur within ten to fifteen minutes. And depending on the dose, that may be all it takes to kill a man. The convulsions are so strong, they arch the body and can stretch the face into a rictus grin."
- He opens an old-fashioned black apothecary's kit, displaying antique bottles and tins. Wyatt pales. "The strychnine. It's gone."
- "The last time I saw the bottle of strychnine was at my nine AM lecture. I showed it to the crowd, then returned it to the apothecary case."

- "There were about twenty people at my presentation this morning. A bunch of them came up afterward to chat with me. Someone could have pilfered the strychnine when I was busy then.
- I couldn't tell you who any of the guests at my presentation were. But some of them did sign up for my author newsletter afterward." He shows you the list. You recognize two names – Helga Jones, the wife of the victim and owner of Aether Couture, and Tasha Teasdale, owner of Deadwood Teas.
- Want to buy a cracking book? It's only $11.99. Imagine a young, orphaned Englishwoman, bound to San Francisco to meet her uncle. But when she arrives, the village of San Francisco has been abandoned by its men, who've left for the gold fields. Little does she know the danger she'll encounter there...

Do you buy a book? If PCs buy a book, they earn +1 charisma for the next round.

You decide to pay a visit to Deadwood Teas, where Tasha Teasdale works.

Deadwood Teas

A giant Nautilus machine, polished sides gleaming, trundles past along the faire's twisting dirt road. Its wheels squeal loudly. You make your way to a small tent with a sign above it reading: *Deadwood Ritual Teas*. Inside, brushed nickel cannisters of tea are stacked in neat pyramids at the sides and back of the tent. Glass display jars with colorful teas line the counter. A thirty-something woman in a blue corset, bowler hat, and western-style skirt and blouse smiles at you, lines crinkling around her eyes. "Can I help you? We have Nevada's finest selection of ritual teas."

TASHA TEASDALE

If a player asks you a question and you know the answer (i.e. it's below), you must answer the question honestly. Make the players work for it and have fun with the character. Ham it up!

Mood: Tasha is horrified and worried. Word about Commodore Jones's murder is making its way through the fair, though she isn't sure about the details. Everyone knows she and Commodore Jones did not part amicably. Is *she* a suspect? And she's a little worried Amarinta might have been behind his death. When she researched the non-profit, it looked a little sketchy to her. But Tasha doesn't have any proof, so she's not going to say anything to anyone but the police, when they get around to interviewing her. They haven't interviewed her yet.

Objective: Don't get arrested and learn what the PCs know. You're here at the fair to promote your online tea shop.

If Tasha doesn't know the answer, she should say, "I don't know," and ask the PCs the same question they just asked her. She doesn't know anything about the murder, so the PCs will have to explain a bit to her before she'll answer any questions.

If PCs ask about her ritual teas, she should get defensive. "Ritual teas are teas that are high enough quality for ritual. I'*m* not trying to mislead anyone."

If PCs ask about flavor combinations with tea and baked goods, she should suggest jasmine tea with mixed berries.

If PCs ask about the medicinal qualities of the teas, she should say it would be unethical for her to make any claims that the herbs treat specific medical conditions.

PLAYERS EACH MAKE ROLLS TO ASK TASHA QUESTIONS. Players with + charisma can add that number to their die roll. Tasha will respond to every die roll over 3.

Clues:

- "Commodore Jones was a con artist. He sold what he called "wellness teas." He made all sorts of claims about their health benefits that there are no studies to substantiate. But he was making money hand over fist selling them online, so he didn't care. It's why I left Commodore Teas."

- "He tried to look like the good guy by partnering us up with that children's charity, Araminta, but it was just phony virtue signaling."
- "There was something wrong between Commodore Jones and his wife. They were constantly arguing. I don't know what it was about, but it happened a lot when I was working for him in Reno."
- "Are you sure it was strychnine? Commodore thought he knew a lot about tea, but I could see him accidentally mixing a poisonous herb into one of his *wellness* blends."
- "I saw his wife, Helga, at the Victorian Poisons lecture this morning. She would have known all about strychnine."
- "I came directly back to my booth after the lecture and have been here ever since, so I didn't see anything."
- "You might want to ask Gemma at Gothic Jewels. She and Helga were good friends until they had some sort of falling out."
- "I was the creator of all those teas, but would Commodore give me credit? No. He made me do all the work. I managed everything for Commodore Teas—not just the blending, but also the business side." [She frowns]. "Is it true Commodore's last words were *it was a fraud*?"

It is now twelve-thirty. You decide to pay a visit to the victim's wife, Helga Jones, at Aether Couture. As you glance over your shoulder, you see Tasha hanging a CLOSED sign on her tent and hurrying away.

Aether Couture

You see two policemen leaving Aether Couture's red-and-white striped tent. You walk inside, your footsteps muffled by a thick Persian carpet. A chandelier hangs from the center of the tent. Racks of steampunk clothing in silk and leather form aisles in the tent. A woman in an elaborate emerald-colored Victorian gown, her brown hair done up in a bun, approaches you. Her eyes are red, but she forces a smile. "Hi, I'm Helga. How can I help you?"

You give her condolences over her husband's death.

HELGA JONES

If a player asks you a question and you know the answer (i.e. it's below), you must answer the question honestly. Make the players work for it and have fun with the character. Ham it up!

Mood: Helga has been informed by the police of her husband's murder and is still in shock. But their marriage was in trouble. She's convinced her husband was having an affair with that hussy Lina Love. She continues to work to keep her mind off the murder, and she doesn't want to talk about Gemma or Lina.

Objective: Learn what the PCs know.

If Helga doesn't know the answer, she should tell the PCs she doesn't know. If PCs ask her about Gemma or Lina, Helga should say she doesn't want to talk about it. She's too traumatized by her husband's murder, and she wasn't an active part of Commodore Teas. She had her own business to run.

PLAYERS EACH MAKE ROLLS TO ASK HELGA QUESTIONS. Players with + charisma can add that number to their die roll. Helga will respond to every die roll over 3.

Clues:

- "I just can't believe he's gone. We came to the faire together in our minivan. I didn't think when I said goodbye to Commodore this morning at eight that I wouldn't see him again."
- "Commodore packed his own tea things at our house. No one helped him, and no one else had access to our minivan."
- "The only person I know who'd have wanted Commodore dead was that Tasha Teasdale. He fired her, you know."
- "Tasha thought she was entitled to some sort of profit sharing agreement just because she gave him a little help

in creating his tea blends. She was enraged when he turned her down."

- "He fired Tasha when he caught her sabotaging one of his tea blends. I don't know exactly how she did it, but he was furious."
- "I saw Tasha at the Victorian Poisons lecture this morning. After the lecture, she was standing near the table where the lecturer kept his poisons."
- "When we arrived at the faire yesterday, that actor who runs the Vampire Cowboy improv group tried to start a fight with Commodore. I don't know what that was about. Commodore said it was nothing."

A customer arrives, and Helga walks away from you to help the newcomer. You leave the steampunk clothing shop and walk back toward Deadwood Teas to ask Tasha more questions. Dark clouds mass over the faire. Wind whips down the dirt road, kicking dust in your eyes and flapping the sides of the nearby tent. Thunder cracks, and freezing rain bullets downward. There's a blinding flash, and a woman shrieks. It's a lightning strike!

EACH PLAYER ROLLS TO DETERMINE HOW MUCH DAMAGE THE STORM CAUSES. Players with + strength may add that number to their die roll.

Roll 1 - 2: You are injured, losing 2 life points.

Roll 3: You are injured, losing 1 life point.

Roll 4-6: No injuries.

The storm ends as abruptly as it began, and you continue toward Deadwood Teas. A paramedic races past you, and you fear someone's been seriously hurt by the sudden storm. When you reach the Deadwood Teas shack, the two police officers you saw earlier are there. One is on his radio. The paramedic emerges from the shack and shakes his head. "She's dead. Ms. Teasdale bled out fast. That bowie knife cut an artery. There was nothing I could do. I'm guessing she was stabbed about fifteen minutes ago." It is now one o'clock.

PCs should consult the brochure and decide where to go next.

Araminta Children's Charity

The Children's Charity is in a small polka-dot tent. A man darts around in front of the tent picking up brochures, sodden from the cloudburst earlier. He looks up and swipes his longish brown hair from his eyes. "Hi, I'm Haskel Radley. Can I help you?"

HASKEL RADLEY

If a player asks you a question and you know the answer (i.e. it's below), you must answer the question honestly. Make the players work for it and have fun with the character. Ham it up!

Mood: You are the killer, and you're a conman. Your charity is a fraud. You need to stay cool, or someone may suspect you slipped poison into Commodore Jones's tea and stabbed Tasha Teasdale.

Objective: Learn what the PCs know and cover your tracks.

If Haskel doesn't know the answer, he should tell the PCs he doesn't know, unless the question is about his bogus charity. Then feel free to make things up.

If PCs ask what Araminta means, he should tell them he knew a girl named Araminta. It means prayer and protection, so he thought it was a good name for his charity.

PLAYERS EACH MAKE ROLLS TO ASK HASKEL QUESTIONS. Players with + charisma can add that number to their die roll. Haskel will respond to every die roll over 3.

Clues:

- "What a horrible thing. Commodore Jones was a great man, a real humanitarian. I and the charity I serve are indebted to him. A portion of the profits from Commodore Teas went to Araminta, you know. Commodore would deliver the money to us himself each month. He cared that much."

- "Araminta sponsors children in foster care. Would you like to make a cash donation? Cash has so much more impact since we don't have to pay credit card processing fees. We don't take checks."
- "I did see Commodore wandering around earlier today. He walked right past the Araminta stand. We said hello to each other, but that's it. I wish I'd seen more, but I've been stuck here all day."
- "I have no idea who might have wanted Commodore dead, though I suspect he and his wife were on the outs."
- "We're running a sweepstakes for donors at the faire. It's for a good cause. Kids in foster care can be so lost. We provide them with new clothing, toys, and have volunteers who provide emotional support and guidance."
- "We have a corporate donor which is doing a donation match this month, so every dollar you donate becomes two. Don't you like children?"
- "Ten percent of Amarinta's income goes to administrative costs."
- "I've been here most of the day. I did stop by the food court to get a funnel cake for lunch. Have you tried them? They're amazing."

PCs should consult the brochure and decide where to go next.

Gothic Jewels

You stop in front of a small stand. The rickety wooden sign above it reads: Gothic Jewels. Glittering broaches, earrings and necklaces in steampunk designs cling to brass stands shaped like gears. A smiling woman with graying hair done up in a loose bun stands behind the counter. "Welcome," she says. "I'm Gemma. How can I help you?" How do you respond?

GEMMA GOLDEN

If a player asks you a question and you know the answer (i.e. it's below), you must answer the question honestly. Make the players work for it and have fun with the character. Ham it up!

Mood: She's heard about the murders and is shocked and saddened.

Objective: Sell jewelry.

If Gemma doesn't know the answer, she should tell the PCs she doesn't know.

PLAYERS EACH MAKE ROLLS TO ASK GEMMA QUESTIONS. Players with + charisma can add that number to their die roll. Gemma will respond to every die roll over 3.

Clues:

- "Commodore Jones was too trusting, if you ask me. He put a lot of work into getting that children's charity into the fair, but I've heard the money the charity collects isn't very well spent. I've heard they have high administrative costs."
- "Poor Helga. She was certain Commodore was having an affair, but she wasn't sure with whom. I didn't want to say anything, but I saw him with that woman from Hoopskirts and Honeys, Lina Love. The irony is Helga accidentally introduced them. She was so worried about Lina's business cutting in to her own, she made Commodore go check out the competition last year. Insecurity is the devil. She actually blamed *me* when I told her."
- "That Tasha Teasdale... She worked hard. She was the backbone of Commodore Teas. She was involved in *everything* and got few rewards for her labor. It was probably for the best she started her own business. Commodore was a bit lazy."
- "Can you believe Helga thought Tasha and Commodore were having an affair? Poor Helga."
- "Commodore's business must have been in some trouble without Tasha. He stormed past my stand early this morning muttering about the IRS. I said *hello* to him,

and he just kept on going, as if I hadn't spoken at all. It was quite rude, if you ask me."

- "I got to the faire at eight and haven't had a chance to leave my stand since I got here, not even for lunch. As you can see, I don't have any help."

A customer appears at her booth, and Gemma turns her attention to the newcomer. Where would you like to go next?

PCs should consult the brochure and decide where to go next.

Hoopskirts and Honeys

You walk to a booth bracketed by dressmaker's mannequins wearing elaborate corsets. Racks of steampunk women's clothing stand beside the old-west booth. A woman with honey-blond hair and dressed like a vampire in a lacy red and black Victorian gown smiles at you from behind the counter.

LINA LOVE

If a player asks you a question and you know the answer (i.e. it's below), you must answer the question honestly. Make the players work for it and have fun with the character. Ham it up!

Mood: She's heard about Commodore's murder and is torn up inside. She loved Commodore and is certain his death is his wife, Helga's, fault. She's unaware of Tasha Teasdale's death.

Objective: Stay outwardly calm. She doesn't want anyone to know about the affair with Commodore Jones and will indignantly deny the affair.

If Lina doesn't know the answer, she should tell the PCs she doesn't know.

PLAYERS EACH MAKE ROLLS TO ASK LINA QUESTIONS. Players with + charisma can add that number to their die roll. Lina will respond to every die roll over 3.

Clues:

- "I didn't know Commodore Jones very well. We saw each other now and then. When you're on the steampunk circuit, you tend to get to know everyone. And of course, I knew Helga. I heard Helga was the one who forced Commodore to fire Tasha Teasdale. She was a very jealous woman."
- "She thought Commodore and Tasha Teasdale were having an affair. Ridiculous, isn't it? He despised Tasha."
- "I'm on the volunteer committee that helped organize the steampunk section of the faire. Commodore was so proud of his work connecting Amarinta Children's Charity to the faire. Haskel stopped by the tent this morning to show me photos of some children they helped—that must have been around eight-thirty. The pictures made me want to cry. Amarinta's a wonderful cause."
- "I'm sure Helga killed Commodore. That woman made his life miserable."

You leave the tent and discuss where to go next. A woman screams, "Look out!" The Nautilus machine is bearing down on you. You try to dive out of the way.

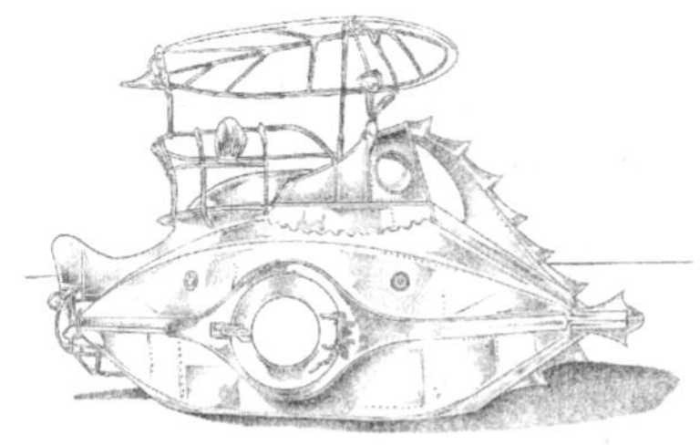

EACH PLAYER ROLLS TO DETERMINE HOW MUCH DAMAGE THE NAUTILUS CAUSES. Players with + strength may add that number to their die roll.

Roll 1 - 2: You are injured, losing 2 life points.

Roll 3: You are injured, losing 1 life point.

Roll 4-6: No injuries.

You dust yourselves off and hurry to the open door of the Nautilus. No one is inside. An man with a long gray beard and wearing a vest and waistcoat hurries up to you. "My Nautilus! Someone stole it!" You question the man, but he didn't see or hear anything.

Where do you go next?

PCs should consult the brochure and decide where to go next.

Lasso Emporium

The Lasso Emporium is a small, old-west style stand with lassos hanging from every possible surface. Located in the bend of one of the faire's dirt roads, it has a good view of the Commodore Tearoom, Amarinta Children's Charity, and Hoopskirts and Honeys. A man dressed like a guacho leans over the counter and grins. "Hi, I'm Larry Lasso. Want to see a lasso trick?" he asks.

Do the PCs stay for the trick? If yes, all PCs gain +1 charisma for the next two rounds.

LARRY LASSO

If a player asks you a question and you know the answer (i.e. it's below), you must answer the question honestly. Make the players work for it and have fun with the character. Ham it up!

Mood: He's heard about the murders and is shocked something like this could happen at a family faire.

Objective: Sell a lasso.

If Larry doesn't know the answer, he should tell the PCs he doesn't know and offer to sell them a lasso - directions included! He's also got links to online videos with lasso demonstrations.

PLAYERS EACH MAKE ROLLS TO ASK LARRY QUESTIONS. Players with + charisma can add that number to their die roll. Larry will respond to every die roll over 3.

Clues:

- "I didn't know Commodore Jones or Tasha Teasdale well. I'm just here to sell lassos. I have a range of wide range of prices for any cowpoke."
- "I saw Commodore Jones storming down the road there around 8:45 this morning. He looked like he was about to blow his stack. I heard him say something about a tax ID number. I've got *my* sales tax license, but I'd be willing to bet not everyone at the fair does."
- "I didn't see anyone suspicious go into Commodore Teas before Commodore was killed, but a killer could come in through the back. It's not like those tents are tough to get into. Also, I wasn't paying that much attention." [Wink] "I was more interested in Lina over at Hoopskirts and Honeys."
- "Lina didn't leave her stand all morning. And she *couldn't* have snuck out of that little stand. It's wide open. There's nowhere to sneak."

An older woman with dyed black hair and one-inch white roots stops you. She introduces herself as Mrs. Malone and insists on telling you all about what Nowhere was like when she was a girl. Roll to escape.

EACH PLAYER ROLLS TO ESCAPE MRS. MALONE. Players with + charisma may add that number to their die roll. Any roll over three is a successful escape.

PCs should consult the brochure and decide where to go next.

Stagecoach Stop

Four horses stamp in their harnesses in front of an old-west stagecoach. The whiskered driver leans down from his perch and grins. "Want a ride?"

If players take a ride, they earn +1 strength for the next two rounds.

The stagecoach driver knows nothing about the murders or the victims.

PCs should consult the brochure and decide where to go next.

Steampower Creations

You walk through an open-air enclosure filled with fantastic steampunk creations, including a giant contraption that's half house, half steam engine, a twelve-foot tall copper hoop with wings. The Nautilus that nearly ran you down is there too.

A woman in a corset, skirts, and top hat drives slowly past on an four-wheeled contraption. You stop in front of a man in a vest and top hat. He flexes a giant, wooden articulated hand. His eyes bulge. "Terrence, Terrence Madoff. And my Big Things are art," he snaps.

TERRENCE MADOFF

If a player asks you a question and you know the answer (i.e. it's below), you must answer the question honestly. Make the players work for it and have fun with the character. Ham it up!

Mood: Terrence has heard about the murders and doesn't care that much. Art is more important than life, and these steampunk people are weirdos.

Objective: Educate people about the importance of his art.

If Terrence doesn't know the answer, he should tell the PCs he doesn't know or care.

PLAYERS EACH MAKE ROLLS TO ASK TERRENCE QUESTIONS. Players with + charisma can add that number to their die roll. Terrence will respond to every die roll over 3.

Clues:

- "I saw a man lurking around the Nautilus earlier, but I didn't get a very good look at him. It was definitely a man, but who cares? He was just rushing through anyway, didn't even take the time to look at the art. Not that there's much of it in this place. You won't find many conceptual entrepreneurs like myself at a steampunk faire."
- "I admit the Nautilus is an interesting interactive device. If you ask nicely, the owner may let you drive it. That woman Helga Jones was driving it earlier, at the start of the fair. It took her about an hour to figure out how to get it going."
- "Helga was fooling around with that Nautilus between nine and ten, I'd say. But that Nautilus is just craftwork. It's not art. My work interprets the human experience. I created all the Big Things in Nowhere, you know."
- "My work defies the boundaries of space and forces the viewer to reassess his relationship with the environment and society."

PCs should consult the brochure and decide where to go next.

Telegram Office

You enter an elaborate old-west shack the size of a walk-in closet. A man in a charcoal-colored frock coat points at a stack of papers on the counter. "You can fill out your telegram there, and we'll deliver it free. I'm Joachim, by the way." The telegram boy runs into the office and blows his whistle.

JOACHIM YORK

If a player asks you a question and you know the answer (i.e. it's below), you must answer the question honestly. Make the players work for it and have fun with the character. Ham it up!

Mood: He's heard about the murders and is shocked something like this could happen at a family faire.

Objective: Joachim's a bit lazy, so he's happy to gossip with anyone who stops by.

If Joachim doesn't know the answer, he should tell the PCs he doesn't know.

PLAYERS EACH MAKE ROLLS TO ASK JOACHIM QUESTIONS. Players with + charisma can add that number to their die roll. Joachim will respond to every die roll over 3.

Clues:

- "Commodore Jones sent a telegram to Tasha Teasdale at Deadwood Teas around nine-thirty this morning. I'm not supposed to look at what the telegram says though."
- "I'm not *supposed* to look, but of course I looked. Everyone knows those two hated each other."
- "His telegram to Tasha said: *You were right. I'm going to stop this.* I thought it was a little weird, which is why I remembered it."
- "He also sent a telegram to Lina Love at Hoopskirts and Honeys. But I can't repeat what it said at a family faire." [Wink]
- "Wyatt Westcoat got a lot of telegrams today, and they all said the same thing: "I'm a huge fan!""

PCs should consult the brochure and decide where to go next.

Western Stage

As you approach the stage, the audience bursts into applause. Vampires and cowboys storm the stage and bow. A vampire leaps from the stage and passes a cowboy hat around the audience for tips. You wait until the audience disburses, then approach the vampire. "Howdy, folks," he says. "I'm Jack Hammer. Are you looking for an autograph from the star?"

JACK HAMMER

If a player asks you a question and you know the answer (i.e. it's below), you must answer the question honestly. Make the players work for it and have fun with the character. Ham it up!

Mood: He's heard about the murders and is shocked something like this could happen at a family faire. The shows take place every two hours, at 10, 12, 2, and 4 o'clock, so he's too busy to worry about it much though.

Objective: Get someone to ask for your autograph.

If Jack doesn't know the answer, he should tell the PCs he doesn't know.

PLAYERS EACH MAKE ROLLS TO ASK JACK QUESTIONS. Players with + charisma can add that number to their die roll. Jack will respond to every die roll over 3.

Clues:

- "Yes, it's true. Like I told the police, I *did* get into a shouting match with Commodore Jones yesterday. But I didn't kill him."
- "We were going to have a performance at his tearoom, but he backed out at the last minute, said he was going to go with some local murder mystery theater instead. He said he'd arrange for another place for us to perform later. We'd already sold tickets."
- "He moved us to a fundraiser for the Araminta Children's Charity. Then this morning he told us that was off too. He came by with the bad news just before 9 AM. I'll bet that mystery theater skunked us again. We can't

cancel two shows in a row that we've already sold tickets for. It makes us look unreliable and unprofessional."

- "He should never have let Tasha go. *She* was organized."
- "Each of our shows lasts exactly 60 minutes, and I'm on stage during every one of those minutes. I'm one of the biggest draws."

Whodunit?

You decide you've gathered enough information. It's time to go to the police with what you know.

Whodunit?

The players should vote now on who killed Commodore Jones and Tasha Teasdale.

Concluding the Mystery

You're not getting any signal on your phone, so you walk through the faire in search of the detectives you saw earlier. A vampire on an old-fashioned bicycle tells you he saw them headed for the vendor parking lot. You stride to the dirt parking area and see Haskell Radley from the children's charity hurrying away with a thick backpack beneath his arm.

You shout to him. He drops the pack and whirls, aiming a gun at you. You look around for help, but the parking lot is empty aside from yourselves and the Nautilus beneath a nearby tree.

PLAYERS ROLL TO STALL BY ASKING QUESTIONS. EACH ROLL OVER THREE GETS AN ANSWER. Players with +charisma may add that number to their roll.

- Do you think I'm stealing from the charity? There is no charity. I made the whole thing up.
- Tasha Teasdale was suspicious of me from the start. She was the real manager of that business, but then Commodore fired her.

- I don't know what set Commodore off this morning, but for some reason he checked with the IRS and found out Amarinta didn't have a tax ID number.
- He confronted me. I managed to convince him it was all a mistake. But I knew he'd start thinking again, and I had to get rid of him.
- I stole strychnine from that fool Wyatt Westcoat this morning. Of course I didn't sign up for his email list afterward. I'm not stupid. Then I snuck around the back of the Commodore's Tea Parlor and added it to Commodore's tea.
- But after he died, Tasha grew more suspicious. She came to see me and asked if I'd spoken to Commodore this morning. I knew something was up. I followed her back to her tent and killed her there.

Still training the gun on you, he backs toward his Audi and gets inside. He guns the engine and roars off, dust spewing from his tires. You race to the Nautilus. The door is open, and you crowd inside. There's no key to start the engine—there's a key code.

PLAYERS ROLL TO GUESS THE KEYCODE. A ROLL OF A 5 OR 6 WILL GET THEM THE CODE: STEAM.

Fortunately, the Nautilus starts easily. You race forward, bumping across the uneven lot, and block Haskel's car. He jumps from the car and shoots wildly at the Nautilus. Bullets ping off its metal sides. The windshield shatters, showering you with glass.

PLAYERS GET THREE ROLLS EACH TO AVOID GETTING SHOT. Anything totaling over six is a success. Players with + strength may add that number to their roll. If the players roll a number under three, they deduct that number from their Life Points. If Life Points reach zero, the PC dies.

You push the lever to move the Nautilus forward, and you race toward Haskel. He leaps away at the last minute. Unfortunately, he leaped in the wrong direction and collided with a tree. He lies unconscious at its roots.

The police, alerted by the gunshots, race across the parking lot toward you. You explain what happened. The police take you to the station to make a statement. The mayor of Nowhere, a little old man wearing thick spectacles, congratulations you on catching the killer. You are heroes!

More Kirsten Weiss

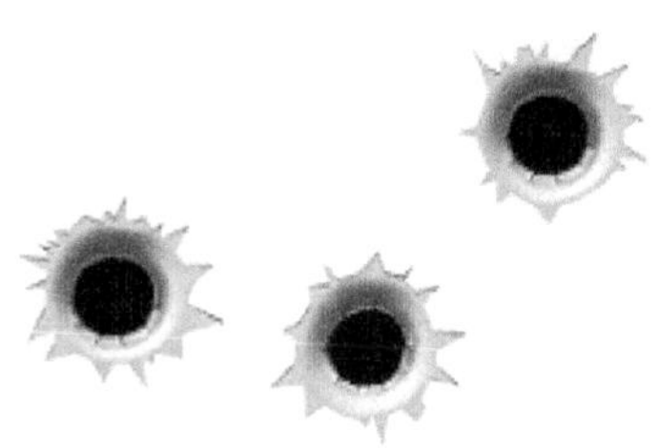

The Perfectly Proper Paranormal Museum Mysteries

When highflying Maddie Kosloski is railroaded into managing her small-town's paranormal museum, she tells herself it's only temporary... until a corpse in the museum embroils her in murders past and present.

If you love quirky characters and cats with attitude, you'll love this laugh-out-loud cozy mystery series with a light paranormal twist. It's perfect for fans of Jana DeLeon, Laura Childs, and Juliet Blackwell. Start with book 1, *The Perfectly Proper Paranormal Museum*, and experience these charming wine-country whodunits today.

The Tea & Tarot Cozy Mysteries

Welcome to Beanblossom's Tea and Tarot, where each and every cozy mystery brews up hilarious trouble.

Abigail Beanblossom's dream of owning a tearoom is about to come true. She's got the lease, the start-up funds, and the recipes. But Abigail's out of a tearoom and into hot water when her realtor turns out to be a conman... and then turns up dead.

Take a whimsical journey with Abigail and her partner Hyperion through the seaside town of San Borromeo (patron saint of heartburn sufferers). And be sure to check out the easy tearoom recipes in the back of each book! Start the adventure with book 1, *Steeped in Murder.*

The Wits' End Cozy Mysteries

Cozy mysteries that are out of this world...

Running the best little UFO-themed B&B in the Sierras takes organization, breakfasting chops, and a talent for turning up trouble.

The truth is out there... Way out there in these hilarious whodunits. Start the series and beam up book 1, *At Wits' End*, today!

Pie Town Cozy Mysteries

When Val followed her fiancé to coastal San Nicholas, she had ambitions of starting a new life and a pie shop. One broken engagement later, at least her dream of opening a pie shop has come true.... Until one of her regulars keels over at the counter.

Welcome to Pie Town, where Val and pie-crust specialist Charlene are baking up hilarious trouble. Start this laugh-out-loud cozy mystery series with book 1, *The Quiche and the Dead.*

A Big Murder Mystery Series

Small Town. Big Murder.

The number one secret to my success as a bodyguard? Staying under the radar. But when a wildly public disaster blew up my career and reputation, it turned my perfect, solitary life upside down.

I thought my tiny hometown of Nowhere would be the ideal out-of-the-way refuge to wait out the media storm.

It wasn't.

My little brother had moved into a treehouse. The obscure mountain town had decided to attract tourists with the world's largest collection of big things... Yes, Nowhere now has the world's largest pizza cutter. And lawn flamingo. And ball of yarn...

And then I stumbled over a dead body.

All the evidence points to my brother being the bad guy. I may have been out of his life for a while—okay, five years—but

I know he's no killer. Can I clear my brother before he becomes Nowhere's next Big Fatality?

A fast-paced and funny cozy mystery series, start with Big Shot.

The Doyle Witch Mysteries

In a mountain town where magic lies hidden in its foundations and forests, three witchy sisters must master their powers and shatter a curse before it destroys them and the home they love.

This thrilling witch mystery series is perfect for fans of Annabel Chase, Adele Abbot, and Amanda Lee. If you love stories rich with packed with magic, mystery, and murder, you'll love the Witches of Doyle. Follow the magic with the Doyle Witch trilogy, starting with book 1, *Bound*.

The Riga Hayworth Paranormal Mysteries

Her gargoyle's got an attitude.

Her magic's on the blink.

Alchemy might be the cure... if Riga can survive long enough to puzzle out its mysteries.

All Riga wants is to solve her own personal mystery—how to rebuild her magical life. But her new talent for unearthing murder keeps getting in the way...

If you're looking for a magical page-turner with a complicated, 40-something heroine, read the paranormal mystery series that fans of Patricia Briggs and Ilona Andrews call AMAZING! Start your next adventure with book 1, *The Alchemical Detective*.

Sensibility Grey Steampunk Suspense

California Territory, 1848.

Steam-powered technology is still in its infancy.

Gold has been discovered, emptying the village of San Francisco of its male population.

And newly arrived immigrant, Englishwoman Sensibility Grey, is alone.

The territory may hold more dangers than Sensibility can manage. Pursued by government agents and a secret society,

Sensibility must decipher her father's clockwork secrets, before time runs out.

If you love over-the-top characters, twisty mysteries, and complicated heroines, you'll love the Sensibility Grey series of steampunk suspense. Start this steampunk adventure with book 1, *Steam and Sensibility.*

Get Kirsten's Mobile App

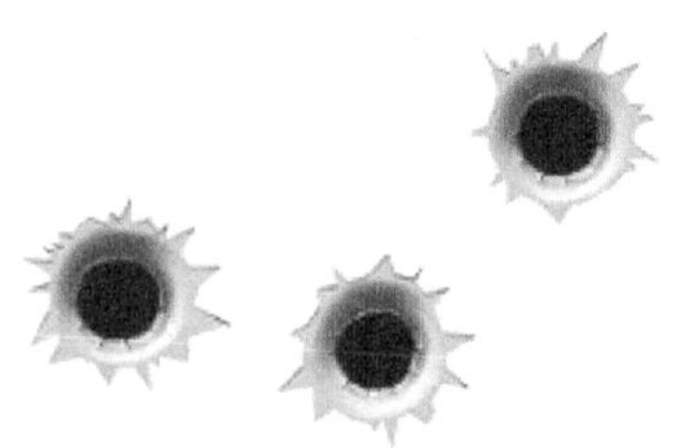

Keep up with the latest book news, and get free short stories, scone recipes and more by downloading Kirsten's mobile app.

Just click HERE to get started or use the QR code below.

Or make sure you're on Kirsten's email list to get your free copy of the Tea & Tarot mystery, *Fortune Favors the Grave*. You can do that here: KirstenWeiss.com or use the QR code below:

About the Author

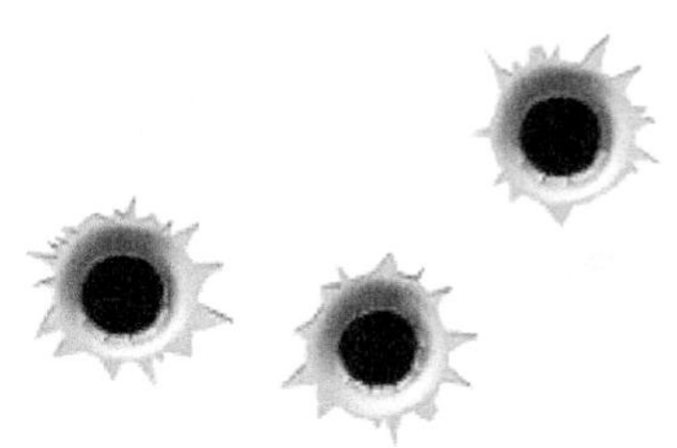

I write laugh-out-loud, page-turning mysteries for people who want to escape with real, complex, and flawed but likable characters. If there's magic in the story, it must work consistently within the world's rules and be based in history or the reality of current magical practices.

I'm best known for my cozy mystery and witch mystery novels, though I've written some steampunk mystery as well. So if you like funny, action-packed mysteries with complicated heroines, just turn the page...

Learn more, grab my **free app**, or sign up for my **newsletter** for exclusive stories and book updates. I also have a read-and-review tea via **Booksprout** and is looking for honest and thoughtful reviews! If you're interested, download the **Booksprout app**, follow me on Booksprout, and opt-in for email notifications.

Connect with Kirsten

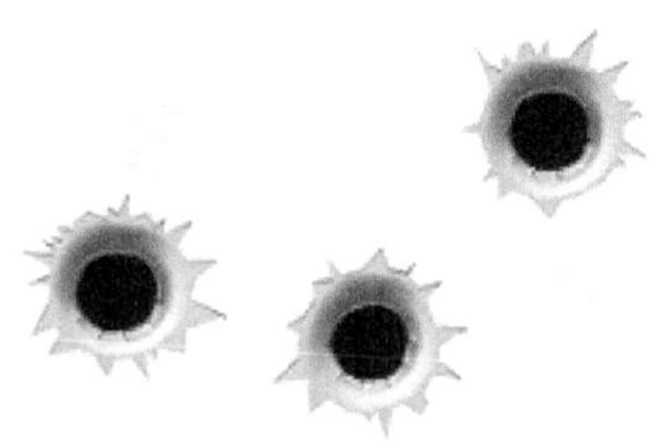

You can download my free app here:
https://kirstenweissbooks.beezer.com
Or sign up for my newsletter and get a special digital prize pack for joining, including an exclusive Tea & Tarot novella, *Fortune Favors the Grave.*
https://kirstenweiss.com
Or maybe you'd like to chat with other whimsical mystery fans? Come join Kirsten's reader page on Facebook:
https://www.facebook.com/kirsten.weiss
Or... sign up for my read and review team on Booksprout:

https://booksprout.co/author/8142/kirsten-weiss

Made in the USA
Middletown, DE
27 April 2023